THUNDERBIRD RISING

A MAXX KING THRILLER

JOHN H. THOMAS

THIS NOVEL IS ENTIRELY a work of fiction. The names, characters and incidents portrayed in it are the work of the author's imagination. Any resemblance to actual persons, living or dead, events or localities is entirely coincidental.

To my mother who inspired me to read, my father who encouraged me to write, and my wife who convinced me to seize the day.

I will stand at my watch
and station myself on the ramparts;
I will look to see what he will say to me,
And what to answer when I am rebuked.

--- Habakkuk 2:1

PROLOGUE

Maxx grunted as he knelt on the dirty tile floor of the ferry terminal and helped Gabby repack the things that had spilled out of her backpack.

Gabby's long hair was pulled back into ponytail to stay cool. Her face was flushed from a long, active day and the unusually hot late-summer weather. She nervously cleaned her sunglasses as she tried to keep the sweat off. She was torn between staying partially hidden behind the dark glasses and the need to watch the people around her.

"Have you seen anyone who looks like they're paying attention to us?" asked Maxx. Gabby shook her head briefly and half grinned, showing her perfect white teeth. "Hopefully, we lost them this time. I still don't know how you picked them out of the crowd before."

"It's my finely tuned bullshit detector," said Gabby as she pointed at Maxx. He laughed a little too loudly and looked around the mostly empty terminal. Her sense of humor, especially during stressful moments, was one of the many things he found appealing about their relationship.

"I know you use it regularly with me, so it's always in tip-top condition." His knees popped when he stood up to start toward the ticket turnstile to board the ferry. "Too many heavy squats at the gym," he muttered.

"That or old age," she added. "Speed it up, grandpa."

As soon as they walked on the ferry, they grabbed a booth inside the passenger area. Maxx wanted to sit by the doors where the walk-on passengers boarded, allowing him to quickly spot anyone who might have followed them. It was possible to drive onto the lower deck, but he'd been on the ferry often enough to know it would be nearly impossible for anyone following them to get into the vehicle line in time to make the rush-hour crossing.

It was still hot and very bright as the sun moved toward the Olympic Mountains to the west. No one would think it was unusual for a couple to be wearing Mariners caps and sunglasses. The air-conditioned ferry was a welcome relief after the draining run down to the ferry terminal from Pike Place Market.

After the last of the passengers and cars boarded, the ferry gave a short blast on the horn and pulled away from the dock. For at least the next hour, more if no one knew they were onboard, they'd have some time to recharge and plan their next moves.

They watched West Seattle pass by the large picture window on the Wenatchee as the ferry accelerated quickly to cruising speed. The ferry was busy, passengers wandering around the decks to admire the view of the mountains and the sun glistening on the water.

"I'm going to grab something from the snack bar," Maxx said. "I hope they have an all-you-can-eat buffet, because I'm going to put them out of business."

"Grab us some waters and protein bars. We don't know when we'll get another chance to stock up," Gabby said as she rolled her eyes. She knew Maxx was always looking out for his next meal. She'd brought a box of protein bars in her backpack this morning when they left, and Maxx had devoured them all before lunchtime.

"Save our seats. I'll grab us some supplies and take a quick tour of the boat to see what I see. Aha, no pun intended." He smirked, picked up his backpack, and walked toward the café.

He doubted he'd been able to lighten the mood much as he watched Gabby lower her cap over her eyes and snuggle herself deep into the corner of the booth.

Maxx grabbed as much of the food and bottled water from the café as he could safely carry in his gorilla-sized arms. His backpack was already full, so it was a juggling contest. He really wanted beer instead of water, but he wanted to stay alert in case they needed to start running again. He had been making a solid effort to cut back on his drinking, and it felt like it was paying off.

They'd been evading people all day, and although he wasn't completely sure why they were being followed, he had a basic idea from one of the guys he'd been able to apprehend earlier this morning when all of this began to blow up. Gabby had downloaded some sensitive files from the computers at work, and someone very badly wanted the thumb drive she had used to copy the data. They needed the information quickly and were willing to do anything to recover it. Only someone very foolish or very desperate would try and grab Gabby when Maxx was within striking distance.

All of the day's efforts at evasion had led them here, and while Maxx doubted that they'd been followed onto the ferry, he'd prefer to avoid another confrontation. It would be better if he and Gabby found somewhere safe where they could review what was on the thumb drive.

As Maxx began to walk back toward Gabby, he saw a group of several young Asian men come up the stairs from the vehicle deck. The group had split up and were clearly looking for someone while trying to remain casual. Luckily, none of them had spotted him yet, so he nonchalantly sat next to Gabby.

"Don't look, but they followed us onboard. Somehow they must have gotten a car."

"I see them," she said. "If we split up for now, it's less likely that they'll be able to grab both of us." Gabby took most of the food and water and put it into her backpack, making sure her Glock could be reached quickly, then handed Maxx the thumb drive. "Hang on to this, grandpa. I'm going to hang out in the ladies' room."

She stood up and pulled her hat lower over her eyes. Maxx casually slipped the thumb drive into his boot for safekeeping.

"If we get split up and it's not safe to get back together, text me or meet me at Anthony's Bar in a couple hours."

Maxx headed for the stairwell down to the vehicle deck, planning on getting behind the guys who were following them. It would also give him a chance to see the kind of car they were driving, because they couldn't abandon it on the ferry even if some of them walked off to try and corner them.

The stairs down to the car levels were tight and steep. Maxx moved quickly to keep from getting trapped in the narrow space if one of the pursuers happened to spot him. It was a full ferry with plenty of places to hide among the cars. He knew it was unlikely anyone else would be walking around down on this deck during the crossing, making anyone down here a potential threat.

Figuring he would be less likely to be spotted if he was seated in a car, he looked for any cars that might be vacant but open. The last thing he wanted to do was set off someone's car alarm by checking doors. Trying to act as casual as he could, Maxx sauntered toward the front end of the ferry, looking for suspicious persons and any open car doors.

About to give up, he noticed an old, rusted Rambler that might work. The car had manual-style door locks, and the knobs were up, indicating that the doors were unlocked. Moreover, he couldn't imagine anyone would spend money putting in an alarm on a car that was one small step from being towed to a junkyard.

The Rambler also happened to be the first car on the ferry. He'd be able to spot anyone coming and could have plenty of time to jump out before they saw him.

Maxx quickly opened the passenger door on the sedan and slid into front seat. He needed to adjust the rear and side mirrors to watch behind him. That way he would notice men chasing him or people starting to come back down to get in their cars early. He'd have to get out before the owner of the car came back.

He also couldn't risk going back up to the passenger decks, because they'd see him when he walked up the stairs. His best chance of getting off the ferry undetected was hitching a ride on one of the cars or trucks before it left then jumping out when they stopped at the light in Bainbridge.

Maxx rummaged in the glove box and backseat to see if there was anything that might work as a disguise. There wasn't much, but the owner kept a bunch of old tools in the glovebox, probably in case they had to do emergency car repairs, Maxx thought.

He switched out his Mariners cap for a beat-up John Deere cap and put on a pair of women's sunglasses that made him look like a professional wrestler in drag. He knew Gabby would get a hoot out of his new look. Hell, he was cracking himself up. Oversized sunglasses were becoming part of his go-to disguise repertoire.

He pulled out his cellphone and found it had virtually no signal out here on the open water. The phone didn't have any texts or messages from Gabby either. When he tried to send her a quick message to let her know where he was hiding, it unsurprisingly didn't go through. All he got for his effort was an error message.

As he was checking himself out in the rearview mirror, he noticed someone moving behind the wheels of a semi-truck on the driver's side of the car. He didn't think it was his imagination, but he ducked down and pulled his hat lower. He had two choices, and neither of them were very appealing. He could either act like he was asleep and try and bluff his way out of the situation, or slide out and try and sneak toward the back of the ferry.

As Maxx decided to open the door and make a run for it, there was a soft tap on the window behind him. He turned to look as a tall man stood up in front of the car and waved at him over the hood. Maxx recognized him. It was the Chinese guy from the bar who had started this nightmare a week ago.

His other hand held a pistol with a suppressor attached. He pointed to the side of the car, where another man appeared. Both men held their guns at their sides, but Maxx had no doubt they would use them if he tried to get out of the car and run.

The short man standing next to the car door pointed to the door lock. "Open the door. Let's have a friendly conversation, and you can return the information you stole," he said.

"It's not my car, and I don't have any of your information. Besides, my mom told me I'm not supposed to talk to strangers, and you seem very strange," Maxx answered. While he was talking, he discreetly checked to make sure all the car doors were locked.

The man tested the doors on the passenger side to see if they'd open. When they didn't, the taller man moved from the front of the car to the driver's side and tested those doors.

The tall man said, "Make this easy for everyone. We can either sit somewhere peacefully and talk, or we can strongly encourage you and your girlfriend to come back to Seattle to meet with Mr. Xi. He's anxious to recover the information you took. It won't do you any good anyway."

"Or here's another idea. Why don't I sit here and honk this horn until a hundred people show up and see you standing here waving guns around?"

"I don't think it'll take that long before my short friend, Mr. Jones, puts a dozen rounds through that window. But I have a better idea. You sit here, and we'll go get some additional transportation and come back." Both men quickly inserted something in the handles of the doors and returned to the truck behind the Rambler.

"What the hell are they talking about?" Maxx grumbled. He tried to open his door, but the handle wouldn't move. He tried the window, which wouldn't open either. He reached over and tried the driver's side door and window, getting the same result. Somehow, they had managed to jam all the doors and windows, trapping him inside.

Maxx really got a bad feeling about being locked in the car when the semi that was parked immediately behind him started its engine. He turned around and watched in surprise as the tall guy waved at him again. This time, the guy's not-so-friendly wave ended with a raised middle finger.

The truck shifted into gear. It occurred to Maxx that maybe they didn't need the thumb drive anymore. Either he'd been mistaken about its importance to them, or they'd caught Gabby already.

The truck moved forward quickly and smashed into the rear bumper on the Rambler. Maxx could see the parking brake was already engaged, but that didn't stop the truck from pushing the car forward, all four tires screeching in protest.

The truck was in low gear and continued to push the car toward the front of the ferry. Maxx watched the two guys climb out of the truck cab and walk quickly in the other direction. His only chance was if somehow the large chain that was strung across the front of the ferry was able to hold the force of the truck pushing into it. Otherwise, both the car and the truck would end up going ass over teakettle into the water.

When the front of the Rambler pressed against the heavy marine chain, Maxx heard the truck engine behind him beginning to strain with the effort. He leaned back in the seat and strained as he kicked at the passenger-side window to no effect. He had extremely strong legs but didn't have leverage at this angle even when stretched across the bench seat. He was quickly running out of options to escape and needed to calm down and think instead of knee-jerk reacting.

If the chain didn't hold against the pressure, he was going to be trapped in this car as it quickly sank to the bottom of Puget Sound with a twenty-ton truck landing on top of him. Being trapped underwater was his worst nightmare. Heart racing, he put on his seatbelt, braced for impact, and hoped for the best.

The car began to shake madly as the truck continued to press forward. With groans and screeching metal, the old car came apart at the joints before there was a thunderous crash. The cable snapped apart into sections, damaging the cars next to the Rambler.

With nothing to obstruct the Rambler and the truck behind it, they accelerated off the front end of the ferry. Any chance of the car floating was quickly eliminated when the truck landed on top of it, pushing it under the water, while the truck floated briefly on the surface. The 6,200-ton ferry loaded with more than 150 cars was still moving at 18 knots, and both vehicles were easily pushed aside by the bow of the ship. Passengers on the upper decks that had heard the truck engine and the chain snapping watched in stunned disbelief as the two vehicles disappeared beneath the murky water.

As the sun set over the Olympic Mountains, an emergency

call from the ferry captain went out to the Coast Guard, and the ferry rapidly came to a stop in the middle of the Salish Sea.

The rescue began in earnest, but they never were able to recover Maxx's body.

RUBY TUESDAY, SIX DAYS EARLIER

It was late in the season for the Mariners, but they were a lock for the playoffs. Maxx didn't have tickets but decided to take advantage of the late-summer weather and make the long walk from his office to Pioneer Square. He would catch the game with the crowd at one of the neighborhood bars. It felt good to stretch his legs and relax after a long day in the office.

With all the excitement about the team, it seemed every bar near Safeco Field had standing room only for the locals and fans who had flown in from Tampa Bay. Maxx found a tight spot for himself at The Double Play, "Home of the Mariners," as the sign in the window proudly proclaimed. Oddly enough, he had noticed the sign was not on display most of the time. Some years it was the "Home of the Seahawks," if they were playing well.

He didn't really think the bar was the home of anything but a lot of fair-weather fans, of which he was one. He was not ashamed to admit that he liked the Mariners but didn't follow them like a "true to the blue" fan. This bar did carry a good selection of locally brewed beers that he had sporadically enjoyed trying, although he was partial to whiskey.

Even though Maxx grew up on a farm on the east side of Washington, he had not really followed the Mariners until he'd been stationed for a couple years at Fort Lewis, the Army base in Tacoma south of Seattle in between assignments to the Middle East. Mariners tickets were generally cheap, and he could either catch a bus from the base or hop on the train to get to the stadium. It was easy to get lost in the crowd and enjoy the weather and occasional beer. Maxx was a loner, and baseball was an easy game for a loner to enjoy. No one hassled a single guy at a baseball game.

The seat he'd found was at the end of the bar where he could watch a couple of the games, but no one would ask him to move. People didn't usually approach Maxx anyway. He considered himself easygoing but had been told others didn't see him that way. It was either due to his size at 6'4" and as big as bear or the scowl he frequently wore when he was thinking about something deeper than baseball.

With all the problems he'd run into lately, he seemed to be wearing a permanent frown.

"I'll take whatever you have on draft from Redhook," Maxx mouthed silently to the nearest bartender. There was no point in trying to yell his order over the noise of the cheering crowd when the Mariners got a hit. He grabbed a drink menu and began to look for a whiskey he could savor while he was relaxing, planning to nurse it for an hour or two while the game played. He felt good about his promise to Gabby to cut back. One day at a time. He still had some things he needed to finish up back at the office before heading home.

He'd called Gabby before he'd left the office. She'd been working late again, so he didn't expect to see her until tomor-row. They were still new in their relationship, and both were trying to give the other plenty of room to figure things out. They'd come out of some messy situations, and Maxx's was still not completely resolved. He was trying to sort it out while keeping his temper in check.

Things had seemed to be going so well for him a year ago. He had found a great woman, and it seemed like they had a lot of things in common. She was smart, a nine on her worst day, and had a great sense of humor. He had met Natalie at a bar near his office, and they had shared a fondness for whiskey, tech advancements, hiking, and about every other topic they talked about except for politics. She was from a liberal family in Connecticut and had her views cemented while attending the sociology program at the University of Washington. With so many other interests in common, they steered clear of anything too divisive. It was easy at first.

After three months of an increasingly satisfying romance, they had moved into an apartment on Capitol Hill and kept the romance growing, even including the workday. Maxx had started a tech surveillance business four years ago that took off. He'd made friends with some of the retired military people who worked at Seattle PD, the local FBI and ATF offices, and they started sending some contract work his way.

With more work than he could manage, Maxx hired a part-time assistant. Natalie's previous experience at Microsoft and TechCom checked all of the boxes. Her looks and intelligence rapidly led to a partnership both at the office and in their personal lives. They often joked that their relationship was a made-for-TV sitcom, except he was not handsome enough to play the lead.

Things went great for a year or two until the time together became too much. They began to spend more time apart after work and found reasons to focus on different assignments. It was a story as old as time, except Natalie was the one who found someone she preferred to be with, and Maxx was left wondering what happened. The breakup was painful, but the hardest part for Maxx was when he discovered she had been siphoning off clients and embezzling funds from the business. When she left, she had taken most of the money from the bank account and left him on the hook for a lot of the outstanding debts.

It had been tough losing a woman he trusted and then having to deal with the flotsam of a once successful business that had been turned upside down financially. People who had trusted him with delicate assignments were now hearing a lot of concerning things from Natalie that were flat out lies. She not only blamed him for their financial issues but insinuated that he had trouble controlling his anger and had physically abused her privately. It had been hell for six months trying to re-stabilize his world, and his business still struggled because of the clients Natalie had taken.

Of course, all of this was bad, and Maxx had made it worse by drinking to escape the pain. The drinking felt good until he had too much. Then his anger took over.

Maxx thought he was heading toward the bottom three months ago when he and Gabby had met. He had to drop off a report at the police headquarters downtown and was having a cup of coffee to take the whiskey edge off in the non-Starbucks next door. He had been enamored by her British accent and wide smile when she'd ordered tea. They'd started talking, which led to a date and more. They had been taking things slow because they both had recent relationship baggage.

But Maxx felt he was recovering for the first time in a year. He had stopped the day drinking and was being more careful about letting his temper get the upper hand.

Today he'd found out he was past due on a project he had never heard of. Natalie had committed to an IT project for a Chinese holding company. The project included steep penalties for nonperformance. He'd already missed deadlines and didn't even know where to begin.

When a group of three young Chinese guys pushed to his

end of the bar, it was all he could do to keep his temper in check. They seemed to recognize him, but maybe he was the type of person they liked to mess with.

He really wanted to watch the game and nurse a shot of whiskey. Instead, he kept getting bumped from behind and overhearing occasional derogatory comments. He had been quick to learn more than a handful of swear words from Gabby, whose parents had immigrated to the United States from Hong Kong. It confused people that a Chinese woman with a strong British accent was from Seattle, and Gabby used the cultural confusion to her advantage every chance she had.

After a particular aggressive push from behind, Maxx's patience was exhausted. Trying to keep the situation from escalating, he turned around and politely said, "Gentlemen, I don't think you realized it, but you keep bumping into me, and I'd appreciate it if you'd be more careful."

He intentionally stayed seated so he wouldn't tower over the short man directly in front of him who was already close to eye level.

"Our apologies," the tall guy said. "My colleague will be more careful about where he places his hands next time." He smiled at Maxx, but the smile didn't quite reach his eyes. He nodded and said something in Chinese to the third man.

The third man nodded at Maxx and leaned in closer so he didn't have to shout.

"Perhaps you should leave, and then we will not have to worry about bumping into you. You look rather delicate and could get hurt by my little friend here."

The smile he put on showed too many teeth, resembling a shark.

Maxx couldn't believe they were threatening him, so he made another attempt to avoid a confrontation. "I might not have been clear enough. Stop bumping me. Move away before someone gets hurt." He gave them one of the dead smiles that they'd been giving him to make sure that they got the message that he was done being polite. He had little doubt that they'd be on the losing end of this fight if it got physical.

"No offense was intended," the tall man said loudly so that people around could easily hear him. "Can I buy you another drink to smooth over this misunderstanding?"

"That won't be necessary. I still have this one to finish, and then I'm going to head out before it gets too dark."

As he looked at his drink, the third man stared at him with a smirk on his face as he slowly inserted his middle finger into Maxx's glass.

Now Maxx understood why the tall guy had spoken so loudly. He wanted everyone to think he'd been trying to diffuse the situation. Anything Maxx did in response now would look like he was overreacting. He couldn't let this slide though. They were intentionally provoking him. And the beer had scraped the thin veneer from his self-control.

Not to be outdone, Maxx stood up and glared at the tall man.

"Perhaps you'd like to step outside, and I'll show you the directions to the nearest hospital as you requested. It seems you and your friends are rather prone to accidents and need to be prepared." He smiled broadly.

People sitting closest to them in the bar moved away as Maxx and the group stood and moved toward the front door. It was clear they were leaving together, not like a group of friends but as people trying to keep their front toward a potential enemy. Maxx could see several people watching them in their peripheral vision. The bartenders had seen enough fights to know when there was the potential for violence on the horizon.

When they stepped on the sidewalk outside, the convivial sounds of the bar dropped off dramatically, and they left the need for coded messages and innuendo behind them. The tall guy looked at Maxx and snarled, "You bit off more than you can swallow. You think you're a tough guy, but you're going to find out that you're a paper tiger."

"I really don't think of myself as tough," he said. "But the people I put on the ground usually have that opinion."

He moved off the sidewalk and stepped around the corner into the alley, making sure to keep enough distance because he could see the three of them trying to position themselves in a circle around him. He hadn't seen any evidence of guns on them as they had moved outside, but he was certain they were carrying knives. And anyone who didn't respect a sharp, quick blade was a fool. Maxx had enough scars to prove that he knew how to survive and win a knife fight.

He took off his windbreaker and wrapped it around his left hand and forearm.

"Last chance to walk away, gentlemen. When this kicks off, you're going to wish your mothers had taught you to be more polite to strangers."

"You talk too much," the third guy with the shark smile said.

He brought his leg up for a jump kick but quickly realized he'd made the first mistake, as Maxx stepped inside the kick quick as a snake. Even though Maxx was built like a gorilla, all the years he'd spent in wrestling, sports, and life-or-death combat had taught him to move quickly with overwhelming force when someone underestimated him.

He put his hip into a full uppercut that caught the shark hard enough to knock his teeth out. The man's head snapped back like he'd slammed chin first into an anvil. Even though he was shaken, it didn't stop him from getting in a couple quick hits to Maxx's face before Maxx stunned him with an unexpected left hook.

Maxx could feel the short guy moving in on his left side. He didn't know where the tall guy was going, but it didn't feel like he was stepping in yet, so he juked left to keep the body falling between him and the incoming movement. This proved to be enough of a distraction to give the short guy's attack a misstep. Indeed, he'd produced a knife in the last few seconds and was aiming for Maxx. He was very quick, but not quick enough.

Spinning, Maxx snapped his knife into his left hand. He carried a knife on his left forearm that snapped into his hand with a flick of his arm. Enemies assumed his right hand was his strongest and tended to move to what they thought was his weak side. By wrapping his jacket around his arm, he effectively hid the motion and the blade.

He drove the wickedly sharp four-inch blade into the short guy's side and grabbed his knife hand by the wrist in a vice-like grip, his thumb pressing deep into his nerves. The double shock caused him to drop his knife.

Maxx pulled out his blade and pushed it in again all the way to the hilt. He could tell he'd hit an artery this time as blood sprayed out of the wound. Keeping him wrapped up as he weakly tried to pull out of his grip, Maxx looked around the alley for the tall guy, who was nowhere to be seen.

The fight had happened so fast and was so quiet that no one could have heard anything over the sound of the crowded bar, traffic, and the baseball game. Maxx had blood all over his shirt and jacket, which were luckily the deep-blue color of the Mariner uniforms, so they looked wet and deeper blue. He saw some water sitting in buckets further down the alley by the back door of the kitchen and walked in that direction. He did a quick look around and didn't see any cameras, but he knew that wouldn't matter once witnesses started talking to the police. He wasn't exactly a forgettable person, and the bartenders had watched him leave. The guy who had taken off was probably calling 911 and giving them his description.

Either he could walk away now and try to explain the circumstances if they caught him, or he could call 911 and report the attack. If he called it in, he could pretend to be an anonymous witness and make it sound like he was the victim.

In better times, he would have trusted the police to sort the situation out in his favor, but he'd been in enough trouble lately that he had little confidence that they would. When Natalie started making accusations against him without any evidence, he had developed a deepening distrust of authority figures. With his recent record of public altercations, he knew things would tilt quickly against him.

The other part of this situation that really weighed on him was how they had seemed to choose him and intentionally escalate a confrontation. Fights usually had a point when they crossed the line from grandstanding and name calling, but in retrospect these three guys had kept pushing the conflict like they wanted violence. He couldn't think of any reason they would have singled him out of the crowd.

After Maxx washed off the blood on his hands and wind-breaker, he made his decision, pulling the burner phone from his zippered pocket and dialing 911. He told the operator that he'd witnessed two Asian guys jump a large white guy in the alley on the other side of the street. He said the guy took off running in the opposite direction that he planned to go and was trying to hail a cab, so they better come quickly. He thought some misdirection might buy him time to get to the nearest bus stop. He could jump in the back of the bus where no one would notice him, another Mariners fan downtown for the game. He was a long way from home but was sure he'd be able to make it far enough to dispose of the burner phone, dump the bloody knife, and call his attorney to figure out next steps.

As observant as Maxx usually was, especially during times of stress, he didn't see the woman in the leather jacket and oversized sunglasses talking to herself and watching him walk away in the reflection of the window across the street. If he had noticed, he might have wondered how she fit into the picture.

She'd known it was going to get messy as soon as she saw Haoyu and his two toadies walk into the bar and head over to Maxx like he had a homing beacon on. They either followed him here like she had or placed a tracking device on him. Either way, they were done watching him passively and were now intent on removing him from the equation too. She knew some of the intelligence agencies had considered removing Maxx, only they had planned to do it with more subtlety. Of course, the agencies had access to Maxx's military record, so she wouldn't have underestimated him like the Chinese team.

She thought the short guy might have seen her in the bar, but things had happened quickly after that so she doubted he would have had time to mention it to Haoyu. She had followed them discretely out of the bar but had turned the other direction and crossed the street so none of them would have seen her face. She'd been able to watch the confrontation in the reflection of the storefront but had missed a few details when it was over from start to finish in under a minute. Maybe thirty seconds.

Using an earpiece and throat microphone, she was able to call it in when Haoyu took off while the third guy was still falling down. "It's Grey. King is leaving. Black Knight is heading north on Second Avenue. Do you have a tail ready for Knight? I'm going to follow King."

"Copy. How do you want to handle the cleanup?" the monotone voice on the earpiece replied.

"Give me a three-minute head start then call 911 and report it in case the Chinese are monitoring," she said quietly. "In the meantime, call Jameson at Seattle PD and let him know to hold off sending a response until then. We don't want Star's prints or description logged in officially. I want it to look like a ghost hit."

Keeping Maxx out of the spotlight would have two benefits. Haoyu was going to be very suspicious when Maxx wasn't named as a suspect. Getting Maxx thrown in jail would have been Haoyu's plan B if they didn't kill him in the alley.

It would also give her a chance to intercept Maxx and take him out of play herself. He'd be looking for more Chinese guys to follow through and would never suspect a petite Hispanic woman with a rhythmic Spanish accent was the person he should be concerned about.

She watched Maxx wash up quickly in the water bucket in the alley, make a phone call, then head toward the train station. She knew that was a move to throw off anyone who might try to track him out of the alley. He had to be leaving some blood spots intentionally to give a false trail, expecting the police to be here soon.

When he turned the corner, she walked casually across the street to see what the situation was and make sure a few more pawns were taken off the board. The Chinese team had decided to move now, so the time must be getting close for them to act.

When she walked up to the guy with the knife wounds, it was obvious he wasn't going to make it for another three or four minutes until the police and maybe an ambulance arrived. There was already enough blood pooling around him that he'd gotten a major artery nicked. Seattle had first-rate emergency services, but he was as good as dead.

The short guy was a problem though. He was still breathing, and while he might have a concussion, he'd likely recover and be able to identify Maxx. She didn't have to worry about Haoyu, who would stay in the shadows and never publicly step forward, but this short guy was a pawn they would push in front of the PD and the media. She had to stop him from acting as a witness pointing to Maxx.

She grabbed the third guy's knife and placed it in the hand of the short guy, so it'd at least look like he was the attacker. They'd be missing Maxx's knife at the scene, but that was a detail she'd clean up later. In the meantime, she took a syringe from inside her jacket and injected it into the short guy. It was a nonlethal dose of LSD to show cause delusions and psychosis with the added benefit of showing up neon on the toxicology screen the police would run.

While it wasn't fatal, it would scramble his memory enough that he'd have a difficult time remembering what was real and what was imagined for the last couple days. She could have made it fatal but figured it would be more problematic for the Chinese to have to explain why one of their guys was dead and the other guy was on drugs and looked to be the killer. The additional confusion would act in her favor.

Sirens echoed from about a half mile away. With these details taken care of, she began jogging in the direction Maxx had gone.

BAND ON THE RUN

Once Haoyu had seen the big, ugly American pull a knife from his sleeve, he knew it was time to leave quickly. Even if the idiot Jiang managed to ultimately win, which he doubted very much, there was going to be police, witnesses, and a lot of questions he didn't have the time or patience for. They had clearly underestimated the American, and he would take care of the oversight when it was on his terms.

He quickly moved in the opposite direction of the bar, away from downtown and toward the docks. He had a driver waiting a couple blocks away in an out-of-service taxi, and no one would think twice about someone jumping in a yellow cab. As he walked quickly toward where he knew the car was parked, he turned on the throwaway phone he always carried for emergencies. He doubted any intelligence agency tracked his phone, but it was better to assume they did and be wrong. He was acting the part of a foreign businessman and kept his primary phone dedicated to communication to support his cover story.

He called the number he had memorized for his contact. Of course, no one would answer the voicemail dead drop, but it was a clean method to relay deniable information.

"We underestimated him. He didn't seem to know who we were, but he was prepared. He could be more involved than what his partner suggested. That may be why he hasn't completed the project we commissioned from his company. He may have figured out it was a ruse."

He continued to walk a route to make sure he wasn't being tailed. An extra minute or two would make no difference, but it would be better to spot any tails he might have missed at the bar.

"Make an anonymous call that routes through Seattle's 911 system. Report three men fighting with knives and possibly a gun outside the bar. That will get the police to respond quickly and keep the American occupied for a while until we can make plans to tie up this loose thread."

After Haoyu rounded the last corner, he could see his taxi waiting in the lot half a block away. The street was empty, but he still took the time to stand in the doorway of a print shop and watch for anyone who might follow him around the corner.

"I don't believe I'm being followed, but let me know if that changes. Also, make sure that we are continuing to monitor the woman."

"TechCom is still a day or two from being able to decipher the code, but they could get lucky. Also, if her boyfriend is alive and able to escape the police, he may call her and give us an idea where he's heading. We need her to keep working on the project and not get distracted. The best way to do that is to intercept him before he reaches her."

Haoyu knocked on the driver's window of the cab as he hung up the phone. "Excuse me, are you able to take a fare?" He could hear several police sirens heading in the direction he had come from. Time to put some distance between himself and the bar quickly.

"Sorry, I'm out of service, champ," the cab driver answered as he pointed to the sign in the window.

"I'll pay you well for a quick trip to the zoo," Haoyu said, delivering the code phrase with agitation.

The driver nodded apologetically and took down the out-of-service sign. Haoyu climbed in the backseat of the cab and pulled the battery from the phone.

"Head toward the airport," he said. "Can you monitor the police scanner with your radio?"

"I'm listening on my earpiece," the driver answered as he headed toward the highway speedily but without driving recklessly.

After they had driven several miles south, Haoyu snapped the cheap burner phone in half and dropped the pieces out the window of the cab. The driver pointed toward his ear and watched Haoyu.

"The first police that arrived are calling for an ambulance and the homicide team. Two males, one is unconscious and the other dead. It looks like they were in a fight outside The Double Play. A third suspect might be involved, but they don't have a description yet."

Haoyu knew where one of the 911 calls came from but was puzzled who else had called it in. Hopefully he hadn't been identified as the third suspect and would remain a mystery person of interest.

"Any more description of the two men at the scene?"

"Both Asian," the driver said as he glanced at Haoyu in the rearview mirror.

The American had survived the attack, making things more complicated. The boyfriend had been a potential threat before but was now an active risk, and he'd clearly seen Haoyu. If he worked for an intelligence service, they'd have no doubts there was a high-level action occurring in the U.S. that was worth a murder. This would set off alarm bells all over the world.

Maxx headed south toward Safeco Field for a few blocks to blend in with the Mariners fans and game traffic. He was much less likely to stand out in a crowd if the police were able to put together a description of him from the bar and the tall Chinese guy who might report him. He took a moment to stop at one of the vendors selling gear on game day. Paying cash, he bought a cheap pair of oversized sunglasses, a couple new ball caps, t-shirts, and a Seattle hooded sweatshirt, proclaiming it was "Rain Town USA." The sunglasses and hoodie were the perfect tourist disguise.

After going a few blocks, he started picking up his pace, moving east toward a more industrial area. He needed to find a place to switch out his blood-stained clothes and get rid of the burner phone and knife. He ducked down a side street and stepped behind some cars that looked to be abandoned. He took off his shirt and used it to wipe off what blood he could, burying the shirt and jacket under some rags in a dumpster.

He went another block north, crushed the burner phone, and dropped it along with the knife down a sewer grate after wiping off any fingerprints. No one would find those among the mountains of mud and junk that had to be down there already. That was the best he could do for now.

Maxx returned to the underground bus station. He knew better than to go inside because they usually had some under-cover transit cops stationed there. But if he was close enough to the station, he could hop on the back of a bus, heading away quickly. The drivers usually didn't pay attention to the passengers in that area because all the rides were free. He kept looking to see if anyone was following him, but so far he felt like he was making a clean break from the scene at the bar. Riding buses would also make anyone trying to follow him easily stand out, since it would be obvious if anyone got on or off the bus with him.

While walking the last couple of blocks, he called his attorney but had to be careful about what he said over the cell line. He knew from his friends at some of the three-letter federal agencies that they monitored much of the cell traffic, and there had been a big push to expand these programs with the increase in terrorist activity since the Gulf War.

"Hi, Delores, it's Maxx. Is Daryl in now, or is he out on the golf course again?"

"He's around here pretending to work," she said, "probably playing that video game *The Sims* on his computer again. I swear he's a twelve-year-old boy in a man's body. Let me put you through."

She transferred the phone call while Maxx hustled across an intersection.

"Hey, Maxx, how's it going?" Daryl said when he picked up the phone.

"I'm glad to hear the retainer I pay you every month is allowing you to live the lifestyle of the rich and famous."

"Damn it, I can't believe Delores outed me on the video game case that I'm researching!" he said as he laughed.

"Two things, I was heading downtown for the Mariners game and heard a lot of sirens. I was wondering if you could check and see if it's something I should be concerned about and then give me a ring back."

"Do I look like the local news?" Daryl responded. "You know I'm going to bill you for this."

"Yeah, I know, but you have access to some of the inside information at SPD, and I might or might not have left my concealed carry license back at the office, and I might or might not be carrying a lawfully licensed pistol."

"Since this might or might not be a legitimate legal issue, I'll check for you. What is the second thing?"

"I was going through old files at the office today. It looks like Natalie had taken on an assignment for us before she left and never told me about it. Now I have some deliverables that are coming due. The agreement is not on our standard contract and looks to be on the client's paper. I hope she at least had you review it. It was with a company called AI Ventures based out of Wuxi, China."

Daryl paused for a few seconds. "I remember that contract. I recall telling Natalie to be sure to cover some of the terms with you, because they were unusual. And they were very aggressive about the penalties for nonperformance. I can pull up my notes."

"That would be perfect," Maxx answered. "Give me a ring when you get the information from SPD."

He ended the call as a double bus pulled up to the curb, and he found a seat in the back. A few people got on the bus with him, but none looked like a potential tail. Of course, they could be shadowing him in a car, but they'd be easy to identify in this heavy downtown traffic. The bus was using the dedicated bus lane, so it was pulling further and further away from the vehicles around it.

Maxx had grabbed a bus schedule from the kiosk at the last stop and looked for a place where he could switch back toward home by making a couple of connections. It looked like a good place to switch directions would be by Pike Place. He could walk over a couple of blocks and be in time for a bus to the University District if he hustled.

When the bus pulled into the stop, Maxx waited until all the other passengers had either gotten on or off. As the door was starting to close, he squeezed out on to the busy sidewalk.

He walked over to the drugstore window and watched the bus pull away in the reflection. There were a couple people who had been on board moving in the same direction he was, but they looked like office workers heading home. Only one woman had gotten on the bus at the same time he had, but she'd been waiting at the stop when he'd arrived, so he discounted her as a possible tail.

After practically running to the next stop, only a group of teenagers boarded with him. Again, no one suspicious, so he was beginning to believe he was out of the target neighborhood that the police might be watching. He might have been lucky... It depended on if they were working off a description of him. Even with a quick change in clothing, he didn't think he'd be overlooked if a police bulletin went out. There weren't many people his size.

Maxx had always been larger than the other kids his age. It was a story his mom loved to tell to anyone who would listen. She had announced she was carrying twins even though the ultrasound had shown that it was one very big boy. His parents had already agreed to name him Max if he was indeed a boy or Maxine if he was a girl and the doctor had been wrong. But after being in labor for six hours, she had finally delivered a healthy twelve-pound, six-ounce boy.

When it came time to fill out the birth certificate, his mother had jokingly said they needed to add an extra X at the end of his name since he was extra-large. Unfortunately, his dad hadn't realized she was joking. Thus, Maxx's nickname became "Extra Large." He had easily lived up to that nickname as he grew up, and the moniker had caused more than one embarrassing moment.

His phone began to vibrate in his pocket as he sat watching the other passengers on the bus and the traffic behind him. The caller ID showed him that it was Daryl, which was a quicker response than he'd expected, and he wasn't sure if that was good news or bad news.

Maxx answered and said, "I'm on a bus at the moment, so I'll have to listen to you."

"No problem. About your first question, there was a fight

down by The Double Play bar, and a couple of guys are going to the hospital. There was a third guy the police are looking for who was apparently known to the other two. Also, a fourth guy might be a witness. Do you know anything about that?"

"Hmm, no, I hadn't gotten that far south," Maxx lied. "Did they give any descriptions?"

"All four were Asian, likely Chinese nationals from the IDs and witness statements."

Maxx was silent as he thought about that information. Clearly something was wrong with the information, but it was to his benefit for now.

"You still there?" Daryl asked after a few seconds.

"Oh right. I was thinking about the second question I'd asked you. Some coincidence about that being a Chinese contract."

"I emailed you my notes. I recall telling Natalie at the time not to take the job. She said you needed the money for some bills. The bottom line was they had some concern about employees from TechCom they were in the process of recruiting and wanted you to do some surveillance and deep background work. It sounded very sketchy to me, and although not illegal, not very ethical."

"She was right. We did need the money, but I wouldn't have taken that kind of work. I know too many people at TechCom, and if word got around I was helping them poach employees, it would cause me to lose more business than what I stood to gain from one contract."

"That isn't even the strangest thing about this," Daryl continued. "You know at least two people they wanted you to review, your girlfriend Gabby and her boss, Dale."

Maxx was confused now. He had been retained to do a thorough background review of Gabby before they had met. Natalie had not mentioned this assignment to him, and Gabby had never told him that she was considering leaving TechCom to go to work for a Chinese company.

"I'll look through your notes and get back to you with a plan," Maxx said. "Obviously, I can't fulfill that contract now that I'm in a relationship with Gabby. But I don't want to get sideways with this company and end up paying nonperformance penalties."

He hung up the phone as he got off the bus and walked the last couple of blocks to his apartment, his head reeling. Maxx's Spidey senses were tingling. There was something very odd about this...before he even considered the events of the last couple hours.

When he opened the lobby door, he recognized the woman from the bus stop, who stood up from the couch. She was short but built like a gymnast with broad shoulders and long, muscled legs. Her face was an oval, her features—brown, almost black eyes, high cheekbones, full lips—bunched into the middle. She wore a dark mid-length skirt, white blouse, and a blue blazer, which made her look like she'd stepped out of a midlevel attorney's office.

"We need to talk in private. Let's take a ride," she said, walking over confidently and offering Maxx her hand. "I'm a big fan of your work."

IN THE HOUSE OF LOVE

She'd had a hunch he'd try and make it home, and it didn't hurt that they'd taken the trouble to put a trace on his phone. When he'd come walking through lobby doors, the look on his face when he recognized her was worth all the running and bus hopping she'd had to do to get here before him. She could almost see his mind racing to figure out who she was and why he was sitting in the lobby of his building.

She wondered if he might argue with her or resist going with her, but her official government identification from the not-yet-official Department of Homeland Security was convincing enough to give him pause.

"I'm Miss Grey," she said with a smile and a light Hispanic accent. "Would you mind giving me a tour of your beautiful city?"

"How exactly am I going to do that? Why don't we chat upstairs? I'm sure you know by now this is where I live."

"I have a ride outside waiting for us. Let's talk where I can be sure we won't be overheard."

"How can I say no to an offer like that? Lead the way, ma'am," he said as they stepped outside.

A black SUV with tinted windows pulled up to the curb. There weren't any official markers, but it might as well have had a bumper sticker that said "Fed." She preferred to be less conspicuous, especially when she knew others were looking for Maxx, but it was the best she could do on short notice. It wasn't like they could go sit in a Starbucks while she explained the current situation. She didn't fully trust him but needed his help, and he was in the thick of the mess now. She'd have to be selective about how much she told him.

When they got in, the overhead lights from the car shined on his short, light-brown hair and prominent forehead, giving her a glimpse of his hazel eyes. Up close, she could see the outline of his muscles even through the heavy fabric of his shirt.

"I know you were at the bus stop. How long have you been watching me?"

"Since the bar."

"You were at the bar?" he asked incredulously. "How much did you see?"

"If your question is if I saw the fight in the alley, the answer is yes."

"And you haven't involved the cops?"

"I'm the reason they are looking for someone else and not you." She could see the look on his face as he thought about what that meant.

After a few minutes of silence, he said, "You were following the Asian guys, weren't you? And you know why they attacked me in the alley."

"I was following them," she said without bothering to add that she'd also been following him. "I don't know why they decided to attack you this evening, but we do know why they are interested in you."

"It seems like everyone knows what is going on but me. Care to give me a clue?"

"You have a friend, girlfriend, named Gabrielle Fisher who works at TechCom."

It wasn't a question; it was a statement of fact. She was walking a fine line about giving him the right information but not disclosing too much. The Chinese team had clearly under-estimated him when it mattered most, and she didn't want to make a similar mistake.

"What does this have to do with Gabby?" he asked suspiciously.

"Everything, I'm afraid."

He nodded. "You're going to have to be more specific. I'm not a fan of riddles."

The SUV, which had been driving for some time, pulled up to a gate in a nondescript industrial area by Boeing Field. She stepped out of the car to talk on the phone at the security booth. It was obvious from their poise and weapons that these were military police at the front gate, despite the absence of uniforms or identifying signs.

After taking him through the front gate, the SUV drove to the rear of the building and down a ramp to an underground garage. The entrance to the garage was hidden from the road and had a second set of guards controlling the heavy gauge steel door. While they looked the same as the crew at the front gate, with the same military crewcut and firm bodies, these guards were clearly US Marines. Even though she had cleared security once, she had to repeat the process again before the vehicle gate swung open and the SUV drove down a few levels to park.

The empty underground garage was a seemingly endless cave of gray concrete and flickering fluorescent light fixtures. The driver parked the SUV near the oversized door that appeared to be the only visible personnel access. After staring at the ceiling-mounted camera above the door, the lock clicked loudly enough to echo in the cavernous garage.

The driver opened the door to lead the way. She motioned Maxx to go next and entered last to make sure the door sealed securely behind them. There was no chance anyone could have gotten past the guards, the gate, and the imposing steel blast door, but they were extremely serious about security here. She'd gotten her ass chewed out the last time she'd let the door close on its own.

The group proceeded down the tiled hallway that was painted an Uncle Sam-discount white color. Even the doors were white, although they each were labeled numerically as B2-001, B2-002 etc.

From a speaker placed in the ceiling, a monotone voice instructed them to move toward door B2-100.

"This place has none of the charm I expect from a top secret government facility," Maxx said.

When they arrived at the designated door, it slid open with a hiss of compressed air. Instead of a room, it was an oversized elevator of stainless steel with no visible controls. Although she had been to this facility a couple times before, they had met in a tasteless conference room filled with cheap furniture. She had never ventured this far into the building and presumed that they were either going to meet someone much higher on the chain of command.

When the elevator door closed behind them, she expected that it would begin to move up, but instead it felt as if it was descending rapidly. Her instincts were confirmed when they stepped off the elevator and she could see the marking on the wall indicating they were now at B9-100. They had come down seven more stories from the underground garage and were deep inside the facility.

Maxx looked at her with a raised eyebrow as he pointed to the floor number. "Good thing Seattle isn't in an earthquake fault zone."

As they stepped off the elevator, they were in a sealed room that had transparent glass walls facing both sides of the hall. Through the glass, they could see several Marines holding rifles in a low ready position. The oldest Marine, presumably in charge, spoke into an intercom, "Please place all your personal effects in the sliding trays in the wall opposite. That includes wallets, phones, watches, and especially weapons."

After they put everything from their pockets into the sliding drawers, they could hear the drawers locking. The Marine then instructed them to proceed through the metal detector in single file to what appeared to be a carbon copy of the conference room she had seen last time she was here. A single table, a dozen uncomfortable chairs, a projection screen on the wall, and a ceiling-mounted projector. There wasn't a pen, piece of paper, or paperclip anywhere, as if the room was never used.

Maxx looked at the ceiling. His meaning was clear. They were being monitored here. He then asked for some water.

The same atonal voice from the ceiling said, "Please be patient. Doctor Smith will be there shortly."

"The famous Doctor Smith?" she responded. When no one answered, she turned to Maxx. "I can pick up the conversation where we left off, but I'd like to hear what Doctor Smith has to say first."

Since none of them had anything to read, they sat silently in the conference room waiting for their host to arrive. Maxx closed his eyes and appeared to be sleeping. Her driver tried to communicate with her using sign language, and she studiously ignored him in case there were hidden cameras, which she knew was the case. She took the time to mentally run through what might be the next steps depending on what they told Maxx. It was paramount that they find out what the Chinese knew at this point and avoid giving them anything more.

After about thirty minutes of waiting, a middle-aged Hispanic man came into the room. Two armed Marines waiting outside the door closed it behind him. Plain looking, the man's only notable characteristic was a pair of glasses as thick as her thumb. He continued cleaning them even though they were already spotless.

"I'm sorry to keep you waiting," he said, clearing his throat. "I'm Doctor Smith."

She stood and started to introduce herself, but he quickly cut her off. He looked vaguely familiar, but she couldn't quite recall where she had seen him before.

"I'm aware of who you and your colleague are. I had instructions to meet with you, but this other person is a bit of a mystery. Let's start with him." He nodded toward Maxx.

Maxx seemed to be as unimpressed as if he were meeting too many people at a church social. "I'm Maxx King. I only came because Miss Grey said you had free booze."

Grey cringed and brushed her long, dark hair behind her ear as she tried to paper over his remark.

"Let me give a quick overview, since Maxx isn't being very helpful," she said to Doctor Smith. "Maxx is a former military officer who owns a private cyber security business here in Seattle. He was unknowingly contracted by the Chinese team to keep watch on his girlfriend, who works at TechCom on Project Hermes. Early this evening, the Chinese broke cover and tried to take Maxx out of the picture. We decided to bring him in and provide some background. Originally, we were observing him, but the Chinese must be ready to move, and we need him actively engaged on our side."

"I have no idea what this Project Hermes is beyond the obvious reference to Greek mythology," Maxx interjected. "This is the first time I've heard about it. I was minding my own business when these three Chinese guys attacked me."

Doctor Smith held up his hand. "Okay, I understand the connection now. I'm authorized to give Maxx some information based on the security clearance you sent over, Miss Grey. But I have to keep the conversation at a high level, and what I say remains confidential. Am I clear?"

"Yes, we are clear," they answered almost in unison. Maxx rolled his eyes.

"Now that we have that administrative detail in the record, let me start with some background." He took off his glasses and began cleaning them again.

"I'm going to presume you all are familiar with DARPA, or Defense Advanced Research Projects Agency. It helps the US Department of Defense create innovative technologies to be utilized for national security purposes. As you might imagine, much of that work utilizes what is commonly known as artificial intelligence or AI.

"Because these capabilities require tremendous expertise that the agency hasn't fully assembled yet, DARPA is occasionally using outside resources at a variety of organizations like TechCom, Microsoft, and local universities. As is the case with Project Hermes. DARPA has a very aggressive timeframe for a specific project, and Project Hermes at TechCom is responsible for some critical processing and analysis. It appears that the Chinese government is working on a similar project. It is a race, and the Chinese are trying to penetrate TechCom because they can't get in to DARPA directly."

Maxx, rapidly trying to connect the important puzzle pieces, spoke up, "I know you aren't going to tell me what this project involves, but what do the Chinese expect me to find out from Gabby? And since they hired my firm to collect information, why are they trying to take me out now?"

She nodded. "I think I'm better suited than Doctor Smith to answer those questions, Maxx. It's doubtful they would expect Gabby to divulge much or anything specific to you. It's highly technical, and there's not a lot of detail she could share that the Chinese aren't already aware of. If it was details they wanted, they'd have to kidnap several people on the Project Hermes team or have a mole inside. We believe it is most probable they have a mole.

"What they are most likely looking for is information about project timing. If there is a mole, they may not be close enough to the project to know when a critical point is reached. They might suspect Gabby would informally communicate a radical change in timing to you because of your relationship. Knowing when is as important to them as what."

Maxx shifted his gaze between the two of them. "That's rational but doesn't explain why they'd take me out of the picture now."

"They either think you're working for the U.S. government or have figured something out on your own through the work they hired you to do. In that case, it's more important to directly find out what you know. They think the best way to get answers is to interrogate you. The clock is running out, and they need answers."

"Fighting them at the bar probably convinced them that I'm a dangerous U.S. intelligence operative protecting Gabby and not an uninvolved citizen," Maxx added quietly as he rubbed the stubble on his face.

"This is all background that we're aware of," she said to Doctor Smith. "The Chinese team has been taking measured, conservative steps for the last year. For some reason, it's accelerated rapidly in the past few days. They are taking increasingly risky actions, and I was hoping you'd provide additional context.

"We've known for the last twenty years that the timing was going to be in this decade but didn't know exactly when. However, last week the Hermes team was able to decipher some information that indicated the critical date is next week, September 11th to be exact."

"Deciphered information from whom?" Maxx asked.

Doctor Smith removed his glasses again, a nervous tick.

"Mmm, we aren't exactly certain of the source," he said with a slight stutter. "However, we are confident the file is not from the Chinese, because they're also trying to decipher the excerpts as quickly as we are."

"You mean this code is from a third government?" she asked.

"An unidentified third faction."

"And both the US and the Chinese are trying to decipher it at the same time...and spying on each other to make sure they aren't late to the party?"

"I think I have the picture, but I don't understand why next week is so important when DARPA has known that a critical date was coming for years. What is going to happen?" Maxx asked.

"All we are certain of is that we will be getting more information on that date. It's an open communication window we couldn't exactly pinpoint. We also needed to make sure we had the technology and the language capability to communicate effectively," Smith added.

Maxx rolled his eyes again. "This is sounding more and more like science fiction. Someone has sent you code that you need to break to be able to communicate with them, and this open communication window has been coming for roughly twenty years."

"That's the gist of it, yes," Smith answered.

"Strange, but I guess that's what you all do here at DARPA. Why aren't the US and China working together if it's that important of an event?"

"That's not my decision and was a choice made many years ago independently by both governments. Perhaps that will change after next week if there is effective communication by one or both governments."

The door to the conference room opened, and a uniformed

Marine said, "Doctor, it's time for your next meeting. I'll escort our guests out now."

After saying goodbye to Doctor Smith, the three gathered their personal items from the locker and were accompanied back to the garage. Other than the Marines, the elevator and hallways were devoid of any other people, giving the impression that the building was deserted. She knew better. If the deadline was next week, they had to be working around the clock deeper in the facility.

Once they were in their vehicle and driving north on I-5 back to Maxx's condo, he spoke up. "Thanks for getting me the clearance to get the background, but I'm not sure I feel any more enlightened after that conversation."

"You're welcome," she answered. "I thought it'd be important to understand that before I asked for your help."

He laughed. "I was wondering when I was going to get the request. No one in the government does anything without a quid pro quo, especially when they work for a mysterious agency named Homeland Security."

She gave him a half smile. "I didn't involve you in this event. You signed an agreement with the Chinese that got you in hip deep. Killing that Chinese agent and putting the other one in a coma put you in up to your neck. I'm trying to dig you out."

"What do you need from me?"

"DHS can handle the direct work with DARPA and the Chinese. What I need from you is to keep an eye on Gabby to see if she changes her pattern in the next few days. That will be a triggering event, and while I don't think the Chinese will take her out of the equation prior to that time, they may do it after. Call or text me at this direct number if you think anything is off."

She handed him a blank business card with her phone number written on it.

"Alright. And if I don't?" he asked, and she lowered her eyes at him.

"I can't force you to do anything. But right now no one knows you had anything to do with the dead person in the alley. DHS has that covered. If you don't want to play ball, we'll have to hand that back over to Seattle PD." She stared at him for a moment to make certain he got the implied threat.

The SUV pulled up to the curb outside Maxx's building, and he opened the door.

"Thanks for the game of hardball. It's been swell," he said as he stepped out. "I'll keep you informed if I hear anything unusual from Gabby."

"Maxx, by the way," she said as she began to close the car door, "you know the Chinese will be actively hunting you now that they think you're working for us. His name is Haoyu, and he's as dangerous as they come."

I GOTTA FEELING

Maxx didn't sleep well despite getting home late and having had quite a workout during the fight and the subsequent flight through downtown. The trip to the DARPA facility had helped fill in some gaps but added an entirely new set of questions. He'd tossed and turned for several hours after texting Gabby when he arrived home, taking a shower, and settling on the couch.

He woke up with a splitting headache later the next morning when his assistant, Bonnie, called him on the home phone to say he had a client holding on the line for his 9 a.m. scheduled call. He had her transfer it to his cell phone and stumbled through the brief call while he looked for something to settle his stomach and headache. After, he told Bonnie to cancel all the rest of his calls for the morning.

He had a light schedule for the day because of a hosted party at a corporate box at Safeco Field for the Mariners game that afternoon. One of his bank clients had given him four tickets for the celebration when the Mariners hopefully secured their 100th win of the season. He'd invited Gabby, his close friend Glen Piper, and Glen's son Scott.

Maxx and Glen had served together in a couple Special Forces units during Maxx's years in active duty, and both shared a fondness for baseball. When he'd gotten the invitation to the party, Glen was the first person he called after he made sure Gabby could get the afternoon off work. Gabby and Scott knew each other at TechCom, so they'd been looking forward to the time to catch up, grab a hotdog, and watch the Mariners win at home.

He hadn't gotten any messages from Gabby that she needed to cancel. After what he'd heard last night about the critical deadline for the work that Gabby was involved in, he was anticipating a message that she'd be late or would have to miss it altogether. When he'd texted her this morning to confirm that he should still pick her up and they'd take a cab together to the stadium, she'd told him that her boss, Dale, had been encouraging her to take the time off, and she didn't want to ask again.

Maxx hadn't told her about last night's events and was planning on telling her most of the story when they were together. He'd tried to clean up the bruises on his face where the guy had connected with a couple solid punches. But when he had his sunglasses off, it was pretty evident he'd been in an accident or fight.

Before leaving the condo, Maxx set a few traps to let him know if someone had been in while he was gone. He guessed that Miss Grey or someone else from DHS had checked through his place before. He'd do a thorough search later for bugs and cameras, but for now he assumed they'd planted some while he was at DARPA last night.

He didn't think the Chinese were also watching him yet, but better to know sooner rather than later. He placed a couple pieces of thread in his home office and a hair between the door and the door jam as he closed it behind him.

The TechCom building was only a twenty-minute walk

from his condo in Capitol Hill, so he decided to walk rather than drive.

After he arrived at the TechCom building, he sat across the street at a coffee shop to watch the pedestrians going by and see if anyone was following him. No one stood out from the crowd, but he'd been fooled by Miss Grey yesterday. He ordered a cup of coffee, black with some sugar, hoping it would take the edge off. If the coffee didn't do it, then he might need something a little stronger.

When he saw Gabby walk out the front door, he called the cab company, left a tip on the table, and crossed the street. While he was still twenty yards away, he took off his sunglasses and watched the look of concern cross her face.

"What happened to your face, Maxx?" she asked.

"I cut myself shaving again."

When she got closer, she reached up and touched his cheek.

"Are you purposefully trying to make me feel sorry for you, Mr. Tough Guy?"

They hugged each other for a moment before she leaned back and looked him in the eyes. "Are you going to pretend you fell down the stairs, or are you going to tell me what really happened?"

He tried to meet her gaze but gave up after a few seconds and looked away. He never could lie to her, which was a good thing for their relationship but made some conversations very uncomfortable. This was one of those conversations. There had been many like this when they had first started dating, which had led to him cutting way back on his drinking. Drinking and fighting, if he was being completely honest.

"I had a bit of a run-in at a bar last night while I was watching the baseball game. I promise I didn't start it, but as usual I finished it."

She continued to stare at him as if she was waiting for him to go on.

"Yes, I had one beer, and I was not even tipsy, Gabs," he said sheepishly. "I tried to walk away from them, but they wanted a fight, and they got it."

Maxx felt conflicted about not telling her the entire story but figured this wasn't the time nor the place for that part. Not only was a lot of the background information confidential, but he was unsure how involved she was in any of it. He decided to give it some time before laying out the full story.

She paused, and then her eyes got big. "This doesn't have anything to do with that man who died in a fight last night near Pioneer Square, does it?"

"What? No, of course not. I heard about that, but this was a friendly scuffle."

"Maxx, what am I going to do with you? You promised me you'd cut back on the drinking and work on your anger. Your drinking almost landed you in jail before, and I can't deal with that. Besides, you might end up seriously hurt. I know you think you can handle any situation that comes along, but one day it will be more than you can take."

"I promise you it wasn't like that. A client had a cow over a contract that Natalie had messed up on. It deescalated once a few punches were thrown."

Now he really felt terrible about telling her the partial truth. He had been doing much better lately and felt that he'd turned the corner on this drinking and fighting. He didn't want to jeopardize his relationship with Gabby, who was the best thing that had happened to him in a long time.

The cab he had called finally arrived, and they climbed in the backseat. He told the driver to drop them off as close as he could get to the baseball stadium with all of the traffic.

Gabby wasn't ready to drop the subject yet. "What did that

witch do this time? I get tired of hearing Natalie's name every time you get into trouble."

"She'd hired us out to do a job and forget to mention it to me. But I found out about it yesterday and coincidentally ran into some of the client's management at the bar. It seems they were angry we had not followed through on the contract and decided a few punches would get my attention. They were right about that."

Maxx really wanted to ask her about the potential job with the Chinese company that she was interested in applying for but knew that would lead to a lot of questions he couldn't answer. It might even lead to an argument about him getting into her personal business.

After a few minutes of silence, they changed the topic to the weather, the game, and the trip to Hawaii they were planning. The normally short cab ride took another twenty minutes and finally dropped them off a couple blocks from the stadium when it became obvious that walking was going to be faster.

The crowds were dense as Maxx led the way up to the side entrance for premium ticket holders. Since the Mariners had moved to Safeco Field from the Kingdome a couple years ago, attendance had grown substantially. And with their record this year, it was looking to be a sold-out crowd. The place was alive with the excitement of more than forty thousand fans eager for the 100th win of the season.

Reaching the upper levels required a lot of stairs. Gabby had never been to a private suite at the stadium and was glad to be out of the pressing crowds. Maxx couldn't afford tickets to the premium booths or the Diamond Club behind home plate, but occasionally a client sent some tickets his way, and he never passed them up.

This was his first chance to show Gabby how high rollers watched the games. Tonight, they were likely going to see fireworks, entertainment, and a very engaged crowd if the Mariners were winning. All the excitement helped him push the events of the last twenty hours to the back of his mind.

The bank's private suite had a fantastic view from the first base line with the downtown skyline in the background. The clear blue sky behind the skyscrapers framing the deep green of the grass made Maxx grin. Sometimes he lost his appreciation for Seattle's beauty, but on an afternoon like this it was easy to remember. With the stadium roof fully retracted, there was even a light breeze blowing in from Puget Sound. As he breathed in the smell of the salt water, freshly mown grass, and food being served, Maxx realized he was famished and hadn't eaten anything since he'd wolfed down a bowl of stale pretzels in the bar almost twenty-four hours ago.

The small suite was only half filled when he and Gabby showed their passes and were let in. He knew a few of the people from the work he'd done for client. They both grabbed a beer from the bar and made the rounds for introductions. After some small talk and more than a few toasts, they went to the buffet and found a seat. Glen and Scott hadn't yet arrived.

Not long after picking out four seats on the outside patio, Maxx heard Glen's booming voice as he entered the suite. Glen wasn't as tall as Maxx but had the shape of a fireplug and the voice of a foghorn. When the two of them were together, they looked like a tall and wide version of two brothers. Scott was a younger version of his dad but was more soft-spoken and still had a full head of hair. While Maxx kept his hair cropped close, Glen had shaved his head bald when he started to lose his hair at the age of thirty.

After they'd had a chance to spend some time catching up, Scott leaned over to Maxx and with a little bit of nervousness asked, "Maxx, I was wondering if I could get some advice from you on a personal cybersecurity issue I ran into. It's probably

old stuff to you, but it's a bit embarrassing to me, so I thought
I'd ask you when we were together."

"Sure, Scott, why don't we find a spot where we can chat in
private?" Maxx replied.

Glen looked at Maxx and said, "He's already told me about
it, so don't worry about being too hard on him. I told him you'd
be an objective expert without trying to get in the middle of his
personal business."

"This sounds really juicy," Gabby exclaimed. "Are you sure
don't want me to tag along for a woman's perspective?" She
winked at Scott.

Scott blushed a little when he mumbled, "Naw, it's nothing
like that. It's not about any girl problems."

"Okay, Casanova, let's see what this is all about," Maxx said
as he stood up and moved to the door to the hallway.

When they found an empty room that was open, Maxx
shrugged while Scott worked up the nerve to speak.

"I hope you don't mind, but I was not telling the entire truth
when we were in the suite. It has to do with something going on
at work, and I didn't want to say anything in front of Gabby,
since she works in the same area I do."

Maxx narrowed his eyes.

"Why are you concerned about saying something with
Gabby around?"

Scott paused. "I know she's your girlfriend, but we are
working on some really crazy things lately. And I don't know if
she knows what's going on in my area or not, so I didn't want to
say something that would be a breach of confidentiality. It is
technically a breach even for me to mention it, but my dad said
I can trust you and that you work with security projects all of
the time in your business."

"I understand, Scott. I trust Gabby, but it's your story, so tell
me what you can. Then we'll see if I can help you."

"I'm working on this project for TechCom. I can't tell you all the details, but it involves using some artificial intelligence that we've developed to try and understand some encrypted information we received. It was so advanced that we had to first try and understand what the methodology is behind the encryption. It's not even next generation stuff. It's like many generations beyond anything we've seen before. It's like we're peeling back layers on an onion, and each new layer is something new and unprecedented."

"That sounds very interesting, but I don't work with any encryption at that level."

"That's where it gets interesting. This code is so complex that it clearly came from somewhere that is using technology far ahead of us in the commercial environment. We've spent the last year and are only now beginning to understand how it works. It's so advanced that it has to come from either the Russians, Chinese, or the US intelligence system, and it seems we are involved in something that may be helping China or Russia crack our own encryption. I want to make sure we aren't working for a foreign government to break our own code."

"You're worried you're involved in something illicit?" Maxx asked.

He frowned, thinking about Maxx's question. "Yes, that's part of it. Do you think I've got some personal risk if the US government finds out we're doing some work for the Chinese or Russians?"

"If you're acting on behalf of your company, and there's a contract to support the work, that's up to the company's attorneys to be concerned about. Even if TechCom is at risk, if you are working within the bounds of the contract, both you and Gabby would be personally protected. That doesn't sound like something TechCom would knowingly take on."

Maxx was beginning to strongly suspect that Scott was talking about Project Hermes. It sounded very similar to the project he had learned about at DARPA last night. Both Scott and Gabby reported to the same boss, so it would make sense that they might be working on different elements of the same project. He couldn't tell Scott that DARPA was outsourcing the work to TechCom.

"I'm still confused why you didn't have this conversation with your boss," Maxx continued.

"Normally, I would have, but that's the other issue I was going to mention. There's something about Mr. Phi that I don't trust. Since we took on this project, he has been acting unusually secretive, and it feels like he's holding some information out of the reports that we prepare internally and for the client. He makes edits that aren't completely consistent with what we're doing."

"Like what?"

After a slight pause, Scott answered, "We think there are three parts to the data that we're deciphering. The first part appears to be some critical dates or times that don't match our calendaring system. That's what I'm most involved in. Then there are engineering specifications that seem like a physical design. And then the third part of the files seem to be instructions or procedure, perhaps how to use the devices. Gabby is working on the third team."

"What do you think Mr. Phi is misrepresenting?"

"He's reporting that the second part of the data is irrelevant and that we shouldn't put any resources into this team. But he has a secret team working on that data segment that doesn't go back into the other two teams or into any of the formal reports. It feels like he knows something the rest of us don't, and none of us know how it fits together."

Maxx wondered who the Chinese mole that Doctor Smith mentioned might be. In his position, Dale could easily curate some of the important findings and feed the information to the Chinese. That would give the Chinese inside access to the results without the need to share raw data.

Following that line of thinking was beginning to make Maxx uncomfortable. If Dale was the mole, then there had to be a connection to Haoyu. If Haoyu was involved, that begged the question of why he had contracted with Maxx to research both Dale and Gabby. Since he'd been retained by Haoyu prior to Maxx and Gabby starting a relationship, it was causing him to wonder if they had really met by coincidence. The topic of the mole – and thinking about Gabby as a possibility – was raising a level of distrust he didn't want to consider.

"Have you tried calling out this discrepancy to him directly?"

"I did confront him about it, but he said I didn't see the big picture and should focus on my areas of the code so that he could manage the overall project. I even tried putting some red flags in the weekly status report that goes to other tech teams, and he pulled them all out and gave me a verbal warning about disregarding explicit instructions."

"Have you ever talked to the other teams or Gabby about Dale's oversight?"

"Gabby and I did talk about it briefly. She said she'd also gotten the same pushback from him. We'd agreed to drop it unless there was something specific we could raise in a team review, where we'd back each other up."

"Do you have any guesses why he might be doing that?" Maxx asked.

"I wouldn't say this to anyone else, but I wonder if he's trying to carve out some of the critical information to make sure he is indispensable if the project gets elevated at TechCom or taken over by the client that hired us."

Maxx nodded grimly.

"I'll talk with Gabby and see if she can provide any additional information, without mentioning you of course."

"Thanks, Mr. King, I'd really appreciate it. I'm new in my

position at TechCom and don't want to cause any problems, but it seems very odd."

He squeezed Scott's shoulder and moved toward the door. "No problem, I'm happy to help if I can. Let's get back into the game before it's the seventh-inning stretch."

The Mariners had entered the season as one of the few Major League baseball teams to have never won 100 games in a season. That night, they removed themselves from that list by easily beating the visiting team and becoming one of the few teams in major league history to reach the 100-win mark in only 140 games. They had previously clinched a playoff spot, so the fans were in a great mood to celebrate.

Watching from such a great panoramic location was especially exciting for Maxx and Gabby, who seemed more relaxed than she'd been in weeks, and it helped him put the events of the previous day out of his mind. That night, Maxx enjoyed spending time with his friends and the enthusiastic fans around him. He felt like his life was getting back on track.

As the celebration was wrapping up, Scott got a text from work, asking him to come back in. Maxx thought Gabby might get a similar message and was glad when she didn't. That meant the two of them would have the chance to catch up and spend the evening watching some episodes of *Friends* that they'd recorded. Hopefully Gabby wouldn't ask him any questions about what he and Scott had discussed. He didn't want to lie to her, but it was quickly getting complicated, and she was involved to some degree.

Maxx and Gabby got a ride home from the game with Glen and Scott. It would be impossible to find a cab with the crowd celebrating, and Maxx was still feeling tired from last night and didn't want to walk home. Scott dropped them off and then drove back into the office. Maxx was glad Scott had taken his dad's advice and gone easy on the free drinks.

On the drive home, Maxx couldn't shake the feeling that

they were being watched. He never saw anyone, but it was crowded and would be near impossible to pick someone out of the crowds and the traffic. If anyone was following them, he hoped it was Miss Grey or another DHS agent, not Haoyu. He needed to be careful, but it was difficult when he didn't know all the players involved.

MESSAGE IN THE STARS

Scott parked his dad's car in the underground garage. TechCom had several satellite offices around Seattle, and this was one of the least visible locations because of the sensitivity of the work that they were doing. It was an old industrial building near Ballard that had been renovated inside and had access to the utilities that had been put in when it was running manufacturing machines during World War II. The outside was unmarked and sat among a variety of other repurposed buildings. The parking lot was underneath the building to further the appearance that it was not heavily utilized.

He wasn't thrilled about coming back into the office after the game, but it wasn't totally unexpected based on the pace they'd been working on Hermes over the last month. He was glad he'd had a chance to talk with Maxx but also felt like he'd said too much about the project. He didn't care about badmouthing his boss, because Dale deserved all that criticism and more, but mentioning that the project was split into three parts was more information than he'd wanted to disclose. From the surprised look on Maxx's face, it seemed like Gabby had told him none of that.

He trusted Maxx not to say anything to anyone but Gabby, but that probably would make her angry. She was more senior than Scott and wouldn't take kindly to breaking any confidences.

Scott had to show his badge to get into the garage, again to get into the elevator, when he checked in with security on his floor, and lastly to get into the office where his team worked. Because of the amount of bullshit the engineers sorted through and the open-cubicle arrangement, they affectionately referred to their work area as the bullpen. They had a large open room of workstations on the fourth floor that was close to the other two Hermes teams but separated so that they had to meet in an internal conference room for cross-team conversation.

When he entered the bullpen, most of his team had already arrived and were working at their terminals. They briefly asked him how the game was and got back to work. Scott turned on his Hermes computer, and while it was booting up, he read the flash that Dale had sent to the team. The Hermes computers were physically connected within the facility but had no external connection to other company systems or external systems. Any Hermes-related input or output was transferred to an intermediary system that made sure it was sanitized before being ported in or out.

The flash bulletin from Dale was coded as extremely sensitive, and Scott had to approve a security release before it opened on his terminal. He had to reread it twice to make sure he had read it correctly.

At 1605 UTC, the Hermes Codex System was able to decipher 27% of data in the Alpha file, a major accomplishment.

What we determined: The largest known star in our universe, hyper giant UY Scuti emits a very distinct set of wavelengths of electromagnetic radiation. Those exact wavelengths were matched to a data block key in the Alpha file. The Alpha decryption key is derived from a specific set of solar wavelengths.

It is unclear if the wavelengths match UY Scuti or different stars. Our partners at the Jet Propulsion Lab are running models to identify other viable wavelength sets. After they have some data for comparison, we will test those wavelengths against the Alpha data.

Expect the potential wavelengths to arrive from JPL in the next several hours.

Scott sat back in his chair. This was an incredible breakthrough. He quickly pulled up the output on the Hermes computer to see what the output looked like. It was impossible to translate the information in its current structure, but he could establish what looked like two sections of independent information based on binary numbers. Once they had a full set of binary data, they would be able to translate it to English. It prompted so many questions. How did they land on the idea to try wavelengths from UY Scuti? They'd been testing trillions of potential source frequencies and wavelengths for months. He doubted they'd found the right wavelength key by coincidence.

The instant messaging system on Scott's computer pinged as he was starting to write down some notes. "Scott, read my message then stop by my office ASAP."

That was interesting. He'd never been called into Dale's office in the three years he'd worked here. After he had been elevated to Alpha section leader on the Hermes project, he'd expected he'd be invited to his personal space. Instead, Dale had continued to meet with him in the team conference room, even if it was only the two of them. Scott hoped this was a good sign.

Dale's office was basically a cubicle with walls covered in whiteboards. Some of them were covered with information that made sense to Scott, and some were obscured with a shade. There were a couple of extra guest chairs that were stacked with reports, additional evidence that Dale rarely had anyone else in his office. There were no personal pictures or effects on his desk or the walls. It looked like his life was completely devoted to work, his desk a chaotic mess with piles of printouts and unread reports.

After entering, Dale pointed to a chair while he finished a phone call. It sounded like it was a brief summary of the email that he had sent to the Hermes team. He said something noncommittal as he hung up the phone and swiveled his chair to face Scott.

"You read my email?" asked Dale.

Dale was dressed in his unofficial uniform of khaki pants and a plain blue shirt that looked like it was recently grabbed off a clothes pile at Costco. His greasy, shoulder-length hair was unusually messy, and his bloodshot eyes darted from screen to face but never settled on anything for long. He attempted a smile that didn't quite reach his eyes as he looked at Scott expectantly.

"Yeah, very exciting. I was jotting down a few questions that would help me to plan out the next steps once we start receiving some of the wavelength data. Can I run those by you now?"

"No, let's hold that for a team huddle after we're finished in here. I called you in because I'm getting concerned about the questions you're raising about me supposedly withholding information about the Omega file from the weekly reports. It looks like we're about make a significant step forward, and I don't want this issue left unresolved."

Scott took a deep breath and looked his boss in the eye.

"I raised this concern to you directly. A lot of us don't agree with your assessment that the second data set is less critical. I told you this, and you told me to drop it. I don't know what other questions you're referring to that have happened since our conversation."

The condescending look from Dale was withering.

"That's not what I'm hearing from others, and I want to

make it clear that if you continue to pursue that line of questioning with other people, in or out of the team, I'm going to escalate this into a formal action through HR. Am I clear?"

Scott was stunned since he'd only talked to Maxx about this a few hours before and no one else. Dale's comment was either an unbelievable coincidence, or somehow his conversation with Maxx had been overheard and reported to Dale. That was almost too bizarre to contemplate.

"I hear you. But since this is between us, I would like to raise my concern one more time. It's clear to me that the Alpha data includes some translation key to deciphering both the Delta and Omega files, and therefore they are related. It makes no sense that we would completely disregard the Omega file and only focus on Delta."

"I've explained this to you before, and I think your lack of experience is leading you to suppositions that won't hold true. Not all things on this project are equally important, and I have to choose how to deploy the available resources to get the maximum results. It is my call on how to prioritize resources and focus on the project in its entirety. Your job, Scott, is to focus on deciphering the Alpha data."

"I understand what my job is, Mr. Phi, but it's a mistake to compartmentalize the data before we understand the potential interdependence."

Dale shook his head.

"I don't think you know what a mistake looks like if you're continuing to press this issue. I've discussed it with more senior engineers that have forgotten more than you'll ever learn. They all agree with me that this is the right approach here at Tech-Com. Their recommendation was to cut you from the team since you seem to be overstepping your boundaries."

"Cut me from the team?" Scott exclaimed. "I don't see how being inquisitive is grounds for transfer."

"Inquisitive is one way to describe it, but I see it as trying to undermine my authority. And on a critical program like Hermes, I won't tolerate it. Consider this your last warning to keep your focus on your job and out of mine. Clear?"

Scott was seething but knew he couldn't push the conversation any further at the moment. He would see what the data showed after they were able to decipher the Alpha file and then see if it vindicated him or not.

"Is there anything else we need to cover right now?" Scott asked.

"Plan on staying as long as it takes to make meaningful progress on Alpha. If we're at 27% already, I think we can get over halfway in the next day. If you find anything significant, report back to me first. Don't leave the building without checking out with me."

As Scott was walked out, Dale told him to assemble the team in the conference room and he'd be there shortly to update everyone. "And this conversation stays between us. No more chances."

The team meeting went on for several hours, during which they used the whiteboards to diagram the likely options and how they would proceed. There wasn't a lot that the team could do to prepare without some additional frequency inputs that they were expecting from the Jet Propulsion Laboratory. The files would be extremely large, so they had prepared to break them into multiple segments. Then they would run them through the security screening process, upload them into Hermes, and then begin the analysis process.

Because UY Scuti was one of the largest known stars by radius, the artificial intelligence engine had begun mapping the maximum brightness of magnitude with some significant events on Earth. Another team at JPL was tasked with looking for similar stars in comparable constellations, based on a similar size distance from Earth. There was a lot of speculation by the team that there was at least one other similar star that would correlate, and the coordinates of that star would fill in missing gaps in the code.

He had learned that the Alpha file had been around since the 1980s. However, the various teams working on the analysis and decryption had only begun to make significant progress in the last year with advancements in AI capabilities and the availability of granular astrophysical data.

He'd also been told that the Delta and Omega files had been around even longer than the Alpha file. It was difficult to believe that another government had been that far advanced compared to the US in its ability to encrypt and crack code. Assuming the data came from either the Russians or Chinese, it was perplexing to consider what information the files might contain that would still be relevant two or more decades later.

In the very early morning hours of Thursday, the Alpha team received the first files from JPL. An hour later, they had been cleared by the security team for upload into Hermes. Scott was told there would be at least seven more similar files arriving over the next several hours. He went to the cafeteria to grab a giant mug of coffee and head downstairs to the processing center.

The processing center was on the sub floors beneath the underground garage. It was only accessible by a dedicated set of elevators that required a separate security clearance. Employees, like Scott, could access the floor that housed the processing center but were restricted from entering the center that contained all of the supercomputers that handled the AI processing, due to the strict security and environmental conditions required. The series of processors had been dubbed MaGiC by the technology department. The tech employees who worked in the processing center were affectionately known as wizards, and they preferred not to have to interact directly with the rest of the employees at TechCom.

A series of cubicles lined the outside of the center in which employees not assigned to the tech teams could view the wizards at work. They could also chat directly using an instant messaging system. This allowed them to communicate in real-time on sensitive projects and still maintain the separation of the center from the rest of the building.

Scott logged on to the system and pinged the MaGiC team to see how the processing was progressing. He needed to give Dale an update. A terse answer came. "On second batch. Zilch so far. Hold tight in observation area."

He pulled up his email to send a message to Dale and didn't get an immediate response, so he pulled up the data they had processed earlier to see if he could spot any patterns that he'd missed. It still looked like there were two independent sections in the data: instructions, a time event, and a translation key. Unfortunately, with only 27% translated into binary code, it was mostly undecipherable with the occasional series of characters that might be a word.

Scott dozed off while looking over the data. The zeros and ones along with the beer from the baseball game had relaxed him enough that he put his head down on the desk and fell asleep.

A chime from the processing center communication system startled him awake. When he glanced at the clock, he saw that he'd been asleep for more than an hour. His inbox indicated that he had five new messages.

Four of the messages had been sent over the course of the last hour, giving him a series of short updates. It was the fifth message from NOUCRZY99 that caught his attention. "Call me ASAP at extension 9999."

It must have been sent with priority, which had generated the chime that woke him. He picked up the internal phone and dialed 9999. After three rings, a female voice answered. "Li Jing. Hold."

After a few minutes, Li Jing picked up the phone again. "I

apologize. I wanted to transfer the call to a secure room. This is Scott?"

"Yeah," he answered with a raspy voice, sounding like he'd been asleep. "You messaged me to call you as soon as possible."

"Thanks. We've been running the files we received a few hours ago and got a hit against Alpha in the fifth data set. The correlation is perfect, like the frequency we had processed yesterday evening. My guys ran both variables against Alpha concurrently and came back with a combined success rate of 74%. The two variables must be working in combination."

"Then we only need one more variable to achieve 100% decryption. That's much quicker than we expected."

"That's what we think too," she said. "Hopefully the final matching variable is in one of the remaining files."

"It seems likely that the next variable would be from a similar star, right?" Scott asked.

"Yes, that is what JPL believes. We first narrowed the search criteria to Wolf-Rayet stars, a rare subset of supermassive stars. Due to their strong emission lines of gases, they can easily be identified in nearby galaxies. We have narrowed the search to a smaller set of coordinates with WR stars that meet our desired profile."

"What are the coordinates based on?"

"JPL thinks it's an equilateral triangle with Earth at the calculated center," she answered.

"What is the corresponding date then?"

"This is where it gets a little weird based on the date of the files." She paused. "The time and date that correlates with UY Scuti is July 28, 1976, the day of the great Tangshan earthquake."

"What's the second date? Another major earthquake?"

"Not exactly. The date is May 18, 1980."

"When Mount St. Helens erupted?" he gasped.

"Yes, both events show a relationship of the exact time, date, and location with the wavelength data of the two independent stars. However, the files are from the 1950s, so they were using two dates in the future to calculate the frequency for the stars and the dates of the events. The likelihood of that happening is zero, Scott. It's simply impossible."

"And yet it has happened. It's not impossible, but we don't know how it was done. Is there something else you you're not telling me?" he pressed.

After a long moment of silence, she answered, "Based on the limited set of coordinates of the third star, we believe we know approximately what the corresponding date will be."

"What was the event?" He was quickly trying to recall a list of the most significant natural events in the last twenty years, and the most notable event he could recall was the devastating cyclone and flood in Bangladesh. While there was a terrible death toll caused by that disaster, it didn't fit the pattern of the other two events. Both of those events were caused by seismic activity, and Bangladesh had been the result of a devastating cyclone.

"It's not a date in the past... It's next week."

BLURRED LINES

Scott crafted a brief email summarizing the details of the work over the last several hours in the processing center and sent it to the Hermes team. He then prepared a separate email for Dale's eyes only that provided additional detail from his conversation with Li Jing. He didn't get a response back from Dale but did receive a number of questions back from the Alpha team, all of them centered around what they should be prepared to do if a complete translation arrived in the next day.

In the absence of direction from Dale, Scott told the team to assemble in the Hermes conference room in an hour. He'd stay down in the processing center in case there was news from Li Jing.

He waited for an hour and messaged Li Jing before taking the elevator up to the fourth floor. She responded, "We finished processing. I have notified Dale of the results and have been instructed to report in person in your team conference room thirty minutes from now."

It wasn't odd that Dale had gone directly to Li Jing or her boss after reading Scott's email. He'd expected that might be the kind of end run Dale would make. What surprised him about Li Jing's message was that she was going to be presenting in person. It was very unusual for a senior person to leave the processing center during work hours for a face-to-face meeting. Typically, they joined via video conference to avoid the process of going in and out of the security check during a shift.

It was clearly a signal that the findings were meaningful enough to warrant a visit to their team room. Scott jumped on the elevator then stopped for some more coffee, since the first mug was cold and hadn't done enough to keep him awake all night.

Everyone began arriving in the conference room and grabbing seats as far from Dale's usual seat as they could. Everyone knew he'd be in a cranky mood after being awake all night and likely being bombarded by email and calls from executives.

Li Jing came in, made brief introductions to the team, and sat at the head of the table in the chair Dale typically occupied. Her straight, black hair was pulled back into a ponytail, and stylish glasses pushed on her forehead. She was much more attractive and professionally dressed than the typical employee that they had worked with in the processing center.

Her presence and choice of a seat created a bit of a stir with the rest of the team, who were curious to see how Dale would respond to the unintentional usurping of his authority. If Li Jing noticed the ensuing tension, she ignored it and continued to type on her laptop. She connected it to the presentation system in the room but left the screen blank while everyone waited for Dale to arrive.

When Dale entered the room, it was clear he was thrown off by someone sitting in his traditional seat. After a moment or two, he went to one of the other vacant seats by Li Jing and introduced himself. She acknowledged him with terse nod and then asked if she could start, seemingly in a hurry to get back.

She projected her laptop onto the screen.

"As you are aware, early this evening we found the correlating code to begin translating the Alpha file to a binary language. With the data sent to us by JPL, we had MaGiC looking for additional code that would correlate to Alpha. Scott emailed you about that finding, which greatly accelerated our search for a third and final code.

"We found the third code and have been able to determine the date, time, and Earth coordinates. The results are different than the two previous codes. It differs because it is a future date, and the location is not the site of a known earthquake, fault line, or volcano. There is no reason to link that location to any past seismic events. The time is 0937 EDT on September 11, 2001, and the coordinates are 40° 46' 58" N / 73° 58' 15" W."

When Li Jing pulled up a graphic showing the three dates and locations, there was an audible gasp in the room. In addition to the markers on Tangshan, Hebei, China and Mount St. Helens, Washington, the third marker was placed over Manhattan, New York.

Dale cringed at the screen. "I'm finding this to be a bit of a stretch. The encryption keys were formed by correlating the wavelength data from three unrelated stars in three different galaxies and then matching that data with the latitude, longitude, and times from two past events and one future event on our planet, correct?"

"Yes," she said. "There is complete certainty and no other set of variables that correlate with those data points. MaGiC ran quadrillions of alternative iterations and could come nowhere near to the same level of correlation. That those variables create a key resulting in a deciphered Alpha file makes it difficult to believe it was random. Impossible really."

Lyza, one of the data scientists on the Hermes team, said, "I have some questions. Do we have a theory about why the variables from the three codes correspond to these three specific stars?"

"We don't know why these three stars exactly, other than that by mapping them relative to our sun, we see we are located in a triangulated position. There is no other star that is in a position that can be at the center of this triangle. Our sun is figuratively the needle in the middle of a universe-sized haystack. This calculated universal position was how the JPL team derived the location of the third star so quickly."

"This makes sense," Lyza continued, "but that leads to my next question. How did we identify the location of the first star? Because our logic flows from the location and characteristics of the first star. If that was an incorrect assumption, then everything that follows from that assumption is likely wrong."

Li Jing nodded. "I agree, but the first coordinates were embedded in the Delta file. Also embedded was a set of numbers that correlates to a specific wavelength of that star's output. In fact, it was the only information in the Delta file that was translated when the files were first received. We didn't realize this is what the data represented, the first portion of a master code."

"If we knew that information, then why did it take us this long to discover the code's other two stars?" asked Dale.

"We didn't have the capabilities of machine learning to try to determine what variables that data might correlate with. We also didn't have the processing power to attempt the iterations required to solve for the missing portions of the Alpha key. Knowing that the starting point was UY Scuti told us we could determine the relative times and locations on Earth, and it allowed us to identify the characteristics we were searching for in a similar star.

"It was like the Alpha file was written in several different numeric languages intermixed. Once the file was in a readable binary language, it was easily translated to a nonnumeric language that most of the world can understand."

"The Alpha file has been translated to English?" Scott asked.

"It translates to English in addition to Mandarin and Spanish," Li Jing answered. She brought up a new slide on the screen that read,

Five Primary Elements of the Alpha File

1. *Three dates/times and geo locations on Earth that correspond to the wavelength data of the three identified stars.*
2. *Requires that contact only be made during the sixty minutes following the times indicated in the star codes.*
3. *Requires that communication only uses the protocols as described in the attached information. [Delta file]*
4. *Requires that communication must use the appropriate translation device as described in the attached specifications. [Omega device]*
5. *A strict warning that if we do not do as instructed, a punitive event will be triggered at the locations indicated in the star codes.*

"When were these files received?" Scott asked.

Dale glanced at Scott and addressed the room. "The initial files were received in 1957, but the source, exact date, and method of transmission are still highly classified. The Alpha file was amended in 1982 when several new lines were inserted into the file. No one in this room is cleared for more than this information."

"Do we at least know why we were given the files?"

"No, we don't. That raises additional questions," Li Jing answered. "This is an extremely complex code system that has taken us forty years to decipher. What country had that kind of technology available over forty years ago?"

Lyza spoke up from the back of the room, "No one on this planet was capable of this at the time we received these files. This also would be consistent with the information that is used to provide the locations and details of the three stars. This kind of complex coding based on information unavailable in 1957 could only have come from an external civilization."

Li Jing nodded. "We and JPL concur with that conclusion. It's a message from an alien source. This message was encrypted in a manner that required us to advance technologically to understand.

"We've suspected that source for years, and the evidence seems to support that thesis. But there is another oddity. The Earth coordinates correlate to two past cataclysmic events, one in China and one in the United States several years apart. The coordinates for these events are built into the coding system.

"Do the creators of the codes have knowledge of future events, or did they somehow trigger the events on the predetermined dates and times to match them up?

"We don't know the answer to that, but we can assume that some event will occur in New York on the morning of September 11. Incidentally, that was the information that was inserted into the Alpha file in 1982. I wouldn't be surprised if these events were examples of the 'punitive events' that they reference in the Alpha file."

"You mean that we humans did something incorrectly to trigger the previous two events?" Dale asked.

"Exactly. That seems like historical information someone in the program would have. Hopefully that doesn't mean that what occurs next week in New York is also a catastrophic event. Let me finish up the final slide, because I think it's relevant."

Li Jing projected a new slide on the screen.

In addition to the five elements, the Alpha data also includes

- *The decryption keys to decipher the second (Delta) file.*
- *The decryption keys to decipher the third (Omega) file.*

After reading the slide, Dale said, "It seems to me that the next steps are clear. I'll bring our liaison at DARPA up to speed on the latest findings. I'll also ask DARPA if they know what might have triggered the events at Tangshan and Mount St. Helens. That may get them thinking about what they expect to happen in New York."

"I also have approval to start decryption on Delta and Omega, once DARPA tells us to move forward," Li Jing added.

Scott doubted that Dale meant to reveal that TechCom was performing the Hermes Project under the direction of DARPA. But now that he better understood that the files were linked to an alien civilization with potential catastrophic penalties for mistakes, it made sense that DARPA would be at the center of the effort. The stakes for involvement in this project got a lot more serious and helped explain the pressure the Hermes team had been under the last month.

The meeting had been a lot more productive than Scott had expected. On the way out of the conference room, Li Jing asked him to stay behind for a moment to get his opinion on one other item. Scott was surprised she hadn't grabbed Dale, but he practically ran out of the room after they wrapped up the meeting.

When the room was clear except for the two of them, Li Jing closed her laptop, stepped closer to him, and whispered, "There was one item I didn't bring up in the presentation, and I'd like your opinion – between you and me."

"I'm sure you know I'm the lead person only on the Alpha team," Scott said. "Dale is the team leader of Hermes and can give you a more informed opinion."

"Perhaps he's a little too informed," she said as an aside. "As I said, the file translates to two other languages. And of course, the initial event is related to an earthquake in China. Do you have any idea why this would be?"

"I'm still trying to process this, but my guess is that maybe we aren't the only country that received the original files."

"My team thinks that's a natural assumption too. China and possibly a Spanish-speaking country are also working with this information. Maybe Russia too, although there has been no evidence of their involvement.

"Here's my question, Scott, and why I came to you directly," she continued. "When MaGiC is examining the available information, it looks at all public and some private information that it can access. It found no information relevant to the Alpha or Delta file in any private domain."

"I would hope not," said Scott. "We have lots of safeguards to keep it confidential."

"But it's very concerning that we did find a substantial amount of information related to the Omega file that was "informally" sourced from some recently obtained Chinese communication. My sources tell me you've been raising concerns that we should be pushing on the Omega file harder. They also tell me Dale has moved this task outside of Hermes and that the Omega file team is working independently of Alpha and Delta. Is this true?"

Scott glanced at her, trying to figure out how much he could trust her.

"Yes, it's true. I have raised concerns that we were not pressing forward on the Hermes team with Omega. But what does that have to do with the information you got from China?"

"There might be an information leak on the Omega team, I would speculate."

"That would make sense why Dale would want to keep it

isolated from the rest of the team. I still don't understand why you're asking me this instead of him."

"I did speak with him," Li Jing said, "but his answers weren't very convincing. And since you have been raising concerns about the isolation of the Omega team and transparency, it seemed to me that you might have some off-the-record insights that would help me sort this out. And if you see something unusual going on, feel free to ring me directly at the processing center...not through email."

"I will keep my eyes open, but Dale has made it clear that I am to keep my nose out of this. I'll contact you if I notice anything that might be relevant."

Scott took a moment to consider everything he'd learned before heading back to his desk. While he had suspected that Dale was not being upfront regarding the Omega team's separation, it made sense if he was trying to keep the Alpha and Delta teams from any external leaks. He tried to imagine Dale as the source of a leak in light of his strange behavior. But if he was the source, it wasn't obvious why he would only relay information from the Omega team and not Alpha or Delta.

This was becoming very complicated if the US government was behind Project Hermes and if the Chinese government was also on a similar path. If there was information passing to China, there very well might be information moving from China to the US. It seemed that there was not only a race to communicate with some alien contact but to prepare for some major event occurring in New York in a few days. He knew they got the occasional severe storm with flooding there, but he wondered how bad that could be as he pulled up the New York City weather forecast for the next week. The flooding there had never been on the scale of the either events and historically had never been the result of a seismic event.

The forecast looked benign, safely ruling out the possibility of an earth-shattering storm forming in the north Atlantic.

Scott was looking out of personal interest because he was sure somewhere there would be entire teams of people looking into the possibilities in New York.

In addition to the main headquarters in Virginia, there was a DARPA satellite office here in Seattle and one in New York. That was a bit of an odd coincidence, but certainly they'd have a vested interest in looking at it.

He texted Maxx a cryptic message to alert him about the odd warning Dale had given him last night. One or both of them might be under surveillance, and now that Li Jing had told him about a potential leak, it made sense that they were being watched closely.

"Thanks for the pep talk earlier. I wonder what it would have sounded like to be a fly on the wall. What do you think? I'm tied up here, but let's catch up ASAP."

His new Nokia 6310 cell phone reset shortly after sending, and he set it aside when it wouldn't restart. It was cool that everyone on the Hermes team had gotten the new phone as a business perk earlier that year, but the Bluetooth connection seemed to make it operate erratically whenever he was in the office. He hoped Maxx had gotten his message before his phone crashed.

The mole stepped into the vacant room and closed the door. There was no lock, but at this time of the morning no one would have reserved the conference room for a meeting.

Using a mobile phone, the mole dialed a number memorized months ago. The number was linked to the after-hours exchange for a local physician's office, if anyone ever bothered to try to trace it. After the fifth ring, the mole hung up and called the number again, directing the call straight to a voicemail box. The voicemail recorded a detailed message that would be immediately transcribed and inserted into a classified email. Its contents would raise quite a few eyebrows. The email would be distributed to everyone on a selective email list before the sun lit the rooftops in Washington D.C.

After hanging up, the spy made a separate call to a different memorized number. "Scott Piper has become a problem that needs to be permanently removed."

He is someone else's concern now.

CREEPIN', NEVER SLEEPIN'

Miss Grey made the trek to the DHS offices early in the morning. The cab she'd grabbed to take her from her hotel downtown to the federal building dropped her off at a nearby coffee shop as the sun was peeking over the Cascade Mountains.

There was enough light to see the city starting to stir, and she definitely needed the caffeine after being up all night monitoring the communication traffic between TechCom, DARPA, JPL, and a half-dozen government security agencies that had an interest in the unfolding events. Drawing a deep breath, she took in the smell of the roasting coffee beans and the bakery across the street.

One thing at a time, she reminded herself. *Keep your eye on Haoyu, and let the scientists do their job.* It was good advice but difficult to follow when she was getting pulled in so many directions. One way or another, she had the feeling this was going to come to a head soon, and she'd have to pick a clear path through the politics in Washington, DC.

As for Maxx, she hoped he would heed her advice and take care of Gabby.

She needed to focus on Scott Piper, who was likely in danger. One of the internal contacts at TechCom had called in a warning last night that two people were being scrutinized and in danger from Haoyu and his team. She knew Scott, and they had monitored him while he was with Maxx last night. He'd made it clear he didn't trust his boss, Dale Phi, who they had done a thorough check on, clearing him of any connection with Haoyu, but there could be some other connection they were missing. She'd get someone else to investigate after she'd talked to Scott in person.

While she was at TechCom this afternoon, she also wanted to spend some time with the other person whose name she had been given, Li Jing. She had pulled up a quick jacket on Li Jing, who had an extremely high security clearance but hadn't been investigated specifically related to Hermes in the previous year, since she was in the tech department and not specifically assigned to the project. *One thing at time.*

Carrying two large coffees, Miss Grey opened her unlocked office door and promptly stopped halfway inside the door.

There was a man sitting at her desk typing on her computer.

He barely looked up as she stood there gaping at him. Before she could ask him what the hell he was doing at her desk, he stopped typing and put his hands up.

"It's okay, Miss Grey. You may not recognize me, but we have talked often in the past year."

Grey walked in and kicked the door closed as she juggled the two cups of coffee. Her eyes never strayed from the large man wearing a bow tie as she calmed her nerves. "Mr. Green, I presume."

"Correct on the first guess." He stood slowly and held out his hand as she set the coffee on her desk. "It looks like you brought refreshments. Expecting someone?"

"No, it's been a long night. Is there something I can help you with on my computer? I was expecting that we'd chat on the phone with your boss."

"I don't trust the communications of late. Someone at DHS is getting suspicious that you may be playing both sides of the field and doing a little extra curricular monitoring. That's what I was checking for on your computer."

"And what did you discover?"

"Someone at DHS is tracking your conversations. It's an open secret in Washington that senior politicians are trying to avoid a misstep with Hermes. DARPA, DHS, and the Department of Defense want to remain ahead of the political conversation. As careful as you are, they must suspect you are feeding information to a political source...me."

Grey pursed her lips.

"I've been clear with you and your boss, the senator, that I am not going to actively undermine DARPA or DHS. They may see it differently, that I am providing you information directly, but my intent is to only shorten the communication path."

As she looked around her office, she was glad she'd been checking frequently for listening devices. She was also aware of the back doors that had been put on her computer. This was a dangerous situation, but she felt it was a risk she had to take when the potential for a miscalculation was so high. It was best to cut through some of the bureaucratic red tape.

"What I don't understand, Mr. Green, is why different people in the government have an interest in taking control of communication with the aliens. I respect that there are varying points of view about what should be messaged, but I would think that would be managed with one unified voice representing the US government."

"You and I agree on that point, Miss Grey. Many in the government feel they should make that decision because they are better informed or have more insight. You happen to work for one of those areas of the government.

"I hope the Chinese don't have a similar problem. It could be catastrophic if competing factions from multiple governments are communicating conflicting messages to an alien civilization. We don't even know what their intent is in communicating with us, and we could really create a disaster for ourselves and the rest of humanity.

"We aren't spending enough time thinking that through. Why are the aliens going through all this effort to communicate with us now, and why did they create such a complex coding structure? The complex cryptography seems as if they were afraid the communication might be intercepted by someone other than us."

After Mr. Green moved from her office chair, she sat down and pulled some tablets from the drawer and a pen.

"This is how I see things," she said as she began to diagram out her thoughts.

On one side of the paper, she wrote the three dates and locations with a blank space above them, ordered in time from Tangshan, Mount St. Helens, and lastly New York City.

Along the top, she wrote, "Who, What, When."

In the first row for Tangshan, she wrote "Chinese government" under "Who." She then proceeded to fill in each of the boxes.

"It seems quite clear that the Chinese and US government each made an attempt to contact the aliens unsuccessfully. Those unsuccessful attempts triggered a disaster as a warning. The problem is we don't know who is likely to trigger an event in New York, as it hasn't happened yet. But the location seems to indicate it will be initiated by someone in the US, and we both know that DARPA has a facility in Manhattan."

"If that's the logical conclusion, shouldn't we avoid any contact and let the Chinese take the risk? Then we wait to see when the next open communication window is and prepare for that," Mr. Green said.

"That would be sensible, but for some reason both countries are pressing forward hastily. It's either blind competitiveness or that someone in the government knows the potential benefit of the communication and hasn't revealed it to others. I could imagine it is merely international competition, like the race to the moon with the Soviet Union, except we know there is a stiff penalty for an incorrect move. Part of the story has been closely guarded within our government from the start. The reason *why* we would contact the aliens is the missing piece of the equation.

"Since the aliens initiated this attempt at communication back in 1957, it stands to reason that they told us about their intent at that time. Because that information is such a closely guarded secret, I believe we need a political counterbalance to any military objectives, making sure that the interests are not only in the best interests of the US but the world. I think taking the alien's motives at face value could be an unrecoverable mistake.

"And that is why I am here this morning," she said, "to see if we can get whoever is pushing to make a move before I go to TechCom. Let's take a walk and grab something to eat. All of this caffeine and speculation is making me jittery."

As they walked out on Second Avenue, the traffic was beginning to get too busy for her to keep an eye out for any potential threats. It was unlikely that Haoyu would try and make a hit on her during the day on a busy downtown street, but it was evident he was willing to take some risks considering the attack on Maxx the other night. However, Maxx was not an armed federal agent. Haoyu would be raising the bar in the international tension between intelligence agencies quite a bit.

After walking a few blocks with no sign of a tail, she and Mr. Green began more active countermeasures, stepping into stores suddenly, splitting up at random times, and taking different paths.

As she stepped around a corner and out of sight of Mr. Green, a tan Ford with heavily tinted windows pulled up to the curb and slowed down. The back window rolled down enough for her to see the barrel of a long gun poking out the window, a man in a mask behind it.

She quickly threw herself to the side and began to pull her pistol from under her jacket. It was a quick action operating on adrenaline, and she hoped her response would prevent her from getting hit in the drive-by shooting. She barely had time to act, let alone think clearly.

I didn't think they'd be this brazen.

Before she had been able to target the passenger in the car, it sped away. No license plates. She heard a man laughing as the car turned the corner and yelling at her what sounded like, "Goodbye, Clarice!"

It must have been a reference to agent Clarice Starling in *The Silence of the Lambs.*

What did that mean?

She was standing up and putting her pistol back in the holster when Mr. Green came running around the corner.

"I heard someone yelling and a car racing by. Are you okay?" he huffed, out of breath.

"I'm fine," she said. "I'm not surprised they sent a warning, but I don't think it was my old friend Haoyu. He wouldn't bother with a warning. It has to be someone in one of the US security agencies letting me know I'm in physical danger if I'm not careful."

"Let's get back to the office and call it in," he said. "We need a secure line."

"Why don't you do that? I'm going to grab my car and go catch Doctor Smith first. I think he might be able to help me understand the genesis of this. Although this began before his time at DARPA, he had access to the origination files. Then I'll get over to TechCom before traffic gets too heavy. I need to talk to a couple of people who might have some missing background, and unfortunately one of them might be a little too close to the dangerous side of this. And the other might be feeding the Chinese inside information. I just don't know which one is the white hat and which is the black hat yet."

Miss Grey went through the DARPA security process at the underground facility near Boeing Field much more easily than the last time she visited. Being alone and having been a visitor multiple times in the last few weeks didn't minimize the process, but it wasn't new to her, so she anticipated the questions. She even recognized a few of the uniformed guards, although they treated her as if this was here first time at the facility. She imagined they wouldn't let their guard down regardless of who was at the checkpoints.

It struck her again that if she didn't know better, she would have driven right by this complex and not given it a second thought. It could have been any vanilla government building in the world with its bland, utilitarian furniture. She knew that it progressively got more distinguished as one descended into the lower levels, but she guessed it looked a lot like any other high-tech office building if you ignored the absence of any windows and an overabundance of armed security guards.

Making certain the door to the garage was secured behind her, the escort in the public announcement system instructed Miss Grey to a conference room a few doors down from the entrance. She had been authorized to meet with Doctor Smith again, so she was surprised she wasn't going to a lower, more secure floor.

When she was first assigned by the DHS to work on this investigation, the nature of the assignment piqued her interest. Her previous experience in working for federal law enforcement had been as an FBI agent on cases that involved influence pedaling to the Defense Department by right-wing governments in Central America. The government had learned some hard lessons during the Iran-Contra affair that they didn't want repeated. Her sharp mind, Hispanic heritage, and ability to speak several Spanish dialects led to a several promotions and eventually to her reassignment to the fledging DHS.

Her lack of previous experience with technical cases and limited exposure outside the defense industry initially made her question the wisdom of her assignment to Seattle. But after she had grasped DARPA's involvement and was introduced to Doctor Smith, she began to suspect why she had been selected to head this project team. In several previous investigations that she had been assigned to, there were rumors about Doctor Smith's motives, but nothing tangible had ever been uncovered.

She'd barely gotten seated at the conference table when a uniformed guard entered. The female guard quickly verified her credentials again then exited.

Miss Grey had created a list of topics she wanted to cover with Smith on the drive over. While she was most curious about the implications for New York, she wanted to start with the question of how this all began. She knew it had begun in 1957, but how was it uncovered, and by whom? That might help her understand the motivations involved.

Doctor Smith entered the room and started talking before the door was fully closed. "You must realize I'm extremely busy, Miss Grey. I hope this is related to your attempts to prevent the Chinese intervention and not another social visit."

What a pendejo.

"Doctor Smith, I'm doing my job the best I can with the little information I have. Being in the dark regarding the motivation of the Chinese team and the apparent mole at TechCom makes that difficult. Can you tell me anything more about the source of the files? That may help me understand what they may be looking for."

He proceeded to explain that the files had been received in 1957 but was not at liberty to say how that occurred. He could tell her that the files came with a readymade communication device, the one outlined in the Omega file.

"After determining the files and device were from an alien source, ARPA (now DARPA) was formed in 1958 to try and decipher the files and determine how to use the device. There was much speculation and significant fear that it could have a negative purpose, and caution was used to relocate the device as far from Washington, DC while remaining in the continental US. That's when the Seattle office was established, and the federal government funded a technology and aerospace resource pool to support the project in the geographic region."

"Through intelligence assets, we discovered that the Chinese had also received the same files and a similar device. Like the US, they handled their project with the utmost secrecy, since the implications weren't clear. In 1980, we learned that the Chinese had made a failed attempt to communicate with the aliens in 1976."

"When we learned that Chinese also had the same information, why didn't DARPA accelerate its efforts?" Miss Grey asked.

She could tell that struck a nerve by the way he glared at her before answering.

"Ah, but we did. Even though we only had a partially deciphered file, DARPA rushed an attempt at communication in 1980, which also was doomed to fail. Our rush to trial led to the eruption at Mount St. Helens. The original communication device was destroyed in the eruption. At that time, we came to the realization that the Tangshan earthquake in 1976 was related to the Chinese failed communication."

"After the disaster at Mount St. Helens, we received a revised Alpha file but did not receive a new communication device. The Delta and Omega files have stayed consistent since the 1957 version. For the last twenty years, we and the Chinese have been trying to decipher the initial alien communication to make certain we don't cause another natural disaster by botching an attempt. The technical capabilities that were necessary to solve the complex computations required quantum leaps in processing speeds, networking, inexpensive data storage, and ultimately machine learning, or what we now call artificial intelligence. All of that had to be ready by the time another communication window opened."

Miss Grey mused about this. "If the Chinese also have the same files and device, why are they suddenly so aggressive in interfering in our program?" she asked.

"There are two reasons," Doctor Smith answered smugly. "Their AI capabilities lag a decade behind ours, and therefore they are concerned that we'll decipher the files before them. They can't afford to miss the communication window if we're ready. If that happens, they won't have another chance for a decade or two...if ever."

"That would justify spies anywhere they could infiltrate." *TechCom.*

"The second reason is not so obvious and probably the missing piece of the puzzle for you. We know the device is a conduit for communication that relies on tremendous amounts of energy from natural sources. If it is used incorrectly, it results in a devastating energy backflow."

"How does that affect the Chinese?"

"It doesn't necessarily affect them directly, but now that we know the date and time of the next event, wouldn't it encourage them to make sure the device operates incorrectly? Then, not only do we miss the communication window, but it results in a third disaster in one of our largest cities and primary financial center," he said with grim look. "It would be more effective than a nuclear device, and we couldn't very well blame them publicly."

"We can't afford to allow the Chinese to succeed before us, nor can we make a mistake. Now that they know the time and the place, they have every incentive to make our attempt at communication fail."

Now she understood why Haoyu was willing to kill Maxx during the early evening hours in the middle of downtown Seattle. She knew she had better get to TechCom quickly before Scott Piper, Gabby Fisher, or Li Jing also got caught in Haoyu's crosshairs.

POEMS, PRAYERS, AND PROMISES

Scott kept searching the internet and any secured files that were not on the Hermes computer for information related to what Li Jing had shared with the team earlier today. Any searches related to the stars JPL identified didn't provide him with any additional insight.

He also conducted an internal and public search for significant events that had occurred on those two dates, which didn't reveal any other possibilities. MaGiC had already done this association, and he wasn't finding any other possible events of significance. The past dates that MaGiC had identified were only closely linked with the Tangshan earthquake and the eruption of Mount St. Helens. *Two strikes*.

He took a closer look at the information for potential natural disasters that might occur in the New York area and came up with nothing beyond references to storms and flooding. There were no faults or geographic anomalies that he found publicly or as he dug through the secured scientific data he had access to. As his searches became more complex, it took increasingly longer for the results to appear.

He guessed that the IT team was using all the available

processing power to work on completing the decryption of the Delta and Omega files. That would explain why any secondary processes and searches would be pushed to the back of the queue. It was creating a real bottleneck, but Scott was doing these searches informally to pass the time while he waited for the results to come back from Li Jing and MaGiC.

After getting nowhere on the question of natural disasters in New York, he thought about trying another approach to his early line of thinking about the first two dates. He had been told that the correlation with the dates of the two natural disasters was certain, so he created some code that would begin looking though the secure files he had access to using that date as a key parameter. The results were too large to process.

He leaned back in his chair and thought about any other parameters he might add to the search to narrow down the results. He tried *alien* in English, Mandarin, and Spanish and got no hits, but that didn't surprise him, as that would have been too easy. He tried every combination of words he could think of from the names of the three stars to the wavelength data and still got no meaningful results. Either no related information was contained in the files he had, or the files had been scrubbed of meaningful identifiers.

He closed his eyes, ran through all of the interactions he had over the last month, and sat up when he had a realization. *Omega.*

He quickly looked up how to spell Omega in Mandarin and Spanish. A few results came back, but nothing that was very informative. However, a few of the results referred to the number 800. Of course, Omega had a value of 800 in the Greek numeric system, so that wasn't terribly shocking.

He input 800 as the next variable in the query, trying it both as a numeric value and spelled out in all three of the languages in the file.

"My oh my... Home run!" he said excitedly.

The results came back with a subset of files in both Mandarin and English. He began scanning through the emails and reports that were in English. Every document was clearly marked "TOP SECRET – SCI 800." Scott knew that SCI meant Sensitive Compartmented Information, and he was seeing documents that he was not cleared to access. In them, he learned that DARPA had been involved and had lost the alien communication device at Mount St. Helens. *Omega is the key.*

Scott realized he was in serious trouble when his computer screen went dark, and he couldn't get past the login screen when it rebooted. His credentials were blocked. He checked his computer connected to Hermes, and it was frozen. He couldn't even get a login screen.

This can't be good.

While reading the documents before his computer shut down, he had noticed several common themes. Both DARPA and the Chinese counterpart, The Commission for Science, Technology and Industry for National Defense (COSTIND), had been trying to replicate the Omega device following the eruption of Mount St. Helens in 1980. Based on what he read, the US device had been on site during an attempt at communi-cation, and the US was unable to recover it afterward.

Additionally, the COSTIND documents had alluded to the fact that the Chinese team had suffered a similar loss of their device at Tangshan. Consequently, COSTIND had been formed through a reorganization of the ministry in an attempt to recover the US device or rebuild a replacement using technical information they had gained from the first device. It appeared that neither approach was entirely successful.

When his computer had been reset, Scott wondered if he should go talk to Dale and give him a heads up or stay at this desk and wait to see what happened. Rather than sit patiently, he began to put some of his personal items in his backpack. It only took a few minutes before two security people opened the door to their office and walked in. They were talking on handheld two-way radios as they made eye contact with Scott and made a beeline for his desk. They didn't appear to be armed, but they did look seriously agitated. They gave him instructions to only take personal items and confiscated his security badge and his Nokia phone that had been given out to the team. They then told him they were instructed to escort him to see his boss, Dale.

Dale's face was a bright red when Scott entered his office.

"Don't bother sitting down. This won't take long," he said. "You breached security access, and a formal investigation was initiated."

Scott was visibly shocked and tried to object. He was immediately cut off by Dale.

"Have you removed anything from the office that is work related?"

"Of course not," Scott answered with disbelief. "Look through my bag if you don't believe me."

After a thorough search of his backpack, which didn't reveal anything important, Dale shook his head in dismay.

"I don't know what you were thinking digging into files that were clearly marked top secret. You shouldn't have been able to override the security protocols, but tech will do a thorough review to see if it was intentional or an unforced error."

Dale and security escorted Scott down to the garage to get his car, forcing him out of the building. His parting words when he closed the door behind him were terse. "You're temporarily suspended. Go home, and I'll contact you after I discuss the situation with HR and security."

It had all happened so quickly that Scott was reeling from the sudden change. He was finding it difficult to process what he'd learned and that he was no longer on the Hermes project, potentially fired or worse. He had an idea what happened to low-level employees who breached national security. On a project like Hermes, jail was certainly a possibility.

He wasn't paying close attention to his driving, the recent turn of events and lack of sleep distracting him. Nevertheless, it didn't take him long to spot the car that was following him. The black sedan didn't even make any attempt to be inconspicuous, following him at every turn. The car was close enough that Scott could clearly see two men wearing sunglasses and white shirts. He suspected they were FBI agents by their appearance, but that was a guess. Definitely Feds though.

It wasn't shocking that TechCom had already contacted the government about the breach, but he was shocked that they had responded fast enough to already be following him. This must be much more serious than he could have imagined. He had given up his cell phone and didn't have any way to contact his dad to get some advice.

He could drive home and call him from there, but if they were already following him, they might have a wiretap on his phone. He hadn't intentionally done anything wrong but wanted to avoid giving the government any wrong impressions.

Scott recalled there was a pay phone at the convenience store up ahead. He occasionally saw people talking on it, so he presumed it worked. He pulled into the parking lot. Before making any phone calls, he went inside to get some change for the pay phone. He bought a coffee and something to eat to help calm his nerves and settle his churning stomach.

The Feds had parked around the side of the building, so Scott couldn't see them from inside. When he came out of the convenience store, he was surprised to see they weren't there. He hurried to the pay phone and tried calling his dad, but there was no answer, and the call went to voicemail. Rather than leave a detailed message, he told his dad he wasn't feeling well, had left work, and was driving home.

On a whim, since he couldn't reach his dad, Scott called

Maxx on his cell. Maxx picked up and answered gruffly, "I'm with a client. I'll call you back in a few minutes..."

Before he could hang up, Scott interrupted him. "Hey, Mr. King, it's Scott. Please don't hang up! I'm in a bit of jam and can't reach my dad. I was hoping you'd have time to talk with me in person."

"Okay, Scott, no problem. I got your text earlier but couldn't call you back. The message says your number is out of service."

"Yeah, that's related to my problem. Can I see you in person?"

"Got it. I can wrap up with this client and meet you in a couple of hours. Meet me at the pig in front of Pike Place. Don't worry. We'll get it all worked out."

Scott hung up feeling somewhat relieved. He didn't want to head home and wait, so he decided to go find a parking spot and find a place to wait near the market. Being able to watch all the activity in Pike Place might help take his mind off the trouble he was in.

Despite the cool morning and the summer tourism dying down, there were still a lot of people walking toward the market. The smells of the fresh seafood, coffee from Starbucks, and the salt air on the breeze blowing in from Puget Sound was making his stomach growl.

He realized he'd been living off junk food since he'd left the Mariners game last night. It was difficult for him to believe that was less than a day ago.

Walking through the crowd, he had a strange sensation he was being watched and wondered if the federal agents were still following him.

Exploring the shops, he tried to see if anyone was paying attention to him but didn't see anyone who looked suspicious. The usual mix of retailers, shop owners, locals, and tourists were all his untrained eye saw. He used a few techniques he had seen in the movies or on television shows, but they were amateurish and unhelpful. He tried changing direction abruptly, stopping in front of glass displays and watching people in the reflection, and using revolving doors to see if anyone followed him in and back out. He felt like a kid playing a game of spy, but he couldn't shake the feeling that he was being followed. The hair on the back of his neck kept tingling.

He thought since he was here and had some time to kill while waiting for Maxx that he'd grab a coffee from the original Starbucks store. Like most locals, he had avoided it for years because there was usually a long line of tourists, but the line was relatively short this morning. He had the time to spare and could use caffeine and some real food.

While he was waiting in the line to order, he borrowed a pen and made some notes on a napkin. He was tired and stressed and wanted to make sure he remembered to cover all the important points when he was talking with Maxx. *He'll cut to the important parts of the story.* Scott had to be careful not to put anything confidential in writing, but his notes would help trigger what he wanted to say. He also made a note that he put in his back pants pocket to remind himself to tell Maxx and Dale about his conversation with Li Jing.

He grabbed his coffee and Danish and walked toward Steinbrueck Park. The park wouldn't be too busy yet, so he'd be able to pick a good spot and watch the ferries come and go on Elliot Bay on a beautiful September morning.

Being surrounded by people and watching the sun on the water helped Scott relax a little, even though there was no way to completely forget what had happened at work this morning. He knew he hadn't done anything intentionally wrong, but he should have stopped reading immediately and notified Dale there was a problem. That had definitely been a screw-up on his part. Everything that had happened during the last day had been so shocking, so surreal.

He hadn't even found a place to sit on the grass when two

Asian men approached him. They looked like more Feds but different than the ones who had followed him from work earlier. The aviator sunglasses, white shirt, and sport coat must be like a uniform to these guys.

"Scott Piper, I presume?" the taller man said as he approached. He was the older of the two men and looked like he was at ease with a hint of a smile around his eyes.

Scott stuttered a bit, his nerves on edge. He'd never been in trouble before, and to now be followed by the FBI was unsettling. "Yes, that's me. Who are you?"

"Agent Neo, Federal Bureau of Investigation," he said as he showed Scott an official-looking badge.

The badge looked real to Scott, but he didn't know what he a real one looked like. "Neo like in *The Matrix*?"

"Yeah, I get that a lot," he said with a disarming smile. That wasn't exactly the behavior Scott had been expecting from a federal agent, but he couldn't help but return the smile.

"I can understand you're probably a little thrown off," Agent Neo continued. "We were told to make sure you're safe. This thing you're working on is very high profile, and there have been foreign agents getting their noses in places they shouldn't."

"That's the first time anyone mentioned that to me, but it explains why people are kind of edgy at work. I'm meeting a friend here in a little bit, so I think I'll be okay."

"We were asked to make sure you get home safely and keep an eye on you there. It's probably nothing to worry about, but better safe than sorry. We replaced the pair of agents who were assigned to watch you when you left TechCom earlier."

Increasingly concerned, Scott had never considered the possibility that there might be other countries or spy agencies attempting to intervene in Hermes beyond China's technical team. As he had told Maxx last night, he wanted to be certain they weren't unwittingly assisting the Chinese. But the idea that there might be foreign spies in Seattle watching him made him more anxious.

"Gosh, I'm a project manager. I don't know why any spy would care about me," Scott said. Maybe that was why Dale had told him to go straight home and the other agents had followed him from the office. If anyone had told him about potential danger, he would have went directly home and locked the doors.

"We don't know of any immediate threats, but I think it would be safest if we walked you back to your car and then followed you home. We can make sure your house is safe too."

Scott was really getting concerned now. He'd call Maxx to let him know about the change in plans when he got home. He was sure Maxx would understand.

The agents walked Scott back to his car. The quiet one walked ahead, and Agent Neo walked a half step behind him, making certain no one got too close. It felt strange to be escorted by two FBI agents, but under the circumstances it was comforting to know someone was watching out for him. Agent Neo's humming was also helping him relax.

As the three of them approached Scott's car in the parking lot, the quiet agent stopped at the rear window to make sure that there was no one inside.

When Scott went to get in the driver's seat, he was confused when Agent Neo pulled his head back. He never felt the razor-sharp blade move across his neck. His last thought was to wonder where all the bright-red blood was coming from.

Scott was pushed the rest of the way into the car and slumped down over the center console, out of sight. Unless someone was looking closely through the tinted windows, all they'd see was a man sleeping.

Agent Neo closed and locked the car doors. He casually moved down the street, humming to himself.

Maxx finished his meeting with the client and was pulling out of the parking garage when his cell rang. He'd set the ringtone to play "The Imperial March" because Darth Vader's theme seemed appropriate for calls from Miss Grey. He smirked at his inside joke and pulled over to the curb to take the call.

"Good morning, Agent Grey. What's the good word?" he asked with unnecessary enthusiasm to irritate her.

"Don't call me agent, Maxx. I'm not officially an agent, since DHS is not recognized as an official agency yet. It's miss or ms."

"Sorry, sorry." He couldn't help but look at his grin in the rearview mirror.

"I wish I had good news, but this is a serious call. Are you somewhere you can talk privately?"

That is a concerning start to the conversation. "Go ahead. I'm sitting alone in my car."

"We had another homicide, and we think your friend from the bar was involved, although he was more successful this time."

"Why are you telling me? I'm not involved this time at all. I've been working all morning."

"I'm telling you because he killed someone that you know."

Maxx's stomach did somersaults. He was partly in shock but also began to run through the possible scenarios before he answered, "Tell me it's not Gabby before I explode."

"It's not Gabby. She's still at TechCom. I talked to her boss, Dale. He's keeping the team on lockdown in the building."

He breathed a sigh of relief. "That's great news. Then who was it?"

"Scott Piper. I know he texted you this morning and asked to meet you shortly."

Maxx listed in his seat, covering his face with his free hand.

The grin was long gone and replaced with a tightly clenched jaw.

"I'm not going to ask how you know all that, but you're sure it was him? And you're sure Haoyu killed him?"

"Yes to both questions. Someone called SPD about an hour ago. Scott was found in a car registered to him. The picture on Scott's drivers license matches the body. Several eyewitnesses described Haoyu at the scene. It's not a formal identification, but the homicide detective knew enough to call it in since Scott was on the FBI watch list. They called me."

"I appreciate the call, but why'd you call me other than that Scott was planning to meet with me shortly?"

"He had some notes in his pocket with your name and information that is highly sensitive to national security. It seems he wanted to talk to you about some things that are way beyond your clearance."

Gritting his teeth, Maxx glanced at the phone before putting it back to his ear.

"No offense, Miss Grey, but that is the least of my concerns right now. I'm getting real tired of your secretive spy games. Scott's father, one of my best friends, is going to be devastated. Has he been notified yet?"

"The police haven't contacted Glen. I asked the detective to wait until I talked with you."

"Do me a favor and let me go with the police to inform him. I want to be there. I'll tell you right now that this is going to end very badly for Mr. Haoyu. I will keep Glen out of this so he can grieve the loss of his only son, but Haoyu started something that I will finish. He can run, hide, or come after me, but I will write his ending."

COME SPY WITH ME

The homicide detective had taken photos of the Starbucks napkins that they recovered from Scott Piper's back pocket. She could go down and look at the originals that the detectives would put into evidence, but rather than wait she asked him to send the photos to her email. She'd asked the detective to contact the FBI to make sure the evidence was kept in a secure location. Chances were low someone could decipher Scott's scribblings unless they had a background that included the Hermes project, but she didn't want to take a risk.

The crime scene technician was also looking to match any latent prints with the copy of Haoyu's prints that the FBI supplied. The eyewitnesses had described him pretty accurately, and they were also looking for any security cameras in the vicinity that might be able to tie him to the crime. While it might matter at some point if there was any prosecution, she doubted it would come to that. Haoyu would never let himself be taken alive, and if he was, he'd never see the inside of a courtroom.

She received an email from the homicide detective a few minutes later. The pictures that were attached to email weren't the highest-quality resolution, but she was able to make out the gist of what Scott had written on the napkin. On one side, he'd made several lines that stood out to her. He'd probably written them in the sequence that was important to him.

The first note simply read, "NYC next Tue." Clearly, he planned to tell Maxx that the third location for a potential event was next week in New York. Knowing when and where a potentially catastrophic event might happen was an extremely distressing development. She was disturbed and could understand why Scott might also be overwhelmed and want to talk to someone about the news, but why would he think it was critically important to communicate those details to Maxx, even before going home?

If Scott had friends or family in the New York area, it would have made sense to talk with his dad, not Maxx. She was missing an important piece of information, and with Scott dead she hoped Maxx could clear it up for her.

Perhaps he had learned some other details and hadn't had a chance to let anyone else know about them. She knew other branches of the intelligence community were deep into analysis, but if Scott knew anything, it had died with him.

The second bullet point was a little more descriptive. "What happened to O devices? Both US and Chinese destroyed?" Doctor Smith had told her that the US device had been destroyed at Mount St. Helens, but no one said the Chinese had experienced a similar loss. Had both devices really been destroyed for both countries? If one country or the other had retained a working device, they'd be much further ahead than the other in preparation for the communication window next week. In fact, she didn't see how they'd have time to construct a replacement device in time using the Omega file that was now being deciphered.

This point also raised the question of why the Hermes team,

under Dale's direction, had put the Omega file on the back burner. His rationale that he thought it less important wasn't logical in light of the absence of a device. His decision to side-track work on Omega only made sense if he was trying to delay readiness for next week or if the device had not really been destroyed and was available. That would mean Dale was acting under the direction of someone who wanted to avoid communication or already had a device. She was confident that DARPA did not have it, but that still left the Chinese or some other group inside the US that was acting out their own agenda.

She needed to talk to Dale to see if she could ferret out the motivation. She had heard the recording of the conversation at the Mariners game when Scott had told Maxx he didn't trust Dale. Scott clearly got in over his head, and someone had informed Haoyu. As far as she was concerned, Dale and Gabby were both on her short list of possibilities.

There was no indication in Scott's note that he planned to tell Maxx that the source of the data and device was the result of alien contact. While it was possible Scott had already shared that information with Maxx, she was doubtful. There must be a reason Scott didn't want to tell Maxx or hadn't had a chance to write it on his note. Hopefully it was another question Maxx could shed some light on.

On the back side of the napkin was a single sentence. "Tell Maxx and Dale about conversation with Li Jing last night after the meeting."

She had seen the slides Li Jing had prepared for the meeting with the Hermes team, giving her a good idea what was covered. However, the SCIF was not wired to record conversations, so she had no idea what exactly was said. It was odd that Li Jing would talk to Scott and not Dale, since she and Dale were peers. It was possible Li Jing was also suspicious of Dale, but then why would Scott tell Dale about the conversation? There was a missing piece of the puzzle she'd have to ask Li Jing about.

She was aware that a confidential informant at Hermes had passed along Scott's name. Initially she had been concerned about Scott being the Chinese mole, and his unauthorized access into the file system had seemed to support that suspicion, but his death ruled that out. It was highly unlikely that Haoyu would burn an inside source unless he was worried about him breaking. It was more likely Scott had been targeted for being close to revealing something or exposing the real mole.

That would mean Li Jing was still an unknown. She could possibly be the mole or also be in danger. Miss Grey hoped she would be able to get some indication when she interviewed her shortly. A good place to start would be to ask Li Jing about the conversation she had with Scott after the meeting. She'd have to bluff that she knew more than she did, but she was a damn fine poker player.

Before she talked to Li Jing, she needed to talk with Scott's boss, Dale. She'd called ahead, and security was waiting for her at the front door of the TechCom building to give her a visitor badge and escort her up to Dale's office.

She'd visited several of the TechCom offices in the last year, but this was her first time at the Hermes office. Like the DARPA building, it was essentially in disguise. Anyone looking at the square concrete low-rise structure would have never guessed it housed some of the most high-tech processing capabilities in the world. It looked like a forlorn industrial structure that had seen better days. The entire complex had several layers of fencing, but she guessed many of the security layers weren't even visible. They certainly weren't visible to her, and she knew the telltale signs.

At the front entrance, she was vetted in a reception area that looked more like a high-security prison than an office building. In fact, there were no noticeable markers that this was even a TechCom building except for the employee badges. She could see that they were embedded with an RFID chip, which would track their location at all times in the facility.

Given the exceptional physical security, she was even more surprised that Scott had somehow *accidentally* gotten access to secure information. That seemed even less likely as she observed the layers of scrutiny she was going through simply to meet with a mid-level executive.

When she got to Dale's office, it was very sterile looking. She was surprised by the lack of personal effects in a place where she knew he probably spent long hours. It made her wonder how emotionally invested he was in the company. It looked like the space where a person was going or coming, not someone who had been at the company for three years as his profile stated. *Very curious.*

After clearing off a chair for her to sit in, he didn't waste any time with small talk or niceties. "You are here about what happened to Scott, I presume?"

She jumped right in too. "He was your employee, and I understand he was sent home several hours ago."

"That's correct," he said.

Sensing he was not going to willingly provide more information than he had to, she took a harder approach. "Why was he sent home? It seems unusual when you're under significant pressure to translate and analyze the Hermes files."

"I'm not authorized to cover that with you, Agent Grey."

"It's Miss Grey, not agent," she corrected him. "You are authorized. Read your email. The authorization from the head of the division to answer any of my questions is in there."

Dale grunted, spun his chair around, and read through his email quickly. Then he turned back to her and said, "I sent Scott home under the direction of HR and security, because he intentionally accessed top secret files that were outside his purview."

"You're certain it was intentional?"

"He had to write some very complex queries using classified search terms. That doesn't happen by accident. He was accessing files that he had no authority to review, and if he'd gotten retrieved classified information by accident, he should have immediately notified me. Which he didn't."

"Fair enough. But don't you all have security protocols to prevent unauthorized access *before* it happens?"

Dale ran his fingers through his disheveled hair and sighed loudly. "We do."

"He was able to disable those protocols?"

"We already checked, and there's no record of him disabling them. But the protocols were overridden by someone in this building, and the audit trail to determine who had overridden them were both disabled earlier this morning."

Grey squinted at him.

"Who has the ability to disable the audit trail and protocols? Scott?"

"Not Scott. Only a handful of people in this building. Me and a few people on the tech team. And it wasn't me, obviously."

"Do you realize how this looks to me and others outside this building?"

"We already knew there is a mole here. Maybe it was Scott, and we haven't discovered how he did it yet," he offered.

"Or Scott wasn't the mole and the Chinese wanted us to spend time focused on him instead of the real mole."

Dale shook his head, but she could see a small tic under his right eye. "That would be smart. I should have considered that."

"I just don't see Scott as the mole," she emphasized. "If Scott didn't have the necessary access as you said, that leaves the obvious explanation as the most likely. Someone perceived

Scott to be a potential problem and wanted him gone under a cloud of suspicion."

"Scott had FBI protection when he left the building. Were they involved?" he asked.

It was her turn to sigh. "No, they were reassigned to another emergency and left him unprotected." She didn't mention that the other emergency had evidently been a red herring.

"It's awful, and I feel like I sent him into a trap. I looked at the information he'd accessed, and he really didn't have time to get too deep into the details. It was a problem, but in the end it was only worth a written warning, possibly a suspension, but certainly not worth his life. He was either the mole and got caught or was set up."

"I have one other topic I want to cover with you. Do you know Li Jing from the MaGiC team?"

"Of course. What does she have to do with this?"

"Nothing that I know of yet, but Scott had a note in his pocket to remind himself to talk to you about a conversation she and Scott had after a department meeting last night. Do you have an idea what that might have been about?"

Dale paused and thought deeply. After a minute, he answered, "The only thing I can think of is about Omega. Both she and Scott have been pressing the issue of putting more resources on the Omega files. I had told him to drop the topic, but maybe they had new information he wanted to relay to me."

The security guard knocked on the office door and reminded Miss Grey that he needed to take her to meet with Li Jing.

"I'll ask her and see what she says. I'm already late, but when I have more time, I'd like to hear you explain why you disagreed with them."

"Let's chat when you're done with Li Jing," he said as he

spun around in his chair and logged into his computer. The conversation ended as abruptly as it had begun.

Dale Phi was still high on her list of possible suspects, and his lack of emotion about Scott's death only exacerbated her suspicion. He was hiding something, but what?

She followed the security guard to the secured elevator to the processing center. The security guard explained this restricted elevator only stopped on select floors in the building and required special clearance to access. Even with all the limitations to accessibility, there were cameras constantly monitoring the inside of the elevator cars and matching passengers to a small list of employees. It was clear there were strict, redundant security procedures in place to limit physical access. A clearer understanding of the physical restrictions only increased her belief that electronic access would be as restrictive.

She had been assured that there was no direct access to MaGiC from outside this building. There was literally no means to bring information in or out without being at this location and having the information screened through various highly secretive proprietary algorithms. Someone at DARPA had told her they demanded the same level of security from any outside agency as they had deployed themselves. That was the one of the security efforts implemented after the failure at Mount St. Helens.

When she was ushered into the conference room outside the processing center, Li Jing was already seated and waiting for her. She was much younger than Miss Grey had expected and looked like she had barely graduated from college, and yet she was already a senior manager at one of the world's most competitive technology companies. When Miss Grey extended her hand to shake with Li Jing, she didn't take her eyes off the keyboard of her laptop. *Why the hostility?*

Miss Grey ignored the slight and opened her own laptop.

"You don't mind if I take some notes of our conversation, do you?" she asked.

Li Jing shrugged. "Feel free, I'm going to do the same. Do you mind telling me what this is about?"

"First, I have some bad news to share. In case you haven't heard, Scott Piper from the Hermes Alpha team was murdered this morning."

"We heard about it from the security team when we went in lockdown. It's too bad. He seemed like a nice kid."

There was some irony in Li Jing referring to Scott as a *kid*, when she looked like she was at least five years younger than him. Maybe Li Jing was older than she appeared.

"We don't know the nature of the attack, but we don't want to take any chances that it was related to yesterday's events with Hermes, so we're talking with anyone he had contact with in the last day."

"I was his primary contact from processing when we were decrypting the Alpha file last night, and he was in a meeting with the team when I presented the results. Perhaps a conversation with the leader of the Hermes team would be more helpful."

"I already talked with his boss Dale and got his perspective on the meeting. Nothing stood out to him regarding Scott's behavior in the meeting. Did anything stand out for you?"

"No, Scott didn't say or do anything that seemed unusual, not more unusual than the entire topic warranted at least."

"What about the conversation you had with him after the meeting ended? What was that about?"

Li Jing looked at Miss Grey quizzically. "What meeting? I went to the restroom to freshen up and then returned directly to my office."

Miss Grey didn't want to divulge the details of Scott's note, so instead she said, "Perhaps I misunderstood something Dale had said about the two of you having a private conversation after the team left."

"Dale would be mistaken. I didn't talk to Scott after the meeting. That's easy to verify. Pull up the badge location logs to see our locations. We were never alone together last night. Or ever. I barely knew who he was."

Grey nodded halfheartedly.

Ji Ling closed her laptop and stood up. "Unless you have more questions, I need to get back to work. Are we done here?"

"That's all. I apologize for any misunderstanding. Getting insight on your one-on-one conversation with Scott was the primary reason I had set a time for us to meet."

While she waited for security to come and escort her back to Dale's office, she accessed the badge logs to validate Li Jing's statement. She was correct. The log showed the team meeting ending and her back in the processing center within minutes. Scott's badge indicated he'd stayed in the conference room for an extra ten minutes by himself.

Miss Grey had no reason to doubt that Scott's last note was correct. If so, not only was Li Jing lying about not having a conversation, but she had also found a way to manipulate the badge logs. Where there was smoke, there was usually fire. Where there was a lie, there was usually a motive. *What had Li Jing and Scott talked about?*

After waiting fifteen minutes, security knocked on the door and stepped into the room. "Miss Grey, unfortunately Mr. Phi had a critical issue arise. He said it could keep him tied up for quite some time and that perhaps you could set up another time to meet. It might be even better to call him."

She couldn't help but think that it was more likely that Dale was avoiding meeting with her rather than tied up in some emergency, although with today's turmoil she concluded that a soft touch might be the better approach. She didn't have the time to wait here, and pushing Dale to meet would only lead to a stalemate.

"Thank you. Then I'll ask that you escort me out of the out of the building and let Mr. Phi know I'll drop by another time to go over a few open items."

She'd come here to get answers and instead had more questions than she'd arrived with. Dale and Li Jing were both hiding something and were competing for the top spot on her suspect list. She didn't know if it was a good or bad thing yet. The bright side was that both of them were locked down in this building and couldn't disappear. The dark side was that both were in this building with critical information.

If only she had been able to help Scott before Haoyu tracked him down and killed him. Now she had to worry about who was next on Haoyu's target list.

THE TEENAGE QUEEN, THE LOADED GUN

Maxx opened another beer and handed it to Glen after the police left.

Glen had broken down when he saw the detective and Maxx on his porch. He'd been on both sides of those kinds of conversations, and it was a terrible, empty feeling to know that someone you loved died. The trite saying that no parent should have to outlive their children came to Maxx's mind. Watching Glen be crushed by the loss of his only son was almost more than he could take.

Maxx and Glen had served together in the Rangers and were no strangers to losing friends and fellow soldiers. It was always a devastating feeling, but this was an entirely new experience. Glen had always been the one above it all even when the shit was hitting the fan. Somehow, he stayed as steady as a rock when everyone else was losing it. And here he was, a shattered man.

Maxx had given him some space but stayed in the room to offer Glen some support. They asked him if he'd known of any trouble that Scott might have gotten into or if there were people he'd expressed concern about. Any substance issues, gambling, girl problems. Maxx let the detectives do their job and ask the questions to make sure they didn't miss any area of concern. Glen and Scott were very close as father and son, so it was easy to close any of those lines of questioning.

Maxx told the detectives once again for Glen's benefit that Scott had contacted him to talk about work when he couldn't get a hold of his dad, that there was a big project at work that he had gone in to work on last night. The detectives needed to talk to Scott's boss about that, and Maxx wasn't going to get in the middle of that conversation.

The detectives had told Glen that Scott had been taken to the King County Medical Examiner's Office. After the coroner contacted them, they'd meet Glen there for the formal identification of the body, although they already identified Scott through fingerprints he had on file at TechCom. It was a formality they had to go through. Maxx offered to go with him, but Glen declined the offer.

After the detectives had finished their questions, they had headed back to the scene to help with the questioning of witnesses and look for cameras that might give them more information about what had happened. They had been given insight into the potential killers, but they were still following procedures in case it turned out the primary suspect was not guilty.

Maxx and Glen grabbed a couple more beers from the refrigerator and slumped in the lawn chairs in the backyard. The alcohol helped take some of the edge off, but it still felt surreal when he had spoken with Scott a few hours ago. The cold beer also helped temper the warm afternoon sun. It didn't make it any easier to talk about what had happened.

Maxx had some suspicions about what might be happening but had to be careful what he said to Glen. While Haoyu was the primary suspect, it would be difficult to explain Maxx's involvement with the case without talking about Project

Hermes, the Chinese intelligence agency, and Scott getting sent home from work. It was too much to unravel when Glen was still struggling with the news that his son had been murdered.

Maxx ran his hand through his crew cut for a moment while he figured out where to begin the conversation.

"I can't imagine how this feels, Glen, and I'm not going to act like I do. It seems to me that the most important thing for you right now is to focus on taking care of Scott's funeral and final arrangements. Say goodbye to your boy."

Glen paused for a few moments and then nodded.

"While you take care of Scott, I'll keep in touch with the police and keep you informed if there is anything you need to know about."

Glen nodded again and then sat quietly for a few more minutes. He was often mistaken for a professional athlete, but right now he looked like he had shrunk three inches and lost twenty pounds in the last day. With an Army green, hooded sweatshirt pulled over his head and cinched tight around his neck, he looked like he was trying to withdraw from the world.

When he finished his third beer, he angrily crumpled the aluminum can. He squinted at Maxx directly.

"I need one thing, Maxx, and want to make sure I can count on you like I always have."

"There's no question, Glen. Anything you ask, you know I'll do."

Glen nodded. "Yes, there's never been a question in the past, but this time might be a little different. I need to know I'm not alone on this."

"Glen, before you ask, let me tell you something. When I heard from the police that they had found Scott, I told them I was going to keep you out of this so you can grieve. But I will find out who did this. There's nowhere the killer will be able to hide that I won't find them."

"I really appreciate that, but that wasn't going to be my ask."

Maxx took a deep breath.

"You want to know if I will help you finish what got started."

"Yes, deep down we are men of violence, and I believe in an eye for an eye."

"Let the police do their job for now. When the time comes, I will help you do whatever it takes to balance the account. No matter what the cost."

Glen closed his eyes and bowed his head. "I never dreamed it would come to this, but there is no one else I'd rather have shoulder to shoulder with me, Maxx."

Glen stood, turned, and headed into the house.

Maxx called out, "I'll swing by later this evening to see if you need anything."

Glen acknowledged Maxx with a thumbs-up and disappeared into the house, letting the screen door slam shut behind him.

Maxx sat staring at the deep-blue sky. Somewhere far out there, something was getting ready to talk with them. How something so remarkable could be affecting him on such a personal level was a mystery. Three days ago, he'd been sitting quietly in a bar, and here he was caught up in international intrigue, murder, and a plot from a science fiction novel. If someone else had told him this story, he'd think they were ready for a tinfoil hat and a padded suite at a mental hospital.

On his way out, he took a moment to look though the photos of Glen and Scott on the entry wall. He couldn't help but get a large lump in his throat. This was going to be incredibly hard for Glen to come to terms with, and the sooner that the police could bring in the killers, the less likely it would be that he and Glen would have to take things into their own hands.

He didn't have any qualms about killing Haoyu, having killed plenty of people in combat, and as far as he was concerned this was combat. Haoyu had already shown he was willing to eliminate Maxx and had murdered an uninvolved friend, not only a friend but a nice kid. And he had no doubt that if Haoyu perceived Gabby to be a threat, he'd kill her too.

What he didn't want to have happen was to get caught and spend time in jail, where he couldn't do anything to help anyone. Being trapped in jail was already a possibility since Miss Grey was covering for him to hide his involvement in the fight outside the bar. Right now, the homicide detectives had another murder to deal with, and it probably wouldn't be long before they suspected there was a connection that involved Maxx. Hell, he was involved, and trying to explain would make him sound insane.

Gabby had texted him that she was getting off work soon and that TechCom was lifting the lockdown, so she wanted to go home. He didn't trust that she'd have any kind of security to watch her even if there was a chance she was at risk. There were too many people on the Hermes teams to give them all protection, and it wouldn't have stopped Haoyu anyway, if what had happened with Scott was any indication.

He'd be the best security Gabby could have; not only was he armed and extremely dangerous, but he was also more motivated than any paid protection. Maxx wasn't looking out only for Gabby and himself. He was itching to retire Haoyu permanently.

He parked in the visitor lot at the TechCom Hermes office and waited in the car to avoid all the security checks. The place was essentially a solid concrete block in the best of the times. With the Chinese threat, there was no way he was handing over his Springfield .45 1911 to have it sit in a locker. The best place for a pistol was in the holster under his windbreaker.

He'd been given the gun when he was a teenager. His dad had carried it with him in the Marines, and when his parents had divorced, it was the one thing his dad had given him. Maxx didn't have a lot of good memories of his dad, but the pistol was one of the few things that made him realize that even though he didn't trust his dad, there was a bond between them. A bond of violence as it turned out, and the Springfield had followed him through a difficult adolescence, to the Middle East, and back to Seattle.

While he sat in the cab of his truck with the air conditioning running, he saw Miss Grey talking on her phone as she walked out of the front door. She was parked in the small visitor lot and heading right for him.

He shut off the engine and hopped out. Waving her over, he took a moment to see if he'd gotten a text from the detectives. No text but a missed call from Miss Grey.

As she drew closer, she said, "Just the person I was looking for. How'd it go with Scott's father?"

"Rough, real rough. I've seen Glen handle some extremely difficult situations, but that's the most distraught I've ever seen him. We better hope the police catch Scott's killer before Glen gets a hold of him, or there won't be anything left to question."

"Maxx, you need to convince him to let us handle it. It's messier than he, or you, can imagine. You take care of Gabby like I asked and let me deal with this."

"Yeah, yeah, I hear you, jefe," he said with a smirk.

"I'm not your boss. Saying it in Spanish sounds even dumber. The reason I called was to let you know that I talked to Scott's boss and one other person in his office. Also, he'd written a note for you before he'd died. He'd wanted to tell you and his boss about someone he'd had a conversation with last night. Has he ever mentioned a person named Li Jing?"

"Nope. What did she talk with Scott about?"

"That's the strange thing," she said as she showed Maxx the picture of the note on her phone. "Scott clearly indicated there was a conversation with her, but when I interviewed her, she insisted they didn't have a conversation. And when I looked at the badge logs that track people's movements in the building, it corroborates her story. She and Scott were never alone."

"Is there any way she could have altered the audit logs?" Maxx asked.

"I suppose it's possible, and I have someone chasing that possibility down. But why go through all that trouble when she could admit they talked and say it was about the weather or any other topic?"

"It does look bad," Maxx agreed.

"You know we have at least one high-ranking mole within TechCom, and this places Li Jing at the top of the list. I'd make sure Gabby steers away from her. If can she clear out audit trails, there is nothing to stop her from inserting or removing information to make Gabby look culpable."

Wincing, Grey focused on Maxx and continued, "I know this is a tough question, but I need to ask..."

"Don't," Maxx said.

"Are you sure Gabby isn't involved on the wrong side of this spy business?"

Maxx didn't mention his own concerns stemming from the Haoyu contract to research Dale and Gabby. Instead, he answered with certainty he didn't entirely feel, "Absolutely not. I'd focus on Li Jing or Dale. Don't waste time wondering about Gabby."

"I'll trust you on this for now. But if you get any inkling of a doubt, you need to let me know."

"That's fair. How do you think Scott got twisted up in this?"

"TechCom has tight security protocols. I spent time reviewing them, and they would send all kinds of alarms if anyone like Scott was accessing top secret information. Somehow Scott blew right through those safeguards, which then triggered him being sent home. The FBI was tracking him after he left the building and then were called off by a false flag, leaving him wide open for Haoyu.

"Scott must have really triggered an event for both the mole and Haoyu to expose themselves like this. Unfortunately, we don't know what the event was," Miss Grey finished.

"Since we don't know what Scott stumbled onto, we can only make sure Gabby isn't being set up for a similar trap. Let me talk to her and see if I can get any clues. She may not even be aware of the link between her and Scott," Maxx said. "I don't know how I got involved in all this, but I appreciate you keeping me up to date and telling me more than you probably should."

She smirked at him.

"I do trust you, Maxx. On that note, I've got to follow up with Doctor Smith at DARPA. There's something out of alignment with the Omega files and the device, and I can't seem to make all the puzzle pieces fit. I'm hoping he'll help me think it through."

After Miss Grey left, Maxx thought about what she had said and remembered Scott's initial intuition that there was something awry about Omega. That'd be a good topic to start his conversation with Gabby.

When she climbed into the passenger seat of his truck, she took her long black hair out her ponytail and began to twist it nervously around her index finger. Her eyes were slightly puffy, as if she'd been crying. It was evident she was shaken by the news of Scott's death. Even though they hadn't been friends, they'd been coworkers, and spending time with him and his dad at the baseball game last night made it more personal.

They sat in silence, thinking about how Scott had looked a few hours before, happy, young, and excited about the baseball game. Maxx felt another surge of anger, grief, and disbelief. How could this have happened? How could someone knife him to death for no reason? He was still in his mid-twenties and had so much to live for. He was their best friend, their coworker, and the only child of Maxx's best friend.

They embraced each other tightly, Gabby trying to choke back the tears. Maxx realized he needed her more than ever. At times it was difficult to imagine a time when they hadn't been in each other's lives. He felt her heartbeat, her warmth, but most of all her pain. But he knew he had to be strong, to carry on, to protect Gabby from the danger that had caught up with Scott. For now, they hugged.

When she caught her breath and leaned back in the seat. They hadn't had the chance to catch up since he'd dropped her off at work this morning. She was surprised to learn that Scott had been sent home and was planning to meet Maxx before he was killed.

There hadn't been an official announcement about Scott. The rumor was he'd gotten into an argument with Dale. She was alarmed by what Miss Grey had told Maxx about Scott accessing top secret files. Gabby had occasionally run into fire-walled information, and it was improbable that anyone, especially someone as relatively new to TechCom as Scott was, could circumvent the procedures to get restricted information. The few times she had come close to accessing restricted data files on the Hermes project, she'd gotten her hands slapped immediately by IT security.

It was her opinion that someone had given him access intentionally or accidentally. Then when it was discovered, that person went back and removed the access. These kinds of changes would have been recorded in the security logs, but she also knew the audit logs could be altered by someone with enough authority. That would mean whoever had changed the logs had to be a senior manager with the intention of getting Scott in trouble.

Maxx then told Gabby about Miss Grey's conversation with Li Jing and her denial that she'd talked with Scott after the meeting, despite Scott's claim that they had. And the logs that

Miss Grey had reviewed were consistent with Li Jing's statement.

Gabby explained it was a similar issue. If someone was removing data, they'd also have to clear the audit logs. It didn't make sense that Scott would lie about the meeting, but someone was going out on a limb altering the audit logs. She'd learned from one of the programmers that there was a way to verify this, depending on when it happened.

If there had been a data backup performed after the initial event but before the logs were altered, there would be a discrepancy between the two versions. Gabby called one of the members of her team to see if he could pull up the backup files from last night without triggering any notifications. Those backups would include the audit logs. She made sure he would not tell anyone but her if they found anything—it was a hunch that could clear Scott's name.

While waiting for Gabby's coworker to pull up the files, Maxx told her about his visit with Glen. He purposefully didn't mention the promise he'd made to make sure the killer was punished, because that was something between himself and Glen. And he hoped it wasn't something he'd have to make happen.

Gabby got the call back and put him on speakerphone so that Maxx could hear.

"Good and bad news, Gabby," her friend said. "The bad news is that backup files were corrupted for a twelve-hour timeframe last night. There is no way to tell what the differences are between the current events file and what was in the files from last night. We have to accept the files we have as correct."

"That doesn't help at all, because we don't know who granted Scott access and why it was taken away. What is the good news?" she asked hopefully.

"The audit file isn't corrupted. It shows that changes were

made to the events file and the badge log this morning. We don't know what the changes were, but there were deletions."

"Who made the deletions?" Maxx asked.

"Li Jing from the data processing department made three event deletions and two other changes."

"She must be the mole," Maxx mouthed to Gabby as she was wrapping up the call.

"Maybe, but how do we prove it?" Gabby asked.

CAN'T BELIEVE ALL THEY SAY

It was the third time in the last week that Miss Grey had been to the DARPA facility. She had little patience for the amount of time she was spending driving back and forth on I-5 through Seattle, especially during rush hour. It still made her smile every time she drove past the Rainier Beer brewery and imagined pulling off for some quick samples.

She didn't think anyone would find it quite as humorous as she did though, so she crept along in the bumper-to-bumper traffic until she pulled off into the nearly deserted industrial area that housed the top secret DARPA complex.

She had to admit she was getting much more proficient at the security protocols getting into the facility. Soon she might be calling the Marines by their first names as they let her into the underground parking lot. Even though they were all business, the thought made her blush a little bit. She'd been doing this job for so long that it was hard to remember the last time she'd made time in her life for dating.

Doctor Smith had to be getting irritated with her interruptions, since she knew he was under severe time constraints with the deadline next week. She still wasn't clear what they did at this facility beyond working on the Poseidon Project. TechCom called their portion of the project Hermes, dedicated to the decryption of the three alien data files. Poseidon entailed taking the output from Hermes and other tech companies and assembling them into a functional capability to communicate effectively when the appropriate time came. That required having a working Omega device that matched the design criteria in the Omega file.

No one explicitly told her that the Omega device was being constructed here, but from the number of engineers located at this site, along with other scientific specialists, she'd come to that conclusion on her own. She hoped that when she pressed Smith today he'd be able to clarify for her why Haoyu might be so concerned with Scott's recent inquiries into the Omega device and why Dale had been slow walking TechCom efforts into the Omega file.

There might be a rational explanation for Dale's delays and secretiveness about the Omega file if he was working directly with DARPA. Otherwise, it raised the question of if he was acting on behalf of the Chinese.

Unless DARPA had been able to construct a working version of the Omega device, she didn't see how it was possible to attempt communication with the aliens in less than four days. Her instincts told her Haoyu was here primarily for the device and secondarily to see what else he could learn from insiders at TechCom.

When Doctor Smith pushed into the conference room, it was evident he was agitated with her. He made no attempt at small talk or formalities and practically shouted at her before he was even seated.

"Miss Grey, you better have a good reason to interrupt me again. I'm tired of your fishing expeditions, and next time I suggest you send a formal inquiry instead of driving over."

She wanted to remind him she was here to investigate the

Chinese attempts to intercede, and since they were not above using murder, they clearly took it seriously. Instead, she took a deep breath and ignored the way he struck out to deescalate the situation. She needed information, and agitating him further would lead to a short conversation.

"I presume you've heard that one of the TechCom employees was released after accessing top secret files related to Hermes? That employee was subsequently killed by the Chinese team early today."

"Yes, nasty business. But what does that have to do with us here at DARPA?"

"The root cause of this *business* seems to be the Omega device. The employee was concerned that Hermes was dragging its feet on reconstructing the Omega file and that there was some inconsistency in what was in the files regarding the Chinese and US devices."

"As I told you and is evident in the top secret documents that you have access to, the official position of the US government is that the Omega device was destroyed in the earthquake at Mount St. Helens in 1980. We have resources trying to reconstruct that device based on the file that is being deciphered by TechCom and others now. I'm not aware of any efforts at TechCom to drag their feet on this. It has been moving along quite rapidly in the last several days. It would be moving along faster if you'd stop interrupting me."

"Would it be possible that the Chinese mole is trying to delay TechCom's efforts to make the US miss the communication window?" she asked.

"If that was their intent, I would say they failed."

"Can you think of any reason that would be their intention? Are they that determined to establish first contact?"

"I don't know what China's motivations are. America's motivation has always been to establish a narrative that shows we are peaceful and open to a constructive relationship."

"It appears from the classified information that China also lost their original device at that time of the Tangshan earthquake. Could it be that they want to make sure we don't have a device ready for operation before them?"

"That would explain their efforts to subvert us. However, I would not be certain they don't already have a working Omega device."

The shock Miss Grey felt must have been evident on her face as she processed Doctor Smith's implication. "That's stunning. As you know, I have been read into the SCI compartment on this topic. Every report indicates that Omega was indeed destroyed at the time. If it wasn't lost, then they did an excellent job misleading our intelligence services us for the last twenty-five years."

Doctor Smith took off his glasses and cleaned them. "Oh, I believe that was a factual account, and it was destroyed at Tangshan. Despite the official position of the US and what you read in the SCI compartment, I personally doubt that the US device was destroyed at Mount St. Helens."

"Then DARPA still has an Omega device and we've fooled the Chinese this entire time?" she stammered.

"No, that's not what I'm saying. DARPA didn't recover the Omega device from Mount St. Helens. However, rumors have it that the Chinese recovered our device and are simply waiting for the appropriate time to use it. Imagine what will happen if they inappropriately utilize our device in New York City at the right time. We know how the aliens will respond: disaster."

Doctor Smith had no more to say and dismissed her. She then called her boss to let him know she would be in the office in the morning with an update. Although her cell phone had a special application to encrypt voice calls, she had been instructed to avoid relaying information on this case over the phone. Instead, she texted Mr. Green about meeting tonight so she could get his advice before talking with her boss. She was trying to protect DARPA from the Chinese interests, but at the same time she didn't want DARPA getting too far ahead of any political counterbalance.

Mr. Green told her to meet him at Mike's Chili Parlor in Ballard. It was an old-school dive bar that he'd discovered while doing some undercover work. Mike's was an institution in the area since the 1920s when it had started by serving chili to the Greek dockworkers who lived in the Ballard area. No uppity Feds on an expense account would ever be seen there. They only take cash.

When she walked in, the bartender pointed to a booth near the back. It was a place where people minded their own business, and they had a jukebox instead of always playing one kind of music. She liked the atmosphere already. It wasn't too busy at this time on a weeknight, so no one was really paying that much attention to her. Mr. Green was dressed like a regular customer in jeans, a gray hooded sweatshirt, and a new Seattle Seahawks cap.

He was nursing a beer and eating some of their famous chili with saltines when she spotted him. As she was making her way to the table, Mr. Green pointed to his beer and held up two fingers. She hadn't planned on drinking, but it wouldn't hurt to nurse a beer so she didn't stand out as much from the rest of crowd. She'd much rather have a shot or two of tequila, but beer would do at the moment. Naturally, a Nirvana song was playing on the jukebox. It was easy for her to see why Seattle had become the epicenter of the grunge scene.

Miss Grey filled him in on her conversation with Doctor Smith, making certain she was talking in enough code that if anyone overheard her that it would be meaningless. Mr. Green nodded along and didn't say anything until the waitress had brought over the beers and another bowl of chili.

"Are you sure you don't want to try this chili? It's amazing," Mr. Green said as he offered her a clean spoon.

"Another time," she said. "All the stress lately has given me an upset stomach, and I'd rather go back to my hotel and get some sleep. It's been a crazy few days."

"Your loss," he said as he blew on the chili to cool it down. "Regarding what Smith told you, that's interesting, but he's way off base about a few things."

"He did say it was an unconfirmed rumor. But it would explain some things."

"He's wrong though. I know for a fact the Chinese didn't recover the Omega device from Mount St. Helens. The device was recovered after the eruption by a group of former intelligence officers who didn't want it to go back to DARPA."

Miss Grey almost spilled her beer when she put her glass down.

"What group?" she hissed.

"The same group you and I work for," he said with a smirk.

"You mean all of this time we've had the alien communication device and nobody told me?"

"Need to know, and you didn't need to know before now. Long before you and I became involved, a group was formed to securely store the original device in a secure location here in Seattle. The group we work for is aptly named Team Tacoma. We only have one priority, to make sure the Omega device is secure and operational when needed."

"Why Tacoma?" she asked.

"Because Mount Tacoma was the indigenous name of Mount Rainier. The mountain is central to the culture of many tribes around Puget Sound. And it's also where the Omega device was originally discovered back in the 1950s."

"That makes more sense than the usual names the spooks come up with..like Omega."

Mr. Green smiled broadly and continued, "Without the device, the military and DARPA can't attempt another unprepared communication with the aliens. It seemed they were being rather reckless in the way they were planning to use Omega. Their intent was to get ahead of the Chinese and use the device for a preemptive strike at the Chinese. What better way than to create a crisis in China without having to take any blame?"

"Not to mention that the Chinese would think we were on equal footing if both ours and their communication devices were destroyed. It was a brilliant move to freeze DARPA and the Chinese in one stroke. Unfortunately, it looks like the temporary freeze is about to thaw quickly."

Miss Grey was still struggling to understand. "So we've been holding on to the original device all this time, while DARPA was trying to build a replacement. We haven't made any more attempts to use it, or did we figure out how to use it correctly without creating another disaster?"

"We needed the Delta file to be fully translated before trying to use it again. That was where DARPA and the Chinese agency made their initial mistakes with their respective devices. They had the original devices and the correct initial dates. They hadn't fully translated the protocols and went ahead and tried anyway...resulting in disasters for each of them. Rather than try to use it again, the team has been using the original device to build a backup device again. Having the translated Omega file available is like getting the answers to the test so we can verify our work."

"Since we have the original device secured, I don't understand why we'd want a backup," Grey said.

"In case it gets destroyed, taken by the Chinese, or compromised by DARPA. A backup would allow us to continue communication to counter either DARPA or the Chinese. It's an insurance policy to maintain ongoing communication under every scenario. We believe the aliens provided us with design specifications in case we needed to construct a replacement."

"Even with the specifications they provided, is it possible to create a duplicate device? I would assume it would require tools and materials we don't have on Earth."

"That's a natural assumption but totally incorrect. The file includes instructions on how to build the tools and forge the required materials out of rare metals on Earth and in select meteorites. Some of the raw material wasn't easy to locate, but it seemed the aliens expected we might want to create additional devices."

She needed another drink. She was getting a headache from all of the twists in this case, and while she knew she was looking out for the best interests of the US, it was becoming questionable what those best interests really were when looked at from all of the angles. Scott, Maxx, and Gabby were in the middle of a deadly political chess match that included two competing factions of the US government, the Chinese government, and an unknown alien civilization.

"So why did the Chinese kill Scott? Wouldn't they want to find out what he knew if he was suspicious that the Omega device hadn't been destroyed?"

"They would, which makes me believe Haoyu killed him because he was misled by an insider at TechCom about the potential risk of what Scott uncovered. We know his boss Dale was the one who discovered Scott's access to the confidential files and sent him home. He wanted Scott silenced so he couldn't mention that the device might still be accessible."

"Silenced so he couldn't mention there might be an original device?" she asked.

"We know Dale isn't working for us, so that only leaves the Chinese or someone at DARPA. If Dale is spying for the Chinese, then I think he'd want them to know there was a device. If Dale is spying for DARPA, I think he'd want them to know that too."

"Maybe he wants one of them to know but on his terms," she said.

"What do you mean?"

Grey took a deep breath, thinking it through carefully.

"If Scott found out and started telling everyone at Tech-Com, and maybe even his friend Maxx, that the device hadn't been destroyed, then it's out of Dale's control. We know he's been slowing down the Omega file work at TechCom and has been called out on it. Maybe it's to position himself for a payday."

"Selling the information to one or both of them..." Mr. Green speculated.

"By slowing the Omega file work being done at TechCom, he makes the device more valuable as next week's deadline approaches. DARPA and the Chinese would pay a fortune to know its location."

"That still doesn't make Dale the Chinese mole at Tech-Com, but it makes him a leading suspect along with Li Jing. I still haven't completely ruled out Gabby Fisher either. Maybe more than one of them works for Haoyu."

Nodding grimly, Grey needed to wash that one down with a sip of beer.

"Smith told me he thinks the Chinese have the device because he doesn't know I am working for you on the side. He wants me to stay away from DARPA and chase the Chinese, because Dale is probably his source inside TechCom, and he doesn't want Dale compromised," she said.

She finished her second beer and said goodbye. It was becoming clear that there were circles within circles on this, and ironically the only person she trusted in this web was the person she knew the least. Maxx King.

The spy had to be careful about continuing to make clandestine calls from vacant conference rooms. Two events in as many days were likely going to become noticeable to anyone monitoring unusual behavior using the employee badge tracking. It was possible to alter the audit logs, but that would only increase suspicion and result in more uncomfortable interviews. People were beginning to ask too many questions.

The mole had been able to see the material Scott was looking at before being rescinded. How Scott had gotten access to the material was unknown. Any documents related to Omega, 800, or Mount St. Helens were behind the firewall. When reviewing the audit logs this morning, there was no evidence that someone had granted Scott access, but that was impossible based on Scott's search history and the documents he'd accessed.

Another call to the local doctor's office followed, this time with a different message indicating that it was a medical emergency requiring a return call as soon as possible.

After a few moments, the phone rang. The caller ID was blocked, but the spy knew who it would be and quickly verified that using the predetermined code that only the two of them knew.

"Thanks for calling me back, Doctor. I thought you should know my Chinese friend has learned we know his old device was not lost and is still working."

The voice sounded like it was going through some electronic filters. It never sounded the same two times in a row.

"Who told your Chinese friend?"

"Someone who found the information in some old records."

"Unfortunate. I presume he's not able to give your friend any more information."

"Sadly, he passed away suddenly, so I don't know everything that was said."

"Did your friend say what he plans to do with the device now that he found it?"

This was the crux of the information that needed to be

delivered. "I believe my friend plans to take the device to New York to see if works. If it doesn't work, then no one will know he was testing it there."

"That might be a dangerous outcome."

"He's trying to keep it a secret so no one can blame him if things go badly."

"It's good to know what your friend is planning. We must do everything to stop him from doing this test. In fact, I think it would be best if I held onto this device. Can you tell me where I might find your Chinese friend and this device of his in New York?"

"I need some more money, and then I can get that information for you."

"Get me the device. I can reimburse you considerably more than your friend."

"I'm sure you will," the mole said, ending the call.

MASTERS OF WAR (MAY 18, 1980)

El Herrero checked the calculations one more time. He'd been using the proprietary software system they had spent billions of dollars on to run the calculations in as many iterations as possible, but he still liked using a slide rule to check some of the math.

He knew it wasn't logical, as the software programs were designed to continuously verify all calculations at least three times. But the slide rule had been the preferred tool of many of the engineers who he'd been trained by, and it was comforting in his hands. It grounded his thinking in physical motion.

He'd begun working for ARPA in the 1960s and had originally been assigned to projects like ARPANET, or what had been commonly called the internet civilian population. When ARPA was renamed DARPA in 1972, he was brought along for the work that he'd been doing on global positioning systems using a constellation of satellites for tracking and communication.

This expertise, along with his experience in developing some of the more forward-thinking weapons systems like Nike, Harpoon, and Tomahawk missiles, had led to his nickname of

El Herrero – or the Swordsmith. He was proud of his past achievements, which had put him in the unique position to work on the current project, known as Poseidon.

While Poseidon was best known as the Greek god of the sea, it was his fighting capabilities that had led to the selection of the project name. Poseidon's trident was a distinctive symbol, but even more relevant was his weapon's ability to call up water, natural disasters, and even cause earthquakes. Literally translated, they referred to it as "Earth Shaker."

When ARPA had initially secured the alien device and communication protocols, they learned it was designed by aliens to be able to contact them if Earth or critical civilizations were threatened or been conquered. The holders of the device would then be able to trigger natural disasters such as flooding, earthquakes, or volcanoes to destroy the invaders and enemies without the aliens having to physically be present on the planet.

Along with the Omega device, the Alpha file was intended to indicate when the next communication period would be open and was set at predetermined random times about every fifteen to twenty Earth years. If contact was made during one of those times and not at the location indicated and NOT using the correct protocols in the Delta file, then it would trigger a disaster at the location that the Omega device was calling from. This failsafe design was intended to keep a conqueror from using the device as an offensive weapon rather than a defensive one, as it was intended.

DARPA had not fully translated the communication protocols but had determined that the initial contact date that would open to them was today, and the coordinates fell at Mount St. Helens. The decision had been made by the Secretary of Defense that the attempt at communication would proceed. The majority of the DARPA team was connected remotely with a small team that would be on site with the Omega device.

The specific site at Mount St. Helens was chosen because the amount of thermal energy required was astronomical and could be collected naturally near the dormant volcano.

El Herrero remained with the remote team at the Johnston Ridge Observatory. The observatory, which was normally open to the public, had been closed temporarily, and the ARPA team had set up a short-term management location. They were close enough to the exact coordinates that they could be on site quickly if necessary but far enough away to evacuate if there was a minor eruption. He'd calculated the risk multiple times and felt that the potential benefit of direct communication with the aliens would outweigh the risk of a natural event if they'd gotten the protocols wrong.

He'd been up all night preparing for the initial contact. They'd originally planned to initiate the device at sunrise, but a few approval delays from the east coast had forced him to push things back to 8:30 Pacific time.

They had been testing the powering up of the Omega device over the last year. Initially, they had tried to begin the process in the controlled setting of the DARPA lab in south Seattle. It was buried deep underground and connected to industrial-grade power utilities that serviced the port and the Boeing production plants. However, they'd learned from experience that even with access to power at that level, it hadn't been adequate to fully initialize the device. Even though the device was not large, it somehow absorbed enough power to take the grid completely offline.

Under the cover of night, they had transported the device to the area that had surface access to the volcano vents below. By constructing a geothermal power plant in the course of a year, they had determined that they could draw enough continuous power to keep the device operating without affecting any civilian utilities, so it was essentially off the grid. That wouldn't be a sustainable solution in the long term, but for the primary test he was satisfied.

They would initiate the operating sequence at sunrise, which was 5:30 a.m. That would allow the device to be at full power by 7:30 a.m., giving them an hour to ensure that the monitoring devices were functional and the appropriate satellites were synched in orbit to locate and track the incoming and outgoing deep space signals. He had also arranged for several observatories to be watching the star coordinates that he had calculated. They had theorized that there might be visible evidence that the observatories might capture during contact.

Lastly, he'd made sure there was military support on standby from Joint Base Lewis-McChord. No one had suggested there would be any appearance by the aliens in person, but having Army and Air Force assets already in motion was an insurance policy he couldn't refuse, since it had come directly from the president. *Politicians, always covering their asses.*

That left them with thirty minutes to get the final approval for "Go" and to start the countdown at exactly 8:30 a.m. He'd rather have time for one last review of the checklist than be rushed into the start.

They had run multiple scenarios based on the various responses. The most likely scenario that the team had agreed on was that they would send the initial signal at 8:30 and then at some time in the future there would be a communication "handshake." They had estimated that could last anywhere from hours to months depending on how far the signal had to travel. They were not even sure how the signal traveled, since it apparently was operational when buried deep underground. Since it wasn't a direct light beam but some other form of energy, and they didn't know where the alien communication source would be located, it was a wide-ranging guess.

After the handshake verified that the connection was secure and emanating from the appropriate location and time in the

Alpha instructions, they were expecting the aliens would send a greeting or burst message with instructions. From what they could interpret from the directions, they were to wait for communication and then respond accordingly. This was the largest unknown in the process. They weren't sure what the communication would entail beyond a greeting. Perhaps, a series of questions about who they were and the purpose of the contact, so they had used game theory to construct a communication protocol based on expectations. The theoretical protocol had been vetted against the Delta file to ensure it was consistent with what they had been able to translate thus far.

El Herrero was the point person for those conversations. He was on site but had positioned himself behind a blast structure far enough from the device that even if there was a malfunction, he would be safe and able to continue to communicate.

He had been running through scenarios with the Poseidon team for the previous year and felt they were as prepared as they could be. Many on the team had suggested they weren't ready yet and should wait for another communication sequence. He had convinced his superiors there might not be another communication cycle, or the Chinese might beat them to initial contact. They were well aware they were racing with the Chinese, and many were calling this their "moonshot." No one wanted to take the blame for letting the Chinese take the glory for the first successful contact with an alien civilization.

There was a lot of speculation about how communication with the aliens would proceed, but there was vocal certainty that the US had to establish that relationship first even if it was exploratory and could eventually be detrimental to Earth. Bridging communication was the safest path, as long as the Chinese failed. But if they didn't fail, then the US would be relegated to the sidelines and would have to live with the consequences anyway. El Herrero had become comfortable with the notion that there were many risks – some of them known but most unknown. In his opinion, the worst outcome, even at the risk of creating a natural disaster, would be missing the opportunity for first communication.

He'd like to think he'd come to the decision objectively, but he knew that wasn't completely true in the rare moments when he was being honest with himself. He was prioritizing the politics of the project at the expense of the scientific hazards. He'd had some interaction with the Chinese on some projects before and had been embarrassed by being outflanked publicly.

He and Mr. Xi, a rising star at COSTIND, had written several technical articles for a scientific journal years ago. The media, never one to pass up a good story with some international drama, had positioned them as forward thinkers in the various fields. It was annoying to have it elevated to a public feud when he was trying to keep out of the public eye. It was frowned upon by the old-timers at ARPA, who were more interested in the project outcomes than political visibility.

It happened that both Xi and himself got put on a panel at a conference in Geneva and had come to radically different positions about how they believed artificial intelligence will be deployed in science. El Herrero had seen early success in select areas of astrophysics and felt there would eventually be widespread commercial applications.

Mr. Xi shared some of the findings from the Chinese projects that supported his skepticism. El Herrero was embarrassed to find that his optimism was largely discounted as unrealistic by his peers and communicated "off the record" with the scientific press. Xi's findings made El Herrero and ARPA look widely naïve.

Since that time, El Herrero had tried to minimize his public exposure, but the press latched on to some of the military projects that he'd completed. The two of them became linked publicly, as their nations developed forward-looking technology and weapons to change the shape of warfare. America was the current global champion, China the up and comer to replace the position previously held by the Soviet Union.

They soon became known as The Masters of War, much to the dismay of DARPA. The visibility was a double-edged sword for El Herrero, but it was a fight he'd internalized, always cognizant of how success or failure played into that competition.

When it became known that Xi was the head of the Chinese team at COSTIND that was working with the alien device and communication, El Herrero had increased the pressure to move forward rapidly. It fed his competitive advantage, and he used that to force political risks that would have been avoided under different circumstances. If he were able to connect with the aliens first, he could only imagine the scientific breakthroughs that would follow—all attached to his name.

The primary stated intent of advancing Poseidon was to establish initial contact with the aliens to build a positive part-nership. However, there was a more covert motivation for some of the hawks within DARPA and the Defense Department to secure the communication to use the aliens to attack China either intentionally or through manipulation. There was a belief that a significant event might slow their growth and sour any eventual interaction between China and the aliens. El Herrero had convinced senior leaders in the Pentagon that the Chinese were trying to create the same strategy against the US. Now that the USSR was in a steady state of decline, there were many financial and political reasons for China to be positioned as the future global enemy.

At 6:30, the engineers began to shunt the power over to the waiting device. It still put him in awe that a relatively small device could absorb so much power and not even get warm to the touch. They had tried to remove some of the outer shell, but even that had taken some creative engineering, as there were no outside joints. The material looked like dark glass but was impervious to any physical attempts to penetrate it. They couldn't even see beyond the outer skin using the latest MRI, radar, and imaging equipment.

After several years of failed attempts to open it, they had stopped and simply connected the power to the electrical ports that would open from a hidden door when the button was pushed on the control panel.

The control panel was the first thing they had discovered when they laid their hands on the outside of the device. It only became visible when it was touched directly by a human. They'd found that out by accident when someone had tripped in the lab and caught themselves on the device with a gloveless hand. A small control panel had become evident behind the cover material. When it had been touched again, it disappeared. They'd tried many other materials to trigger the control panel, but it would only initiate when touched by a human.

The panel itself only had two potential points of contact. The first contact point when pushed began the charging process. They didn't keep it connected to the power source all the time to avoid any unintended activation. Therefore, when it was time, the engineers connected the positive and negative charges. Switching the positive and negative poles had no reaction, so it had been designed to be foolproof.

The second point of contact lit up when the device appeared to be fully powered. Until then, it stayed grayed out. They had never pressed this button, as they were under the impression it would have negative results if it was done from the wrong location or at an unapproved time. This was also evident as half the contact point had changed colors when it was at the proper location. They had assumed the other half of the contact point would change color when it was within the appropriate time window.

What wasn't evident was how the communication would occur once the device was activated. The team had speculated endlessly about that, but there was no way to know until it happened. They had placed multiple cameras, monitoring equipment, and some team members on site to be prepared for every eventuality they could imagine.

At 8:00, El Herrero began to run through the final checklist one last time. As they surmised, the control point was completely lit up, meaning the device was powered up, in the correct location, and within the timeframe allowed. He could feel the tension in the room, but he was excited. He was convinced this was a pivotal moment in history and that he was meant to be here.

When the digital clock in the control room read 08:29:50, he nodded to the project engineer, giving the final ten-second countdown. It was so quiet in the control booth that he couldn't even hear himself breathing, but he could clearly see the device through the high-powered telescope several miles away. It was strange that the device's surface was shiny but seemed to absorb the light instead of reflecting it. There was so much they didn't know, but there was no turning back now.

He watched the lead engineer press the button on the close-up video feed from the camera recording. Immediately the button changed colors again and began pulsing. When the engineer stepped back and put on his protective glove, El Herrero began to watch the scene through the telescope again. He wanted to get a better sense of the device in the surrounding environment, including his team members who were situated nearby.

None of the monitoring equipment registered any change in audio, visual, or the myriad of other scientific equipment that was monitoring the device and the surrounding area. The only change was the small pulsing light on the console.

No one said anything as they watched their assigned equipment for changes. *Nothing.*

El Herrero had expected something would happen immediately after initiation. No one had guessed the device would remain static. The initiation had clearly happened, as indicated by the change on the console lights, but they had expected the next step would be a response.

After a couple minutes of silence, he spoke over the radio to the engineers at the device location. "This is Poseidon actual. We are seeing no changes in the monitoring equipment. Are you observing, hearing, or feeling any changes at your location?"

He could see the engineer who had pressed the device console shake his head. "No changes noted here other than the flashing light."

Almost immediately after his response, the monitoring equipment began to go erratic, as if there was signal overload at every frequency and wavelength all at once.

At 08:32:11 PDT, a signal was received by the equipment at Mount St. Helens. In English, Chinese, and Spanish, the brief signal translated to, "Improper Sequence. Contact Aborted."

The device and the team of scientists disappeared into the ground when an earthquake opened a gigantic chasm. This earthquake caused the entire north face of the mountain to slip away, beginning the most disastrous volcanic eruption in U.S. history.

Doctor Smith, known to the world as El Herrero, or Sword-smith, realized he had made a terrible miscalculation by under-estimating the warnings that had come with the device.

DO THE TWINE (DANCE)

After Maxx and Gabby left TechCom, they swung by Anthony's for some fish and chips while they talked over their next move. They reviewed everything that happened without revealing confidential information. He couldn't tell Gabby everything he'd learned over the last couple of days, and Gabby couldn't tell Maxx about everything she was working on. It wasn't a matter of trust, more that they thought the other would think they were crazy.

The one thing they both agreed on was that Miss Grey was more deeply involved than she had let on. Maxx told Gabby how he had met Miss Grey after the bar fight and his subsequent effort to escape the police and keep the Chinese from following him. He suspected that Miss Grey had been tracking the Chinese and may have also been tailing him. He left out parts of the conversations he'd had with Miss Grey and completely avoided mentioning the DARPA facility he and Miss Grey had visited that night. He felt some guilt about not telling Gabby everything.

By the time they were finishing the last of the chips, they'd decided they couldn't simply go home to wait and see what happened next. Maxx had told Gabby about his earlier visit with Glen, and she wanted to go with Maxx to check on him. And they agreed it was time to get some answers from Miss Grey.

Before going anywhere, Maxx wanted to switch to Gabby's smaller, less recognizable Audi. Maxx's raised truck stood out like a sore thumb downtown. If they were going to find Miss Grey, they wanted to blend in. He also knew there was a tracking device on his truck, which he'd discovered when he checked for electronics earlier in the day. He didn't know who the tracker belonged to, the Feds or the Chinese, but he really didn't want anyone following him now.

He'd also found a tracking device on Gabby's car but had attached it to the pipe next to her car in the parking garage. Anyone watching them would assume they were staying put in Gabby's house and not out on the town.

Maxx had also taken the precaution to add a tracker to Miss Grey's car when they were in the visitor's parking lot at Tech-Com. He doubted she would bother to check, and on the off chance that she did, she'd assume the Chinese or one of the other three-letter intelligence agencies put it there.

While they were eating dinner and then switching out his truck for Gabby's car, he monitored the path of Miss Grey's travels around town. He knew from her earlier comment that she planned first to visit the DARPA facility in South Seattle. He had made sure his device was inactive by the time it was near that facility so the security teams wouldn't find it when her car was searched before entering the underground parking lot. He'd watched them search her car on the first trip and knew they were very thorough about checking for electronics.

When Miss Grey had left the area of the DARPA building, the tracking device rebooted itself and tracked her to the Ballard area. The electronic map showed it parked at Mike's Chili Parlor, one of Maxx's favorite hangouts. The staff at Mike's knew him as a regular customer, so he decided not to go inside, instead waiting in the parking lot of the little shopping mall across the street. Maxx didn't believe she would be going there on her own, so she must be planning to meet someone. He'd love to know who it was but didn't want to risk going inside. That would be too much of a coincidence for anyone to believe.

Miss Grey was inside the restaurant long enough for a meeting and a couple of drinks. When she pulled out of the lot and started to drive in the direction of downtown, Maxx asked Gabby to hang back a few cars and follow her. He didn't want to spook her, but he also wanted to talk to her tonight, so he'd have to intercept her before she got to her destination.

Before they pulled out of the parking lot, they had also noticed another car that looked like a government vehicle pull out behind. Maxx proposed they hang back even further and watch both of them. When it was clear that Miss Grey was indeed being followed, they decided to call her and ask her to meet at a little bar down the block from Gabby's.

Gabby made a quick call from her cell phone and asked Miss Grey to meet her and Maxx at Cicchetti in thirty minutes. She told her she had something to tell her that they didn't feel comfortable talking about on the phone and didn't want to wait until tomorrow. That would give them time to park, walk over, and avoid the question of why they'd been following her. But now they had another question. Who was following Miss Grey, and why?

Gabby parked in the garage under her apartment building. Maxx removed the tracking device he'd taped to the back of the water pipe near her parking space and reattached it under the rear bumper. He'd doubted anyone was watching to make sure her car was physically matching the tracking device, but better to be cautious.

They then walked two blocks down to the restaurant, taking side streets to avoid being seen by whomever was tailing Miss

Grey. On the GPS vehicle tracking device he was using, Maxx could see her car was parked on the street. If she had already arrived, her tail was probably not far behind. He doubted they'd follow her inside to see who she was meeting, but that was a chance he'd have to take.

Maxx and Gabby ate at this restaurant frequently and felt comfortable coming in the rear entrance off the patio. It was still warm, so there'd be a few people seated outside to enjoy the late-summer evening.

Miss Grey had a bit of a surprised look when they emerged from the back hallway and walked over to her corner table in the dining room. She was watching the front windows and door and had been expecting them to appear from another direction. She quickly dropped her phone in her purse when she saw them. Maxx saw it as a wary movement, like they had caught her doing something suspicious.

Maxx pulled up a chair for Gabby then sat down, Miss Grey between the two of them. He signaled the bartender and said to Grey, "Thanks for meeting us tonight. I know it's kind of late, but we figured you'd still be working on the case. It looks like we were correct."

"Yes, you both know there is a deadline looming in a few days. No rest for the wicked," Miss Grey answered.

Gabby laughed. "Are you the wicked, or were you referring to us or someone else?"

"I was referring to our very busy mutual acquaintance."

After they ordered an ice water for Maxx and wine for Gabby and Miss Grey, she jumped right into the conversation. "What's so important that we needed to chat tonight?"

"I'll be blunt, Miss Grey. We've been talking it over and feel you're not being completely honest with us about this situation. At first it was annoying, but it jumped to a new level of concern when our friend Scott was killed today, killed by our mutual acquaintance, as you called him."

"I understand the concern, Maxx. It's a terrible situation, and I wish I could tell you more, but it's a confidential and ongoing investigation with national security implications. I know you're both involved, and there is clearly risk, but I have to keep some information from you until I'm authorized to tell you."

"How about we go first and tell you something you don't know, and then you do the same?" Maxx proposed.

"I doubt you have any meaningful information that would be news to me." Grey crossed her arms and leaned back.

Gabby spoke up. "After we left the office this afternoon, I went back through the audit logs to see who gave Scott access to the confidential information that got him in trouble."

"There was nothing in the audit logs," Miss Grey said. "It was the first thing we checked."

"That's because they had been scrubbed," Gabby shot back. "Li Jing gave Scott access, and someone later removed Scott's access when he was finished."

"How do you know that if the audit logs were scrubbed?" Miss Grey scooted her chair closer and leaned in, intrigued.

"We compared the backup files that were created before and after Scott accessed them. The files didn't match. After that, we tried to see who removed his authorization, but the data in the backup was corrupted."

"We also checked to see if Li Jing met alone with Scott, as he indicated. You told us that Li Jing denied it, but the evidence was in the log...which had also been scrubbed."

Maxx joined in. "What would make Li Jing give Scott access and then take it away after he had reviewed the files? Does Li Jing work for you, or is she the Chinese mole?"

"Maxx, I warned you to be careful around her. She may be a mole, though I haven't found any hard evidence to support that. And she doesn't work for us, that I know of."

"What does that mean?"

"There are a lot of government agencies with a stake in this project, and there may be players I don't know about yet," Miss Grey said.

"What about Dale?" Maxx snapped back. "Does he work for the government?" Maxx could see Gabby react to that question as if she hadn't even considered that angle.

"He doesn't work for us either. He may be a mole too, but again I have no conclusive evidence."

"Scott seemed think he had some conflicting interests because of his actions to delay the Omega file," Maxx reminded her. "It would make sense if he sent him home."

"I know, but Dale also sent some FBI agents to tail Scott."

"But why would Scott have been targeted unless there was something in the secret files he inadvertently accessed that were behind a firewall? If Dale was the mole, he would have seen those files too. What information did the files contain that would have been an issue for Scott?"

"The files were about the Omega device. The US had an early prototype, and it was destroyed."

Maxx could tell she wasn't telling him the entire truth and pressed her. "Completely destroyed? When?"

"It was officially destroyed in 1980, but there are rumors that the Chinese may have it," Miss Grey replied.

Maxx leaned back in his chair. "This is the reason we wanted to talk to you. It feels like we are getting random pieces of a puzzle that involve us, and you are holding back. All signs seem to point to this Omega device as a critical part of the puzzle, and you sidestep the topic like you're conflicted."

"That's because I'm finding out pieces of the story as I dig further, but I am conflicted. It's important for the country and yet seems riskier the more I uncover. I don't know exactly what the device does and why the Chinese want it as badly as we do."

"It sounds like you have conflicted principles, Miss Grey," Gabby said.

"I'm trying to balance multiple responsibilities because I don't feel like I know the truth yet and what is at stake. I am not confused about the fact that I need to keep it out of the hands of Haoyu. I'm also sure I need to keep the two of you safe. There is more danger than I realized."

Maxx snorted. "Oh, I think I have a good idea of how much danger we're in."

She looked around the room to make sure that no one was close enough to overhear her. "We all know that the Omega device is at the center of this disruption between us and the Chinese. Originally, we thought it was a race to decrypt the files. But the files are the instruction manual for the Omega device. Without that, the Alpha file means nothing, because we don't know where and when to use the device. The Delta file has instructions on how to use the device and what to communicate. The Omega file is essentially an engineering schematic on how to build, power, and repair the device."

This wasn't necessarily new information to Maxx, but it was clear Miss Grey had gotten more clarity around the big picture since they had last talked. What he wanted to know about was the device.

"Is there a newer prototype of the device? Are we trying to get one ready to use next week?"

Miss Grey sighed. "There may be one available, but it's only based on conjecture. We know that the Chinese and the US each received a device in the 1950s with the original files. The Chinese version was destroyed. We're certain about that."

"And the US device?" Maxx asked. "You're not so certain?"

"Up until a few days ago, I was under the impression it was destroyed. DARPA doesn't have it but thinks the Chinese have it. I'm confident that someone has it, but I don't think it's the Chinese. I believe Haoyu has come to the same conclusion, and that's why he's here in Seattle and acting more desperate by the day. He wants the device and knows he only has a few more days to recover it so the Chinese can use it during the open communication window on Tuesday."

Maxx didn't press Miss Grey about how she was so sure a device was still available if it wasn't at DARPA. *She is working at another angle.*

Gabby then said, "That sounds like a reasonable theory, but a device to communicate with whom about what?"

"It's not a theory. I'm confident about what I said," Miss Grey insisted. "We don't exactly know who we are communicating with, but it's an active civilization considerably more advanced than we are. At least the civilization was active in 1982, the last time we received a message and an updated Alpha file. The primary question is why we are expected to communicate with them. We've been speculating about that for decades and are hopeful that the decrypted files will provide some clarity..."

"I'll be straightforward with you, Miss Grey," Maxx interrupted. "I don't believe you're being completely open with us. For example, you are confident the US device was not destroyed, and yet DARPA and the rest of the US government believes it was. Why do you and the Chinese believe it is still active? I doubt you are conspiring with the Chinese, so that means some other faction – probably of the US intelligence community – knows the device is still around. If they know where it is, then it's in their control."

He could tell from the look on Miss Grey's face that he had hit a bullseye, so he pressed on. "Since the Chinese have sent their A-team to Seattle, I'm guessing it's somewhere in the area. They didn't come here for the files at TechCom—they already have insiders there. They need a physical presence. It's probably the same reason DARPA built a location nearby. The device was, or maybe still is, linked to this geographic area."

Miss Grey nodded. "I can't confirm that because I don't know, but your logic makes sense."

Gabby leaned in and looked at Miss Grey and said, "Find the device, and I think you'll find the answers to both of your questions. Why is the Omega device still here, and what is its purpose?"

"I don't know why the device was given to us and the Chinese, but I have an idea how we want to be able to use it. And that's what has made me increasingly concerned as we get closer to next week."

Maxx thought about what Miss Grey said for a moment. "If I was a betting man, I'd say that we think the device has significant military value, and we don't want the Chinese to figure it out first."

"Why do you say that?" Gabby asked him.

"Because DARPA is the primary organization that has been working on the development. Sure, they were the original creators of the internet, global positioning systems, and other programs that have had tremendous commercial benefits for the US and internationally, but the primary function of their advanced research is related to security of the United States. 'Defense' is the first word in their name. And where else could we acquire advanced research beyond interaction with an advanced alien civilization?"

"You're not wrong, Maxx."

"And I think that's why you and whoever else you are working with are trying to keep the device from getting into the hands of both the Chinese and DARPA. You think there's other reasons the aliens might have provided us with the ability to communicate with them. You're trying to hold on to the device until you know what those reasons might be, which will make you a target for the Chinese and the US intelligence agencies."

"And you too, if they think you are impeding their access," Miss Grey added.

"Maybe we can help each other," Maxx suggested. "Gabby and I think Haoyu is the key. He's the lead for the Chinese efforts to find the device, and we know he already wants to take me out of the equation. He'll be especially motivated now that he thinks I am getting close to finding answers. If we can convince him that Scott gave me some information about the location of the device before he was killed and then put myself in an accessible position, Haoyu will find me. I need to know where to look for him."

"That's terribly dangerous. He almost killed you last time, and the only reason you survived was because he underestimated you. He won't make that mistake again."

"I understand, but I'm not going to put my myself in his crosshairs unprepared. If I know where he is, I'll be prepared and have overwatch."

"I'll tell you, on two conditions," she answered.

"Name them," Maxx said.

"First, I want to keep Gabby under protection while you're out playing soldier."

Maxx and Gabby both agreed.

"Second, I need Gabby to get me an original version of the Delta files from TechCom. By the time they get to me, they've been reviewed and edited by DARPA. I want to see if there is something that indicates the original purpose of the Omega device. I can also compare the file versions to see what DARPA is removing from the original."

"I can do that," Gabby said, "but it may take me a day or two. If I can be onsite on Sunday, security is always minimal, and it's a skeleton crew in the processing center. It'll be the best chance I'll have to make a copy and get it out undetected."

"It sounds like we have a plan then. Thanks for trusting us, Miss Grey. I'm sure we'll be in a much better place after the next two days."

∾

When Gabby parked at the curb in front of Glen's house, there were a handful of cars in the driveway, and the downstairs lights were on. That was a positive sign. Maxx had been worried Glen would be alone and depressed this evening when he'd left earlier this afternoon. Glen was a remarkably stable guy, but losing his child, especially his only child, would be an emotional shock for anyone.

Maxx could see Gabby was also struggling to deal with the loss. She'd worked closely with Scott over the last year when they'd been assigned to the Hermes project. Although their interaction had been mostly limited to work, it was still a devastating development. He wished he had more comfort to offer, but mostly he was angry about the situation. And he felt partly guilty that he hadn't gotten over to see Scott when he'd first been called. If he'd been a little bit quicker to respond to Scott, he might have gotten there before Haoyu.

He knew from experience that going too far down this path of what ifs wasn't healthy, so he pulled back and focused on helping Glen and supporting Gabby. He took her hand and walked toward the front porch.

Immediately after Glen answered the front door, Gabby stepped forward to give him a big hug. Maxx didn't see this side of her personality often. She said, "I don't know what to say other than that I'm so sorry. I still can't believe he's gone."

"Thanks, Gabby. I keep expecting him to walk into the room. It's hard to accept."

Maxx stood to the side and put his hand on Glen's back. He didn't feel like he had anything more to add since his conversation with Glen this morning, but he wanted to let Glen know that he was there for him.

When Glen and Gabby finished hugging, Glen walked with them into the kitchen. "Come on in and grab something to eat and drink."

"Thanks, we already ate dinner and can't stay long. It's been a really busy day with the craziness going on at work."

From the other room, a voice called out, "Aren't you at least going to say hello before you two run off?"

Maxx rolled his eyes. "Geez, who let my twin brother in? I thought he was still in jail."

Gabby gave Maxx a confused look.

Glen laughed. "It's Andres. Maxx hasn't introduced the two of you?"

"No, I've been trying to keep him out of the picture," Maxx said.

Glen looked at Gabby. "Andres and Maxx jokingly were called twins because of their resemblance to Arnold Schwarzenegger and Danny DeVito in the 80s movie of same name."

"So is Maxx Arnold or Danny?" Gabby asked with a half smile.

Andres laughed loudly from the other room. "I'm the smart, funny brother."

"Definitely the one with the big ego," Maxx said to Gabby as an aside. "Andres is a professor at University of Washington and is a major know-it-all."

When Andres entered the room, Gabby could see how Maxx and Andres had earned the nickname. Maxx looked like a giant standing next to Andres. There was no resemblance whatsoever between the two men, so it made the nickname even more comical.

"Give me a hug, you big ape," Andres said to Maxx.

"Let me introduce you to my girlfriend first."

Maxx introduced the two of them. They immediately found a common interest in the current record of the Seahawks. While they were deep in conversation about player statistics, Maxx took the opportunity to chat privately with Glen about the latest updates from the SPD. Even though there was little new information to report, they had assigned a support worker to his case that was helping with the details.

As soon as there was a lull in the conversation between Gabby and Andres, she gave Maxx the nod, his signal indicating it was time to go.

Maxx said goodbye to Glen and then pulled Andres aside as he was walking out. "I have a case I'm working on that might be up your alley. How about I swing by your office tomorrow? I'd like to take advantage of that fancy education you're always bragging about."

"Please do, brother. You know I'm kind of like a modern-day Indiana Jones," he said with a wink.

"Good, that may be exactly the kind of wingman that I'm going to need," Maxx said.

UNDERGROUND

Maxx and Gabby woke early Friday morning to get started on their plans to try and connect with Haoyu. Checking outside the window, Gabby could already see a couple of people across the street in a dark sedan. They assumed they were the protection Miss Grey had promised last night, but they would verify that when they heard from her. Maxx had been carrying around his pistol lately, and Gabby had a 9mm Glock in her nightstand with a defensive load. They felt secure in the apartment as long as Miss Grey kept some agents to watch the access points to the condo building.

Unknown to the building management, Maxx had replaced Gabby's door with a solid-core metal version that would stop anything short of an RPG. It was the same door he'd put in his own place. A few years ago, he was getting concerned about the threats he'd gotten from some gangs on a case that became violent. He'd made some of the same alterations for Gabby when she had asked. It was better to seem paranoid than be dead.

On a whim, he'd checked the contract with the Chinese company that Daryl had sent to him a couple days ago. Interestingly, the agreement that Natalie had signed was also signed by Mr. Haoyu. If Haoyu was interested in Gabby at the time he initiated the agreement, he had to be aware that Maxx and Gabby were now in a relationship.

Since they were waiting for Miss Grey to contact them before leaving and driving Gabby to TechCom, Maxx felt like it was a good time to clear the air about that issue.

Treading lightly after a couple cups of coffee, he said, "I've been meaning to tell you that Daryl found out the strangest thing with one of the agreements Natalie had signed, one I wasn't aware of until now."

Gabby gave him the side-eye as she paused her sip of coffee. "Strange? I told you that bitch was a manipulator, so nothing she did should be surprising."

"You won't get an argument from me about that, but a Chinese company named AI Ventures based out of Wuxi had retained us to do a background search on two employees at TechCom. The Chinese signatory was our *friend* Mr. Haoyu. That can't be a coincidence. He had to be sniffing around TechCom but for some reason chose my company. And now he's tried to kill me."

"Okay, that is very odd," she said with a puzzled look. "Who were the employees at TechCom he wanted you to do background research on?"

Maxx coughed and looked away. "Oddly enough, one of them was you. The cover letter states you'd applied for a position at one of his companies in Wuxi, China."

"What? I have never applied for a job with a Chinese company. That's a lie!"

"I'm sure it is. It was earlier this year, so he must have been targeting you as a potential source for contact relative to Hermes. The contract for the background check with the Chinese company also included your boss, Dale."

"What research did you find about me and Dale?" She was

angry now, her cheeks fiery red. Then she paused and growled, "Is that why you met me at the coffee shop...doing some investigative work, and I was your target?"

Maxx raised his hands in surrender.

"No, that was my good luck. I didn't even know about the contract until this week. Natalie signed the contract against Daryl's advice, and as far as I can tell, no work had even started. My guess is that Haoyu wanted some dirt on you and Dale to leverage you into giving him some insider information."

"Well, I obviously didn't. Maybe Dale did, which would make him the leading candidate to be mole. There had to be a reason Haoyu picked you for the work. Since you didn't know about the contract until recently, I'll bet Natalie was involved somehow."

"I hadn't really considered that possibility. Maybe she got in over her head with the Chinese and that's the reason she ran."

Gabby smirked at him. "You're so naïve sometimes. I was suggesting that maybe her motives weren't so pure. What if she was setting you and me up for the Chinese? That would be more her typical approach from what I've seen."

Maxx would have to think more about that angle. *Could Natalie be that nasty? Yes.*

Maxx's cell phone began to vibrate as he received a text. It was from Miss Grey. "Will you be ready to go in an hour?"

He texted her back, "Yes. I'll drop off Gabby at work then head to where you tell me. Are these your friends outside in the sedan?"

"They're outside and also covering elevators and stairwells. They'll follow you to TechCom and stay there with Gabby."

Maxx then sent a follow-up text from his burner phone to an unlisted number. "Be ready to go in an hour. I'll give you directions when I get them. Bring some heavy equipment."

An answer came. "Not my first rodeo."

Maxx put the phone down. While he waited to hear from

Miss Grey, he thought more about what Gabby had said. Why would the Chinese want Natalie to track down Dale and Gabby?

As promised, Miss Grey texted him about an hour later to tell him that Haoyu and a few of his team were in the Pioneer Square area of downtown. She had been informed that they were heading over to Doc Maynard's Public House for an early lunch.

Maxx noted that she must either have someone inside Haoyu's team or had been able to bug their houses or cars. She knew more about what the Chinese were doing than she had let on, and it begged the question of why they had not been able to connect Haoyu's movements to the Omega device while he was moving around Seattle.

According to Miss Grey, there were armed DHS agents waiting by the elevator when Maxx and Gabby came out of the apartment. He'd set up the cameras and the apartment before they left to see if anyone made the effort to get in while they were gone. He was becoming less trustful of everyone involved as the week wore on.

The drive to TechCom was uneventful. The government sedan tailed them all the way and parked next to them in the visitor lot. Maxx walked Gabby up to the front door, where she was met by security. They kissed and promised they'd stay in touch throughout the day so she would know how things went with his attempt to track down Haoyu. If everything went as planned, he'd be able to get a bead on what Haoyu was doing in Pioneer Square and how it tied to the Omega device.

By the time Maxx found a place big enough to park his pickup truck, it was nearly 11:30. He'd verified that the restaurant didn't open until 11:00 so thought that would give them time to settle in and order but not so long that they finished eating.

Maxx was familiar with Doc Maynard's, named for one of

the prominent early settlers of Seattle. The restaurant featured a rustic, old-world atmosphere with exposed-brick walls, wooden beams, and vintage décor. It was in a building that dated back to the late-nineteenth century and was once home to a hotel and saloon. The building was later used as a brothel, and many original features, including the distinctive red-light sign, had been preserved and incorporated into the restaurant's decor.

He put on his sunglasses and pulled down his baseball cap as he took a stroll down the sidewalk on the other side of the street to see if one of Haoyu's men might be posted outside as a watchman. When he didn't see anyone who met the description loitering outside or in the cars parked nearby, he turned around at the intersection and walked back.

He was on the same side of the street now and paused by the front door as if he was reading the menu posted there. However, when he looked inside, Haoyu was nowhere to be seen. It was empty except for a few staff and a couple of older tourists sitting by the window. No one looked like spies or federal agents.

After taking a moment to think, Maxx decided he'd step inside and ask the bartender, who said there had been several Asian tourists working for a local bank that had taken the first Underground Seattle tour. The group had gone down the stairs about fifteen minutes ago.

Maxx told her that was the group he was supposed to meet and needed to catch up with them. At first, she refused. But when he discreetly slipped her a twenty-dollar bill, she handed him a ticket and pointed toward the entrance to the Underground.

The Seattle Underground was a dusty and cramped network of tunnels and passageways that ran beneath the streets of Seattle's historic Pioneer Square neighborhood. The tunnels were created in the aftermath of the Great Seattle Fire of 1889, which destroyed much of the city's central business district.

After the fire, the city decided to raise the street level in an effort to prevent flooding, leaving many buildings with their original first floors buried underground. As a result, many businesses and shops moved their storefronts to the second story, which became the new street level. The underground portion of the tunnels had been abandoned and dirty, with junk piled in the unused areas.

When he came down the stairs, he didn't rush ahead into the tour group. He took a moment to adjust his eyesight to the dim lighting and dark corners. He'd been down here before on a tour, but the gloom seemed more sinister knowing that Haoyu was probably down here.

He sent a quick text to his backup that he was heading into the Underground. He was going to take his time and verify that Haoyu was actually on the tour and then trail behind them out of sight. There were plenty of turns and blind corners he remembered from his first tour. The tour guide's voice gave him a good idea where the group was so that he could maintain some distance.

When there was a section that looped back on itself, he was careful to stay out of the overhead lamps and the filtered light coming from the glass blocks set in the sidewalk one story over his head. He caught a glimpse of the group coming around the corner and saw a couple of Asian men but didn't see Haoyu, who was taller than average, so Maxx expected he would be visible in the crowd even from a distance in the gloom.

He knew this was the first tour group of the day, so they had to be in this group. Maxx was getting a little anxious watching the group coming closer and still hadn't spotted anyone that he recognized. A couple of Asian men fit the profile of a young, active associate of Haoyu, but that could be coincidence.

As Maxx started to turn around to go check back with the

bartender to find out when the tour would finish, he spotted some shadows moving away from the tour group. It looked like a few people had waited for the rest of the group to turn and had ducked behind a bunch of stacked crates.

It was too dark to tell if they were people Maxx was meant to follow, but he noticed the two likely men he'd seen earlier were no longer in the tour group, so it was possible he was on the right line. He found it interesting that the tour guide also completely ignored them. They must have made arrangements ahead of time to split from the main group.

Maxx doubted anyone had been able to spot him following the group, so it was odd Haoyu would go through the trouble to slip away to evade him. There must be some hidden tunnels they were using to get outside undetected. He'd heard rumors about the tunnels, but the city always put those rumors to bed by having the engineers certify the layout. It was difficult to believe there were alternative routes that remained connected to this place.

Maxx waited a few minutes to see if anyone returned from behind the crates before he followed them. When it was clear the tour group was moving on without the ones who had slipped away, Maxx moved stealthily over to the crates.

He didn't hear anything and could see well enough into the shadows to see that there wasn't anyone standing around waiting for him. He took the penlight out of his pocket to see if he noticed anything unusual, but other than several sets of recent footprints on the dusty cement floor, he didn't see any other evidence that there'd been anyone in this area. They must have slipped through a door or access point somewhere in the area hidden by the crates. *Why is Haoyu underground, and where is he going?*

The small flashlight that Maxx was using wasn't very bright, so he got down on his hands and knees to see if there were any loose boards or joints in the floor. He didn't need to be very quiet because the wood, bricks, and concrete seemed to muffle all of the sounds. He could hear the tour guide getting further away, but it was barely audible after a few minutes.

After a thorough search of the floor, he started looking along the walls and rapping when he sensed there might be a misaligned joint or section of the wall. Haoyu and his men had disappeared very quickly and quietly once they had moved behind the crates, so the hidden exit had to be easily accessed.

As Maxx was about to get up off his knees, he heard someone cough nearby. He started to stand and felt metal pressing hard into the back of his head. "Hello again, Maxx. How have you been? I didn't get a chance to say goodbye the other evening."

Maxx stood still and didn't dare turn his head to look behind him. There was no need to look, as he instantly recognized Haoyu's distinctive voice. He didn't know how he'd sneaked up on him so silently, but he knew he was in deep trouble with a pistol pressing hard against his neck.

"Is it alright if I turn around so I can say hello properly?" Maxx asked with his tongue in his cheek.

Haoyu took a couple steps back to stay out of Maxx's reach. He wasn't going to make the same mistake his colleague had made at the bar the other night.

"Go ahead and turn around now. I'd like to see the eyes of a walking dead man. Even if you want to cry for help, no one will hear you down here...very soundproof."

"Not to mention the suppressor on your pistol," Maxx noted.

"It wasn't very smart of you to follow me, but you have been getting your nose into all kinds of places it shouldn't be lately, so I'm not surprised to see you. In fact, I suspected it was you when they texted me that a big, ugly American was looking for me in the bar. Government agents usually try to be more discreet."

Maxx kept his eyes locked on Haoyu, looking for any indication that others were backing him up. Even though his vision began to adjust to the dark, he couldn't see into all of the shadowy nooks and crannies, but he got the distinct sense that it was him and Haoyu down here alone. That was the only good thing he had going for him.

He was glad he'd had the foresight to set up a plan B in case he'd need help tailing them after they left Doc's. His only hope was that he could keep Haoyu talking long enough for backup to arrive and get him out of this jam before he caught a bullet.

"Since we're down here, and I doubt you have plans to let me go alive this time, can you tell me why we're here? The villain – that's you, by the way – always reveals the plan to the hero in the movies."

"This is not a movie, Maxx, and you are not a hero. Helping the American government to start a war isn't how hero's act."

"What are you talking about?" Maxx asked, struggling to understand what Haoyu meant. "No one is starting a war. I'm trying to understand why you killed my friend and are trying to kill me."

"I already told you the answer to that. I'm trying to stop a war from happening. Even if you are naïve about what is really going on, and I don't think you are, you are moving us closer to war. Nothing good can come from America attacking my country."

Maxx was thoroughly confused. Either Haoyu was lying, or there was a major piece of the puzzle that he was missing. Why would Haoyu bother lying when he was going to kill him any moment?

Maxx tried again to explain. "I don't know what war you're talking about. I'm not part of the government, and you attacked me a couple days ago for no reason that I know of."

"You should have been more careful about who you trusted.

It will cost you your life. I can't let you live, even if you are only a fool and telling the truth."

As Haoyu glowered, Maxx saw a flash in his peripheral vision and lunged to the floor away from his gun hand. He didn't know what he'd seen, but within a fraction of a second he heard the sound of two suppressed shots. He could hear a round splintering the wooden crates behind Haoyu and a bullet hitting the floor near his head, ricocheting off the concrete floor.

His backup plan had arrived.

The bullet had missed him, but he could still feel the sting of the concrete chips burning his face and neck as he rolled away from Haoyu. He pulled his .45 from his shoulder holster. If he was going to die, he sure as hell was taking someone with him.

Haoyu didn't wait around for Maxx or his backup to get off another shot. He immediately took off around the corner of the brick wall and raced into the dark.

Maxx's first instinct was to try and chase Haoyu, but after taking a few seconds to think it over, he decided that he'd let him go for now. There was no point in getting in a gun battle down here where there were too many places to hide and shoot. Since he didn't have a suppressed weapon, it would be obvious where he was shooting from. He decided it wasn't like the movies after all.

"Are you okay, Maxx?" Glen called out.

"Nothing that some of your sweet kisses can't fix. I was wondering if you were going to show up before it was too late," he answered.

"You're welcome, you big crybaby."

Glen walked over carrying his rifle. He didn't have a night scope on it, so that he could hide it underneath his coat. He used the flashlight mounted on the rifle to see if there was any blood on the floor. "I don't think I hit him."

"It didn't sound like it," Maxx said. "He took off running that way as soon as he got a shot off." He pointed toward the dark tunnels outside the tour area.

"I didn't bring any night vision equipment with me," Glen said.

"He must be familiar with these tunnels and has some friends nearby. I think we should call it quits and come back another time with better equipment."

"Come back for what?" Glen asked.

I'm not sure, but he was down here for a reason. And having that many people down here going through the tunnels means he's either hiding something or looking for something."

"Is this the guy you think killed my boy?"

"Yes," said Maxx, "it's definitely him."

Glen looked into the dark and clutched his rifle.

"Then we're going to hunt him out."

FLY ON, THUNDERBIRD FLY

Maxx and Glen walked back up the stairs to Doc's. At the gift shop, Maxx bought a "I did it Underground" t-shirt for Gabby as a souvenir. She probably wouldn't think it was as funny as he did.

As they walked back out through the bar, the bartender told him that Haoyu was gone, so they made a point of letting everyone else know they were leaving. The "all clear" would get back to Haoyu, if he was still around, making him wonder if they were trying to fake him out and wait for an ambush. Sometimes being too obvious was the better ploy to make people nervous.

Glen had taken a cab over, so Maxx took him home. After that, since it was still early afternoon on a Friday, he made a point to head up to the University of Washington to visit Andres, an instructor in the archeology program and a specialist in Native American cultures of the Pacific Northwest. He'd done a lot of the work in the field and helped as a graduate student on excavating many of the sites in the metro area, including around Pioneer Square.

Maxx parked his car in the garage near Suzzallo Library

and walked over to Denny Hall, where Andres had an office. The archeology program was integrated into the anthropology department, not one of the more high-profile studies at the university. Consequently, it was housed in some of the older facilities built in the 1890s. The brick and stone building itself always reminded Maxx of an ancient relic, especially since Denny Hall had been the first building constructed when the University of Washington moved from downtown to its current location.

Andres's office only added to the picture with the piles of books and the smell of musty paper. Maxx was always nervous watching Andres making coffee on his personal portable coffee maker. One errant spark and it would be an inferno in seconds. No amount of hectoring could get Andres to stop. He lived on caffeine and smoked salmon that he caught off his little trawler in Puget Sound.

Andres was also former Special Forces and a scuba diver. He looked more like a librarian than a lethal military weapon. His dad had been a tunnel rat in Vietnam and had enjoyed sharing the opposite experience of being in the open ocean with his son. Andres had been doing extreme and deep dives before he could legally drive a car. Following his dad's footsteps into the military, he had gone through Special Forces training but had naturally been attracted to the SEALs. That was where he and Maxx had met during the Gulf War.

After returning from the Gulf, Andres had used the education benefits he'd earned in the military and completed the master's and doctoral archeology degrees in record time. His proficiency in the water also allowed him to do underwater fieldwork all around the world, but his passion remained centered in the Pacific Northwest and the Native American cultures that had flourished in the area before the nineteenth century.

When Maxx entered Andres's office, he had to move books

off the only guest chair to the floor. There couldn't be a lot of students who came here for office hours. The musty smell and dust would have triggered anyone's allergies, and Maxx didn't know how Andres could spend more than short periods of time in the office without running short of breath.

When he was moving the stacks of books, one of the volumes caught his eye. "Can a borrow this one?" Maxx asked.

"Sure, although I thought a copy of Guns and Ammo magazine would be more your style."

"Normally I'd agree with you, but it's about a topic I've been thinking about lately."

Andres rolled his eyes. "Can I get you some coffee? I made a fresh pot so I could stay awake while I grade these blue books."

"Honestly, I'm wired already and could use something to take the edge off. I'd prefer a shot of that whiskey you keep in your bottom drawer."

Andres pulled out a flask from his desk drawer and poured a small shot into an empty coffee mug. "Why are you wired, and isn't it a little early to be drinking, even for a Friday? I thought you were cutting back."

"Glen and I were over at Pioneer Square. There is some weird stuff going on, and I need to get some background information from you. And you're right. I don't need this."

Maxx pushed the mug of whiskey away from him and walked over and poured himself a cup of coffee.

"How is Glen doing today?" Andres said.

"He's still pretty shook up. The reason we were in the Underground was related to that."

Andres raised his eyebrows in surprise. "How so?"

"I can't tell you the whole story, but we got information that the person who killed his son might be in the area. The cops can't touch the suspect because he's a foreign national with diplomatic immunity, and the evidence is thin. But thin evidence or not, we thought as private citizens we might be able to incentivize the guy to talk."

"And did he talk?"

"No, he decided to take the chat a different direction and shoot at me. That's why I'm a little on edge."

"I take it you're okay because you're talking with me. Is Glen okay?"

"He's fine, and the other guy got away before we could chat too much. But that's why I wanted to talk to you. We were in the Underground that starts on the tour below Doc Maynard's. A couple times he was able to disappear down there."

"Disappeared, how?"

"I don't exactly know, but him and a couple of his friends were able to go into an area that is off the tour path and seemingly go through solid brick walls without making a sound or leaving a trace."

"I see. When we were working in the Underground doing field surveys, we found several hidden passageways. Plus there are dozens of places to hide. We turned over all that information to the city though. I thought they had sealed all the unused passageways to be safe."

"Do you remember where they were located?"

"I'm pretty sure I could locate the general areas. If they had been sealed up, I think it would be pretty evident."

"I looked as closely as I could but only had a pocket flashlight. Where did the passageways go?"

"Some of the passages were simply extra access to the original street level doorways, so they were essentially first and second floors of the above buildings. They had been cleared out and sealed."

"Some large places to hide?"

"Some of them were large, but not much to see unless you had lighting put in. And no air flow, so they were as stale as a tomb."

"Kind of like your office," Maxx pointed out.

Andres chuckled. "Emptier though. But there were a few passageways we didn't get too far into. They sloped down toward the waterfront and were probably underwater. The corridors were created using natural formations in the bedrock that predated the early settlers. A team from the geology department did some analysis and said the passages are a spiderweb of caves and tunnels formed by seismic activity."

"We were going to get some scuba gear and do some diving into the tunnels to see where they led, but the city wouldn't give us a permit to explore them. We didn't follow through because of concerns about the instability of the Seattle Fault."

"No idea where those passageways went?" Maxx asked.

"No one has ever found an above-ground entrance to these underground passageways, and the early settlers tried. Obviously, we know the fault exists, and it has been partially mapped using ground detection sonar, but with Puget Sound sitting above it, it's not a very thorough map. As far as I know, there are multiple shallow east–west thrust faults that cross the Puget Sound lowland. It'd be an interesting study for one of the graduate students, but so far I haven't got anyone else interested enough to fully research it.

"The Suquamish tribe has oral legends that there was at one time a series of connections to the underground fault line that runs out into Eliot Bay. It was supposed to be a revered way for them to travel to some of the islands without having to come above ground. About 1,100 years ago, it was the scene of a major earthquake of about magnitude seven. It's an event that became legendary for the Native Americans in this area."

"That sounds more like your area of expertise than the answer I'm looking for," Maxx cut in. "I can't imagine these guys were looking for secret passageways on the fault. They were more likely looking for a place to temporarily hide."

"I get that, Maxx. I can pull up some of my notes from the

work we did on the Underground. Then I can give you better details on the passageways we explored. I will dig through my materials tonight. It's in boxes in my attic, so it will have to wait until I finish all the grading."

"That would be interesting, but what would really be the most helpful is if you would come with me and do a walk-through of the Underground space with your notes. Then I'm not trying to interpret what you meant while I'm stumbling around in the dark."

"I'm free tomorrow morning if we can get there early before they start doing tours. That way we'll also have some daylight filtering in and won't have to rely only on flashlights."

Maxx nodded, thinking it through.

"Do you know anyone who will let us in that early? I'm also sure the guys who disappeared down there are working with some of the employees, so I'd like to keep it low-key. I'm sure I can get us in illegally but would prefer not to break in and have someone calling the police on us."

"It won't be a problem. The archaeology department does some pro bono work for them occasionally. I'll tell them I need to update some pictures and posters. It's normal for me to take students in to take pictures and samples without interrupting them during business hours. No one will suspect a thing."

"That sounds perfect. I'll pick up Glen and meet you there around six tomorrow morning."

"Would you mind if I brought one of my teaching assistants? Joseph is a member of the Suquamish tribe and has been begging me to go down there with him. He's the grad student I've also been trying to encourage to do in-depth research on the ancient legends about the Seattle fault and how they influenced the settlements in the area."

When Maxx nodded, Andres picked up his phone and dialed. "Joseph, can you come to my office for a minute? I want to introduce you to a friend. He wants to drop by the Underground tomorrow for a little surveying, and I'd like your help if you're free."

After hanging up the phone, Maxx and Andres talked about the Mariners and the weather while they waited for Joseph. Maxx wasn't too sure about bringing a civilian with them if Haoyu showed up tomorrow. But Andres, Glen, and Maxx had concealed carry licenses, so he didn't think there would be any real risk to Joseph. The risk for Haoyu might be another story.

Joseph was a young man in his mid-twenties who had a serious demeanor. He firmly shook Maxx's hand then leaned against one of the bookcases since there was nowhere to sit.

"You're interested in the Underground?" Joseph asked.

"He's particularly interested in the native traditions that relate to the earthquakes in the area and how they reformed the local geography," Andres answered. It wasn't what Maxx would have said, but Andres knew how to get Joseph talking, so Maxx didn't interrupt him.

"I presume you know the Seattle Fault is a multi-stranded east–west striking reverse fault cutting across Puget Sound, through downtown Seattle, and across Lake Washington. There was an earthquake of 7.4 magnitude around AD 900 that cause more than twenty feet of vertical uplift on the southern side, sent massive block landslides tumbling into Lake Washington, and created a tsunami in Puget Sound. There are plenty of archaeological sites near Seattle that confirm the effects on local communities."

"And this fault connects to the native traditions, how?" Maxx asked.

"They are usually structured as stories about the acts and personalities of supernatural beings, often in the guise of animals. In this case, Thunderbird generally represented the ground shaking or what we call earthquakes. The whale represented tsunamis. It wasn't only in the Seattle area but extended throughout Cascadia. Shaking imagery appears in stories about a variety of supernatural beings, which is not surprising in an area with multiple earthquake sources and active volcanoes. Some stories have generic descriptions of shaking that could occur in any earthquake, whereas others appear to describe specific effects, such as tsunamis or permanent ground level changes."

"Thunderbird and Whale were supernatural beings that explained the events the Native communities experienced?"

"Yes, but they weren't always random acts. The major events were usually initiated in concert with tribal elders to address a shortage of fish or to protect them from other supernatural beings. Then it became customary to attribute any earthquakes or tsunamis as the acts of these two supernatural beings. Since there were at least twelve distinct languages spoken in the region, the stories were part of broader culture that conveyed information through artifacts, dances, songs, ceremonies, and place names. If you've seen totems, artifacts, and longhouses, you see Thunderbird and Whale consistently represented."

Maxx was quickly becoming intrigued. "According to legend, the communities had the ability to communicate with these supernatural beings, and together they would agree to trigger natural events like earthquakes, tsunamis, and floods. How would they communicate with them?"

"A lot of that information has been lost unfortunately. What is clear is that communication occurred in cycles with geological evidence indicating that there were at least seven in the last 3500 years. Knowledge of a repeating communication cycle is implied in the stories. And man clearly has the ability to summon Thunderbird and send him back to the sky. Those kinds of ceremonies only occurred in the longhouses in protective ceremonies using languages that are forgotten."

"What about an event like the eruption of Mount St. Helens?" Maxx asked. "Would they see that as the work of Thunderbird?"

"Absolutely. Tribes would ask, 'Why did Thunderbird visit?' Only a medicine man or elder could call Thunderbird, so who spoke to him?"

Maxx thought about what Joseph had told him. *Could this be connected to the alien Omega device? Or was he connecting random dots?*

"Is there an elder who could tell me more about this? I know it sounds like I'm a bit crazy, but there is something going on that might be related to these native stories, the fault, and the Underground."

Andres and Joseph looked at Maxx like he was pulling their leg. Andres answered him seriously, however. "We are doing some archeological dives off the point at Blakely Harbor on Monday evening. It's related to this topic and Port Blakely's early history. After we finish the dives, we are meeting some of the elders to discuss our findings at Hall's Hill Labyrinth. If you'd like, you could join us."

Maxx nodded and said, "Remind me on Monday, and I'll try to make it. Not for the diving part or your excursion, only for the part afterward. You know how I hate the water. And in the dark...not a chance!"

DEEPER UNDERGROUND

After Maxx left the University of Washington, he texted Gabby to see when she might be ready to be picked up after work. She texted him back while he was driving and let him know she would be working late on "the project" and didn't know when or if she would be getting home tonight. She had made arrangements with Miss Grey for a security escort when she was able to leave. The two DHS agents were going to hang out in the TechCom parking lot, so they'd be able to assist when she needed it.

He was feeling pretty beat after the adrenaline rush earlier and was looking forward to crashing at his apartment and watching some of the Mariners games that he recorded. He had plenty of beer in the refrigerator if he decided he needed a drink and was looking forward to a chance to unwind a bit after the whirlwind that had started Tuesday evening. It had been the craziest three days he'd had in several years, and things weren't likely to calm down.

One of the lessons he'd learned in the military was to never pass up a chance to rest, eat, or pee. And he felt like this would be a good time to catch up on all three, since he was going to be a bachelor for the evening. Not to mention he would need to get up at 5 a.m. to pick up Glen then head back to Pioneer Square to meet Andres and Joseph at 6. He didn't know what to expect going back into the Underground, but it would be stressful wondering if Haoyu was hiding behind every blind corner.

When Maxx got to the apartment, the first thing he did was order an extra-large pizza from Pizza Hut, grab a double of some Macallan twelve-year, and flop down on the couch. He started looking through the game he'd recorded from Thursday to watch while he recorded tonight's game to watch later if he was still awake and Gabby wasn't home.

While the game was playing on low volume, Maxx thought back over the events of the last few days. He jotted down some things that had stood out to him. He didn't really get the entire alien connection. Joseph's news had provided him some information that helped connect some dots if he let his imagination run wild. The possibility that some of the legends could connect to the Omega device strained credulity, too much like a science fiction movie to accept without some hard evidence. Surely DARPA had made this connection before and discarded it as irrelevant.

The other thing that was really bothering him was the relationship between the Chinese and Natalie. It felt like there was some connection he was overlooking beyond the obvious. There had to be reason she had been approached by the Chinese and then never followed through. It could be a series of coincidences, but Maxx didn't believe in coincidences; there had to be a firm connection he hadn't spotted yet. He couldn't very well ask Natalie directly, because if she was somehow involved, she might let Haoyu know that Maxx – and by extension, Miss Grey – were onto whatever he was plotting.

The most important eye-opener that Maxx pondered was Haoyu's assertion this morning that he was helping the American government start a war. In different circumstances, Maxx would have disregarded the statement as misdirection. But Haoyu was getting ready to kill him and had no reason to lie. It was his justification to kill Maxx, to stop a war. Hell, Maxx had killed plenty of combatants for reasons less virtuous than that.

Maxx tried to look at what he'd done over the last three days and couldn't think of any reason Haoyu would think that the US was trying to start a war or that Maxx was part of it. He was a cyber detective with a small agency, not involved with the Omega project through the government or TechCom except for his girlfriend and his friend's now-dead son. He wouldn't even know about any of this if Haoyu hadn't tried to kill him three nights ago.

Maxx got another text from Gabby telling him she was going to be pulling an all-nighter at work. They had a deadline to get some reports completed before Sunday so they could send them back to the client. He knew that must mean they needed to finish the Delta files for the Hermes project and send them back to DARPA. He would have to talk to her face-to-face to see if she'd tell him any more than the basics.

As he kept going over and over the open questions in his mind, he drifted off to sleep. The couch wasn't very comfortable, but he was exhausted, and the low murmur of the baseball game in the background was enough white noise that he quickly nodded off.

The following morning, he sat up with a start when his phone rang. He'd forgotten to set his alarm so was relieved when he looked at the clock on the VCR to see it was only 5:15. Ironically, the call was from Andres confirming they were still planning to meet at Doc Maynard's this morning at 6. Maxx was excited to hear that Andres had found the documents he'd referenced about the Underground.

He gathered a couple of large, waterproof flashlights, some heavy gloves, and his pistol and got his truck. He grabbed four large coffees and some donuts from Top Pot Doughnuts on the way to pick up Glen. After last night, he was still a little groggy and needed the caffeine and sugar to get him going before walking into a bunch of dark tunnels that might be concealing a bunch of trained assassins. Nothing got him focused like a possible gunfight.

They pulled into the lower floor of a parking lot on a side street near Smith Tower. The parking lot always reminded him of a sinking ship, and there were plenty of spots open this time of the morning. He parked there because his truck was easily identifiable, and if Haoyu was watching for him, it wouldn't be easy to spot. They could also cut through the back alley, and Doc Maynard's was less than a block away from his truck. If they needed to disappear quickly, they could drive up the James Street hill to the freeway entrances heading north and south.

When they walked up the alley behind Doc's, they could see Andres and Joseph sitting on a bench in Pioneer Park near the restaurant's front door. There was hardly anyone out walking around this early on a Saturday morning. The home-less residents who hung out in the area wouldn't be getting up for hours, it was past tourist season, and most businesses would be closed on a Saturday morning. There wasn't really anyone nearby to watch them, but that also made them of interest for the occasional car that cruised by.

Maxx handed out the coffees and the donuts to everyone. "Andres, are they expecting us, or are we going to have to climb in through the windows?"

"If you climb in one of those open second-floor windows, I'll give you twenty bucks," Glen dared him.

Andres rolled his eyes. "As much as I appreciate the comedy routine, no one is crawling through any windows this morning. I have the spare keys and the code to turn off the security alarm. We keep them in the department office so we can check them out for archaeology work the university does to support the downtown association."

Joseph looked like he wasn't too sure this was the kind of adventure he'd meant to volunteer for. "Yes, I've been here several times. They don't open for a few hours, so we will have the chance to explore without any interruptions. Not that I expect we'll find anything new. Right, Professor?"

"No, I don't expect anything new. I did bring my old binders from when I was working here on several field projects as a graduate student myself. Some of that may be new to you, Joseph."

Glen rubbed his hands together. "It's a little chilly. Can we go inside and get this party started? By the way, Doc, did Maxx mention we had a bit of tussle here yesterday?"

"He mentioned it. The owner of the restaurant and the Seattle Underground Tour assured me the place was searched last night after closing and that nothing unusual was found. The alarm has been on all night, according to the security company."

Maxx looked at him skeptically. "You know the owner, and it sounds like you trust him. But the bartender gave us the stink eye when we left, so I'm not sure we have the full story."

Andres led the group into the entrance for the Underground. Maxx came in last and took a look around to see if there was anyone in the park who seemed to be showing them any interest. He couldn't see anyone but made sure to close and lock the door behind them. It wouldn't hurt to make sure his gun was cocked with the safety off in case they did get surprised.

After descending the stairs, they took turns looking at the hand-drawn maps from Andres's binder. He'd put them in plastic wrap so they could be handled without smudging any of the old pencil markings. Maxx also had them all put on gloves in case they came across anything unusual, not wanting them to contaminate the site with their fingerprints if Haoyu's team had left evidence behind. Joseph raised his eyebrows at this request but did it without comment.

The first location that Andres led them to wasn't too far from the entryway. To the naked eye, it looked like an old brick wall with a series of arches. Joseph told them the arches had been bricked in because this part of the building had been the original first floor and that mud had settled outside. The bricked-in windows were meant to keep the dirt out, like a solid foundation wall.

Andres consulted his map and walked down to the third arch. It looked the same as the rest, but he started pushing some of the bricks looking for a loose one that wasn't set correctly. After several tries, he found a brick he was able to lift out, exposing a rusted metal handle. It looked like it was fixed into a metal door behind the bricks.

Andres twisted the handle until it audibly clicked into place, and then he was able to extend it out enough so that he could get a firm grip with leverage. He began pulling on the handle, and a section of the bricks began to swing out on some hidden hinges. It didn't take much effort for the wall to open enough to see there was a passageway behind the door.

Joseph pulled over a set of short wooden stairs with only three steps so they could walk into the archway. Andres shined his flashlight into the dark behind the hidden brick door, lighting up a narrow bricked-in tunnel wide enough for two men to walk side by side and tall enough that they could walk without stooping too much.

"This is a good example of the passageways that were built as part of the process of raising the street up a story or two," Andres said. "This particular passageway was put in at the time the Underground was created, but the false door was created later so they could move between buildings or hide from law enforcement or rival gangs."

"Does anyone use it now?" Maxx asked.

"The city surveyed this one back in the 1980s, but because it isn't up to code to handle earthquakes, they don't allow anyone in there, and technically it is sealed off. The average person wouldn't know it was there, and it was sealed on the other end. It can only be accessed by the city through a secured door in the basement of a nearby building."

"It doesn't look like anyone has been through here in a long time," Glen noted. He pointed to the thick layer of dust on the floor. There were a few small trails in the dust left by mice or rats, but other than those the floor was clear of any shoe prints.

"So how many similar tunnels are there like this?" Maxx asked.

Andres consulted his map. "I see six like this that we noted on our survey. There may have been more found since then, but no one contacted the archeology department to have us come out and look at them if they did."

"Let me show you the area where I saw some people vanish yesterday." Maxx walked over to the crates where Haoyu and his team had been.

When they got to place where Maxx had been attacked, it was pretty evident from all the footprints and scuffle marks that there had been a lot of activity in the area.

"This is it," Maxx said. "I saw them go behind the crates, and by the time I got over here, they were gone. That had to be less than a minute."

Andres studied his map. When he was sure he was looking at the correct location, he said, "There's nothing noted on my map. The closest passageway we had found was about twenty yards further along. Are you certain this was the spot?"

"Absolutely. Look at the floor where I was down looking for cracks or openings. You can still see my boot prints."

Andres rubbed his chin as he looked at the ceiling above them. "The reason I'm asking is because we are directly in the center of the building. There wouldn't be a tunnel going to the outside from here on this floor. Nor would there be one above us."

"Maybe they went up," Maxx observed.

"It is more likely they went down," Joseph responded.

Andres's eyes lit up. "Joseph is correct. It's more likely there is access to the tunnels that run beneath the original building. If you recall, Maxx, I told you there were legends about the indigenous tribes who were here using the natural tunnels created by the Seattle Fault."

"The tunnels ran east and west from Lake Washington all the way over to the Kitsap Peninsula. Most of the fault lines are extremely deep under Puget Sound, but there are small offshoots or vents that came to the surface. The tribes would use them as underground highways and created additional access points in key areas."

"But someone would have to know about the access points, since neither of you are aware of it," Maxx pointed out.

"That's true," said Andres, "but we do know where there are some mapped Native American natural fault tunnels, and one of them passes underneath this building. Joseph planned to show us that in a moment, although we don't have the gear to go into it today. It's not for the faint of heart."

"I suggest we keep looking here and see if we can find an opening, then try to determine if it connects to the fault tunnel," Maxx said. "I didn't really look closely at the floor. I was assuming they went through the wall or ceiling."

"Based on floor access and it not being an original tunnel, my guess is that the access point is hidden under these crates. If they can swing out of the way easily, then you could quickly jump down or climb a ladder. Did you try and move the crates?" Andres asked Maxx.

"No, but that possibility makes sense when I have time to think it through and no one is shooting at me."

While they had been talking, Glen and Joseph had been trying to move the crates around. It became evident that they were too heavy and wouldn't budge. Using the brightest flashlight they had, Joseph found a wooden latch that allowed a section of the crates to roll away. Moving the crates out of the way exposed a trap door in the floor underneath.

Maxx told everyone to stand back when he hooked some rope through the door handle. He didn't want to take any chances that Haoyu had gotten creative enough to boobytrap this entrance. He'd seen some nasty wounds from people who didn't show any patience before running into booby-trapped rooms. When everyone was behind a wall or the crates, he used the rope to lift open the trap door.

After a brief pause of silence, Glen walked over to the entrance with a flashlight and his pistol out. He examined the hole in the floor more closely and then gave them the signal to keep quiet in case the tunnel contained someone who could hear them. He tilted back the metal door, and Maxx held the flashlight and his pistol while Glen climbed down the ladder to the tunnel floor below them.

Glen disappeared from sight for a few minutes and explored a short distance into the empty tunnel. There was evidence that multiple people had been through this way recently. All the footprints went in one direction, toward the part of the tunnel that sloped down toward Elliott Bay. Other than the dusty footprints, there wasn't anything else to see down here. Although it didn't have junk lying around like other sections of the Underground, it was obviously less traveled.

When he came back up, he shut the tunnel door so they could talk. "There are multiple tracks, and they all head that way," he said as he pointed east.

"Then this has to be a connector to the Seattle Fault tunnels," Joseph said. "I've never seen this entrance on the map, but it must be a branch that ties into the entrance about fifty yards to the east."

"We have that entrance on the map," Andres said. "It was the primary point of entry for the exploration that was done before the government shut it down."

Maxx and Glen put the crates back the way they had found them while Andres jotted down some notes to catalogue the new entry point. Joseph walked toward the primary tunnel entrance on his map. The primary entrance was unmarked and looked like a large, nondescript pair of gray, metal doors set in the concrete wall.

Maxx twisted the handles. "If you open the lock, we can get in. I had walked right by this before and thought it was storage or a mechanical room."

Joseph took a large set of keys out of his backpack. After checking his notes, he found the key for the door and opened the lock. He pulled open the door and peeked inside, then he shook his head and looked back at Andres.

"This looks completely different than when I was here a few years ago. Were you aware of any construction?" he asked.

Andres stepped up and looked in. "What the hell?" he muttered. Where there had been a tunnel and ladder before, now there was a freight elevator door. There was no call button evident on the wall next to elevator, only a card reader. The light on the reader was glowing red.

"What is this elevator for, Doc?" Maxx asked.

"This makes no sense," Andres answered. "Not only was this closed off because it was unsafe, but why would someone install an elevator?"

As Glen noticed a camera mounted in the ceiling, they heard the elevator growing closer. It could pass by their floor, but they probably had been on camera as soon as they opened the outside door.

When the elevator stopped, the doors opened, and several

heavily armed security guards stepped out. They looked like military personnel but didn't have military uniforms. They had their rifles at low ready, even though Maxx, Glen, and Andres had their pistols holstered. It was only after security had stepped out that Maxx saw someone that he recognized behind them in the large elevator.

"Nice to see you again so soon, Maxx," Miss Grey said, but from the look on her face, it didn't look like she thought it was nice at all.

THIS MACHINE WILL NOT COMMUNICATE

Everyone else in the group with Maxx turned to look at him with bewilderment as Miss Grey spoke to him. Maxx was only slightly less surprised by her appearance here than they were.

"Miss Grey, I told you we were trying to track down Haoyu yesterday. Incidentally it was you who told me he was going to be here," he said with a bit of irritation.

"No need to get snippy, Maxx. I didn't really expect you'd return so quickly after running off yesterday, especially at this time of day when the building is supposed to be locked."

"I happen to have a friend who has after-hours access. Let me introduce you to everyone," Maxx said to Miss Grey.

After Maxx introduced Glen, Andres, and Joseph, she shook their hands firmly. Perhaps a little too firmly with Andres. "I am Miss Grey. I work for the federal government and have been trying to track down a Chinese citizen. Haoyu is the reason Maxx and I first met. It's a long, boring story for another time when we all have more time."

"It's a pleasure," Andres said. "If you were looking for this person, it really doesn't explain why you were on this obscure elevator in the middle of a protected, historic site."

"That's going to be difficult to explain without revealing things that are confidential. I wouldn't exactly call this elevator hidden though."

"Joseph and I work for the university, and I can tell you with confidence that this elevator is not supposed to be here. It isn't on any building blueprints or the historic registry."

Grey scratched her ear, unconcerned.

"This is getting complicated. As I mentioned, I don't have a lot of time to stand around giving you details that are closely held. I'd like to invite you to follow me, and then we'll be in a better position to chat. I'd really hate for someone else to wander in here and discover this 'obscure' elevator."

Glen shook his head. "I appreciate the invitation, Miss Fed —I mean, Miss Grey—but I'm going to decline. I need to get back and take care of some personal business."

Miss Grey stared at Glen for a moment. "To be honest, it wasn't really so much an invitation as a very strong hint. I'm trying to keep this friendly because I trust your friend Maxx, but we are all going to take an elevator ride and go somewhere more comfortable."

"Or what?" Glen asked. "There is usually an *or* at the end of a speech like that when Feds are talking."

Maxx decided he had better intervene before the two of them started butting heads. If Maxx had been in Glen's shoes, he probably would have been belligerent too. However, knowing Miss Grey and the backstory to what was going on, they needed to give her the benefit of the doubt. *Not only might Haoyu be nearby, but the clock is really beginning to count down to Tuesday.*

"We should go with her, Glen. I only met her this week, but I trust her. Let's hear her out for a few minutes."

Glen scowled at Maxx. "Fifteen minutes, then I make like a tree."

Everyone looked confused, until Maxx said, "And leave, I

get it." The bad joke took some of the tension out of the air. Hopefully no one would say anything about dad jokes and remind Glen that Scott was killed so recently.

One of the security team had held the elevator door open during the exchange. Maxx guessed it was their emergency exit plan if things had gone badly. "We can all fit comfortably in there, I presume?" he asked.

"It was made to haul some very heavy equipment. We'll be fine," one of the security personnel answered.

"Then all aboard," said Miss Grey. "I know Maxx has clearance, but I don't know about the rest of you, so we are going to have to make a stop on a secured floor. We will see where we go from there."

Miss Grey told the security person, "Three." He nodded, swiped his access card, and pushed the button for the third floor.

Maxx wasn't surprised that the elevator went down instead of up when it began to move. He'd counted a dozen buttons on the elevator panels and assumed the place must be massive.

"I guess three means the third level underground, not in the building above us. More of your hidey-holes?"

The ride was quick and quiet as they descended. It was obvious from the looks on the faces of Andres and Joseph that they were trying to process the revelation that there was now something below the building and even below the Seattle Fault tunnel where they had never been before.

When they came off the elevator, they were quickly shepherded by the security personnel into a large open room across the hall. After they had taken seats around the table, the security guys stood against the wall. They didn't look completely bored but were certainly more relaxed once the door to the room locked behind them.

Miss Grey coughed to stop the little bit of low-key chatter. "Let's get the administrative details out of the way, then I can get to the more interesting information, like who we are and why we're here."

Maxx noted that the head of security raised his eyebrow when she said that. *That will be a surprise to him*, he thought.

"I have a very short nondisclosure agreement I need you all to sign," she said as she handed out copies to Maxx, Glen, Andres, and Joseph.

It was Maxx's turn to raise an eyebrow. "Aren't I covered by the agreement that I signed the other night at our meeting?"

"No. Separate group," she responded cryptically.

Maxx took a pen from the table and signed it without reading it. He handed it back to her and said, "In for a penny, in for a pound."

Andres and Joseph were still reading the two-page form when Glen stood up and said, "I'm not signing anything until I have an attorney look at it. I guess I can go then so you can get back to your secret squirrel meeting."

"That's not happening, Glen. I understand if you don't want to sign, but then we'll need you to stay in another room while you wait for your attorney to arrive. You've trespassed into a top secret facility, and I can't release you until we are in agreement that you'll keep this highly confidential. That's not negotiable."

"I knew it," Glen growled. "Who's going to stop me? These overpaid mall security guys? No offense, guys."

"As a matter of fact, yes, they are authorized to stop you. You've been around long enough to know how this works. Either sign the document, or things are going to get ugly. Don't make things sticky, Glen."

The security team had tensed up when Glen got out of his chair and were already moving for better angles in case it went sideways. Their weapons were still held at low ready, but it was clear they were highly trained operators and weren't underestimating Glen or the rest of the visitors.

Maxx stood up and put his hands on Glen and gently

pushed him back into his chair. "I told you to trust me, buddy. Sign the paper. It's nothing we haven't signed for some spook a dozen times before."

When Glen signed and threw the paper and pen back on the table, there was a collective sigh in the room. Joseph had watched the exchange wide-eyed. Andres had barely looked up from his reading, having seen this kind of drama from Glen and Maxx before. When the professor signed the paper, Joseph shrugged and signed his paper too. Miss Grey gathered the documents and glanced at the signatures to make sure that Glen hadn't signed "Alfred E. Neuman" as she was warned he sometimes did.

Miss Grey put the papers inside the folder under her arm and gave a nod to the head of the security team. "Let's take a short field trip, folks. Keep your hands to yourselves. Remember, anything you experience is covered under the document you signed."

The security team guided them out of the conference room and back to the elevator they had vacated less than a half hour before. They were careful to bracket them in the hallway so the only open path was forward.

When they were all on board, Miss Grey swiped her access card and pushed the bottom button. Naturally the button wasn't marked with any symbols or numbers, but it had to be the basement of this facility. Maxx watched her closely and had difficulty believing a facility had been dug out at least one hundred feet below downtown Seattle and no one had even suspected.

The elevator felt like it was descending rapidly. Maxx stopped counting when he reached twenty, knowing that in twenty seconds they had already descended more than a dozen floors. With the rapid change in air pressure, it felt more like an express elevator in a high-rise building – except they were descending deep underground and not going up.

Why would they need a high-speed elevator down here?

When the doors opened up, they exited into another hallway that looked like the one they'd just left. They didn't file into a conference room this time but proceeded to a large metal door that was sealed shut. It looked like the door to a bank vault or the access to a missile silo, intended to keep something out or in. Once again, Miss Grey used her security badge to access the door controls. When she pushed the button, it swung open slowly on its massive hinges. In the twenty seconds it took for the door to fully open, Maxx could see it was close to five feet thick in the center. That was adequate to keep any conceivable man-made or natural disaster, including a nuclear blast, from escaping the solid rock tunnel they were entering.

After they were inside the rock tunnel on the other side of the blast door, Miss Grey keyed the door closed behind them. Andres gave Maxx a look of shock, unable to hide his reaction to the size and security of the facility. It must have taken billions of dollars and decades to construct this underground while maintaining concealment.

Miss Grey spoke up once the noise of the door closing stopped. "I'm sure all of you have questions already. I'm not going to answer any of them."

Andre shrugged. "This is amazing already, but I can't imagine this blast door is what you wanted to show us. What are you doing down here?"

She didn't answer him and walked forward to a viewing station ahead that had several small windows like portholes on a ship that were deeply set into the stone wall. There was light beyond the windows, and they crowded around, all trying to see what was on the other side.

The blast door had been a shock, but they struggled to absorb what they were looking at through the glass. It was a huge cavern in which a geothermal power plant was built. The plant must have been constructed to capture underground steam that was emanating from the Seattle Fault.

Miss Grey explained, "What you are looking at is the largest dry-steam power plant in the world. It dwarfs the output of the geothermal energy complex in The Geysers located in California. That complex provides more than twenty percent of all renewable energy in California."

"Why build it here? We're underneath a major metropolitan city surrounded by major seismic fault lines," Andres asked.

"Due to the fractures in the Seattle Fault that are not very deep, it is only a few kilometers below the surface and only one of three places in the US where underground steam is accessible. The first being The Geysers and the second being Yellowstone National Park in Wyoming."

Maxx jumped in. "That sounds great and all, but why doesn't anyone know it's here? It had to be constructed in secret, and hasn't anyone from Pacific Gas and Electric noticed there is a huge amount of electricity being generated from this location?"

"I don't know why it has been kept secret. That's above my pay grade. There is one obvious reason. Concerns might arise if the population found a power plant connected to the fault below the city."

"And did this impact any of the Native American archaeological sites we know are connected to the fault?"

"That's how the location was first discovered. Geological surveys were performed when exploring the access points to the fault that the indigenous tribes had used. But while they are connected, those sites have been carefully avoided and protected from the operations of the power plant."

"Setting aside my concerns as a citizen for a moment, what does this have to do with the Chinese spying that's been going on?"

Miss Grey answered him with a nod. "They're trying to

understand how we're doing this so that they can replicate it in their country. There are several shallow fault lines that have accessible steam vents that they want to utilize for similar projects. Their attempts, all the way back to the 1970s, have been unsuccessful. Their initial attempt caused a well-known earthquake in Tangshan in 1976."

"Is that why we had to sign those agreements?" Joseph asked. "To make certain that the information is kept out of the hands of the Chinese spies who Maxx caught probing around in the Underground yesterday?"

"I'm sure you have all heard of the Manhattan Project. This facility isn't as secretive as the research that went on there, but it is probably similar in many ways. This project has incorporated some scientific discoveries that are extremely beneficial, but it also has some destructive capabilities that could be used for nefarious reasons if it got in the hands of our enemies. It is one of the most valuable assets in America at the present time."

Maxx knew this was not entirely true. While this facility may have interest for Haoyu, it wasn't the primary reason he was in Seattle or even the Pioneer Square area. It must be connected to the Omega device, or Miss Grey wouldn't be here to intervene. What Maxx had difficulty understanding was why the facility wasn't connected to the work at DARPA, which was only about five miles to the south.

Glen leaned over to Maxx and whispered, "I don't understand how this connects to the reason why Scott was targeted by the Chinese. He wasn't working on anything that was related to something like this."

It was loud enough that Miss Grey overheard him. "That was a tragedy, Mr. Piper, and I'm so sorry for your loss. I'd be happy to discuss that with you in private since I'm monitoring that case, because it is connected. Apparently, Scott had inadvertently found out about this project while he was doing some deep research, and it alerted the Chinese."

Maxx didn't know if this was completely true either, but it was plausible based on the information he and Gabby had uncovered and shared with Miss Grey.

"Thank you," Glen said. "I'll take you up on your offer to chat more when we're out of this place. For now, I'd like to get out of this cave. It gives me the creeps."

Miss Grey had the security team escort Glen, Andres, and Joseph up to the building above them. She told them she wanted to discuss something confidentially with Maxx, who would join them upstairs in a few minutes.

When they left and the blast door closed them in again, Maxx asked her, "Why'd you really bring us down here? You could have left us standing outside the elevator, and none of us would have been the wiser."

"That's true, except it was highly likely that Andres or Joseph would have said something about the new elevator in a secret location. By getting them to sign the nondisclosure, they can't. I had to give them a lie big enough to make the secrecy credible."

"What lie?" Maxx asked as he look confused.

"What I didn't tell them was the truth about why there is a geothermal plant here in the Underground."

"Does this have something to do with Omega?" he guessed.

"Bingo. The Omega device requires a tremendous amount of energy to operate, and DARPA knows that. By placing it here, there is no record of the power demand. Pardon the pun, but it's off the grid. And by placing it here, both the device and the power are not discoverable by DARPA and the Chinese."

"But that's crazy to spend that kind of money to build this to hide the device from our own government!" Maxx exclaimed.

"There was another reason it was built here," she continued. "The device needs huge amounts of power generated from the Earth directly, and after testing, this area was found to be a hot spot. Yellowstone would have worked, but it would be too hard to hide. San Andreas was too deep."

"So, this location checked all of the boxes for secrecy and availability. I'd think there'd be lots of potential spots in the country that didn't have to be buried below a major city."

"Except all of those locations were missing one important factor," she said. "The indigenous people who lived in this area had figured out how to use and power a version of the Omega device. They've been talking with the aliens for at least a thousand years, and this location was at the center of that contact."

Maxx paused for a moment, and then he realized what she was referencing. *Thunderbird.*

A STORM IS THREATENING

Doctor Smith cleaned his glasses for the third time in the last ten minutes. He was generally unflappable, but the scrutiny had increased considerably after the death of the young man from TechCom. If there had been any doubt before that the Chinese agents were willing to take risks, that had been settled. Killing a team leader on Hermes had raised the alarm at the key DARPA facilities working on this project. Doctor Smith had made certain that security was raised to its highest level. Personally, he wasn't leaving the facility.

He'd been notified that they knew the time and location of the next planned event. His engineers had been working around the clock to make adjustments based on the design information that they'd obtained from the fully decrypted Omega file.

It had been a tightly guarded secret that he had replicated the original Omega device before they had taken it up to Mount St. Helens for its one and only disastrous attempt at contact. They'd kept the replica here in the Seattle facility and had done everything they could to make it operational without having the source documentation for reference.

It had been nerve-racking work over the previous decade with too many false starts to recall. Fortunately, the technological revolution made it possible. In many ways, replicating this device had been as much a scientific achievement as developing the first atomic weapons. Unfortunately, it was progress he had not been able to share outside of this program. *Yet.*

He'd been in a state of agitation during this week as they had drawn closer to another attempt, and it was looking like the politicians and military leadership at the Pentagon had come to an agreement that they were going to make an attempt in New York despite the risks. Correction, they'd be willing to try if Doctor Smith would sign off that the Omega device was operational.

He had no illusions that if he didn't sign off he'd be replaced. And if he did sign off that it was functional, and there was a disaster, he would never work again. In the worst-case scenario, he'd have an untimely fatal accident or simply disappear into an unmarked grave.

He had made plans to house the device under the assumption that it would be ready. He was waiting in his office for the call from the testing team ten stories below him that the device was ready to be connected to the power and cycled through the initiation phase. There were cameras that he could watch on his office computer if he wished, but he didn't care to watch. He might watch the recordings later depending on what happened. The experience of watching the proceedings and the eventual eruption at Mount St. Helens was burned into his memory, and he didn't want his last thought to be that he was sitting at the epicenter of disaster.

The phone on his desk buzzed. It was the testing center. He listened to the senior engineer give him the confirmation he was looking for. The schematics had been triple checked and matched exactly to the replica device. They had tested all the tolerances as specified in the Omega file and found no variation from the expected results. He gave the go ahead to connect it to the power source and begin the final process.

With trepidation, he said one final word before ending the call. "Godspeed."

It still amazed Doctor Smith that the device was constructed from materials that were available on Earth – some extremely rare – but when treated as instructed they essentially became new elements with heretofore unheard of properties. That information by itself would have been enough to stun the scientific community for generations. Combine that with the potential capabilities of the completed device, and it would be unimaginable to the brightest scientific minds in the world.

He leaned back in his chair and waited for the next call from the testing center. Shortly, he'd receive a follow-up call or would die terribly in some catastrophic event. Heads or tails, he was somewhat relieved to be moving forward again. The last twenty years had felt like he was caught in a endless cycle of fits and starts to get back on the edge of history.

He'd previously arranged a secure location for the device in New York. Presuming that it passed the preparation tests, they would arrange for the transportation from DARPA on Monday evening, loaded on a cargo plane at the nearby Boeing Field and flown to Newark. Under the cover of darkness, it would then be transported to its final destination in Manhattan, where it would be kept in the basement of Building 7 at the World Trade Center. It was an unutilized space below the DARPA facility that would escape scrutiny. It had also been plumbed for the extreme power requirements demanded by the Omega device. The power would be cut over from the port shortly before the appointed time.

Another stroke of coincidence: The coordinates in the Alpha file coincided with a location where they already had manpower, security, and power. It did give him pause that somehow the civilization that prepared the files seemed to have insight into the future. Luck or not, it had allowed them to be prepared for Tuesday. It made him look like a genius, so he didn't bother expressing his discomfort about the coincidence with anyone else.

What excited him most beyond the possibility of contact with an advanced alien civilization was that he'd been able to construct the strategic plan surrounding the use of the device. There had been little resistance from the politicians or military about how to use the communication capabilities with the aliens. After considering every angle, they'd come to the conclusion that it would be targeted at the Chinese military.

They were prepared to request that their enemies suffer a series of earthquakes, tidal waves, and floods that would essentially disrupt the Chinese for decades. He felt some regret that so many innocent people would die, but in the end a preemptive series of events would stop the potential for a much more devastating war between the two countries. The most intriguing thing was that it could never be blamed on the US. What a brilliant stroke of warcraft, he thought. With one blow, they could annihilate their enemy and become the most dominate country on the planet without expending any American resources or lives. And the most satisfying result was that he would thoroughly destroy his archrival. He would become the true Master of War.

His desk phone began ringing, raising him from his reverie.

Xi contacted his committee to meet early that morning to discuss the latest developments relative to the device and their attempt to preempt the American government. They had all been informed earlier in the week that progress had been made with the decryption in the extraterrestrial files. They had long ago cracked the first and second file thanks to insider information from one of the contractors in the United States, and their secretive AI program that was at least on par with the American capabilities.

They had lost the device at Tangshan in 1976 before they realized they were dealing with technology far beyond their comprehension. They had not realized at the time that they were in a race with the US. Xi knew that his nemesis, El Herrero, was working on a similar project but had been led to believe—falsely, as he learned—that the Americans were far behind China in their willingness to test the device. When he learned that the eruption at Mount St. Helens was also a result of miscalculation, he'd understood the stakes. They couldn't let the Americans get ahead of them.

Rumors persisted that the American device had survived and was still in operational order. In fact, the rumors even indicated that Xi had somehow secured it and brought it back to China, which although false helped to create confusion and buy time.

He knew he had a workable device. What he didn't know was if the Americans had solved the issue too. Regardless, he had made arrangements for the device to be shipped to the US so that it went undetected. It was hidden in a shipment of automobiles that were currently sitting in the Port of New York. He was being transferred to the coordinates in Manhattan over the weekend. It was similar in size to an elevator, and it had been easy to have it brought on site as a replacement. There was enough power in the building to handle the demands if it was done on a warm day, as the chillers were coming online at the start of a workday.

The most nerve-racking part of the project had been the

chance they would run into the DARPA team making similar arrangements. They hadn't seen any evidence of them near the coordinates, which led Xi to believe that the Americans did not have a device ready. He hoped he would win this race with finality, having been lucky that he'd survived the debacle at Tangshan.

The only thing missing was the final decrypted file from TechCom. He knew they had finished the work because his mole had informed Haoyu. However, that fool Haoyu had been led astray by the mole and had killed one of their employees to hide their trail. That murder had led to an increase in security that had frightened the mole, who claimed it was impossible to get a copy of the files without being exposed. Haoyu had assured him that he had located another employee he could pressure and had been doing so. He would proceed even if he didn't have the files to verify the engineering and directives, but he would prefer to have them as one final checkpoint before going live.

The other piece of information that Haoyu had relayed to him, and the reason for his unscheduled meeting with his advisory committee, was that he had found evidence that there was an operational communication device in Seattle. Whether it was the initial device that had not been destroyed at Mount St. Helens, or DARPA had also been able to construct a replacement, Haoyu had no knowledge.

Why it was of concern to himself and to the leaders in his country was America's intention in using the device. China's initial strategy had been to contact the aliens and position themselves as the premier representative for the planet. At the very least, they would be seen by the aliens and the rest of the world as worthy of global leadership and not a voice in the crowd.

If the United States also had a working device, there was concern they would at best try and position themselves as the global leader on par with China. However, knowing the Americans as he did, it was likely they'd be planning a strategic maneuver that would negatively affect China at the same time. It would be naive for them to ignore the possibility that the US would consider a first-strike strategy. Now that Xi also had a working device, he needed his committee to consider striking first too.

Miss Grey remained behind at that Tacoma team's front office after Maxx and his friends left. They occupied several floors in the building above the elevator connected to the Seattle Underground.

She knew there were several other connection points near Pioneer Square and the port. When they built the underground facility, they had utilized the cover of various construction sites to minimize any suspicion about the massive amounts of subterranean construction. They had even squashed any local proposals of building an underground highway tunnel to replace the dilapidated nearby highway to avoid anyone noticing their efforts.

She took her time writing up a report for her boss that left out any of the recent activities that involved Omega. If he wasn't so focused on the politics back in Washington D.C., he probably would have started wondering how she was spending her time, since she she'd made no progress in pinning down Haoyu's location.

Unfortunately, Seattle PD wasn't having any more success in finding him after he became the prime person of interest in Scott's murder. The local politics were heated on that case due to the location, time of day, and that it involved TechCom. She heard that they had created a task force with more than twenty people and were getting nowhere. Knowing Haoyu as well as she did, that wasn't a surprise. He'd slipped through her grasp more times than she could count.

Things were moving very rapidly now, and it was looking like it would come to a head in the next few days. There were really three trains heading for the same switch in the tracks, and she didn't know if they'd all collide, slow down, or stop.

According to Mr. Green and the people he worked for, the secretive Tacoma team had a device ready to be placed in position and operational by Monday night. The device was being airlifted out on a C5 Galaxy from McChord Air Force Base. They had tested the device and were confident it was functional based on the specifications of the original communication device that had been recovered from Mount St. Helens. It had been recently adjusted based on the freshly decrypted file from TechCom. How they had obtained that information without DARPA realizing it was a mystery to her. Clearly, they had inside resources too. It seemed that TechCom had more security gaps than a sieve.

It was her understanding that the Omega device was only going to be utilized to intervene if DARPA began to implement their primary plan or if the Chinese also had an operational device in the area. Their objectives were to make sure neither country's military used the opportunity to call for strikes on the other country. Their secondary objective was to make sure that any communication was in the best interests of the peaceful US mission.

DARPA had been authorized to call for strikes in China to destabilize the country and place themselves in the position of undisputed world military power. Failing that, they intended to at least position themselves as the main intermediary with the extraterrestrials. She had learned that Doctor Smith was the architect of the strategy despite his failure at Mount St. Helens. It was not clear if they had an operational device, but she was told they were in the process of testing it and would know shortly. If it wasn't operational, the Tacoma team would reveal themselves when it was time to go live.

The wild card was the readiness of the Chinese device. They had no reliable intel that the Chinese were prepared to deploy an operational device. Haoyu's recent actions indicated a sense of desperation, but she wasn't confident that was the case. To hedge her bets, they had placed a significant number of resources to watch the entry points into the New York area. Thus far, they'd had no signs of penetration, but they could be waiting until the last minute, as the Tacoma team and DARPA were.

If the Chinese didn't show, it would be much less messy. They believed they had access to enough senior politicians in the White House to override DARPA if it came to that. It'd probably confuse the communication with the aliens, but that was a risk they had to take to avert the conflict with China and potentially trigger a world war. It really was not in the best interests of the US militarily, but they believed it was the best choice from an ethical and political perspective, not to mention saving many millions of lives.

That left them with the most concerning topic of all. What if one or all of the devices didn't operate properly and created a disaster in the heart of New York City? There had been considerable debate officially and unofficially, and the conclusion had been not to provide an advance evacuation. They were prepared to rapidly respond in an emergency situation post-event, if necessary, but there would be too many questions if they tried to get people to prepare beforehand. They didn't even know what kind of event they would prepare for, earthquake, tsunami, or another disaster they could only imagine.

If the aliens wanted to trigger some sort of event, there was nothing anyone could do to stop them. There had been advance signals in Tangshan and Mount St. Helens that a failure was evident. They were of the opinion that the lack of preemptive signals was actually a positive indicating one or all of the devices would be functional. She hoped that optimism paid off, or it could be one of the worst disasters the world had seen in a very long time.

Biblical, she thought.

NO PLACE FOR BEGINNERS

Gabby came home from TechCom for a brief nap and a chance to recover some energy after twenty-four hours of nonstop work and sleeping at the office. The team was under tremendous pressure to finalize the decryption of the Delta file, proofread for potential errors, and then cross reference with the Alpha and Omega files. The programs that they'd written on the fly had helped take the brunt of the work off the team's task list, but they were running in sixty-minute cycles that were exhausting.

The security team had escorted her home early Sunday morning with explicit instructions to wake her up at 6 a.m. and bring her back to the office for the final review with the team and her boss, Dale. That only gave her enough time for a hot shower and two hours to fall asleep in her clothes on top of the bed. Maxx had made sure she got everything she needed, despite being exhausted himself.

He risked getting hit by Gabby when he woke her up at 5:45 so that they had a few minutes to plan before the security team started knocking on the door. Handing her a hot cup of coffee helped take some of the edge off, but not enough that she didn't give him a grunt or two.

They decided she'd text him when she was finished with her debrief and any follow-up work that came out of the meeting. She guessed that would be after lunch if everything went well. Then most of the building would clear out for the remainder of the weekend, leaving only her and a skeleton crew behind.

She'd tell people there were some administrative items she needed to wrap up, and no one would give it a second thought. She'd text Maxx that she was ready to go, while he'd be waiting in his car in the visitor lot. She'd tell security that Maxx was bringing in a file that she'd checked out to review last night and would ask them to escort him up to her office.

Security would search and scan them both on the way in and out. With rare exceptions made for executives on call, no electronic devices allowed in the building with the exception of cell phones they'd been assigned by TechCom. Any other devices would be held at security until they left.

There was a trick of the trade that Maxx had used many times in his line of work when he needed to bring in files or copy them and get them out unnoticed. He had built a small, watertight compartment into the heel of his boots that would hold a thumb drive; it was designed to look like reinforcement in the shoe and was effectively undetectable. The boots had steel toes in them, so they'd set off the metal detectors and would be examined separately while he walked through the screening. He'd reverse the process on the way out of the building.

While there was some risk to this method, the chance was very low based on the number of times he'd successfully used it. Even though this was his first attempt at TechCom, he was feeling confident that it'd succeed. The uncertain part of the plan was Gabby's ability to download a copy of the file onto the drive. There were no ports on the computers they used in the building, and so she would have to transfer to the drive wirelessly when it was recognized as part of the local network. This was slow, and she couldn't start until Maxx brought it to her. Meanwhile, the security escort would be hanging about while he waited to chaperone Maxx out of the building.

Gabby was nervous about the plan but had little time to think about it too deeply. When they had initially agreed to get a copy of the Delta file for Miss Grey, she'd assumed that if there was trouble, Miss Grey and the government would back her up. However, as she'd thought about it more when she was less sleep deprived, she realized that had never been explicitly agreed to. If somehow she or Maxx was caught with a copy of the ultra-secret file, there would be hell to pay. She'd expressed this concern to Maxx, and he'd reminded her that Miss Grey was also going out on thin ice and had been true to her word.

Despite being a Fed, he thought for the hundredth time.

Promptly at 6 a.m., the security team knocked on the apartment door, two young guys who Maxx could tell were carrying weapons. He was glad to see TechCom was taking the threat to the people on the project seriously. It was too bad they hadn't taken it more seriously before Scott died. He followed Gabby to the car, kissed her goodbye, and walked back up the apartment to wait.

The morning flew by as he drank pots of coffee and tried to catch up on the work that he'd been putting off since Tuesday. It was a relief to put the events of the last four days out of his mind and focus on mundane tasks like writing emails, paying bills, and going through reports that his assistant had prepared while he was out.

He was finishing cleaning out his work inbox when he opened a cryptic message from his attorney, Daryl, who had sent a message on Friday saying he'd received a call from the attorney representing the Chinese company, AI Ventures. The attorney wanted to talk to Maxx's partner, Natalie, who had arranged the contract. Daryl didn't tell him she was no longer a partner but wanted to chat with Maxx when he had a moment on Monday. Nothing involving Natalie could be good, but he would deal with that tomorrow.

Maxx put on jeans, a polo shirt, a light windbreaker to cover his pistol, and his favorite pair of boots. He was feeling sore from the fights and running around that he'd been doing. Normally he'd get to the gym a couple times a week, but lifting weights was much different than fighting and the adrenaline rush that came with it. He also slipped a thumb drive into the heel and made sure it was secured before putting his shoes on. For the cherry on top of his day of espionage, he threw on his old Mariners baseball cap.

While he was waiting for noon or to hear from Gabby to come to her work and bring her "the file she had accidentally left behind," he took a moment to flip through the news on television. There was an interesting story about tension between the US and China over commercial spying violations. He wondered if the story was a plant by the government to try and create an advance narrative should things escalate over the Omega situation. The government was pretty adept at using unnamed sources in the media to plant positions they could point to after the fact. And if nothing came out of the story, it would be forgotten by the next news cycle.

When his watch said it was noon, he grabbed some salmon jerky and a Dr. Pepper from the refrigerator and walked down to his truck. He didn't know how long he'd have to wait in his car in the visitor parking at TechCom, so it was better to have something to eat and drink with him in case. He thought of this part of their plan as a stakeout and wanted to be prepared to move when Gabby told him it was go time.

Sitting in the car could be boring, so he pulled out a book that he'd been reading. He'd tucked the book he'd borrowed from Andres's office under the seat. He started thumbing through it, reading about cultural traditions around the world that related to natural disasters.

He wasn't being sarcastic when he'd told Andres that it was a topic he'd been thinking about recently. It was uncanny how many disconnected cultures around the world had similar beliefs about supernatural beings causing natural disasters. Certainly, it would be fodder for conspiracy theorists if they ever uncovered what he'd learned during the last week. That there might be a connection to an extraterrestrial civilization would be truth as strange as anything people might dream of.

His phone vibrated with a text message. "Can you bring me that file I left at home? Security will bring you to my office. XOXO"

Gabby rarely signed off her written messages with hugs and kisses, so that had been their prearranged signal that she was ready to copy the file. Maxx waited for ten minutes, took a big swig of his soda, and headed for the building entrance. He would be glad when they had the file out the door and had handed it off to Miss Grey. Looking calm at this stage would be critical, or it would raise the suspicions of the security staff that was already on high alert.

He'd been through the security checkpoint at TechCom several times before so knew what to expect. They'd check his ID against the approved list that Gabby would have put his name on. Then they'd check in his weapon, phone, keys, and anything else that might set off the detectors. He knew from experience that the steel support in his boots would set off the detector, so they always took them off and ran them through the scanner separately. The TechCom office had better security than the airport. They were cautious to make certain that only approved electronic devices came in or out of the building and that any metal objects were thoroughly screened.

He passed through security with only the usual kerfuffle

over his boots. He was worried for a few minutes when a new guard took unusual interest in them. However, a supervisor told him that Maxx was the boyfriend of an employee and was smarter than to try to hide a phone in his shoe like Maxwell Smart. The guard was too young to get the reference to the spy comedy, but it flustered him enough to give up the shoe screening prematurely and wave him through.

After security but before he was escorted to Gabby's office, Maxx told his escort that he needed to use the restroom. The guard made sure there was no one else in the washroom then waved him in. It only took him a few seconds to take the thumb drive from his shoe and slip it into his pocket. The device only needed to be within a dozen feet to effectively transfer the data, but it had to be out of the secure storage location in his boot to work.

He knew Gabby would have the file transfer ready to initiate as soon as he walked in her office. The transfer would likely take several minutes, and they had decided that she'd have to distract the guard long enough for it to be complete, then they'd leave together. The problematic part of their plan was going to be getting the flash drive back in his shoe so he could get it out of the building. He couldn't ask to go to the bathroom again without raising suspicion.

While he sat her in her office, she made small talk with the guard as she started packing her things up to leave. She told him her laptop was backing itself up and would be done momentarily. The status bar on her computer was really indicating the file transfer. When it was nearly done, the guard's radio squawked, telling him to call in immediately. Maxx started to sweat, certain they'd been caught.

The guard walked to a cubicle on the other side of the room and talked low enough so they couldn't overhear his conversation. Maxx tried to ignore the looks the guy kept shooting in their direction, but he could tell he was saying something about them. After a brief conversation, he told them to stay put until he returned in a moment. *Is he going to get backup?*

When the guard stepped out of the room, the file transfer was completed without any concern. Gabby, cool as a cucumber, told Maxx to put the device back. She was done and pulled up the audit logs to remove the traces of her activity. He raised his eyebrows at her as if to ask what was happening, but she put her finger to her lips. So Maxx made small talk about the latest episode of *Frasier* while they waited for the guard to return.

When the guard came back, he escorted them downstairs to go through the search process to leave the building. On the way out to the car, Maxx asked her what happened for the guard to leave them alone at the right time. Gabby smiled and told him that she'd set a door alarm to trip when she hit ninety percent on the download, knowing they'd have to send someone to physically inspect it, and since it was on her floor, it would likely be the guard who had escorted Maxx up.

"A piece of cake," she said.

Whatever suspicions Maxx had entertained about Gabby being the Chinese mole had vanished. He'd never seriously considered it likely, but Miss Grey had placed the seed of doubt, and he'd had difficulty completely letting go of the idea. Gabby had put herself in a position of tremendous risk to grab a full copy of the file when, if she was the mole, she could have relayed the critical information to the Chinese. Even Miss Grey would have to admit she'd been wrong when Gabby handed her the thumb drive.

Maxx pulled the truck into a business parking lot a few blocks from the TechCom building. He'd made sure they weren't being followed by taking a circuitous route that led to a dead end, having checked earlier for eavesdropping devices while he was waiting for Gabby to text him. He was too anxious to know what was in the Delta file she had downloaded and didn't want to wait until they were home to look through the material.

While Gabby booted up her spare laptop he'd put in the car, he turned on the radio. Fittingly, one of his favorite songs from Sade was playing. *Smooth operator indeed.*

They both laughed and sang along while she opened the file. It wasn't very long, about a dozen pages once she imported the file into a word processing document. Maxx adjusted the font size, since his eyesight wasn't what it used to be. They read the entire document once, and Maxx asked if he could reread it to make sure he picked up on the nuances that may have been written by the aliens or a translation issue from the AI.

Gabby started talking when Maxx indicated he was done reading. "The makers of the Omega device intended it to be a communication tool to signal the recipients that they needed protection from invaders. It seems to imply that while it was primarily intended to be a tool to protect the holders of the device from extraterrestrial invaders, it could also be used in situations where their civilization is being attacked from an earthbound enemy."

"The protection was to disrupt an enemy using natural resources on the planet, giving the aliens time to travel here physically for direct warfare if necessary. It was like a punch in the nose to warn potential attackers off. If that wasn't enough discouragement, they'd come running, but it could take quite a long time for them to arrive."

Gabby nodded and sighed as she reached over to turn down the volume on the radio. "It's possible for them to trigger these events because they don't need to be physically transported. Using the device, it is signaling natural elements in the Earth's crust, atmosphere, or bodies of water. But everything seems to be on delayed timeframes because the device only aligns infrequently for communication. They must be far away from Earth."

"Or a long time separates us," said Maxx as he drummed his fingers on the steering wheel.

Maxx's comment caused her to sit up straight in the seat. "Right, I hadn't considered that. It could be space or time dividing us from them. We don't know."

"I think the other reason they are using cycles in time is to prevent the holders of the device from abusing it. It's also why it has such specific protocols to use. They wanted to make sure it was regarded as an option of last resort and was treated with importance, so it was held in high regard by our civilization. That would also explain the penalty for misusing it. If someone took the device and tried to contact them improperly, they'd essentially be punched on the nose."

"It's a brilliant safeguard, since they wouldn't be talking to the same humans over the decades or centuries and had no way to verify if they were the proper owners."

Maxx paused for a moment and glanced out the side window. "One other idea struck me. According to the presentation that Li Jing gave to you the other night, the instructions said to only use the protocols that were provided for this specific Omega device. I wonder if that means each civilization received exclusive instructions that were unique to their situation and paired to a specific device."

"It's possible. If we had access to the Delta file provided to the Chinese, we would see if it differed from our version. What's clear is that our instructions explicitly warned that we are not to trigger an event to preemptively attack an enemy. The device is only to be used as a defensive weapon in the case of retribution. An eye for an eye."

"Is it because they understand human nature or our specific motivations?"

Gabby twisted her hair around her finger. A habit that Maxx knew meant that the conversation was making her very nervous.

"I think Miss Grey will figure that out easily when she compares it to DARPA's version of the file. If that language is removed or edited, we'll have our answer," she said.

"What do you think the Chinese version of the file says? No wonder the Chinese were so intent in finding out what our decrypted file translated to. They wanted to know what our instructions were."

Maxx studied the rearview and side mirrors and started the truck. "One thing is certain. We need to get Miss Grey this file right away."

The mole quickly found another empty conference room and attempted to manufacture a rational explanation for being in on a Sunday afternoon. No one was even supposed to be in the office this afternoon, and everyone else had left earlier when they had concluded the successful review of the files and transferred them to DARPA.

But not everyone had left, it turned out. Exhausted after being up for several days prior to today's deadline, the mole fell asleep on the sofa in the break room. The phone had been vibrating for an hour when it was finally answered.

There were a dozen missed calls and several voice messages. What kind of emergency would have triggered this on a Sunday afternoon when the file had already been successfully submitted?

Rather than try and immediately return a call from the break room, it was better to find a secure location and check the email first. There was the problem, right on the top of the email inbox in all caps and with priority status: "UNAUTHORIZED ACCESS IDENTIFIED."

It turned out the security algorithm had identified unusual activity with the Delta file about an hour ago. It had been transferred to an unidentified network device. By the time the algorithm had identified the unusual activity and security had responded to lock it down, the transfer was complete and someone had cleared the audit logs. They'd be able to do a restore and compare procedure if the backup files hadn't also been corrupted. Whoever had done it had known enough about the security protocol to avoid the compliance traps and had likely timed the transfer to coincide with the time gap that occurred in the backup process.

If someone from DARPA had taken the file, it would indicate that there was no trust in the official file and a need to verify its validity independently. If the Chinese had taken it, that would mean there was a high-level second mole, who was double checking to try to avoid paying for the file. In either scenario, the mole was at risk of being exposed as a source of the inside information.

The most likely culprit was someone from another branch of the government either trying to set a trap or use it as leverage against DARPA. This was the most worrisome of the scenarios, as it would point to the Hermes team, and they'd all be under suspicion. The best course of action would be to let the security review run its course, while giving the Chinese a heads up. There was no sense risking another call to Smith, who could figure out he'd been played after the fact.

That was the primary reason for coming to a secure room away from the team office. The mole needed to give the Chinese as much advance notice as possible when it was this close to the deadline. Sleeping through the alerts might end up being an unforgivable mistake. Going through the connection protocol, Haoyu called back thirty minutes later. That was concerning, because in the past he had always called back immediately. *I am being cut out.*

Haoyu didn't seem to be particularly surprised by the news that someone had taken a copy of the file. He'd probably been notified or already had a copy from TechCom. When Haoyu asked for speculation on who had done it, it was an easy choice about who to point a finger at.

If Scott had been alive, that would have been a natural first choice. But since Scott was already dead, the next name for Haoyu to dispose of was easy.

"Gabby Fisher." With that, the call from Haoyu ended.

I DON'T LIKE MONDAYS

Shortly after reading the Delta file, Maxx attempted to text and call Miss Grey on her cell and her office number.

"Hey, Grey, can you call me back? I have that information you asked for, and I think it's something you'll want to hear. It'll be best to chat on a secure line. Soon."

While he waited for her to call him back, he secured the original file in a place that was easily accessible but wouldn't be obvious if he got detained. Eventually someone would determine he or Gabby had taken the file and want it back. The best place for now was keeping it in the hidden compartment in his boot with a fake flash drive in his pocket as a decoy.

They'd thought about renting a hotel room under a fake name and paying cash to create a false trail, but that idea was quickly forgotten after they realized they only had forty dollars in cash with them. There wasn't much interest in spending the night in a motel that would take forty dollars for a night's stay, even if they could find one.

Maxx and Gabby eventually decided to hunker down at his place and wait to hear from Miss Grey. It wouldn't be unusual for her to show up unannounced. Maxx had left the tracking device on his truck so he could use it as a red herring when he needed to, but he still didn't know who the owner was, Miss Grey, DARPA, Haoyu, or some other alphabet-soup federal agency. During this past week, he was getting to be a bit too popular for his liking. He preferred to stay out of the limelight, and now he'd ended up on the target list for people he didn't even know.

When they got inside his condominium, they secured the solid core door and locked up the windows with the shades drawn even though it was a bit stuffy inside. He replaced the patio doors with ballistic glass during the same home improvement project when he'd changed out the front door and locks on his home and Gabby's. It wasn't impenetrable, but anything short of a SWAT team couldn't breach it before backup arrived. That assumed they made it past the small armory he kept in his bedroom closet. There were none of the usual home security weapons. It looked like he'd raided an ATF storage facility – except it was all legal of course. *Wink, wink.*

It wasn't until later that evening that Maxx finally heard back from Miss Grey. They were sitting down to a dinner of salmon and a bottle of Yakima Valley chardonnay that Gabby had lightly chilled while they sipped on Manhattans. Maxx preferred to buy his fish from Pike Place when it came in fresh off the boats in the morning, and they baked it rather than grilling it on the outdoor barbecue to maintain a low profile. No sense announcing they were here if anyone was watching.

Miss Grey skipped the niceties when Maxx answered the phone. "This is a secured line, but keep things to a minimum in case anyone is listening in. Where are you now?"

"We're at my place, all snug and cozy. Where are you?"

"I needed to make a quick trip to check out the office on the East Coast." *Manhattan.*

"We picked up the information you asked for, and it's something you'll want to see sooner rather than later, so don't dally."

"You read through it?" Miss Grey asked.

"Yes, I'm inquisitive like that. You'll want to be sure to compare it to the doctor's report that you'll get."

Miss Grey paused. "You think there might be a difference in interpretations? For what purpose?"

"A hunch based on meeting Mr. Personality. If they perceive the risk to be high enough, some physicians will attempt to perform preemptive surgery. Even if it's strongly advised against."

"I wish there was some way to get to see the original file myself so I can discuss it with some others in my office. I'd need the original in hand to be able to convince anyone. Is the document in a secure location?"

Gabby laughed when she heard the question. Maxx made a face at her as he answered, "It's near and dear, and I'm keeping it very, very close to me. It's the best I can do at the moment."

"Keep it with you. I'll send some agents to keep a watch on your place for the night. I'll be on a red-eye flight tonight and then back in Seattle in the morning. Let's plan to meet near the city center around eight in the morning as soon as I arrive. Find a coffee shop and text me the address. I'll take a taxi from the airport."

Gabby scribbled a quick note to Maxx, who glanced at her and nodded.

"One last thing," Maxx said as he read the note. "We were careful about how we got the information, but eventually security is going to realize it was taken and connect it to us. The last thing we need is for TechCom, DARPA, or one of your intelligence colleagues at another federal agency to come calling with a sledgehammer. Keep us informed if that's going to happen, so we can get lost before they arrive."

"I'll do what I can, but there aren't any guarantees they'll tell me. I'm on their watch list too," she said, ending the call.

He and Gabby had a nice, quiet dinner and then hung out

on the sofa watching some television shows they had recorded in the last several weeks while they had been busy. Maxx tried to initiate some sexual activity after she'd had a couple of glasses of wine, but Gabby cringed at him. "Really?" She shut the door on that idea quickly.

Instead, she had become increasingly quiet as the television shows droned on. Maxx could tell she was thinking deeply about some topic. He'd learned over the last three months to wait and let her eventually reveal what was bothering her.

At the next commercial break, she paused the recording. "What do they want to talk about?"

"Who?" Maxx asked.

"The aliens. I mean, they are putting us through all these hoops to begin communication, but about what? It seems like they are being awfully evasive about the topic of communication."

"You don't trust them?"

"Why would we? They have set up all of the conditions to communicate, telling us how, when, and if we get it wrong that they are going to punish us with some catastrophic spanking. Why haven't they told us why?"

"I doubt they think like we do, but it's hard to believe they see us as equals. Technologically, we aren't even close. The nicest interpretation I can think of is that they see us as some evolving life form and want to encourage and support our development. Or maybe they see us as their pets and keep us around for companionship and laughs."

"If that's the nicest interpretation of their motive, what's the worst interpretation? Clearly, they don't see us as enemies, or they would simply destroy us with a bunch of earthquakes and volcanoes until we become extinct. Maybe we are expendable resources."

"I think that's a great question, one that people need to consider in any upcoming communication. But I don't think we can avoid communication indefinitely. At some point, they are going to act whether we contact them or not."

"That's what has me worried. I think we are so focused on how to make this happen that we aren't thinking about what their motives are. Maybe we can't do anything to stop them, but we shouldn't go into this blind."

Maxx hadn't really considered that perspective until Gabby raised it. He'd been running all week primarily focused on Haoyu and keeping Gabby safe, not mulling over the reasons at the root of all of this. Keeping Gabby safe would be impossible if they decided to cause an eruption at Mount Rainier.

He checked all the doors and windows, set the alarm, and climbed into bed for the night. When he was about to drift off to sleep, Gabby asked, "Do you think it's true that we'll be communicating with extraterrestrials next week?"

"I don't know if I believe it, but a lot of people seem certain something is going to happen. They're even willing to kill for it."

"Are we going to sit here and wait for it to happen? It's supposed to occur Tuesday morning. Maybe we can get up early and watch the sunrise. No matter what takes place, things will never be the same after that."

Maxx rolled over and took her head in his hands. "We'll still have each other, right?"

"Yes, yes, of course, silly. I love you, Maxx. You mean the world to me."

"I love you too, Gabby. You're the best thing that has happened to me in a long, long time."

"Maybe we should stay here then. Stay in bed, hold each other, and forget about the rest of the world."

"Sure, we can do that. We can do whatever you want."

Gabby snuggled into the crook of Maxx's arm and began to breath deeply as she fell asleep. *Sweet dreams*, he thought.

Gabby rolled over in the morning and told him it was time to wake up. The alarm was going off on the clock radio. Ironically, it was a song about Monday mornings, and all he could think to say was, "I really don't like Mondays." After they had met with Miss Grey, he planned to head into the office to get everything caught up. His client projects were way behind schedule, since he'd done little other than respond to email sporadically. Whatever happened tomorrow in New York, he was looking forward to things getting back to normal.

Gabby got in the shower after he jumped out. He made a big pot of coffee while toweling off. Even though they were going to meet Miss Grey in an hour, he needed to get rid of the pounding headache that had been developing since they'd visited the Tacoma facility. He didn't think that had any effect on him, but he'd seen some pretty strange things this week, and who really knew what effect that extraterrestrial device could have? He'd have to ask Miss Grey about any known side effects before he started growing a third arm. It wasn't like the federal government was fond of openly disclosing the medical implications of their secret plans.

While he was waiting for the coffee, he decided he'd pull together a small backpack for each of them. He didn't think they'd need them, but he had been in the Boy Scouts as a kid, and "be prepared" was a motto that he took to heart. It had been reinforced many times since then in the Rangers. Besides, he was always hungry and would never turn down a quick snack.

Maxx gathered some protein bars, jerky, bottled water, Skittles, and a couple of emergency burner phones from his closet safe. He also grabbed a wild assortment of extra clothes for disguises and in case they get caught outside in the rain. He also put his 1911 and Gabby's 9mm in their bags with some extra ammunition. He learned a long time ago that you can never have too much ammunition unless you're swimming. They both went to the local indoor gun range to practice every month, so they were comfortable carrying. Gabby had never had to use her pistol outside the range, but Maxx had used the concealed weapon several times since he'd left the military. It wasn't a requirement to carry a weapon in his line of work, but it wasn't a hinderance either. *Be prepared.*

After he packed the small bags, he poured each of them a big mug of coffee for the road. He wanted to take some time to drive to the coffee shop by taking a circuitous route to see if they were being followed. He didn't want to show up to meet Miss Grey with an entourage. He was also going to remove the tracker on the car before they left. That would smoke out whoever had planted the device on his truck, because they'd have to scramble to chase him down.

After he pulled out of the parking garage, it didn't take long to spot someone following them. They weren't very covert about it, so his guess was that it was either someone working for Miss Grey or another government agency. It didn't matter to Maxx who they were. He knew right where to dump them and headed over to the highway, which was separated with barriers his elevated truck could clear but that they'd get hung up on if they tried to follow him over the median. Then they'd have to go to the next exit to get off and circle back in the opposite direction. In the commuter traffic at this time of day, they'd be stuck far behind him.

Maxx drove slowly enough that it allowed the black sedan to stay several car lengths behind them. He didn't want to lose them at a stoplight and then have to wait for them to catch him again. When he saw an opening in the traffic going in the other direction across the center divider, he warned Gabby, who ended up screeching anyway when he wrenched the wheel at an angle that would propel him over the curb. He then cut back to merge into the traffic. He got plenty of honks and middle finger salutes, but he never came close to hitting anyone as he accelerated into the flow of traffic. He did get an earful from Gabby, however.

He glanced at the car that had been behind him. The driver slowed down but decided not to risk the same maneuver, anticipating that they'd never get stuck on the high median. As he was going slow enough to decide what to do, another black sedan sped past them and tried to jump the curb anyway. There had a been a second car following them, and they weren't as relaxed about Maxx's maneuver to lose them.

When the second sedan tried to angle across the median, it got stuck, as Maxx had expected. The middle of the car ground to a halt on the high point, and then the rear wheels couldn't get enough traction to go forward or back. The driver spun the wheels, but the car wasn't going anywhere without a tow truck to get them out. The police were not going to be entertained by their move, which was going to cause a nasty traffic jam.

Maxx was pleased with himself for taking the risk. He knew now that they were being tailed by two cars. The first car was likely from Miss Grey's team, and the driver knew he'd catch up with them in a while when she arrived. The second car was the curious one. It had to be DARPA or an agency other than the Department of Homeland Security. It didn't look like a car Haoyu would be using, so they hadn't found him yet or they were further back in the parade.

Since he had lost the cars following him, he took a more direct route to the coffee shop, even though they were still early. He'd checked on the incoming flights and guessed which flight from La Guardia was Miss Grey's. It was scheduled to arrive on time, so he expected a text from her any moment letting him know she was on her way.

The parking lot had small spaces, so he found a full-size parking spot at the curb across the street. He put enough change in the meter for an hour, and they went inside. Gabby ordered a few coffees and something to eat, while Maxx sat at a table near the front of the shop. This vantage point allowed him to keep an eye both on the front door and his truck.

Gabby had returned to the table with some pastries and coffee when Maxx noticed a couple of men walking on the sidewalk across from them. They looked like they were casually dressed, but wearing wind breakers in this temperature caught his eye.

Initially, he didn't pay close attention, then he noticed one of them looking slowly at the license plate for a few seconds too long, like he was trying to memorize it. They kept on walking down the street, stopped in an alcove, and pulled out a cell phone. The entire time the guy was on the phone, he kept looking at Maxx's car.

When the second guy pointed at Maxx's car and the coffee shop they were sitting in, he felt his stomach clench. Somehow, they had tracked them here. He knew it wasn't the tracking device he'd removed from the car, so they must have been following them further back on the freeway and been able to get turned around without completely losing them.

He texted Miss Grey. "On the move, we've been followed. Going to ditch them and will reconnect."

Without waiting for a response, he put the phone back in his pocket. He leaned over and nodded toward the window so Gabby could see what he was looking at. "Grab your bag. It's time to go," he said. "They found us, and I don't want to wait around for their backup to arrive."

Gabby pointed in the opposite direction from the front door. "While I was waiting for our order, I noticed the staff was bringing in supplies through a door in the back. Why don't we head out that way?"

They quickly moved to the back door, getting some nasty looks from the staff. "Hey, that's not an exit," one called. They ignored them all and pushed out into the alley behind the coffee shop. The alley was empty, and Gabby started to move in the opposite direction from the guys on the street until Maxx stopped her.

"We need the truck. If we leave it here, we won't have an easy way to get around."

"Maxx, if we go back out there, they will see us coming. We don't know if they're carrying or not, and it would be ugly."

"You're right. Let's go down a block, cut across the street, and come out behind them. I want to ask them a few questions and make sure they don't follow us again."

They cut through the back alley until they were past the corner where the two guys were waiting in the alcove, partially hidden. Gabby took a quick peek around the corner, and Maxx took his pistol out of the backpack in case they did spot them. When Gabby gave him the thumbs up, Maxx took a couple of long strides around the corner and hit the nearest man in the head with the butt of pistol before he had even fully turned around.

"English?" he asked the second man, who was trying to keep his friend from falling in a heap at his feet.

"Yeah, you jackass, I speak English. Why'd you hit my friend?" he snarled.

"It was a friendly tap compared to how I normally greet people following me."

"We were having a smoke break. We aren't following anyone, let alone someone as mean as you."

The words were barely out of his mouth before Maxx punched his ear. The guy doubled over in pain. Maxx stepped in behind him to pin his arms and put him in a headlock.

"You're getting on my nerves already. Following me and then lying to me is not going to work out well for you."

"Look, Mr. Tough Guy, any minute my boss is going to show up, and he wants to talk to you really badly. He said you stole something he needs. I'm supposed to do whatever I need to do to keep you here until he arrives."

"Is your boss named Haoyu by any chance?" Maxx could see from the way he looked away that he'd guessed correctly.

"No," he squeaked before Maxx choked him out.

"Wrong answer."

Maxx pulled both the men back into the alcove and sat them upright to make it less obvious that they were unconscious, which would delay Haoyu when he showed up. He checked their pockets. They only had wallets with IDs, knives, and a little cash. No car keys or guns, which was a surprise. It was a mystery how they thought they were going to be able to keep him here without guns. He kept the wallets and cash as a finder's fee.

Before Maxx and Gabby could head for his truck, he saw several black sedans come around the corner. The cars slowed down when the drivers spotted his car. One car pulled into the open spot in front of his truck, and the other car pulled up alongside, blocking him in completely. There was no way to get his car now. They'd need to come back later for it.

They waited a few minutes in the shadows until people started to pile out of the cars. When Haoyu stepped out onto the street and started walking for the coffee shop, Maxx knew it was time to go in the opposite direction fast.

They took up a brisk pace, although they didn't want to run and stand out. Getting off the main streets was a priority. People in a hurry drew attention, and they wanted to blend into the background.

They stopped behind a dumpster in an alley a couple of blocks north of the coffee shop. In case Haoyu learned what they were wearing from his men, they changed into some of the extra clothing Maxx had thrown into their packs. It was a such of an odd mixture of garments that they could have passed for homeless people wandering through the area. Gabby tucked her hair under a baseball cap, and they looked like a pair of men going nowhere in particular.

The clothing gave Gabby an idea where to go. Between the Feds watching for them and Haoyu's team on the prowl, they couldn't risk going back home, to their offices, or even to their friends' homes. But there was a tent camp for the homeless a few miles away by Volunteer Park that she had seen on the news a few days ago. There were several hundred people living there now and more arriving daily. It was a political football, and no one was going to do anything about it soon. Even the police were keeping their distance.

While they were walking, Maxx made sure their phones were turned off. He knew some agencies had the ability to track cell phones by triangulating signals off the nearby cell towers and wanted to stay unknown until they had handed off the thumb drive to Miss Grey. He powered on one of the burner phones and texted Miss Grey to let her know they were still on the move and that several people, including Haoyu, were chasing them. He told her in the text that he'd check this phone number in a couple hours after they found a safe place to go to ground.

They were able to get to the homeless camp without incident. They had seen black sedans going by several times, but they were at a distance, and they took precautions to alter their route. What would normally take thirty minutes to walk took them over an hour weaving through Capitol Hill. Once they had crossed over the freeway, it was easy to find side streets and alleyways that would be too difficult to search.

The camp was busy, and the people there didn't pay Maxx and Gabby much attention. They found an empty picnic bench and sat down, making a point of staying in locations that were surrounded by small groups of people. Maxx stayed seated as much as possible to avoid his height drawing attention.

Maxx turned on his burner phone every hour to check for

texts or voicemails. After a few hours without contact, he finally got a text that they should stay wherever they were until it was dark. Then she'd have time to plan to get them to a secure location. Miss Grey told him to check back on this phone after seven this evening for instructions.

"Be safe," she said. "I'm going to stay in New York."

They had settled into the camp and split up responsibilities to watch while the other dozed off. They had to fend off several attempts to sell them drugs, but they also had to look like they fit in. It was difficult to convince the more skeptical sellers, when Maxx looked like a poor attempt at an undercover detective. When he pretended to be asleep, it took the pressure off.

Sometime in the late afternoon, there was a rumor they overheard from several people nearby that a bunch of cops had been congregating a couple blocks away. The camp veterans were convinced there was going to be a sweep of the camp and that they should hide anything the police would confiscate. Maxx and Gabby knew their guns would result in a trip to the station even with concealed carry permits and ID.

Whether the rumor was true or not, they couldn't take the chance of getting caught up in a search. They had already noticed several people packing up and heading out of the park. Watching the general direction they were going, Maxx elected to go the other way toward Belltown, essentially where they had been earlier this morning.

It was much busier this time of day, so there were lots of pedestrians to walk amongst. Maxx and Gabby took their time as they walked and switched out their clothing. They wanted to look like commuters rather than homeless now. There was a baseball game that night, so wearing Mariners gear made them all but invisible.

After reaching Belltown, they kept walking toward Pike Place Market. The crowds at rush hour would be large enough to hide in, and they could hang out there until dark and wait for Miss Grey's next instructions. They found a place to stay out of sight on the lower level of the market. They were hot and tired after running and walking for the last hour. They refilled the water bottles Maxx had luckily thrown in the backpacks earlier this morning. The stress and adrenaline were also taking a heavy toll on them.

They'd argued several times about continuing to wait or to alternatively go to a police station or federal office to ask for help. If they did that and tried to explain truthfully why they were in danger, people would think they were crazy. They needed to hold on to the files until they could hand them over to Miss Grey. After that, they'd drop out of sight.

When they had a chance to catch their breaths and think clearly, they decided that putting some distance between themselves, Haoyu, and whoever was chasing them from the government was the best short-term solution too. Since their cars and homes were being watched, and they didn't want to use a credit card, they were limited by the small amount of cash they had left. That left them with only a few cheap travel options.

"We need to get out of town and put some distance between us and Haoyu so we can rest and think about next steps," she said. She was looking frazzled, sitting with her back against the wall and her arms wrapped around legs.

"We could take a bus, but both of the stations are in the other direction, so we'd have to backtrack with a long walk."

"Can we make it to the train station from here?" she asked.

He wiped the sweat off his forehead with his shirtsleeve. "It's doable, but the trains don't run frequently, so we could be sitting in the station for an hour or more. That's risky."

"The airport isn't an option either, so our best choice is to hop on one of the two ferries that sail every hour. They're cheap, and we can walk on and off at the last minute. In fact, we could keep riding the ferry back and forth for the rest of the day while we're waiting for more instructions."

"From up here at the market, we can wait to see a ferry docking, then run downhill to the terminal, pay with cash, and get on board with only a few minutes left before the ferry departed."

"If anyone did try to follow us, they would have to board behind us, making it easy to spot them," she said with a little more enthusiasm in her voice.

Even though the plan wasn't foolproof, Maxx could see Gabby relax slightly at having an escape plan.

They filled up on the last of the water they had in their bags, Maxx ate the last half of a piece of jerky he'd been saving, and they walked outside to the staircase landing. They stood off to the side and waited for the sight of the next ferry. When it was fifteen minutes from docking, they'd make a run down the half mile of steep hills. His knees were bothering him, so he'd left in an extra few minutes of cushion. That would leave them only a short window to board when they were at risk of being chased. He felt good about their chances.

When he saw the ferry from Bainbridge make the turn for the Seattle terminal, he kissed Gabby and said, "Run."

UNDERWATER BOOGIE, BABY

Attempting to escape from Seattle, Maxx and Gabby successfully boarded the ferry to Bainbridge Island. However, Haoyu had outsmarted them and pursued them onto the boat. Maxx, trying to evade capture, hid in a car parked on the auto deck. However, he was quickly discovered and trapped in the car. When he refused to surrender, Haoyu used a semi-truck to violently force the car with Maxx stuck inside off the front end of the ferry. Maxx, deeply afraid of water, was being pushed off the boat toward the dark waters of Puget Sound, and there was nothing he could do to stop it.

Maxx's seatbelt hurt like hell but saved him from getting knocked unconscious three times in less than a minute. First there was the sudden acceleration when the marine chain snapped in two and the truck pushed him forward. It was such a violent collision that his head bent the headrest when it whipped backward. If there had been airbags in the old car, it certainly would have set them off.

The second collision was moments later when the car landed in Puget Sound from thirty feet above the water. He didn't know how fast he'd been pushed from the auto deck of the ferry, but gravity had added to that speed. It was fast enough for him to see it coming.

"Ahhhh!"

The front of the car slammed into the water but didn't become completely submerged.

Almost instantaneously, the truck that had pushed him off hit the back end of the car. It forced the car under water and pinned it there. The air trapped inside the car kept it floating enough that it was slowly sinking, slower than the truck that was on top of him. The roof of the car was between the wheels of the eighteen-wheeler and wasn't going anywhere.

The next collision occurred shortly after when the ferry collided with the truck. The speed was such that it smashed the rear end of truck and collapsed it like an accordion. The bow pushed them to the front for a few minutes. It then shunted them to the side as the truck sank low enough in the water to escape below the hull.

All these rapid, violent collisions took a heavy toll on Maxx's body. He'd suffered plenty of collisions in football and in his military career, but they were nothing compared to this. It was impossible to think clearly, but he was lucid enough to congratulate himself on having the foresight to put on his seatbelt. Even though he probably had multiple concussions, it had saved his life. For a few minutes at least.

When he began to process what had happened, he realized he was still trapped in a car, underwater and sinking into Puget Sound. The water was so murky that even though he was still near the surface, he could have been at the bottom of the ocean for the amount of light he could see. It didn't occur to him that the car was pinned under the truck and blocking any light there was. In his mind, he'd concluded he was already dropping deep into the sound.

He also counted himself lucky that he hadn't been able to kick out the window when he was trying to escape the car on the boat. He could feel the water rising quickly up his legs, which began to go numb, but he knew he had several minutes of air trapped in the passenger compartment at that rate of flooding. If the window had been open, he'd have no chance to catch his breath, get out of the seatbelt, and exit the car before he drowned.

Maxx got his breathing under control to conserve air and cleared his head as much as possible. It wasn't much, but it allowed him to then consider how to break the window. Relaxing in a car trapped underwater would be difficult in any circumstances, but with his fear of the water, it was all he could do to keep from going mad.

He needed to get out now. He remembered from a survival film that trying to open the door was pointless, even if Haoyu hadn't sealed him in. He thought about trying to roll down the window, but that remained stuck shut too. He'd heard about people using their car keys, but his were somewhere in his backpack, which wasn't on the seat next to him anymore. After the collisions, it could be anywhere in the car.

There were old tools in the car's glove box that he'd noticed when searching for a disguise. He didn't recall clearly what the tools were, but they had to be better than nothing. Keeping the seatbelt wrapped around his arm, he leaned over and forced open the glove box with his fingers. The glove box door was partially bent because of the impact, but by jamming his fingers in, he could get it open enough to slip his hand inside.

He could feel the tools inside, and the water was creeping up to his chest, so he had to move quickly now. He would need room to leverage the tool and if the window was underwater he wouldn't have enough momentum to break the glass. He pulled out the first two tools he could get his numbing fingers around, a wrench and screwdriver. He'd have preferred a hammer, but this would have to do.

He made sure he could escape the seatbelt if the water

came rushing in, took several deep breaths to maximize how long he could hold his breath, and put the tip of the screwdriver against the glass. Using as much force as he could muster, he used the wrench to hit the end of the screwdriver.

The first few swings only made the tip of the screwdriver slip against the glass. He then placed the tip on the edge of the window where it met the door and swung as hard as could, catching his hand in the process. It hurt like hell, but it put a crack in the glass. The water pressure did the rest.

The window flew into the car with a deluge of water right behind it.

The tools were swept away, but the seatbelt held him in place. The water was shockingly cold and further disoriented him. If he hadn't been secured, he probably would have ended up somewhere in the backseat. Even though he had filled his lungs before breaking the glass, he could barely keep it in when he was submerged.

His eyes had adjusted to the darkness under the water. Puget Sound only had about thirty feet of visibility to begin with, and with the setting sun it was even becoming dimmer. Maxx could see enough light to know which direction was up, and the air in the car rushed past him for the surface. But the gray above him was fading, and at first he couldn't understand why it was pitch black directly over him and a little lighter to the sides. Luckily, he didn't try to immediately shoot for the surface as fast as he could, or he would have collided with the truck.

As the car rapidly began to fall away into the darkness below, he grabbed onto a tire of the truck that was above him. He pulled himself up under the truck and found a small pocket of air that was trapped beneath the trailer. The trailer was mostly filled with air, and the weight of the tractor was wrenching the rig apart at the connection. It was going to snap in two, or the trailer would fill up soon and get pulled under by the bulk on the front.

Either way, it was a balance that wasn't going to last more than a few minutes, at which point Maxx wanted some distance between himself and the truck. He also didn't know where he was relative to the ferry and didn't want to make his situation worse by swimming right into its path.

As he watched the Rambler sink, he held on to the truck and took in some of the trapped air, while he coughed and gagged from the salt water in his mouth and sinuses. He'd come this far and didn't want to panic and make the situation worse, so it was better to calm down and get his bearings. He didn't exactly know where he was under the truck relative to the surface, and the little bit of light he had was fading rapidly.

When the light was gone, it was going to be difficult to tell which way was up. Trying to follow bubbles in the dark sounded smart but was not easy to do with no light, getting weighed down by his jeans and boots, and reeling from a concussion.

He had calmed down some and reached the conclusion that he needed to swim out away from the trailer and find the surface while he still had air and before the sun set. He was in the process of clearing his lungs for the swim when something bumped against his legs. His first reaction was that it was a shark or some other sea creature. He knew there weren't many sharks in these waters, but he'd seen plenty of seals and even the occasional orca.

Despite his attempt to think rationally, his imagination got the better of him. He started kicking to get out of the water as much as he could.

He felt one of his kicks connect with something firm, so he knew it wasn't his imagination out to get him. After a moment, he felt something grab his leg again. He couldn't tell if he was getting bitten or being rubbed by something in the water. Terrified, he thrashed about to get away from it. He could hear himself yelling, but that was only making the situation worse.

As he was trying to calm himself down again, he saw a light beam in the water shining up through the air pocket from below. He wondered if the headlights on the car had been on. No, this was something new. The light flashed on and off several times and now had his complete attention. Then the flashlight was held up under the chin of a scuba diver, and he realized what he'd been feeling on his leg was a rescue diver trying to get his attention.

He was so relieved that it wasn't a shark that it took him a moment to realize that he was being rescued. His next thought was how they had got a rescue ready on the ferry so quickly. He didn't think he'd been underwater more than several minutes, and here they were already. Maybe he'd been underwater longer than he'd realized. Or perhaps this was a delusion.

It didn't seem like a delusion when the diver flashed him again with the light and signaled an okay. Maxx recognized that hand gesture and signaled an okay back. *I'm great, now that I know you're not a shark.*

The rescue diver signaled to Maxx that he should swim toward him while he held out a secondary breathing regulator. It was obvious he didn't want to get hung up under the truck and was trying to get Maxx to come to him. Maxx had to leave the safety of his temporary air pocket, but this person seemed calm and in control, which gave him the motivation to move.

He hoped that he wasn't imagining this, or he was going to drown. Maybe he was already drowning and this was his mind's last attempt at coping with the craziness of the situation. It wasn't that long ago when he'd been sitting on the ferry, and now he was living his worst fear.

Maxx took a deep breath and reluctantly swam toward the scuba diver suspended in the water. With his wet clothes and shoes, swimming ten feet was much harder than he would have imagined. It took maximum effort to keep from sinking.

As soon as he got within arm's reach of the diver, he was pulled in and could feel himself stabilizing. The diver put some air in his buoyancy vest to compensate for Maxx's weight then handed him the regulator so he could breathe.

Maxx had taken some diving instruction when he was in the military. He hated the experience and never got over the fear of being underwater, but he understood the principles and knew how to help the rescue diver help him rather than fighting. As he took in the oxygen, he fought the instinct to try and swim to surface. He didn't think they were very deep, but he could take some time to stabilize now that he was clear of the truck, had some air, and wasn't going to sink to the mud at the bottom.

After getting past the initial shock, he realized there was another diver behind them. He didn't have a light on but had several glow sticks and some equipment in each of his hands. This must be the first diver's buddy. In the murk, he couldn't tell what it was that he was holding, but they looked like bombs with a fan at the bottom. After a moment of puzzlement, Maxx recognized them as sea scooters. That explained how they were able to maneuver over here so quickly.

The first diver pointed toward the second diver and the scooters, indicating the direction that they were heading. When they were close enough, the first diver had Maxx hold on to his tank, and he took the scooter in his hands and started to move away from the truck quickly. The second diver was a bit faster and shot ahead of them to lead the way. The first scooter turned on a light to shine ahead of them, and they rapidly moved forward. Maxx didn't know where they were going, but it seemed they were getting farther from the ferry, not closer. They must want to clear the area before surfacing, he thought.

After what seemed like an eternity to Maxx, they slowly

began to move toward the surface. He could see some underwater lights up ahead highlighting the bottom of a boat. That must be where they were heading, and he was glad he was about to get back above water. Not solid ground yet, but a big step closer.

When they reached the back of the boat, several hands reached down to grab Maxx and help lift him onto the swim platform on the back of the boat. He reclined on his back with his eyes closed, catching his breath. People kept asking him if he was okay, and he could only grunt an affirmation because his throat was burning from the salt water he had swallowed. He could hear the divers handing up their equipment and climbing on board.

When everyone was onboard and had removed their equipment, the first diver dropped down next to Maxx. "That was crazy stuff, man. How're you feeling?"

Maxx's eyes snapped open when he realized he recognized the voice.

"Andres?" he croaked out.

"The one and only. We were wrapping up the archeology dive when we got a call from Gabby. She said you were on the ferry and being chased by that Chinese guy who has been on your tail. She wanted us to meet you in Bainbridge to help."

"But you were under water."

"We saw the truck and car go off the front of the ferry, and Joseph and I grabbed the scooters and jumped back in. It was faster than bringing up the anchor and trying to move our boat."

"Why didn't you take me to the ferry though? Did they see you?"

"When I realized it was you trapped under the truck, I decided to bring you back here first. If you were in trouble, it would be better if people thought you didn't make it out."

"Smart thinking. Let them think I'm dead or drowning, but

let's give Gabby a call so she doesn't worry. She might not even know I was in the car that went overboard. And if she's hiding from Haoyu, she won't report me missing yet."

Maxx took Andres's phone and called Gabby. When she answered, he said, "Guess who?"

Gabby gasped in surprise. "Where are you?"

"It's a long story for when we have more time, but are you in a safe place to talk?"

"Yes, I'm hiding up on the top deck. It's chilly out here, but I'm out of sight."

Maxx breathed a loud sigh of relief. He was trying unsuccessfully to stop his teeth from chattering from the combination of adrenaline and the cold.

"Maxx, I don't understand why you're calling from Andres's phone. Where are you hiding on the ferry?"

"Did you see the accident on the front of the ferry? That was me. Well, me with a lot of help from Haoyu."

"What?" She practically screamed into the phone. "I heard the crash and saw the truck sink in the water but had no idea you were involved. That was horrible!"

"I was trapped in the car that went overboard but Andres and Joseph rescued me. I'll tell you the details when we pick you up."

"I'm so glad you're okay," she sighed with relief. "I don't know what I would have done if something had happened to you."

"It was scary... I was really close to getting eaten by a shark."

She laughed nervously. "I know you hate the water, but I'm skeptical about you running into a shark. I'll ask Andres."

"It swam away really fast when I punched it. I don't think he saw it." He grinned mischievously, knowing from the skepticism in her voice she wasn't buying his fish story.

"I hate to interrupt your underwater adventure, Jacques

Cousteau, but the captain is making an announcement on the intercom, and I need to listen."

After a brief pause, she came back on the phone.

"He said they're going to do a search and rescue. All of us passengers are going to be evacuated on small boats to the Bainbridge terminal while they wait for the Coast Guard."

"What is the Coast Guard going to do?" he asked as his teeth chattered.

"They're bringing in divers and a small submarine to see if there was anyone in the vehicles. Should I tell them you're safe?" she asked.

"No, no. They'll keep you for questioning, and we need to keep you hidden from Haoyu."

"Okay, you're right. I'll stay hidden as long as I can then evacuate with the other passengers. And let Haoyu keep believing he drowned you."

"After you get to the Bainbridge terminal, Andres will pick you up, and we will all head over to Blakely Harbor. Even if the Chinese spot you evacuating, they won't have a way to follow us out of Bainbridge."

She sounded relieved now that they had plan. "I can't wait to see you. I'm glad this is almost over and we don't have to worry about Haoyu anymore!"

"Me too, babe. See you soon!" Maxx ended the call and tossed the phone back to Andres.

He climbed in to cockpit of the boat to try and warm up as they raced past the ferry toward the marina to pick up Gabby. *I really don't like Mondays.*

GHOST RIDERS

Joseph took the wheel of the boat as they pulled into the marina at Bainbridge Harbor. The university paid to keep a slip at the marina while they were working on the research project off Rockaway Beach so that they didn't have to take it through the Ballard locks every time they wanted to do a research expedition outside of Lake Union. They didn't want to tie up for the night in their assigned slip, opting instead to use the temporary dock so they could get in and out quickly.

They had been secured at the temporary dock for an hour before the water taxis started to unload the passengers who were being brought in from the ferry, Wenatchee. With several hundred passengers on the vessel, they were loading fifty people onto a boat for each trip, unloading and then making another run. The passengers were then dropped off at the terminal to either get picked up or wait if they had a vehicle that was still on the ferry.

As each group of passengers were dropped off, Maxx used a set of binoculars to scan the crowd for Gabby and any of the men who had been chasing him. He was hidden out of sight so that Haoyu would still believe he drowned. He wanted to maintain the belief that he was no longer a threat so he and Gabby could drop out of sight. Since he didn't have a way to contact Miss Grey, they'd have to address that problem once they got Gabby off the ferry without being spotted.

As extra insurance, Andres had parked at the terminal, dressed like every other local person waiting there. He and Gabby would recognize each other, but the men chasing Gabby wouldn't know him. He and Maxx were each carrying a walkie-talkie in case they needed to coordinate in an emergency. Andres had slipped a pistol in his jacket for additional insurance. Haoyu was getting desperate, and Andres didn't want to be unarmed if things got ugly.

Their plan was that simple. When Gabby arrived, she would either be alone, escorted by Haoyu, or followed. If she was alone or followed, Andres would connect with her, take her to the boat, and they'd be away quickly. If she was being kidnapped, it would be up to Andres to intervene with force. In that situation, Maxx would abort his attempt to remain hidden, come up behind, and ambush them. That was their last-ditch effort, but Maxx couldn't afford to let them leave with Gabby. Haoyu had killed Scott and tried twice to kill him. He had no illusions that he'd hesitate to kill Gabby if it suited him.

Andres was waiting by the railing at the terminal when the water taxi pulled in and people started unloading. This was the first group, so Maxx knew she was either going to be in this group or the last group. It was at her discretion as to which group she tried to join depending on her assessment of the situation on the ferry. He was afraid that hanging back until the end would leave Haoyu's men on both the boat and at the terminal so there would be little chance to make a quick escape. Their prospects were better if they only had to deal with a couple of people who were unprepared at the terminal. Even a small element of surprise would help.

Gabby knew Maxx and Andres would be waiting for her at

the terminal but had not used her phone to call them once she came out of hiding on the boat or in the water taxi. She'd slipped in as the last person with the first group when she had switched places with one of the other passengers at the last moment. She'd lied and told them she had a relative who was dying, requiring her to get there before he passed away. Some sobs and tears sold her story, and she got on.

She'd texted them a description of her outfit and tried to see if there was anyone on the water taxi who looked like those chasing them earlier. She hadn't seen the first group go from the ferry to the taxi, and it was dark out and on the other boat. She hoped they had missed her getting on, but even if they hadn't, she knew they didn't get on after her.

The short ride to the island terminal was nerve-racking. As they passed by where they were searching for Maxx underwater, she felt guilty not telling them they could stop looking. Maxx was right though to leave the impression that they had killed him, giving them the chance to get the files to Miss Grey. If they had to keep running and hiding to stay alive, they'd miss the chance to get them to her tonight when they might be of use. The clock was ticking for whatever was going to happen in New York in the morning.

When the taxi docked in Bainbridge, she tried to get in the front of the line. That would allow Andres to get to her before anyone else intercepted her. As she hurried off the ferry and on to the dock, she could see Andres up ahead, waving her over. She was practically jogging when he put the walkie talkie to his ear and said something. She couldn't hear what he said but could tell from the look on his face that it wasn't good.

When she was only a few feet from him, he said, "Keep moving fast. There's a boat waiting for you up ahead. I'll be right behind you."

She nodded and jogged past him, looking for her ride. When she was a few yards past Andres, she could hear footsteps coming up fast behind her. She started running, and so did the person behind her. Starting to panic, she heard a shout.

Taking a chance to glance back she saw that Andres had waited until the man was running next to him and pushed him off the dock into the water. There was no way he would get back on the dock easily. Also, if he had a phone or gun on him, it would be completely soaked. Any chance Haoyu's men had to capture her was ruined.

Gabby slowed down, and Andres quickly caught up to her and grinned. "Be careful. This wood is slippery, and it's easy to fall in."

Once they were both on board the archeologists' boat, Joseph revved the engines, and they accelerated for Blakely Harbor. Maxx shouted to her from the cockpit, "You won't believe it, but I was almost bitten by a shark tonight while I was swimming. It was like *Jaws*!"

Andres shook his head, and Gabby rolled her eyes. They both sat down next to Maxx on the deck to catch their breaths and watch the intermittent lights on shore roll by.

They pulled into a slip at Blakely Harbor and unloaded a monitor and the camera equipment they would need with their meeting with the tribal elders. Andres held a quick meeting with the rest of the archeology team that had been on the boat. They decided that their best option was to take the boat back to the home dock near the University of Washington campus. They wouldn't need it any more tonight, and if they had somehow been followed from the Bainbridge marina, it wouldn't take someone long to rent a boat and get here.

It was better to leave no trace of where they went. Andres and Joseph could grab a ride from any of the tribal members who were heading back to Seattle, since the ferry would be out of commission for a while.

The four of them walked up the road to the meeting place at Hall's Hill Lookout and Labyrinth. Andres explained that the signature feature was a stone mosaic labyrinth based on the thirteenth-century French Chartres Cathedral labyrinth. The creator had also incorporated the Native American medicine wheel into his mosaic pattern through the orientation and coloration of stones. The tribal leaders enjoyed coming here to meditate, and Andres quickly agreed when they suggested the location.

When they arrived, a handful of the tribal elders were already waiting for them and sitting spread out in small groups on the granite sitting stones and the stone bench. They were talking in reverent tones, barely audible over the summer breeze blowing in the surrounding pine trees. They were anxious to hear what Andres was going to tell them about what they had found during the dive. They had pointed them in the direction and were sure there was something to the stories that had been passed down by their grandfathers. What they didn't know was if the truth was going to be found or forgotten.

There was a brief round of introductions, and then Joesph held up his hand to begin the meeting. "Thanks for joining us tonight. I know for some of you it was not the easiest trip to make."

Maxx shook his head and waved half-heartedly while Gabby tried not to laugh.

"Andres and I would especially like to thank the council elders for your trust and sharing your tribal beliefs with us. We took all of the information you shared with us as the beginning of a search for hidden truth."

He told them that it had taken them several months to scan the bottom of the sound for the sunken ships off the shoreline of Blakely Harbor. In the late 1800s, the site was the location of Port Blakely Mill, one of the world's largest sawmills. It was said there were so many ships in the harbor that one could walk from deck to deck and get halfway to Seattle.

"Yes, this is true, and before the mill was built, our tribe was the largest tribe in the area," one of the elders interjected.

"But what of the artifact?" another elder asked. "One of the ships had sunk carrying a special relic that had been stolen from us. The Mouth of Thunderbird."

The tribe had passed the oral traditions about the artifact and how it was lost for a hundred and thirty years. They had avoided speaking publicly about the lost relics because they were afraid that someone less trustworthy would take the item and use it for evil purposes. Part of the folklore was that it was their responsibility to protect the artifact and use it only for the good of the tribe.

There was concern that if the relic was used by their enemies they would be punished. Therefore, they had let it lie somewhere in the sound, thinking at least it was not gone and that they would recover it when the time was right.

When the tribal council had learned Joseph was in the archeology program at UW, they had spoken with him to make sure he could be trusted to help them find and recover the relic. It was of sacred significance for them, and they didn't want it to be sitting in a museum or, even worse, in some rich person's home. It belonged to the tribe, and they wanted it to be returned to them in private.

Joseph continued, "As we agreed, we have been searching and are here tonight to share with you the results of our search. We don't know if it's the sacred object you asked us to recover for you. If it is, then we would like to know the history behind the artifact."

"We will do as we agreed. The knowledge must remain confidential and not be written down. You must use only this information to help protect the Native American history in the area that had been lost during the previous century."

While Joseph was conversing with elders about the background, Andres set up the small screen and projector they had brought with them from the boat.

When he was ready, Joseph turned the meeting over to Andres. He went into detail what they had been doing over the last two months by mapping out the sunken ships that were within a one-mile radius of the bay. That was much further out than the anecdotal evidence they had, but they had decided that casting a wider net was a better start than having to perform a second search if they didn't find what they were looking for right away. The first survey had identified two-dozen potential wrecks.

Using sonar and quick searches, they were able to eliminate all but of a handful of the remaining possible vessels. The remaining searches used an unmanned submersible that allowed them to verify if the wrecks were still intact enough to store items in the holds. These extensive surveys allowed them to catalogue what was visible and match against the ships' manifests that were available in the port records.

This detailed review left them with two potential targets that they had been diving in for the last two months and creating a log of all the items, locations, and possibility of recovery. It was extremely interesting to Andres and Joseph from an archaeological perspective but didn't provide any answers that would satisfy the request from the council, until they had found a number of ancient tribal artifacts in the hold of one of the ships.

The initial discovery had warranted a more thorough dive, which was what they had been doing today. And they had filmed the dive so they could show the results to the council without removing the items from the wreckage.

Andres played back the video of the dive from that afternoon. He fast forwarded through the initial dive to the ship and entry into the hold. As the video played, there were murmurs from the audience, because no one had seen these items for 130 years. It was obvious there were hundreds of Native American objects packed into the hold of the ship. The cold water had kept many of them remarkably well preserved despite the effects of time.

During the video, one of the divers moved toward a large chest pushed into the corner and covered by silt and a jumble of items. Being careful not to disrupt the placement of the items around the square container, a gloved hand brushed the sediment to reveal the item underneath. It was a dark metal that absorbed the camera lights. One square corner was evident. At this point, Andres paused the video and turned to the group.

"This looks like the item you described to me. Is this what you wanted us to find?"

Gabby looked at Maxx but didn't say a word, only nodded back at her. *That's an Omega device.*

The tribal elders were quiet, but from the looks around the circle, it was evident they had found the sacred artifact that their fathers had described to them.

After a pause, Sammy, the head of the council, cleared his throat. He was dressed in a pair of chinos, a light jacket, and hiking boots. Up close, he had the unmistakable look of someone who had spent a lot of time on the water. His face was dark brown and deeply weathered, highlighted by his prominent cheekbones. His long, graying hair was brushed behind his ears.

He began softly, "I believe we are seeing the Mouth of Thunderbird. It is as our traditions describe it. We cannot be certain until it is on shore and brought to life, but it seems you have kept your end of the bargain."

Maxx spoke up, "I apologize for interrupting, but what about this object makes you believe it is what your legends describe?"

"Mouth of Thunderbird was dark as the sky and hid the light, even in the noon sun. It is made from a material that is not metal but looks and feels smooth like metal. It cannot be damaged by fire or water or the hands of man. It is indestructible. It feels cool and warm to the touch at the same time. It is shaped as a cube and looks the same from all angles. One side has an internal light when it has the right power and is ready to speak with us."

"Have you ever seen it before?"

"No, we did not draw or attempt to carve a replica from wood or stone. It is too sacred to our people. As part of our history, we are also told how to make the relic work and what we should not do. It is an instrument of the gods, and we treated it with respect. When the item was stolen from our ancestors, we were devastated but were overwhelmed and unable to stop the army that took it from us. We followed them and watched them load it on the ship. Nature intervened that day, and the ship was sunk by a series of large waves. Whale intervened."

Gabby nudged Maxx. "Tell them."

Andres perked up at her comment. "Tell them?"

"I have seen another device like this. It seems the gods have made more than one."

Sammy grinned. "Of course. We have always known other people have such a way to communicate with Thunderbird. That was part of our pact, that we should take care not to use it against others, lest it be used against us."

"And that is why we are here," Maxx continued. "Some people are trying to use their device to harm others, rather than for protection, and we are trying to stop them."

"I suppose that is why you have been led here to meet us then."

"I don't believe in coincidences, Sammy. I believe we were brought here at this time too. And I think I know why."

"This other relic that looks and seems to work similarly to

the Mouth of Thunderbird also came with instructions on how to use it," Gabby added.

"Do they seem consistent with our legends?" Sammy asked.

"Yes. There are clear warnings about when and how the communication should occur. What was implied but is not clear is when to start a conversation. It seems it must be at a specific time and location. Is that consistent with what you learned?"

"They would hold a council ceremony when they believed they needed to speak with Thunderbird. Then they would receive a vision that told them when and where they should have a conversation. The location was always somewhere close to the Earth's power that the mouth would draw from. The time was in the future. The elders believed the time was to be spent trying to solve the problem ourselves. If it was solved, then there was no need to speak with Thunderbird."

"And if the time arrived to speak and someone did not follow the instructions but tried to use the mouth without the proper practices, then there would be punishment from Thunderbird or Whale. This did happen from time to time until the people followed the word of Thunderbird correctly."

Maxx sat up when a thought came to him. "Did these punishments destroy the Mouth of Thunderbird?"

"Oh no," Sammy answered. "The mouth is indestructible. The artifact in the ship has been in our tribe for over a thousand years. It has been buried in earthquakes, floods, and volcanoes. Our people always find a way to recover it. We have learned some hard lessons. Punishment for disobeying Thunderbird or Whale is swift and harsh."

"We are afraid our people are about to learn these same lessons the hard way too," Maxx said. "The time and place for us to use the device is tomorrow. Unfortunately, we believe the leaders plan to use our device in an unintended way."

"Then they will be punished. Whoever is using the device

and any people nearby will suffer a catastrophe. You must try and stop them."

Joseph stepped forward. "Sammy, would you talk to the person who is trying to stop them? She is someone you can trust."

The elder hung his head in thought for a moment. It was a huge ask for him to share this with outsiders. But he did believe Thunderbird had prepared them for this moment.

"I will help her," Sammy said softly.

TRUST NOBODY

Miss Grey sat in the temporary office they had set up in Brooklyn last week. When the files had indicated Manhattan was going to be the contact point for the Omega device, DHS and a number of other government agencies had spun up additional resources in and around New York City.

She'd been made aware that DARPA had established a secure location in the World Trade Center. She hadn't been invited to visit, nor did she have plans to visit. She was officially tasked with finding if and where the Chinese were operating and if they were making attempts to intervene with DARPA. The NSA had intercepted secure traffic that indicated they were in the area, but it seemed they were being extremely careful not to reveal their plans.

Unofficially, she was also running interference for the Tacoma team that was installing the backup device in the second tower of the World Trade Center. DARPA and the other official government agencies seemed to be unaware that this plan B was running literally right under their noses. There was significant political cover, but it would not protect her if it was discovered that she was aiding an alternative to the official government attempt to communicate with the aliens. In fact, she would expect that the words "treason" and "sedition" would be bandied about privately and publicly.

While she was watching the camera feeds from various locations around the city, her cell phone rang. The caller ID read, "Gabby Seattle." It was curious that Gabby was calling her at 11:00 in the evening in Seattle instead of Maxx. The last time she had spoken to Maxx, they were going to find a place to hand over the illicit copy of the Delta file that Gabby had taken from TechCom. She'd tried to call Maxx several times, but it went to voicemail. Even the texts didn't seem to be going through. Something was wrong, but there wasn't much she could do when she was on the opposite side of the country. He'd have to figure it out on his own for now.

"Gabby, it's great to hear from you, even if it's two in the morning here," Miss Grey said when she answered her phone.

"You can get your beauty sleep another day," Maxx said gruffly.

"Nice to hear from you too, Maxx."

"We've been a bit busy here getting chased around by your amigo Haoyu. We've been running and hiding from them all day and finally ditched them a few hours ago, I think."

"Then why did it take you this long to call me?"

"My phone dropped into deep water, and Gabby and I got separated for a few hours, so I didn't have any way to reach you."

"You know Gabby's phone is trackable, right?"

"We know, but we didn't think you'd answer if the caller ID was from an unidentified number. It won't matter though. We're not in Seattle and won't be here long enough for them to find us."

"We still need to get the information you have. You do still have that, or did that go swimming with your phone?"

"We have it, and it's more important than ever that we get it to you before things get underway this morning. Is there any way you can call me back at this number using a secure line?"

She agreed, hung up the cell phone, then grabbed the phone on her desk, selecting one of the encrypted land lines that bypassed the NSA.

"Why the secrecy, Maxx?"

"There's someone I want you to talk with. They have some relevant information about the device you need to hear before someone attempts to use it."

"Someone? You know I can't say anything confidential to someone who's not been cleared."

Maxx sighed over the line. "You don't need to tell him anything. He has some information to tell you. But let me give you a little background, and then I'll hand the phone to him."

"Alright, this better be good. The clock is ticking, and I don't have time for goose chases."

Maxx proceeded to explain that they had found what appeared to be another Omega device, one that was the property of the Suquamish tribe but had been taken and then lost. He said, "As crazy as it is to learn that there is another device, that's not the most important part of the story."

She interrupted him, "Where's the device now?"

"I'm not going to tell you, Miss Grey. That's up to the person who I'm going to put on the phone. As soon as someone realizes where it is, there will be a mad rush by the government to grab it and hide it away in one of your secret underground labs."

"Yes, because it is insanely dangerous in the wrong hands."

"I think he knows that better than you or anyone else. This isn't new to them. They've been dealing with the implications for generations. That's what he wants to talk to you about."

"Enough with the cryptic setup, Maxx. Let me speak to him."

"I'm handing the phone to Sammy now. Good chatting with you, Miss Grey."

While she waited for Maxx to pass the phone to the next person, she kept watching the video feeds from around New York City. There were several feeds from the port area, Times Square, Central Park, Grand Central Terminal, and the World Trade Center. They also had put as many agents as they could muster in strategic spots around the city looking for any unusual activity. Thus far, it had been a typical Monday night, and they hadn't encountered anything out of the ordinary.

Most of the attention was centered around the World Trade Center, as these were coordinates that were listed in the deciphered Alpha file. They were certain the Chinese had obtained a copy of the file with that location and would be present if they wanted to disrupt the American Omega device. It wasn't probable that they would know exactly where it would be located, so they were just as likely to run into the Tacoma team as they were to find DARPA.

"Hello, this is Sammy." The voice sounded a little hesitant.

"Hello, Sammy. I'm Miss Grey, and I work for the US government. Would you please identify yourself?"

"I already did. I'm Sammy. I'm a high school math teacher and on the Suquamish Tribal Council. Maxx told us a little bit about you and told us we can trust you. To be honest, I'm not that trusting of anyone in the government. I'm sure you understand."

She laughed politely. "Understood. How can I help you?"

It was Sammy's turn to laugh. "The most dangerous words from a government official."

"Pardon me?"

"The most dangerous words in the English language are 'I'm from the government and I'm here to help.'"

"Very funny, and generally I agree with you. In this case

though, Maxx said there was something I should hear from you."

Sammy took a long pause. "I got the impression from Maxx that you're in possession of one the ancient relics that were used to communicate with the gods. I don't know how you obtained it, but if you aren't already aware, there are many of these devices. I know from the tribal legends that several of tribes here in the Cascadia area had a device."

"I can't confirm or deny that I have a device like the one you're describing. If there were several like this, where are they now?" she asked.

"The only one we know for certain is the one that we redis-covered. All the rest have been lost over time, buried by the disasters they caused when they were used improperly."

"They've been destroyed over time, and the one you have is the last one you know of?"

"No, they are indestructible. They've been buried or lost at sea many times over the centuries then recovered. Our legends are very specific that man or nature cannot destroy it."

This revelation startled her. If this was true, it was possible that the Chinese had also recovered their device after the Tang-shan earthquake, as Omega had at Mount St. Helens. They'd always assumed they'd been lucky, but this man claimed it was a feature of the device, not an anomaly. Obviously, DARPA hadn't realized this since they didn't know the device had survived at Mount St. Helens, but the Chinese may have suspected the same.

"That is interesting news. Is there anything else I should know?"

"You probably know by now that the misuse of the device or attempting to use it to attack an enemy has led to many histor-ical examples of retribution. Earthquakes, volcanoes, and floods are the result. If you are planning on using the device except for the specific reasons you've been provided, it will result in disaster."

"Thank you, and we will be careful if we are in that situation. What did you mean when you said, 'reasons you've been provided?'" She held her breath, tapping her finger steadily when he took a moment to answer.

"If you have one of these artifacts, you must know two things. You will be told where and when to communicate with the gods. It's not like you can contact them on a whim."

"Yes, we understood that requirement. But how do they know you want to contact them?"

"Somehow, they are able get the message from whomever has the device. It can be many years in the future, however. The measurement of time is different for the gods, it seems."

"What's the other thing we must know?" She could feel a headache starting behind her eyes from the tension. Sammy's even, measured tone was making her more tense as the conversation went on. It seemed that they had not understood many basics of the device.

"Each tribe had slightly different instructions that matched their device. These instructions are sacred and unique to each tribe. The gods knew what was important to us and what challenges we face, so we are limited to the uses they have given us. Our tribe's oral history tells us of the uses we are limited to but also how they have changed over time."

"If we have a device, then we will also have unique instructions." She tensed as she waited for his confirmation of what she'd just heard.

"You must have specific instructions for your device, or you will trigger punishment by not adhering to them. You cannot mix and match without suffering the wrath. They are very strict about man adhering to their rules."

This explained why both the Chinese and DARPA had failed in their initial attempts to communicate. It also raised the hair on the back of her neck. DARPA was planning to use the guidelines that were created for the original device. If they veered from them, it would result in a catastrophe.

"Sammy, this is great information, and if we have one of these artifacts that you're referring to, I will make sure we take this all into consideration." She couldn't admit that they were already neck deep confronting the challenges he'd pointed out. She needed to get the copy of the untouched Delta file that Maxx and Gabby had taken and compare it to what Doctor Smith was planning to use with the DARPA device.

"Good luck then," Sammy responded. She could practically hear the irony dripping from his tone. "I'm handing the phone back to your friend."

"I hope you take him seriously," Maxx said to Miss Grey when he got back on the phone.

"I do. That was very helpful, but you know I have to be cautious about what I do with the information. I've only got a few hours until the communication begins, and I'm trying to manage the situation with DARPA and the Chinese. A misstep could end up with a huge disaster in New York this morning... that we cause."

"Do you still need the thumb drive with the Delta file?"

"It's even more critical now that I know each device has differing instructions. I have to be sure that Doctor Smith hasn't edited the instructions to justify whatever plans the military has devised. Comparing what they have with the original version will provide insight into their plan."

Maxx paused then asked, "Do we know what the Chinese instructions are?"

"No, we don't. I would guess they are similar to the original Delta file and similar to what Sammy relayed. In short, only use the device for protection, supporting progress, and not for attacking enemies. That's my guess."

"I hope you're right."

"There is no way to know at this point. What we do know is that the Chinese want our version of the Delta file. That should give them confidence we won't initiate an attack."

"How do we know they don't already have it?"

"We've been carefully monitoring TechCom. In the last week after the Alpha file was deciphered, we've intercepted several suspicious data transfers. We are certain that the mole has been actively communicating with China. But the Delta file was not transmitted last night after Gabby took a copy."

"If the mole knows Gabby took a copy, that will explain why Haoyu has been aggressively following us. But they have to be wondering why we would take an official copy."

"That's a good point. They know that DARPA would get an original, so they must be curious where Gabby's copy is going. They must be pondering what they've overlooked."

"When Haoyu had me cornered, he said Xi wanted the file, so they must not have it yet and were trying to bypass the mole or wanted a separate copy to verify against what the mole sent them."

"I think there's a way to kill two birds with one stone," Miss Grey said. "Have Gabby go back to TechCom and turn herself in. We know she's not the mole, but the real mole will try to find out what she's doing."

Maxx took a deep breath. "That seems extremely risky for Gabby."

"Hear me out. Since you're going back to Seattle, I'll coordinate with our office to have one of my team meet you at Tech-Com. You can give them the thumb drive."

"Okay, we are leaving as soon as I finish this call, so it will be a couple of hours."

"In the meantime, I'll get a copy of DARPA's Delta file so we can do a rapid assessment after we upload your version of the Delta file."

"Then what?"

"After you have gotten rid of the evidence, head to TechCom security. She can tell them she has downloaded and hidden an original copy because she is concerned that DARPA is going to improperly use the file. That will send alarm bells to Doctor Smith that someone is observing him and expressing worry about how he might use the file."

Maxx interrupted her last thought. "And it will also alert the mole that Gabby has some inside information that would be worth risking exposure to get access to."

"When someone shows up to security, they won't want to have the conversation in front of outsiders. They'll want to talk privately. That will be our mole."

"You don't think she'll be in any danger, do you? Because I won't put her in that position if she is."

"She won't be in danger if she stays in the building with TechCom security. Once this is all over in the morning, I will explain to TechCom that she was acting under my direction, and they will release her. She'll be safer with security at TechCom than wandering the streets with Haoyu looking for her."

"Okay, I'll hang around outside TechCom in case things go sideways. It sounds like a plan, and we are running out of time."

I TRUST YOU TO KILL ME

Maxx turned off Gabby's phone and handed it back to her. He wanted to reduce the chance that if anyone had been trying to locate her using the GPS signal from her phone that the trail would end in this out of the way park on Bainbridge Island. It had been a long day, and he was tired of being chased around.

The next step in their plan was to catch a ride back to Seattle, since it was going to be a while before the ferries were back on schedule. The drive would be less than two hours with the traffic at this time of night, but they needed a car. There were no taxis out here in the woods, but maybe one of the tribal elders was heading in that direction.

Maxx addressed the group. "We need to get back to Seattle in the next couple of hours. Is there anyone heading back that direction who we can carpool with?"

Sammy looked at his tribal colleagues for a moment then said to Maxx, "Let us chat among ourselves for a moment. I think we can work something out."

"That would be great, especially if you can accommodate all four of us and our gear."

The tribal elders walked to the other side of the clearing

and began to talk in hushed tones. Sammy was clearly proposing something that was making a couple of the elders very agitated. They talked for longer than Maxx expected, which was confusing.

It felt like he was missing some detail and couldn't imagine what it was, other than no one wanted to give him a ride. Maybe he looked and sounded too much like a government agent and had blown his credibility by introducing Miss Grey to the situation. He couldn't blame them for being distrustful.

Maxx was eating a piece of jerky that Andres had given him when Sammy walked over and sat down on the stone bench next to him and Gabby. He motioned to Andres and Joseph to join them. Meanwhile the rest of the tribal members began to walk off toward the parking lot until it was the five of them. *This doesn't look promising.*

"I have a way back to Seattle for you."

Maxx sighed with relief. "And we can all squeeze in?"

"Yes, I can accommodate all of you. But it's going to be more involved than hopping in the back of a pickup truck."

Gabby looked at him and raised her eyebrows. "We aren't riding horses, are we? Because I love horses."

"No, I have a couple of golf carts we're going to use. A little bit slower, but we're going to stay off the main roads and take a shortcut."

Joseph laughed loudly. Andres looked at him out of the side of his eye. There must be some joke that only Sammy and Joseph were in on.

"Sammy, there is no shortcut back to Seattle from here that you can take golf carts on. It's freeways and bridges the entire way unless you're in a boat."

"It's easier to show you than explain. Grab your stuff and follow me," Sammy said as he stood up and headed into the woods.

They hiked on a barely identifiable trail through the dark,

dense forest undergrowth. Sammy led the way, and Jospeh followed from the back using small flashlights. They moved through the woods as if it was a familiar walk in the dark for them. Maxx tried asking where they were going but gave up when Sammy said, "You will see soon enough."

After stumbling along for what seemed like eternity but was only thirty minutes according to Maxx's watch, they came upon a small, stand-alone utility building. It looked like dozens of these buildings he'd seen throughout the years, gray cinder block, sheet metal roof, and heavy gauge steel door with industrial locks. Sammy took some keys out of his jacket pocket and proceeded to open the locks.

Sammy opened the door, stepped inside, and turned on the lights. "Come on in and I'll explain," he said.

When all five of them were inside the building, Maxx eyed the metal stairs that descended from an opening in the floor. It was well lit, and he could see the bottom of the stairwell, but it was a long way below him.

"Have you all heard the rumors about the tunnels created by the fault lines that were used by the native people to move between Seattle and outlying areas?"

Andres looked at Sammy and Joseph as if they had gone mad. "Are you about to tell me this isn't a rumor?"

"Bingo. This is one of the few remaining entry points. I'm going to allow you all to use it as long as you give me your word that it remains a secret, like the sacred device you have found for us. I don't know what is going on with the other device that the lady on the phone talked to me about, but my instincts tell me someone is about to cause a disaster if they aren't careful. The government is dealing with forces way beyond their ability to control. And I think you all are here because you are trying to help."

"Yes, that is true," Maxx said. "Can we really get back to Seattle by walking through these tunnels?"

"I will show you the way," Joseph responded. "The tribe keeps several electric carts at each end of the tunnel. There is a car parked in a garage near the exit we can use temporarily."

"If I have your word you will never reveal the existence of these tunnels, then Joseph will escort you back, and I will lock up behind you."

Maxx, Gabby, and Andres all gave Sammy their word and shook his hand. He then turned and went out the door they had come in, locking it behind him.

Joseph led the way down the stairs, and Maxx counted a dozen levels before they reached the bottom of the stairwell. The tunnel looked like it was formed naturally with no visible manmade reinforcement. It was wide enough to fit the carts in single file with little room to spare. It sloped down for some ways in the distance, but it clearly went further than was visible.

They drove in the rock tunnel for fifteen minutes before the slope began to rise again. Other than the sound of tires on the smooth granite and the whine of the electric motor, it was eerily quiet. No one uttered a peep. It felt as if the weight of the world was on their shoulders and they had stepped inside a mysterious secret within the planet. A couple of times they sped past a side tunnel that branched off to the left or right. They were dim, but with the ambient light from their tunnel it seemed obvious they went to other entrances around Puget Sound. *Then again*, Maxx thought, *do we really know what mysteries are buried here?*

When they finally stopped at the other end of the tunnel, Joseph hopped out of the cart and began to open the metal exit door. "Pretty cool, huh?" he said with a wide grin.

"You've known about this the entire time?" Andres asked him incredulously.

"Yes, but I'm sworn to secrecy, like you are. It's been around for many centuries, but the carts were Sammy's idea. It beats the ten-mile hike each way. Our legend says these tunnels were created by Thunderbird so that tribes would be able to remain hidden from enemies when they were threatened."

"Threatened by what?" Andres asked.

"Could be other tribes or invaders. According to legends, malicious gods were visiting Earth."

After Joseph had shut off the tunnel lights and locked the doors behind them, he started climbing the stairs.

Maxx didn't bother to try and count the number of flights, because it was too exhausting after the fifth level. "Maybe you should get Sammy to invest in an elevator," he said as he paused to catch his breath.

"It's good exercise, and we get to see how motivated you are to come back and visit," Sammy said with a smirk.

By the time they reached the top level of the stairwell, Maxx was dripping with sweat. At least it was cool here, even if the air was slightly stagnant. Joseph opened the outer door, and they exited into an underground parking garage.

Joseph opened the trunk on a Suburban and loaded the equipment in. Andres climbed into the front seat, while Maxx and Gabby hopped into the middle seats.

"Where can I take you guys?" Jospeh said as he drove the car up to the exit. He entered a code into the exit kiosk, the gate opened, and they pulled out into a deserted alley.

It took Maxx a minute to get his bearings and realize they were only a few blocks from Pioneer Square. *This place has more secrets than anyone can imagine.*

Maxx had explained the plan to Gabby during the drive over in the tunnel, so she answered, "I need to get to the office to clear up some confusion. Please drop us off in Ballard. Maxx is going to hang around outside and wait for me."

Maxx texted Miss Grey the name of a bar in Ballard where he could meet the agent she was sending to collect the thumb drive. It was after midnight on a work night, so places would be open but not so busy that they would have a difficult time making contact. The place was also close to the TechCom office, so he'd find a spot where he could wait for Gabby without being seen.

When Joseph dropped them off at the bar, they all joked about what a crazy day it had been. Andres and Joseph were going to meet in the morning and discuss a plan to recover the Mouth of Thunderbird, as they had promised Sammy and the Suquamish tribal council. They were counting on Miss Grey not to get involved but wanted to get the job done before others caught on, especially with all the interest that would arise after tonight's drama.

Miss Grey's colleague was waiting by the door when Maxx and Gabby walked into the bar. It only took a moment for them to confirm their identities and hand off the thumb drive. Maxx was relieved when he watched the agent climb in a waiting car and speed away. He hoped it would give them the evidence they needed to ensure communication went smoothly. This was potentially a pivotal moment in world history, and it was overwhelming to think what had happened in the last week.

But there were still some large puzzle pieces still missing, and they needed to find one of those now. Identifying the mole inside TechCom would close off the leak of information to Haoyu and Xi. That needed to happen as quickly as possible before they reached the deadline in New York.

Rather than grab a cab, they decided to maintain a low profile and walk the six blocks to TechCom. Maxx found a place to sit in the dark outside the gleaming building lights and wait for Gabby. They stood in the dim light, holding each other tightly. This could be the last time they ever saw each other. She was jumping into a dangerous situation that could very easily send her to prison. He could only wait for her to come back.

She looked into his eyes, trying to memorize every detail of his face. He kissed her softly, whispering words of encouragement and he told her to be careful. He told her he loved her more than anything in the world and would wait no matter what happened in the morning.

While this week had been crazy, he had learned the importance of trust and having a partner in life who would stand by your side no matter what happened.

She nodded, unable to speak. She felt a lump in her throat and tears in her eyes. She hugged him tighter, feeling his strong heartbeat. She told him she loved him too and that she would see him soon. She told him to be patient and that he was her everything.

She handed her backpack and pistol to him so she would be able to clear TechCom security. She opened her eyes and wiped her tears. She picked up her bag and walked away. She tried to be strong and have faith.

From his vantage point across the street, he watched her walk across the street and stride confidently through the front door. "Here we go," he texted Miss Grey.

Gabby marched into the lobby at TechCom on a mission. She not only wanted to clear her name but also find out the identity of the mole leaking information to the Chinese. Miss Grey had some prime suspects, but there was no solid evidence. As the stakes became clearer, it was becoming more critical that they stop this spy before the Alpha deadline in the morning.

She didn't have a clear plan on how to expose them, but Maxx had given her a few ideas on the car ride over.

At the check-in kiosk, she asked for a supervisor then swiped her badge. From the looks on the faces of the security guards in the lobby, they knew who she was and said something like "Code Yellow" quietly into their walkie-talkies. She'd never heard this code before but guessed it was at least a step below "shoot her on sight." She kept her hands visible in case one of the guards got overzealous about their instructions.

It didn't take long for a supervisor to come around the corner at a fast walk. With short brown hair, tinted glasses, and a deep-blue windbreaker with "Security" stenciled on the front and back, it was clear he was not here for a casual conversation. He looked at several of the guards standing by and pointed at her. "Take her through the metal detector and then search her. When you're finished, escort her to Holding Room 1."

He sounded gruff, but she had expected that. They were considering her a threat and didn't know what her intentions were by showing back up at the office.

Holding Room 1 was a slightly larger, nicer version of the interrogation rooms she'd seen on television shows. It had a table, chairs, ceiling cameras, and a one-way window on the wall. It made her stomach clench walking in. The door didn't lock behind her, which she took as a positive sign. The locked door might come later, but for the moment she was here of her own free will.

He sat down and took off his glasses but never took his eyes off her. He kept his hands out of sight below the desktop. She wondered if he had a weapon underneath his jacket or in a drawer.

"Thanks for coming, Miss Fisher. You must know we've been trying to get a hold of you all day. There was a security breach in your office yesterday, and we wanted to ask you some questions about it."

"I know I must be a person of interest in yesterday's lapse in security. I'll gladly tell you everything I know after I speak with my supervisor, Dale Phi. He will be able to answer some questions for me that will clarify the situation."

"You aren't in a position to be making requests. Perhaps you should tell me what you know, then I'll determine what the next step is."

Gabby smiled and shook her head. "Here are the choices, sir. Either I talk to Dale, or I will call my attorney down here and leave with him. Then all future conversations will go through him. Which will it be?"

The security supervisor leaned back in his chair, glanced around the room without making eye contact with her. She could see from his body language that he was irritated. Although it sounded like she had left him a choice, he knew she really hadn't. He couldn't hold her here against her will.

He picked up the phone and dialed. "Mr. Phi, this is Bill Kopit, the security supervisor in the main lobby. We have an employee of yours who is on our high-risk list. She's with us in Holding Room 1 but wants to speak with you before talking with us. Would you like to speak with her?"

He listened to Dale for a moment. "Yes, sir." He hung up the phone. "He said he'll be right down."

A few minutes later, there was a soft knock on the door, and then Li Jing stepped in.

Kopit looked at her in surprise and said, "I'm sorry, ma'am, but this room is occupied."

She ignored him and continued into the room. "This is the Gabby Fisher meeting, isn't it?"

"Yes, but we're waiting for her supervisor to arrive. She wants to talk with him first."

Dale pushed the door open and entered the room. He looked at Li Jing and asked, "Why are you here?"

"Since this is my area of concern, I thought I'd sit in on the conversation, if you don't mind. We both have the same security clearances on Project Hermes, so anything she can say to you can be said to me too. If Miss Fisher doesn't mind, it would be best to have a witness. Security has to leave the room, and the cameras shut off for this topic."

Dale's face was a light shade of purple, but he knew she had him cornered.

Gabby, sensing there was a power play going on between the two of them, didn't see any reason that Li Jing couldn't stay. Maxx had told her the mole might try and get involved in the situation. Li Jing may be the mole after all, and here was an attempt to get more inside information. Gabby nodded. "It's fine if she stays, but only the two of you."

After Kopit left the room, Gabby took her time explaining how she absconded with the file, being careful to leave Maxx out of her version of events. When Dale inquired about Maxx's participation, she claimed he had just escorted her as her boyfriend and wasn't aware of what she was doing. It was a lie that probably wouldn't stand up under scrutiny, but Dale didn't press her on that point any further.

She said she had been working with an agent of the government to identify a spy on the Hermes team. She then explained that she took the file and had given a copy directly to a government agent, because she was concerned a copy or version of the Delta file had reached the Chinese government. The government wanted to compare what the Chinese had received with the original.

From his reaction, it was evident the information was shocking to Dale. Li Jing was either a better poker player or didn't realize Gabby was lying. Gabby knew it had to cause a reaction, because she substituted China for DARPA as the primary sponsor of the spying.

"That can't be true," Dale responded when he recovered his composure. "The Chinese have their own Delta file that must sync to their Omega device. Why would they want a copy of the original DARPA files when they don't even have a working Omega device?"

Gabby knew from the call with Miss Grey that only the Chinese would know that the Delta file was unique to each

Omega device. She kept her face from showing any emotion when she realized the only way that Dale would know that was if he has been in contact with the Chinese. And if they wanted the Delta file, they either knew or strongly suspected that the American Omega device was available.

Dale is the mole at TechCom.

She told them that was all she knew and that they could verify her story with Miss Grey.

Dale and Li Jing left the conference room. After a several minutes, Kopit opened the door and stepped inside with Gabby.

He looked more uncomfortable than when she had met with him a short while ago. "I just got a brief update and wanted to let you know that your government contact, Miss Grey, informed us that she'll contact you in the morning."

"Then I'm free to go," she said with her jaw slightly clenched.

"Yes, but she said to tell you that it would be best if you stayed here for the night. She said there would be a lot going on, and this would be the safest place to stay until things are cleared up with Dale."

"She's probably right. Do you have a more comfortable room I can stay in? Preferably somewhere I can lie down. It's been a very long day."

Dale needed to get out of the building and contact Haoyu immediately. The fact the US government knew there was a Chinese spy at TechCom passing them the files not only put him at risk but would also put the Chinese attempt to use their Omega device at risk. Even if the Americans were incorrect about why they wanted the Delta file, the result would be the same.

He grabbed his backpack from his office and his burner phone from the locker at security. As he exited the building, he told the security guards he was walking around the block to get some fresh air. He had no intention of coming back now. They were too close to catching him.

And after the events in the next few hours, the government would do whatever needed to be done to get the facts. He'd be thrown into a dark hole until he told the truth or died, whichever came first.

After he was clear of the bright lighting of the TechCom campus, he began to walk faster. He'd left his car in the underground parking garage to slow down the search for him. He needed to get to a safe spot and call Haoyu to come pick him up. The evening air felt brisk as he walked quickly. He had a sense that things were going to be over soon. He'd been planning to live the life of a very rich man in a country without extradition rights, and his moment had arrived.

Dale barely registered the sound of the silenced gun as something sharp hit him in the neck. The pain was excruciating. But he was rapidly becoming paralyzed, so only the occasional grunt escaped his lips. His body twisted when his legs gave way, and he fell backward. The last thing he saw as everything faded to black was a face he had learned to passionately hate in the last three months, Li Jing's.

EVE OF DESTRUCTION

The transfer of the device from the container onboard the small freighter had been nerve-racking. Xi had the foresight to bring the device on a ship registered to a neutral country to minimize scrutiny. He had routed the ship to the Port Newark Container Terminal before it became known that Manhattan would be the epicenter of activity. His foresight wouldn't stop random searches and extra attention from port security, police, and intelligence agencies.

They took the movement in steps and had done the final stage of the transfer after hours on the weekend so that there was minimal oversight by the building authorities. When the device was finally placed in the secured section of the basement, he'd breathed a sigh of relief. They had finished connecting the power and double checking all the parameters outlined in the schematic, so now it was a waiting game.

Xi had struggled with the decision about where to place the device when they had realized the coordinates indicated that the communication would be centered in Manhattan. They had tested the device multiple times to determine the sensitivity to moving from the given coordinates, and the connection was lost with minor variation. Buildings, geography, and infrastructure above or below ground had little impact within a one-kilometer radius. But outside of that radius, the device didn't make any connection. The lights on the control panel only glowed red until it was moved within range.

This created a challenge for the team, as they had limited options for where they could place the device. They didn't know if the Americans understood the parameters, but they would be exhaustively searching for them near the coordinates. Eventually he made the decision not to risk getting too far from the epicenter but to go as far underground as possible. He had speculated that the Americans would choose an elevated position and would focus their search for them above ground. It was a dangerous game of cat and mouse that would cost him the device and his life if he miscalculated.

They had set up the main device in the basement of Building 7 of the World Trade Center, because it was within the effective radius of the device the Americans called Omega. It was also several stories beneath the building but had easier entry and exit access than most of the complex, so they could come and go with much less scrutiny. They had designed the device container to replicate the materials needed for the ongoing replacement of the building elevators. This building also had access to the backup power generator for the WTC complex and would not need any additional power sources.

His objective was straightforward. There were too many variables outside his control, so he had kept it as simple as possible for the initial contact. The device would establish a connection, and he would provide the required verbal sequence. After that, he would ask that they receive protection from the Americans, who were planning an attack on their country. Then they would repack the device and fly it to a ship waiting for them in international waters.

In the meantime, he had kept Haoyu in Seattle to search for

signs of the device being moved. He knew that was searching for a needle in a haystack, so he had been working under the assumption that Smith was here in New York and planning to communicate with the aliens in a few hours.

Haoyu was also looking for Gabby and trying to keep in contact with the spy at TechCom. Either one of them could supply him with the American version of the operating file, so he could compare his instructions to theirs. That insight would allow him to fine tune his communication with the aliens. It would be beneficial but wasn't a necessity.

The worst possible outcome would be if they were caught in New York after they had finished the communication. If that happened, even if he survived, they'd lose their device to the Americans. They had been unsuccessful in countless attempts to duplicate the device. This was likely going to be his only chance to make first contact, and he was willing to risk it all.

The device had worked as expected in Seattle when Doctor Smith had the DARPA engineers run through all the tests they reasonably could without the appropriate connection with the alien contact on the other side. The information appeared to match the Omega and Delta files they had received from Tech-Com. He was feeling very confident they were ready for a successful connection in a few hours. The first failed attempt at Mount St. Helens had only been a temporary setback that wouldn't be repeated.

They had loaded up the device and the supporting team last night at Joint Base Lewis-McChord on to a scheduled Galaxy C5. It also carried a company of Rangers who were added for extra security in case there was an attempt to intercept the device en route. He and a few key members of his team had flown separately on a passenger jet that was reserved for senior government officials. Not only was it much more comfortable than sitting in the hold of the cargo plane for eight hours, but it allowed him to arrive in New York City in advance of the device and rest of the team.

They had taken over the north side of the 100th floor of the north tower of the World Trade Center. Based on their tests at the DARPA facility in Seattle, Doctor Smith knew the device functioned as well underground as it did above ground, but there were vacant spaces within the tower that they could secure easily without suspicion. Having extra power brought up from the utility channels had been completed over the weekend, so they only had to come in through the freight entrance and use the maintenance elevators on the night shift. He didn't plan to be here very long, assuming the connection was successful and brief.

The only downside was that he would have to be watching from a location in the other tower. He had been rewarded at Mount St. Helens for creating some distance between himself and the device, and he was going to set himself apart from the device again. He had secured a suite in WTC 2 on the 101st floor that allowed him direct visual and communication connection with the team that was operating the device. He expected that this operation would go smoothly, but the extra precaution would allow him another try if something went wrong. He'd see it happening and be able to evacuate before anyone realized there was a problem.

He had taken measures to make sure that all his superiors in the military and political structure had signed off on the potential plan. They didn't know that he had taken the liberty to alter some of the language in the original decrypted instructions. Where the language had specifically forbidden preemptive attacks, he removed the restriction. The changes he made gave him the latitude to initiate an attack at his discretion.

He knew Xi had a device and wouldn't hesitate to use it

against the United States as soon as he had the opportunity. He had assumed the Chinese instructions also forbid them from making a preemptive attack, but he didn't believe Xi would honor those instructions. And therefore, he didn't intend to honor them either. He was nicknamed "Master of War" for a reason.

The approved plan of communication after initiating contact was to request intervention in attacking the Chinese capital to forestall their aggressive maneuvers around Taiwan. Doctor Smith had made certain that there was plenty of real and fabricated evidence to support his assertion. There had been enough saber rattling by the Chinese over the last couple decades that it was deemed imminent. It looked like the US was trying to avoid a global conflict without a direct attack. Add in the potential for nuclear escalation, and he was certain he had a believable case that wouldn't veer too far from the given instructions. It would be a terrible disaster for the Chinese people, but in the end there would likely be less loss of life than if a real invasion of Taiwan were to occur. Not to mention that the Chinese Communist Party would be crippled as a world power for at least a decade.

The only fly in the ointment had been at TechCom. First there had been the mole feeding information to Xi. The spy had been extremely crafty in avoiding detection. Initially, he had suspected the person overseeing the Alpha file decryption. When it was rumored that he'd been killed by the Chinese, Smith had been convinced. Then the communication had continued after his death, eliminating that theory.

Li Jing had finally tracked down the mole relaying the information to the Chinese, and it had turned out to be the Hermes project manager, Dale Phi. The irony was that he had also been using him as a source of information. The man had turned out to be a double spy and got caught in his own web. He'd met the fellow several times in meetings but had no remorse when Li Jing disclosed that she had killed him a few hours ago. It was good to have that door closed.

That only left one thread. Li Jing had discovered that Gabby Fisher, the project manager over the Delta file, had made a copy, and it wasn't for the Chinese. She had given it to another branch of the government. Li Jing didn't know who or what agency yet, but she was tracking it down. If everything went well in a few hours, it would be immaterial.

If there was a question of why they had been using altered directives, it could be messy. He had made certain to erase any evidence that he'd altered the instructions, but it would be best if there wasn't even a hint of suspicion about his pushing for a preemptive attack on China should a disaster occur in New York today.

After Miss Grey had hung up the phone with Maxx and Sammy, she had used the remaining resources in New York, Seattle, and Washington D.C. to try and locate Doctor Smith and the DARPA device. She also wanted to locate the Chinese device but wasn't confident that it was in the area. She was certain Smith would be here trying to push the aliens into striking China, so he had to be her priority.

She'd received the original Delta file from her team in Seattle within an hour of Maxx and Gabby handing it off. They had compared the original instruction file Gabby had downloaded from TechCom and the file that DARPA was using. The DARPA file did not match the original. She'd passed the information along to her contact with the Tacoma team, Mr. Green. His reaction was more guarded than she expected.

He had questioned whether it was certain which was the unaltered edition because of the presence of the mole at Tech-Com. There was considerable pushback from the technicians at

Tacoma about which one was the file that they were to be using in a couple hours if they needed to contact the aliens to circumvent DARPA. It also was questionable who had edited the DARPA file once it had been received. The effect of the confusion was that no one was certain which was the correct instruction file without rerunning the translation from the alien file. That was going to be another hour before it was ready, and they were cutting it very close to the deadline. But they also couldn't risk a mistake and having the aliens start an event in the middle of Manhattan.

Initially they had tried to find the leader of the Hermes project at TechCom, Dale, but they'd been unable to locate him. Both he and the leader from the processing center, Li Jing, had disappeared suddenly. They'd then had to scrape together a team to rerun the Delta file, and it was taking much too long. She knew Gabby was locked up by security at TechCom until she authorized her release, which could wait until later. The clock was ticking, and Gabby was safest there.

What she did know from the comparison was that the file obtained from Gabby had been very clear that any preemptive measures against an enemy were forbidden and would result in punitive action. That restriction was consistent with the historical lore Sammy had passed along, although he had also been convinced the instructions for each device differed, so it was possible there was more latitude than she imagined.

She was confident DARPA's version of the file allowed for a preemptive attack if there was certainty that the enemy was planning an attack that would result in an escalation into a much larger conflict. This definition aligned with the information DARPA had been sharing in Washington D.C. about an imminent attack on Taiwan using limited nuclear weapons.

Miss Grey realized she was in a very difficult position by intervening. If she shut down DARPA's attempt to communicate and a war in Taiwan did occur, or the Chinese initiated a preemptive attack, they would have missed the opportunity to stop it before it began with minimal loss of life. But if there wasn't going to be a war, DARPA would have started one unnecessarily. They had not been able to obtain a copy of the Chinese instructions or confirmation that they were able to communicate.

The Tacoma team had set up the original Omega device in WTC 2 on the 80th floor. It was an empty set of offices that had required some last-minute alterations to obtain the massive amounts of power that would be required to power up the device if it was necessary. This was only supposed to be an authorized backup if it was determined that DARPA was pushing for war and they could intervene in time to stop it.

She knew Doctor Smith was also in this tower. They'd identified him flying on an unregistered aircraft into JFK late last night. They hadn't been able to get any information about the plane, which meant it was probably CIA operated. He didn't have the device with him, but they had followed him to the World Trade Center. They assumed the device would be set up near his location, but they had been wrong and therefore still hadn't located it. If it was here in New York, it had to be near to their location to work, and they had done a thorough search of the towers and surrounding high rises.

If they hadn't located the device, and Smith refused to halt the sequence when he was ordered to stand down, there wasn't anything more they could do. In that case, it would be in the hands of the aliens to either fulfill Smith's request, ignore it, or send a catastrophic message that they had veered from the instructions. The least likely option, that the aliens ignored the request, would be their best-case scenario.

She had spoken with Mr. Green, and they were prepared to transmit if given the signal to proceed. They had decided not to communicate before DARPA started going off-script, or DARPA did not have a connection. Plan B was to tell Doctor Smith to stop, and if he didn't then to either shut down the device or cut off the power supply in the area. Then they would begin communicating as the rightful owner of the original device, representing the United States government. They all understood that an unsuccessful result would be perceived as sedition. They were convinced that was a better outcome than initiating an attack on China.

They had no idea how to determine if the Chinese began to communicate unless they saw a power spike somewhere in the area that wasn't attributed to DARPA. In that situation, they would attempt to shut off the power supply. Without knowing where the DARPA device was located, they were taking a risk to shut down their own device. It was a critical decision Mr. Green and Miss Grey would have to make at the time.

As the sun began to rise over the East Coast, she knew they were only a couple hours from beginning the power-up of the device. Based on the contact time of 8:30 ET this morning, they had planned to begin the initiation process for Omega. They had been told that DARPA had a similar timeframe. That left them only two hours to make sure Smith wasn't going to attempt to initiate a conflict. With the confirmation from TechCom that the original instructions did not match what DARPA was using, it was time for a crucial conversation.

Miss Grey walked briskly out of her office and waved over a cab. "Take me to the World Trade Center, Building Two. And here's an extra twenty if you can get me there in under fifteen minutes."

Ready or not, here I come, Doctor Smith.

TRUTH AND HONESTY

When she pushed the elevator button for the 101st floor, the elevator didn't move, even after pushing the button several times. She tried the button for the 102nd floor, and it immediately began to rise, speeding past the floor she wanted to get off on.

She gave up pushing the buttons and stepped off to find a floor plan that showed where the stairs were. If the elevator was broken or, more likely, blocked from stopping on the floor that DARPA was occupying, then there was no point. If they'd seen her on the camera and had declined to give her access, it was intentional. She'd try to get in the old-fashioned way.

She found the stairwell and quickly descended to the floor below. She anticipated that the door might only open out to the stairwell to discourage someone from bypassing the front entrance. On the other hand, that seemed like a breach of the emergency exits, one the DARPA employees wouldn't tolerate with the potential risks they were anticipating. If something went wrong, they'd want access to every means of exit they could find.

When she reached the fire door out of the stairwell, she was relieved to find that the door handle worked. Slowly opening the door, she was able to see through the crack that the hallway was empty. Holding her breath, she walked into the vacant hallway and pulled the door quietly shut behind her. She assumed the layout was similar to the floor above and walked toward the elevator hoping there would be an indication of the suite that DARPA would be occupying.

When she got near the common area by the elevators, she could see that she was getting close because of the presence of armed security personnel who weren't wearing any identification except a badge with their picture and some unreadable information. No logos, lettering, or flags usually indicated that they were members of a clandestine intelligence agency that wanted to remain anonymous. Security was escorting people on and off the elevators, so they were working but had been restricted to Miss Grey.

She kept her badge out and walked toward them with her hands visible and held away from her body. When they saw her come around the corner, they immediately repositioned themselves between her and the office entrance on the other side of the lobby. They brought their hands toward their weapons, but no one unholstered. A large man with a handlebar mustache and a Yankees baseball cap moved quickly toward her.

Before she could get a word out, he said, "I'm sorry, ma'am. This is a restricted floor. You can't be here. Let me show you out."

She kept her badge visible, extending it toward him as she walked forward. "I'm Miss Grey assigned to the Department of Homeland Security. I'm looking for Doctor Smith and the DARPA team."

"First off, I've never heard of the Department of Homeland Security, although it has a nice ring to it. Secondly, I don't know what makes you think I know where Doctor Smith or DARPA are."

She offered him her badge and ID. "This will tell you more about DHS. There is a number at the FBI you can call if you have questions. And you can stop the fake ignorance about Smith and DARPA. I know he's on this floor this morning, and I need to talk to him about an urgent matter."

"Sounds impressive, but I suggest you give him a call first. I have firm instructions not to let anyone, and I mean anyone, on this floor who hasn't been cleared."

"Officer, Agent, or whatever your title is, I'm not leaving willingly until you contact Doctor Smith and let him know that I'm here and need to meet with him ASAP. Emphasis on soon."

He looked over his shoulder and handed her badge to a slightly smaller man, dressed similarly even down to the same baseball cap. "Bob, can you take this to the big cheese and tell him Miss Grey is very insistent on talking to Doctor Smith at DARPA. She's sure he's here, despite my firm denial."

Bob took her badge and ID and disappeared into the offices behind him. She leaned against the wall and looked at her watch, wondering how long this was going to take and if Smith would make this harder than it had already been. The man who had intercepted her kept her in his peripheral vision but generally ignored her while he kept the people moving on and off the elevator.

It didn't take Bob long to come back out of the office. He said something quietly to the man in charge and then took over for him as he walked over to Miss Grey.

"I was mistaken. There is a Doctor Smith here who seems to know you. He said it's your lucky day, and I'm supposed to escort you to his office for a chat."

"Indeed, my lucky day... A beautiful morning, isn't it?"

He grunted as he led her down the hall. She could see glimpses of the north tower through the windows as they went to one of the corner offices overlooking the other tower of the World Trade Center, Manhattan stretched out beyond it. He closed the door behind her, leaving her standing in front of Doctor Smith's desk.

Smith didn't bother to look up from the computer screen. He continued typing and scowling as he pointed toward a chair, indicating that she should take a seat.

Other than the million-dollar view, the other indication that she wasn't in a mid-level office buried in the basement of a government facility was the electronic equipment arranged by the window. The stack of equipment included scopes, flashing lights, and controllers. There was no indication of the equipment's purpose, but it was certainly busy monitoring something or somethings. It flashed, hummed, and made the occasional beeping sound, reminding her of the machines she'd seen attached to her dad in the intensive care unit at the hospital shortly before he died.

She sat in the chair and tapped her fingers on the arm rest, measuring the passing time without looking at her watch. It was a power move by Smith, and she wasn't going to give him the pleasure of getting aggravated by his inattention. He was intentionally showing her that she was entering his domain and that he had the upper hand. It wasn't going to work with her, as she had an ace in her hand.

After a few minutes of watching him type and ignore her, she started to hum a couple of her favorite Aretha Franklin songs. They might have been unconscious choices, but they certainly fit the circumstances. She doubted Doctor Smith would get the irony of her music selection, but it made her laugh inwardly. It may have even been a bit of an audible giggle, because he finally looked up from his computer screen with a glare.

"How odd that you came to visit me, Miss Grey. I thought I made it clear during our last chat that you were overstepping your authority and interfering with an extremely sensitive project of national security."

She smiled. "It's nice to see you again too, Doctor Smith. Yes, you did make that clear."

"Then why are you here?"

"I wanted to provide you with an update. Because of the critical nature of the timing, and since I was in the area, I thought you'd appreciate the conversation in person rather than an emailed report."

"Fine. Make it quick, as I have a deadline to meet."

"Ironically, the information is about your deadline. As you know, we've been working on tracking and stopping the Chinese interference at TechCom. During our analysis, we were able to determine that there was some manipulation done on the Delta file you received from them."

"How did you determine that it was manipulated?" he asked as he started to clean his eyeglasses.

"We were able to review and recreate the original file, and it didn't match the Delta file that DARPA is using to guide the interaction you have planned here today."

Smith stared at her for a long beat before responding. Despite his attempt not to show any overt reaction, she could see the anger in his eyes with his glasses off.

"I am not going to engage with you on the topic of why I'm here and the project that I'm working on. That is a highly compartmentalized, top secret matter that is beyond your purview."

"That may be true to some degree, but my main point remains that you are utilizing a file that has been compromised. I'm presuming it was due to the efforts of the Chinese, but it could possibly be the work of someone else."

"Why would the Chinese or anyone else modify the contents of the Delta file?"

"I can think of two potential reasons for the changes. The first is if someone wants to engage in behavior that is not allowed by the protocols. It would look like they have been given that leeway by the aliens," she said.

"I think you are grasping at straws, Miss Grey. You are assuming intentions that are beyond your scope. Why don't you give me the two versions and I'll review them and make my own conclusions?"

She handed him a copy of a USB flash drive that contained the two versions of the file.

"As you'll see, they are verified to be authentic versions, and I've taken the liberty to highlight the sections that have been altered. It's evident that the version DARPA has allows a preemptive attack on verified enemies. The original forbids that kind of action."

"I have verified that the DARPA file is the correct version, so I think we're fine. Whatever you have from TechCom must be corrupted, therefore there is no risk."

Doctor Smith stood up from his chair as if he intended to dismiss her. "Thank you for bringing this to my attention, but it appears to me that the Chinese mole removed the language from the TechCom file so that they would be able to initiate an attack without any concern of repercussions on the behalf of the United States."

Miss Grey stayed seated. "We both know there are severe consequences if the communication with the extraterrestrials varies from the prescribed protocols that were supplied with the Omega device. If DARPA has a file that has different instructions, then it will result in a cataclysmic event here in New York."

He sat back down. "I don't think that's a fact. The Delta file is intended as general communication guidelines and not a one-to-one match with each device. We now know that what happened at Mount St. Helens was a result of us attempting to communicate with Omega at the wrong time in the right place, based on a mistranslation of the Alpha file. Due to our improved ability to decipher the revised file, we know this is the correct time and location. We've tested this device multiple times without any negative effects. Where did you get this information?"

"From a reliable source that links various events with improper use of these Omega devices," she explained while he lowered his eyes at her.

"Miss Grey, there is only one device under the control of the United States that I am certain of, and I watched it disappear into a volcano decades ago. The current device has never been used in a live environment with the aliens, so there is nothing to support your outrageous claim."

Smith picked up the phone on the desk and pushed some buttons. "Bob, can you please come to my office and escort my guest back to the lobby? We are done speaking."

He hung up the phone, and said, "After I finish with this test this morning, I'm going to make it a priority to find out who you really work for, Miss Grey."

"I work for the DHS. You know that already."

"I know that's what your official badge says," he answered. "I've been made aware that you are also working for another agency trying to undermine this project, despite it being sanctioned by the president himself. Whoever you work for wants to derail this effort, and I will find out who is behind it and why."

It was her turn to act surprised. They thought they'd been able to maneuver around DARPA and whatever intelligence agencies they were using, but the Tacoma team hadn't been as discreet as they'd hoped. "Let's see how this progresses today, and I think a lot of people will be asking questions about who knew what and when."

Smith shook his head.

"I've had the FBI trying to determine who has been trying to undermine this project for the last year. Your name keeps showing up as a person of interest, so I am going to begin with you. The fact that you showed up here this morning in an attempt to accuse me of falsifying information is evidence that you are working against me, not with me."

"I'm representing the interests of the United States and to a degree everyone on this planet. I am only intervening to make sure the truth is underpinning this effort and isn't being used to address personal vendettas or facilitate a misguided military action with China."

There was a solid knock on the door, and Bob stuck his head in. "Are you ready to go, ma'am?"

Miss Grey picked up her badge and identification off Smith's desk. "Yes, I've said all I need to say. He thinks he can manipulate this his way, and I don't want to be around when he finds out he's wrong."

Doctor Smith put his glasses back on and focused on the computer screen. "One last thing, Miss Grey," he said as she was closing the office door behind her. "Dale Phi was the Chinese spy at TechCom. It's a shame you didn't do your job and catch him."

"How do you know that?" she asked. "Dale and another employee disappeared from TechCom a couple of hours ago, and the FBI and Seattle police are still searching for them."

"Ah, I never thought you were competent enough to find the source of the leak, so the CIA had inserted another asset at TechCom to watch him. After we were done with him, he was removed from the project permanently."

"Removed how?"

"As a casualty, I'm afraid. I couldn't risk that he'd communicate any valuable information to the Chinese or whomever you're working with on the side. Loose lips and all of that..."

Bob began walking ahead of her down the hallway, indicating that she should follow. Her brief discussion with Doctor Smith confirmed her suspicion that he had no intention of altering his plan to attempt to use the Omega device he'd reconstructed to get the aliens to attack China preemptively. He had falsified the Delta file to convince the president and others. Regardless of the risk of it backfiring and creating a catastrophic event in New York, he was willing to move forward with his plan.

She had to convince Mr. Green and the Tacoma team that they needed to stop Doctor Smith before he brought down the wrath of Thunderbird on Manhattan.

KNOCK YOU OUT

Bob escorted Miss Grey down to the main lobby of WTC 2. He used his key to bypass her floor on the express ride down. She didn't bother asking him to stop and let her off, because she was reluctant to give Doctor Smith any indication that she and Team Tacoma were located in the same building. If he wasn't already aware that the original Omega device was ready to intervene, she didn't want to be the one to tell him.

As soon as she stepped off the elevator, she powered up her cell phone. There were texts from Maxx and several of her agents asking her to call about developments back in Seattle, but her priority now was to bring the Tacoma crew up to speed on her conversation with Smith and get some advice about how to address the situation. The likelihood of an imminent disaster had risen sharply if Doctor Smith was committed to using his version of the Delta file. Her stomach was doing flips.

Smith's path only had two potential outcomes. If he was successful in communicating with the aliens, he would be using them to make the first strike in a global conflict. If he was unsuccessful, then New York was only hours away from calamity. Both were terrible outcomes. The best path, but the most difficult, was to stop Smith from communicating at all.

Mr. Green answered on the second ring. He must have been expecting her call.

"I heard you went up to visit Doctor Smith. What did he say?"

"I told him we knew that the Delta file version he was using was incorrect. He denied it and said the original from TechCom was a fake planted by the Chinese mole. He's committed to proceeding with his current communication plan and assured me that the president had given him authorization."

Green sighed. "Yes, he does have authorization to attempt to convince the aliens to attack China to prevent an attack on Taiwan. But that sign-off is based on the authenticity of his edited version of the alien instructions in the Delta file."

"We have checked that file several times, and the DARPA version Smith is using is not correct. The other thing he told me is that he found the mole and had him killed to keep him from warning the Chinese. It also avoids the possibility that we can quickly provide counter evidence. The mole was Dale Phi."

"Isn't that convenient?" he growled. "It's going to be difficult to get the ear of anyone to stop Smith in the next hour. Without the president's approval, we aren't going to get DARPA to stand down."

"And I don't see us stopping him with an all-out assault. He has a large group of armed operators guarding him and the device, I presume. The real kicker is that he's aware there is a possibility the aliens will send a punishing attack on New York, but he's convinced they won't, so he will risk it all to proceed."

"I'm going to call the senator and see if she can get to the president right away. We thought this might be a possibility, so she'd made plans to be at the White House this morning for an early meeting. It's going to be a difficult conversation for her to explain all of the background in the next hour. Then the president will have to call Doctor Smith in time to shut the device down before the 8:30 start. It's going to be really tight. I'll call you back as soon as I hear anything."

After Mr. Green ended the call, Miss Grey dialed Maxx. It was a little after four in the morning in Seattle, and she figured Maxx would be asleep, but she was hoping not.

To her surprise, Maxx immediately picked up the call and cut to the topic he was most interested in discussing. "Have you heard from Gabby?"

"Good morning to you too," she said as she watched the early morning sun gleaming off the windows of the Manhattan high rises. "She's being detained in the security holding room at TechCom. It's the safest place for her until we track down Haoyu."

"Do you think he knows where she is already?"

"Yes, most likely. We found out that Dale was the Chinese mole, and he was killed at the request of DARPA, but he talked to Gabby before leaving the building. I would assume that Dale contacted Haoyu before he was killed."

Maxx went quiet on the line for a moment. "If Haoyu knows that, then he is probably waiting for her to exit. And since he thinks he killed me on the ferry, he won't hesitate to make a move in the open."

"That's what I'd presume," Grey agreed.

"I'm sitting outside TechCom across the street from her office."

"I wouldn't take any risks at this point, Maxx. He's going to be desperate. Wait for this morning's events to be over, then I can send a specialized team to Seattle to focus on finding and removing him."

Maxx scoffed, seeming to enjoy it.

"Nah, this is personal. He tried to kill me three times in the last week, he killed Glen's boy, and now he's after Gabby. Not to mention he made me swim in the ocean at night with sharks. It's time for payback."

She snorted. "You're a weird guy, Maxx. Watch your back."

She put her cell phone back into her pocket and walked across the street to a bodega to grab a cup of coffee while she waited for Mr. Green to call her back. It was likely going to be a while before she heard from him, and there was no point in trekking back up to the Tacoma office.

It was clear to her what needed to be done about Doctor Smith, but it wasn't her decision to make. This would have to be sorted out in the White House. She'd done more than she'd been asked in tracking down the Chinese spy at TechCom and keeping Haoyu away from DARPA and their Omega device. What she hadn't anticipated was that the original Omega device was still available and that Doctor Smith had his own personal and political agenda.

If Maxx was able to stop Haoyu, that only left her with the questions surrounding the Chinese device. Was it here in New York? Did Xi know about the DARPA plans to communicate with the aliens, and what did Xi plan to communicate? It seemed to her that she'd not get any insight into the Chinese plans, so her primary objective was still finding them if they were here. A very big if, considering it was a tiny needle in the haystack of New York City.

She fell deep in thought, reviewing the events of the last week and wondering what tomorrow would bring after this morning's events. It could change the course of the country and probably the world. Would she remain an unknown participant that had helped or hurt in the end? Would she even be alive to see any of it? Taking long, slow sips of the coffee, she tried not to get overwhelmed with all the possibilities. The one thing she was sure of was that she had done the best she could with the information she had. The rest of it was out of her hands.

Her phone vibrated. It was from Mr. Green, which was

surprising. She hadn't expected him to get an answer that quick, which probably meant the answer was not to intervene.

"I don't have any answer for you about how we're going to proceed with Smith," he said.

"Then what's up?" she wondered out loud.

"We have eyes on the Chinese. We've been reviewing any video we could get from security cameras around the World Trade Center in the last week. No luck, but some old-fashioned detective work from NYPD gave us a break."

"What did they see?"

"They spotted some muscle with ties to the local Chinese gangs. The odd thing was they were wearing uniforms from an elevator maintenance company that does installation and repairs in this area. These guys have never done an honest day's work in their lives. We looked into the company they were working for, and they are permitted for an installation in Building 7 this week."

"Did anyone make contact with them yet?"

"No, we didn't want to alert them that we were close, but we pulled up all the video from Building 7 over the last week and watched them bring in a bunch of new equipment over the weekend and store it in a secure area of the basement. Working backward from there, we could trace the equipment back to the port and the ship they brought it in on."

"You're certain it's the Chinese device?"

"I wasn't sure until a senior analyst from the CIA assured us that the lead person is Xi from COSTIND. He's Doctor Smith's archrival and has been leading their program related to their version of the Omega device. There is only one reason he'd be here in New York. He is persona non grata in the United States and is risking a huge international incident by being here."

"What's the plan to intervene? Are we trying to make sure they don't use their device or secure their device and detain Xi?"

"If we try to arrest Xi, that would lead to a shootout. There is no way he'd come with us alive. He's smart enough to know he'd never be seen again once the CIA got their hands on him. He'd be flown to some black site outside the country and interrogated for the rest of his miserable life."

"Then I'm confused why you're telling me this. My job at DHS was to stop Xi and his henchman Haoyu, and if I'm not going to do that, then I can't help."

"Let the FBI worry about collecting him. Our objective, which they don't know about, is the implications of him using the Omega device. The best-case scenario is that he contacts the extraterrestrials but doesn't create a conflict when we also contact them. Worst case? He triggers a war or causes an earthquake in the middle of New York City. I don't see a lot of upside in letting him try to make contact."

"And how do you propose I stop him without directly confronting him?"

"Cut off the power that he'll need for the device. We know it takes a tremendous amount of energy to work. Shut down power that he's drawing, and he'll be sitting there with a big, black, metal cube that doesn't work."

She stood up and started hustling toward Building 7. "I'm on my way over there now. Make sure the FBI doesn't get trigger happy while I'm trying to figure this out. If Xi gets a whiff of something going down before his Omega device is offline, he'll disappear."

When Miss Grey strode into the lobby of 7 World Trade Center, she went immediately to the security desk and asked for a supervisor. She realized why they had overlooked the building when looking for signs of a Chinese presence. The building was part of the campus, but it was across Vesey Street and right next to the federal building. That took some gall to set up an illegal operation right next door to the FBI.

Showing her badge, she told the security supervisor that

there was information from an intelligence agency that there were some elements of an international crime ring present in the building. She didn't have time to get a warrant, as there were unconfirmed rumors that they were planning an event in the next hour. When security balked at giving her access, she asked for the building manager, saying it could be a matter of national security.

The building manager showed up five minutes later, disheveled and short of breath like he'd climbed multiple flights of stairs in a rush. He was holding a two-way radio in one hand and trying to straighten his hard hat with the other. He had a plaid shirt under his bright-yellow vest and a name tag identifying him as Tom.

"What's the problem here?" he said while trying to catch his breath.

She showed her badge again and repeated what she'd told the security supervisor. "I'm going to tell you more than I should, but we have credible intelligence that there is likely to be an attack initiated inside the building using a very powerful weapon. You don't have time to evacuate the building, and giving them a warning could result in them moving the time-frame forward."

Tom rubbed his temples. "Where is this weapon located in the building?"

"It's in the basement. My understanding is that it's in a secured area dedicated to elevator maintenance."

"Yeah, I know where that is. It's on the bottom floor. The contractor has been working on that project for the last week."

"That's the group we're looking for. This device that they're setting up requires a tremendous amount of energy to operate. Is there any way we can see what the power situation is to that area?"

The security supervisor looked over at Tom and raised an eyebrow. "The contractor got permission from engineering to reroute the backup electrical line from the generators to that area in case of a power outage. Apparently they couldn't afford to have elevators down during an emergency."

"Are the generators online now?" she asked.

Tom looked at the computer terminal on his desk. "Nope, they're on standby though."

"If there is a way to shut down all the power to that area, their device essentially becomes a huge paperweight with no way activate it. That would then give us a chance to get some people here to keep them isolated and evacuate the building if things get ugly."

After Tom thought for a moment, he nodded. "Sounds like the best we can do under the circumstances."

"Is there any way to see into that room with the cameras?" she asked.

"No, there are no security cameras in that area, only in the hallways," the security supervisor said.

"Let me get an engineering team on the line and figure out how to isolate power to that area, even from the backup generators."

"It has to be done remotely too," she said. "They are armed and definitely dangerous. An FBI SWAT team is on their way and will be here in thirty minutes. But if we can cut the power quickly and completely before then, we should do it."

Tom picked up the phone and started giving orders.

Xi had gotten a call from one of his spotters watching the tunnels. There was an FBI team organizing outside Building 7. One of the US intelligence agencies must have finally been able to track them to this location. He assumed they would know why they were here and try to stop him from using the communication device in about an hour. He had to hold on that long.

He'd arranged for the power to be drawn from the emergency generators when they came on if the main power was shut off. Hopefully they wouldn't figure his plan B before he had a chance to use the device. He'd also put armed agents at various entry points to hold the Americans back if they tried a frontal assault. They didn't have to hold them off forever, only long enough for him to communicate his message. In fact, an attack might even add credibility to his message.

He'd had a plan to get the device evacuated from the building if they had the opportunity, but that didn't look like it was going to be feasible. They'd be surrounded by then, and getting it into the van and out through the tunnel ports would take more than luck. A diversion would have to distract the FBI so his team could exit during the chaos.

He had no intention of getting trapped in New York and no illusions what would happen to him if they caught him here. He was irritated that they had found him so close to his moment of glory, but he wasn't going down without a fight. They called him the master of war for a reason.

HANDS OF LOVE

The running had been the worst part. There was some irony to being in this position, because it was not how he had been used to living his life. Growing up, playing sports, and serving in the military, his approach had always been to go on the offensive. Even in his business, it was Maxx's job to take the initiative and take out the bad guys. He never waited for them to come to him. Taking the offensive was as much a part of his personality as breathing.

This last week had taken him by surprise. A situation he didn't understand brought him a violent, prepared enemy he hadn't expected. So he'd taken a more passive approach. The biggest concern was the implications for Gabby. If it had only been him caught in the middle, he would have gone full steam ahead. But from the beginning, Miss Grey had made it clear that Gabby was at risk too.

It had been frustrating, which made him want to kit up and go hunting for Haoyu regardless of the consequences. He hadn't done that of course, because it would have left Gabby exposed. He couldn't live with himself if she was hurt or killed while he was out hunting Haoyu.

So he had waited for the right moment to strike.

That moment was now. Haoyu had to believe Maxx was dead after the incident on the ferry. There would be no way he would know how Maxx survived that wreck. He even had a hard time believing he'd gotten out of that situation alive. Then getting back to Seattle quickly and without being spotted by using the tunnel under Puget Sound meant he hadn't been tracked.

Haoyu would think that Gabby was at TechCom by herself, and with time running out he would take the initiative. He'd shown that was his preferred approach since he'd attacked Maxx back at the bar a week ago. That had been Haoyu's first big error; he'd badly underestimated his target and made Maxx an active participant in his own undoing.

When Maxx had finished the call with Miss Grey, he was certain what Haoyu would do in this circumstance. He was going to rectify the oversight and make Gabby pay for the problems she and Maxx had caused him. Call it professional pride or arrogance, but it was a loose thread he couldn't ignore. And with no time left to waste, he would take aggressive action, regardless of the risk.

He knew Haoyu had plenty of muscle in the city, so he expected they'd show up in force soon enough. Trying to warn security at the TechCom building would be pointless. They were already on high alert, and a warning call would only cause them to focus their search on finding him instead of reacting to whatever was coming.

He could call his friends at Seattle PD or ask Miss Grey to send some federal agents, but they wouldn't get here in time even if they took his suspicions seriously. And they were more likely to ask questions than provide help. This was going to be on him to take the initiative all by himself when they showed up. He had a loaded gun and the element of surprise – much better odds than he'd faced in many fights.

His finger was figuratively on the trigger, and he had been itching to pull it all night long. All he needed now was a target.

He heard them coming from a block away. There were several cars and what sounded like a truck engine in low gear. That would be the smart way to come to the facility if they weren't too concerned about getting back out again. Lead with a heavy truck, take out the front gate, go full speed into the lobby, then follow on foot into the building with the foot soldiers riding in the vehicles behind it. It would shock the security team. Even if they were well trained, they'd be unprepared for a brutal assault of that scale.

Maxx crept out of the shadows and crossed the empty street. He wanted to be moving under cover in the visitor parking lot when the vehicles came barreling up the main driveway. The Chinese team would be focusing all eyes forward and not watching for movement among the cars that weren't directly in front of them.

He took his pistol out of the holster and made sure there was a round in the chamber and the safety was off. He had ten rounds in the pistol now and two spare magazines with another eight rounds each. He always carried hollow points in his 1911. Even if they had ballistic vests on, a direct hit would knock them down and out for a while. But he'd be shooting for the bodies below the vest if he could and a head shot if he had to. He couldn't afford to waste too much ammo until he could get close enough to pick up one of their rifles. If his previous experience was an indicator, soon enough there would be an abundance of guns lying on the ground.

The cement truck took the corner a little fast, and he could hear it groaning as the load shifted. But the driver was careful enough that he didn't tip over before he was able to adjust for the turn. It would be a tight angle to the security gate, but the driver seemed to have a handle on it. The truck started accelerating after the corner and aiming for the gate as soon as it was heading straight.

Following closely behind the truck were three full-size SUVs. Maxx guessed they would each have at least four guys, all heavily armed and carrying automatic weapons if they had them. Possibly a few RPGs or LAWs if they had time to get loaded up. Add in the truck driver and someone riding shotgun in the truck cab, and he was looking at twelve to fourteen attackers.

If the guys Haoyu had with him were combat trained, the security guys in TechCom would be screwed. They might hold them off for a while, but by the time SPD SWAT arrived, it would be a hostage situation or a running battle moving out across town. Maxx would take a few of them because he'd be coming from behind, but no one in the lobby would survive. All he could hope for was that the local troops Haoyu had access to wouldn't have the training and communication to carry out a rapid, coordinated assault and then exit.

Out of the corner of his eye, as he ran at a steady pace for the entrance, he saw the cement truck take out the gate without even slowing down. The two security guards took a few shots with their handguns before running to get out of the way of the truck, which had swerved to take out the guard building. It was difficult to tell if their bullets even hit the truck. It didn't really matter. Unless they hit the driver, it was like shooting a pellet gun at a charging rhinoceros. Pointless.

The SUVs followed behind, avoiding the debris from the guard building. A couple of the passengers pointed their guns out their open windows and fired at the fleeing guards. Maxx watched as both were shot down. As he suspected, Haoyu's team didn't care about consequences and were going to kill anyone who got in their way. It was meant to be a punch in the nose for TechCom to punish them for intervening. And Gabby was their primary target now that they thought Maxx was already dead.

Maxx was about to emerge into the lighted area parallel to the circular drive when he heard the truck slamming on its brakes. It had been running through the gears seconds before and now completely locked up the brakes. That didn't make sense, as he expected that the truck would hit the glass and cement entrance at full speed to penetrate the building lobby and collapse the entry. Then he realized he was seeing something he and the truck driver had not anticipated. A series of vehicular pillars rose out of the ground ten feet in front of the building.

The pillars looked like reinforced concrete and metal about two feet square with two feet between them. They pushed out of the sidewalk, presumably using a hydraulic system. It only took a few seconds for the four-foot-high pillars to appear, seemingly as if by magic. It certainly was too fast for the truck to slow down before smashing into them at full speed.

The pillars were strong enough to disintegrate the engine compartment of the truck and lift the back end off the ground as the forward momentum was transferred to the cement in the back. The back end must have lifted several feet off the ground before it slammed back down. It was off the ground long enough and high enough that the SUV that had been immediately behind it was able to slide underneath before it slammed back down on top of the car.

That's got to hurt, Maxx thought, wincing.

Not only was the first SUV completely crushed under the cement truck, but the second SUV slammed into the rear end of the first SUV at almost full speed. The driver had made an attempt to stop but had merely slowed down enough to save the people in the backseat. The driver and whoever else was in the front were ejected through the windshield into the rear of the now-stationary cement truck.

The third vehicle was able to stop before hitting the truck. Three of the occupants immediately scrambled out and began advancing toward the entrance, firing as they went. Much more slowly, a couple of others exited from the rear of the second SUV and moved toward the other side of the truck. They were clearly dazed by the impact and completely focused on the entrance, so focused that they didn't notice Maxx walking up.

When they caught sight of the movement behind them, they tried to swing their weapons around. Neither were fast enough to get their guns pointed in his direction before he shot them point blank.

The three passengers on the other side of the truck were moving forward using the vehicular posts as cover to shoot at the entrance. Apparently, they hadn't known the glass was reinforced. It should have dawned on them when it barely spiderwebbed when it had been hit with parts from the violent truck crash. They kept firing on full auto as they switched out magazines, looking more and more confused about the lack of effect on the glass.

It hadn't dawned on them that they needed to try a new tactic when a TechCom security guard started sniping from the roof down on to the remaining gunners from Haoyu's assault team. Crouching behind the anti-vehicle barriers provided little protection from the person firing the rifle from the roof. Even if the bullets were not striking the men on the ground directly, they were ricocheting off the metal and concrete, creating a maelstrom of lead and fragments.

They couldn't retreat nor advance and were pinned down behind the only cover within yards. Their only choices were to surrender, retreat, or get next to the building for cover.

One of the men tried to make a dash for the only remaining SUV and was cut down before he made it three feet. Another man dashed forward to get next to the building below the windows, where he was out of sight and out of the view of the shooter on the roof.

While the two remaining Chinese attackers and the shooter on the roof continued to take shots at each other, Maxx crouched and ran for the open passenger door on the SUV. It was turned at an angle behind the cement truck so that it was not in the direct line of fire from the roof or the last of the Chinese shooters. He figured this was the best place to avoid getting hit by a stray bullet. He also wanted to make sure neither of the last two would be able to get back to the car and escape.

When he slid into the backseat of the car, he was startled to find Haoyu in the front seat. It looked like he was trying to move the unconscious or dead driver away so he could take the wheel. The driver was dead weight, and he couldn't get a good angle on moving him without climbing out of the car and putting himself in view of the TechCom roof. Haoyu was caught without a weapon and pinned between Maxx and the shooter on the roof.

Haoyu stared at Maxx like he was seeing a ghost.

"Well, well, well," Maxx said with a grin, "you underestimated me again. This is your third strike."

Haoyu's gaping stare curdled into an angry sneer.

"You have been the biggest pain in my ass since the bar. My biggest regret is that I didn't get to kill you and your girlfriend."

"And now you won't get another chance."

"Is this the part where you tell me I'm under arrest and read my rights?"

Maxx laughed. "You think I work for the US government or the police?"

"Don't you work with Miss Grey? Why else have you been involved in this business?"

"Because you killed my friend, tried to kill me, and were

coming here to kill my girlfriend. I don't care about your rights. Your sad story ends tonight."

"Not really, because I will win. Even though I am not with Xi, he will eventually win, and America will lose. You may have stopped me, but you will lose when Xi makes contact with the others."

"I wouldn't count on that chicken hatching yet. This affair has been going on for longer than any of us realize, and it won't be over today whether you or one of the other devices make contact"

"What do you mean, other devices?"

"You don't know, do you? There are many of these devices and have been for many thousands of years. You have been playing a game you didn't even understand."

"You are smarter than your girlfriend gave you credit for. She underestimated you too, it seems."

"My girlfriend?" Maxx asked with a growl.

"Not the one inside," he said as he pointed toward the building. "I would kill her. She was annoying and loyal to you for some reason. I meant your other girlfriend. Natalie."

"What about her?"

"She set both of us up, it seems. I thought she was trying to get back at you by sending you to me. But maybe it was to see which of us would win. She's a crazy lady who must have really loved you to make you die for her."

"We have that in common, Haoyu. She tried to ruin both of us. She screwed me over, but she is going to cost you your life. Would you like me to tell her anything the next time I see her?"

"Yes, tell her I have a present for her. Something to always remember me by." He smiled an evil smile as he closed his eyes.

"I will do that," Maxx said as he pulled the trigger three times. Once would have been plenty to kill Haoyu at this range with his .45, but he wanted one bullet for Scott, one for Gabby, and one bullet from him, making sure the devil got his due.

He climbed out of the SUV and started walking back through the parking lot toward the street. He could hear the last man from Haoyu's team surrendering to the men from TechCom, who came outside with guns drawn. Even though his ears were still ringing from the three shots he had fired inside the SUV, Maxx could hear sirens in the distance. He wanted to be far away by the time the police, the FBI, or anyone else with a gun showed up.

He could see some light in the eastern sky as he began the long walk home. When he was a few blocks away and gliding safely in the shadows, he took out his phone and texted Miss Grey.

"The Chinese knight and all the pawns are off the board. My queen is safe. Good luck."

COME AS YOU ARE

At exactly 8:00 a.m. ET, Xi gave the engineers preparing his device the command to switch on the power from the backup generators at Building 7. According to the manufacturer instructions and his engineers, it would take at least five minutes for them to generate enough electricity to be switched over to his device. Based on the many tests they had run, it would take about fifteen minutes for the device to be cycled on and ready for communication.

As soon as the generators were turned on, the building employees would know there was something unauthorized going on. He was counting on them to try to consult each other and get approval before trying to retake control and shut them down. His team had rerouted as many of the overrides as possible without creating suspicion in advance. It wasn't a foolproof plan, but it was the best they had been able to do with the little time they had to prepare. He hoped he would have at least twenty minutes uninterrupted once the power sequence began.

He'd also taken precaution to place some of his men in locations that would slow the employees. And they'd also help to distract the FBI if they tried to make an assault before they were done with the communication with the aliens. And for one last safety measure, he'd prepared for a last-minute distraction to hold them at bay.

Xi had no illusions that they'd be able to hold the Americans off for very long. That was a sacrifice he was willing to make, even if it did cost him men and the device. The most important thing to accomplish was the initial communication. Safe exit for the device was his secondary priority. The men were all expendable and had viewed this as a potential suicide mission from the very start.

He was closely monitoring the start of the generators as they spun to life. He started his stopwatch when he saw the first light go green on his dashboard. His engineers in the room confirmed that the huge generators were building up to operating levels. The first step had begun without incident. He felt a sudden rush of excitement as he recalled how difficult the journey had been to get here again after his first attempt at Tangshan.

When his stopwatch read 5:05, he checked the monitoring equipment to determine that the generators were running at peak and would be ready to take on the electrical load required to begin to power the device. Two of the three generators were at peak, but the third generator was not reaching the proper capacity and seemed to have stopped short. He called the generator room, and they confirmed what he was seeing. He told them to wait another minute. If the third generator was still not at peak, they needed to increase the power to the first two generators in order to make up the shortfall.

He knew that the excess power would still be in the appropriate range, although it would be cutting it close. After waiting, the instruments for the third generator begin to show a slow increase again. When the gauge showed green, he breathed a sigh of relief. It had only cost them an extra minute, but they were back on schedule. He gave them the order to begin to divert the power to the device now.

He reset his stopwatch, knowing it would take time before the engineers gave the signal that it was ready. There were no remote methods to monitor the condition of the device, so he was dependent on the men who were in room with it to give him routine status reports based on their observations.

When his stopwatch indicated he was only six minutes into the device power up, he received a call from the men in the generator room. There had been several failed attempts to enter the room by the building employees. Despite using fire axes and battering rams, they had not been able to get past the barricade that Xi's men had created at the outer door.

"You must keep them out, no matter what it takes," he snarled at the soldier that had answered the radio.

"We are saving most of our ammunition until we can see them, so we are having trouble holding the doors."

"You fool, it is too risky to use your guns now. If you damage one of the power generators, the power sequence will abort early and defeat the entire operation."

"Without our guns, we will be fighting with axes and knives," the soldier tried to shout over the sound of chaos.

"I don't care if you are stacking your bodies in piles to slow them down, do not use the weapons until I tell you. Do you understand me?"

"Yes, yes, I understand," the radio squelched as it cut out. He could hear a lot of yelling in English, so he presumed they were still in control of the generators.

Xi slammed his fist into the wall. This was going to slow.

He was closely watching his stopwatch to see when he might be getting a signal from the device team that it was powered up and ready to begin the final sequence. He didn't want to keep asking them about the status, afraid it might make them tell him it was ready prematurely.

As Xi was getting hopeful that they would be successful in getting the device ready to use, he heard yelling from the radio in the device room. At first, he thought the Americans had also found the location of the device and were storming that location in addition to the generator room. But then it became clear the power between the generator room and the device room had been stopped. There was no more power flowing to the device. The project was dead without power.

Xi took a breath and moved to plan B.

He called the radio on the single frequency that was monitored by both the teams in the device and power rooms. "I need you to continue to hold the enemy as long as possible, and you are free to use weapons now. Since our primary plan has failed, I will use the explosives to distract them so you can withdraw."

The soldier in the power room answered, "I don't know that we can escape. We are trapped in here."

"Then you are to keep the Americans engaged until the last possible moment. The team in the device room will exit using the vans in the tunnels that lead to the port. Get to the port with the device within the hour, and they will get you to the transport ship waiting in international waters."

"What if we take longer than an hour to get to the port?" the man on the radio in the device room asked.

Xi angrily pushed the talk button on the radio while wondering how he had been assigned a team of fools for this project.

"If you aren't on the ship by noon, it will sail without you. And if you don't have the device with you, don't bother coming back." He turned off the radio and smashed it to pieces with the butt of his pistol.

When Xi finished the radio conversation, he walked out of the air terminal building and climbed into the waiting helicopter. It had already been cleared for a flight to the transport ship waiting off the coast. He wanted to be in international waters as quickly as possible, and the helicopter would be his fastest route clear of Manhattan.

The helicopter door slammed shut as he put on his headset. As instructed, the pilot wasted no time getting airborne and making a direct route for the coast. It was a beautiful morning, and Xi was disappointed that despite all the planning, they would not be making contact with the aliens today.

He made his final call back to the city and told his contact to call the fire department that covered the World Trade Center district. They would tell the NYFD there were bombs in Building 7 and that they had better evacuate before he started detonating them. After he heard from his men that they were clear or that the Americans had captured his device, then they would bring down the building and any evidence left behind. With a tight smile, he waved goodbye to New York and El Herrero, who he knew was somewhere nearby.

We shall see who is the true master of war.

Doctor Smith stared at his phone. It had been ringing on and off for the last several minutes, and he had refused to answer it. He recognized the number of Andy Card's cell phone. Andy was President Bush's chief of staff, and he had kept it in his contacts when they had been in discussions about how to handle the initial conversations with the aliens. He'd first had to convince him that pushing for a preemptive attack on China was the best option. Andy had been extremely skeptical about the entire plan, and until he was convinced of the strategic value, Smith wouldn't even get an audience with the president.

When Andy didn't leave a voicemail, Doctor Smith had a bad feeling about the call. He'd initially thought the president was calling him for some words of encouragement or a last-minute pep talk. But after the call had ended and then restarted the second and third time, he decided to ignore it and proceed with the plan everyone had signed off on. Technically he was told to get last-minute clearance to make sure there were no late breaking developments, but he'd always planned to conveniently forget that step. He'd come too far to walk away at the last minute because of some politician's crisis of conscience.

He was watching the monitor screen and got the signal that the device was powered up and going through the initialization sequence. Through the telescope in his office, he could see clearly into the windows of the other tower. Everyone seemed focused on their tasks, and the initial sequence appeared to be going smoothly. He had a good feeling and wasn't going to let a minor glitch derail this at the last minute.

He heard a knock on the door. He ignored it until he heard his assistant nervously call out, "Doctor Smith, your door's locked. Are you okay?"

"I'm fine, Charles, but very busy. That's why I locked the door. What do you want?"

"Doctor, the office of the president is trying to reach you. They said your phone is not working."

Damn it, they aren't going to make this easy.

"Thank you, looks like I had my phone muted. I will check it."

He sighed and pressed the button to answer his cell phone. "Hello, this is Doctor Smith."

Andy picked up on the other end and said with a note of exasperation, "Doctor, I'm glad I was finally able to contact you. I spoke with the president. We have learned Xi is in New York with the Chinese Omega device. Local agents were able to intercede at the last moment and abort their attempt to contact the aliens."

"That's fantastic news," Doctor Smith exclaimed. He breathed a sigh of relief.

"It certainly is. The president asked me to call you and tell you to stand down for now. Since the pressure is off on the timing, he wants to take some time and reconsider our strategic options. He feels that our greater concern is the terrorist threat in the Middle East. Accelerating a confrontation with China now would create too much of a drain on the military."

Doctor Smith sat in stunned silence.

Andy waited and then asked, "Doctor, are you still there? I need you to take the device offline."

Finally, he answered. "Yes, that's great news, Andy. I agree with the president. I'll give the command to shut everything down."

"Fantastic. I'm glad I caught you before it was too late. Give me call when you're back at a DARPA facility, and we'll schedule a session to talk through the options."

Andy hung up, leaving Doctor Smith reeling from what he'd heard. It didn't take him long to decide on a course of action. There was no way he was going to stop now regardless of what he was told. He was less than thirty minutes from initial contact and was not going to tell his men to stand down.

He shut off his cell phone and dialed the device team in the other tower using a secure, direct line.

"Mike, it's Doctor Smith, and we have an urgent issue. I heard from security that the Chinese are in your building and will try to stop you from activating the device."

He could hear Mike take a deep breath. "How did they figure out our location?" he stammered.

"I don't know how they discovered your location, but it's too late to find out now. Barricade the doors and under no circumstance let anyone into the device area, even if they claim to be security, police, or the FBI. Ignore any instructions unless they come directly from me. There have even been attempts by the Chinese to impersonate the president."

Mike sighed, "That explains a lot. I didn't want to bother you, but I had several calls from DARPA and the White House in the last hour. I've been too preoccupied to call them back. I thought it was strange that they were reaching out to me instead of you."

"Those calls sound exactly like the false attempts by the Chinese that I was warned about. Ignore them and proceed with the initialization as planned."

"Thanks for the heads up. We'll get it done," Mike said, ending the call.

He was trying to remain calm despite the distractions, knowing he'd need to be ready to address the extraterrestrials very soon. He'd deal later with the consequences of lying to Mike and ignoring the directive from the White House. By the time he had to face that conversation, he'd have started the ball rolling, and it would be too late for the president to walk it back. What was the president going to do, tell the aliens they'd changed their minds?

He was watching the device and could see it was powered up and ready to go live. It was 8:46, the time they had been told to begin contact. He removed his eye from the telescope and began to type in the initial message, as he had decades before at Mount St. Helens.

As he was preparing to press the "send" button, he saw a streak in the sky coming into his peripheral vision. It happened so quickly that it didn't register exactly what it was, either a flash of light or light reflecting off a metal object. But that realization was quickly replaced by the explosion and fireball that emanated from the area that had seconds before held the device. In less time than a heartbeat, the entire side of the building collapsed and was engulfed in flame.

He didn't know what he'd seen, but it was clear that either the device had exploded or something had hit the building. He'd have time later to figure out what had happened. For now, he grabbed his briefcase and headed for the elevators.

The team in the hallway was in shock as he rushed past

them. If they hadn't seen the explosion, they certainly saw the effect. They were shouting questions at him, and he had no answers. All he knew for sure was that he wanted to be far away from here by the time anyone came looking for him.

Mr. Green received a phone call from the senator shortly before 8:30 am. She had spoken to the president, and after laying out the concerns for him, he had agreed there more risks than he had been made aware, no thanks to Doctor Smith. When they had discovered Xi and the Chinese device were at Building 7, it had escalated the importance of quickly and boldly adjusting the plan. Apparently, Miss Grey had warned the building engineers on site in time to stop the initialization sequence and shut down the device. The FBI was in the middle of trying to arrest Xi's team and secure the device.

There were no good choices, but the senator had convinced the president to act quickly. The event that had finally moved him to act was initiated by Doctor Smith himself. The president's chief of staff had made multiple attempts to contact Smith, and it became obvious he was actively avoiding communication. When Andy had finally spoken with him on the phone and told him to terminate the operation, Doctor Smith agreed, but the FBI had intercepted Smith's communication with the DARPA engineers instructing them to ignore any directives from the White House and proceed as planned. The power sequence on the DARPA device continued unabated.

The senator instructed Mr. Green to proceed with contact at the appointed time, using the agreed-upon protocol. She told him there had been arrangement made directly within the military to stop the DARPA project if it appeared they were taking actions beyond their authority. The president, at the insistence of the senator, believed that the risk of a rogue element taking the initiative was too high not to have a contingency plan ready to be executed. After the Mount St. Helens disaster and the persistence of rumors in Washington, there was concern that Doctor Smith had a hidden agenda that would result in a conflict with the Chinese. The discovery of the alteration of the Delta file was the evidence that they needed to confirm it.

The Omega device engineers had powered up the device and were ready for contact at 8:46. They had given Mr. Green the final nod when there was a tremendous explosion in the north tower. No one had seen the cause, but the team assumed that the DARPA device had malfunctioned. There had been much speculation from the Tacoma team that this might happen if they were using improper protocols or the device had been defectively constructed. Mr. Green privately speculated that the explosion might have been caused by the "contingency plan" that the senator had mentioned earlier.

In any event, they now had a good idea where the DARPA device had been located. Mr. Green also knew Doctor Smith was stationed on the floor above him in WTC 2. Knowing Smith, he'd probably considered the possibility of a catastrophic event with the device and purposefully situated himself at a location where he could monitor the device and communication and yet escape the consequences of an adverse event.

Mr. Green was the designated lead for the initial contact with the aliens. He had been chosen through careful manipulation by the senator to oversee this critical part of the operation. He'd been with the senator from the beginning and been selected to lead the Tacoma team because he was one of the few people who understood the genuine implications. The senator would have preferred to make the first contact herself, but it would have raised to many questions about why she was chosen rather than the president. When the risks were clear, the politicians wanted a pawn in play. And Mr. Green was the senator's most trusted lieutenant.

He pressed the button on the device when he'd gotten the nod from the engineers. Immediately the button changed from yellow to green and began pulsing. None of the equipment monitoring the device and the surrounding area registered any changes in the dozens of scientific indicators that were being assessed. The only change they observed at first was the colored pulsing light on the console. It felt anticlimactic.

At 08:46:11 EDT, a signal was received by the Tacoma team's monitoring equipment at WTC 2. In English, Mandarin, and Spanish, the brief signal translated to "Proper Sequence. Contact Confirmed."

Immediately after the signal was received, the device took on a hyper state of activity. The lights in the room began shimmering on the smooth skin of the device, making it look as if was vibrating almost too fast for the eye to focus. But the floor and walls were still. It seemed as if all the energy in the room was being absorbed into the cube of iridescent metal. The metallic device that had been absorbing light only moments before seemed to be iridescent now. There was also a distinct odor in the air, like an electrical storm was heading toward them. It was similar to the smell of ozone preceding a summer thunderstorm. The atmosphere in the room felt like a combination of restoration and imminent danger.

Mr. Green ignored his sense of exposure and managed a quick, tight-lipped grin. He felt like shouting in surprise from the sudden change in atmosphere but didn't know if the device acted as both a microphone and speaker. He clapped his hand over his mouth, not wanting to create any misunderstanding with the aliens.

He took a moment to calm down and take a deep breath before speaking. As many times as he had imagined this moment, the fact that he was interacting with an alien species was overwhelming. It was hard to get his mind around the implications.

"I represent the people of the United States of America. We were instructed to contact you at this time and location." He'd practiced his opening lines in Spanish and Mandarin too but decided to speak in English first.

With barely any pause, a slightly distorted voice came from the device. "I represent the people of a galaxy you know as Thunderbird. Are you the leader of this people?"

He not only heard the voice but could see it reflected in the vibrating lights on the device. It was a surreal experience to hear, see, and feel the alien's communication.

Fighting off a wave of dizziness, he answered, "No, I am not the leader, only an emissary."

"We have sent a message to many of the contact devices on your planet. Your people have been the first ones to respond in a great number of your time cycles. We were beginning to suspect that your race was extinct and that we may need to reset your planet."

Mr. Green struggled to respond to that statement without sounding frantic. "There are still many, many people on this planet. We had difficulty understanding how your contact devices work. That knowledge was lost."

"We are a long distance away from your planet and cannot maintain contact easily, so we depend on you to initiate contact at the predetermined times and locations. Do you need assistance?"

He sat down on an office chair next to the monitoring equipment to catch his breath and focus. He was having difficulty thinking clearly enough to answer. *What assistance?* he wondered to himself.

"We are only contacting you as requested."

"Your planet was created as a distant watchtower for Thunderbird. Your people were placed there to watch for the return of our enemies."

"Then we definitely don't have a need for your assistance now," he stammered.

"If you don't know, you will soon. Our enemies have been detected by other watchtowers in your galaxy. We hoped to speak to your leader to prepare for their arrival."

"I apologize," he said as he gulped. "Our leader is not here at this time."

He could feel the sweat beginning to form on the back of his neck during a long pause. He wondered if they were communicating between themselves.

After a drawn out delay, they answered, "There is also another device that is active, but they didn't communicate as instructed. We need to communicate with the leaders of both peoples."

He didn't know if they were referring to DARPA or the Chinese device, but he'd figure that detail out later.

"I cannot speak for the other people, but our leader will be prepared to communicate with you next time."

There was another long pause by the aliens. Mr. Green detected a change in the lights on the device. The smell of electricity in the air grew stronger, and the hair on his arms stood up.

"We need to hear from both leaders. We will send instructions about future contact."

After the concluding message, the metal skin on the device stopped reflecting light, and the smell of electricity in the air wafted away, like the storm had passed. The room was silent and still. All of the energy and sound that the Omega device had been absorbing and reflecting seemed to dissipate in an instant.

No one in the room said a word until Mr. Green spoke. The

unbroken silence felt eerie after the overwhelming sensations a few moments ago.

"Send the video and audio directly to the senator. In the meantime, let's move the device out of here. The explosion at the north tower is going to cause a catastrophe in this area of the city. We want to be ready to move quickly."

Doctor Smith stood near the back of the elevator. It was filled by the time it had reached the middle floors, but people kept trying to climb on despite there being no room. They hadn't given any announcements to clear the building. In fact, the instructions were to remain in place. But people had seen and heard the explosions in the north tower and were frightened enough to exit despite the instructions to shelter in place.

He was anxious to get out of the building too. He had a better idea of what was happening than the rest of the elevator passengers did, but he wasn't going to speak up. He tried to remain as inconspicuous as possible. If the elevator got stopped on one of the upper floors, he would use the stairs. He'd memorized the exit options when he'd picked his command center, so he was as prepared as he could be given the fluid nature of events.

Despite his effort to mislead Miss Grey, Doctor Smith was aware of where the Tacoma crew had placed their device. It wasn't a secret that they could sustain long once he had placed some sources in the local FBI office. He knew it would be in this vicinity and the office he'd chosen had allowed him to monitor his device in the other tower and have easy access to the Omega device on the floor below.

The largest source of agitation in this process had been the inability to discover the location of the Omega device before arriving in New York. He'd known for years that his original device had survived the eruption at Mount St. Helens. At the time of the eruption, it had simply never occurred to him that the device was indestructible. It was a lack of imagination that had caused him untold anger through the years. By the time he'd learned that the original Chinese device had survived, someone with a great deal of money had already returned to Mount St. Helens and recovered his device.

He'd spent the better part of a decade searching for it with no success. He speculated that perhaps it was taken by the Chinese but had no evidence to support his theory. It wasn't until the last week that he became suspicious that there was more to Miss Grey's questions than mere curiosity. Her heavy-handed intervention had led him to the Omega unit and Mr. Green. From there, it was easy to follow their movements to this building.

When he had determined which suite the Omega device would be housed in, he'd had some of his team prepare explosives on the floors above and below them. He had anticipated they might try and terminate his communication with the aliens if they believed the conversation was becoming too risky. If that were to happen, he had planned to exit the building and detonate the explosives, thus stopping their device from operating. It would be the kind of revenge he'd been dreaming about for years. After all, he was the master of war.

What he hadn't considered was that his device would be destroyed before communication with the aliens had even begun. That oversight had delayed his exit from the building and consequently the detonation he'd planned. It had been tempting to set off the explosives immediately, but that would have trapped him in the building. It was better to exercise some restraint and get outside first. Unfortunately, that would leave time for them to communicate, but it was unavoidable unless he was willing to risk dying here today. And he would rather live to fight another day.

The elevator stopped on the ground floor, and he pushed his way out into the lobby. It was chaos with people trying to get out of the building, emergency personnel trying to enter, and the smoke from the fire next door making it difficult to see. He checked his location and decided to walk in the opposite direction, toward the park. He had a car parked in a garage several blocks away and had time to get clear of the area before the explosives above him increased the panic.

He looked at his watch as he exited the building. It was 9:00 a.m., and the three-minute timer started running. He picked up his pace and admired how he could still see patches of clear blue sky despite the smoke.

He smiled as he disappeared into the crowd. *This isn't going to be such a bad day after all.*

ONE LAST KISS

The two weeks following September 11th had been a series of nonstop debriefings and efforts to put together all the pieces of the puzzle to the full story of what had happened that morning and in the months leading up to the catastrophe in Manhattan.

Miss Grey went through a chain of what were a series of commendations then reprimands from her chain of command at DHS as the events were eventually sorted out. Initially she was praised for her quick action to stop Xi and the Chinese team from using their device. Then as her role in working with the Tacoma team to circumvent Doctor Smith was revealed, she was reprimanded. She had not only avoided telling her superiors but had also been actively undermining the work at DARPA. Their criticism was that if she had brought in the leadership at DHS, they would have intervened earlier and prevented the eventual confrontation.

Thankfully, the president had intervened on her behalf and told her leadership that she was confidentially acting under the direction of the senator and himself. It wasn't entirely true, but it was true enough that they couldn't press the issue without overtly challenging the White House. They kept the reasons for the commendation vague and presented it in a low-key ceremony. The circumstances around the Omega device and contact with the aliens were still considered a compartmentalized top secret that she could only discuss with a handful of people on a very short list, one that didn't include her boss.

She'd written up at full report for a presidential briefing and then watched while the report was destroyed after the reading. Everyone was not only covering their tracks but creating a plausible cover story to explain the events in New York, without mentioning aliens, the implication of China, and most importantly how the towers had really been destroyed.

Eventually an explanation that could be supported by the intelligence agencies was settled on and pushed out through the media. Everyone was looking for a scapegoat, and the recent terrorist activities in the Middle East became the easy target.

She had bouts of survivor's guilt that she had been the only person from the Tacoma unit in Manhattan who had survived. She was grateful Mr. Green had sent her to Building 7 to stop the Chinese. On one hand, she regretted that she hadn't been there for the final communication with the extraterrestrials using the Omega device. What an amazing experience that would have been. On the other hand, she knew the few people she had gotten to know from that team had all been killed. As far as anyone knew, they had been killed by the explosions that had presumably been triggered by Doctor Smith, although there was no direct evidence available once the tower had collapsed after the explosions. Due to the location of the explosives, it was only possible that they had been planted in advance and was not a result of any other event.

Some of the leadership at DARPA and in the military had tried to assign blame to the Chinese, but that was quickly ruled out. In review, it was evident that Doctor Smith had used a small team of operatives from the intelligence network to install the explosive devices. They had been trained for other potential bombings, so it was a minor redirect to assign them to the Omega location. What was not known was if Smith was able to detonate the devices before he escaped or if he was trapped with his team on the floors above. All security recordings from inside the building had been destroyed, and the smoke and crowds outside made it impossible to identify anyone.

They believed the Omega device remained buried in the rubble. It had survived the eruption of Mount St. Helens decades earlier, so they had every reason to believe it would survive the explosion, fire, and collapse of the tower. They'd been told that the devices were indestructible and were going test that premise. There was a specialty recovery unit on site that was looking for the device. It was a manual search, as it gave off no visible heat, radar, or metal signature.

There was no immediate need to excavate the device, since they had no instructions about plans for follow-up contact with the aliens. From the recording of the communication, the next communication would be on their schedule when the aliens made an updated Alpha file available. Without that file, they were missing a planned date, time, and location. Right now, it was more important to concentrate on the recovery efforts and avoid raising any suspicion. There were a lot of people and governments watching the site. Not everyone had accepted the official narrative, and there were already plenty of conspiracy theories springing up.

The DAPRA team was never in the public eye, and therefore with their sudden disappearance there were few if any questions about them. It was not uncommon for some of the more secretive teams to drop out of sight for months at a time with no notice. Some of the family members would be making inquiries soon, but they could put that communication off until it could be dealt with individually and within the scope of the nondisclosures that everyone on the team had already signed. Even if some were able to connect the dots to the events in New York, they wouldn't benefit by going public. Without knowing the nature of the project, it would appear to be a small part of the larger tragedy.

The only exception might be the sudden disappearance of Doctor Smith. He was certainly more of a public figure frequently seen on Capitol Hill. With all the surrounding activity, it would likely take a while before his absence was noticeable. The assumption would be made that he was working secretly on some developments related to the War on Terror. The government could let this open question sit with no comment until he was lost in the bigger story.

There was a special team from the FBI assigned to determine if Smith had died at the World Trade Center or had taken the opportunity to go into hiding for his involvement. But matching DNA samples was a long process and unlikely to be conclusive. The FBI had also placed discreet searches through the CIA and friendly foreign intelligence agencies. This was a very wide net that had to be cast without urgency so as not to raise any suspicions. It had been buried along with several other inquiries related to the events of 9/11 so that it didn't raise any immediate doubts.

The one item that had been determined quickly as part of the search process in the wreckage of the north tower was that the communication device DARPA had built to replicate the original Omega device had not survived. Despite building the device using the engineering specifications in the file supplied by the aliens, it had not been indestructible.

They had been able to locate the device fairly easily due to its unique signature on ground-penetrating radar. It was buried in a section of rubble that was accessible using cameras and was badly crushed. There had been speculation about whether this was caused by improper engineering or because the specifications were unique to each device and therefore not replicable. It also raised the question of what the effect would have been had DARPA tried to contact the aliens using the device. When they recovered the replica device, it was likely to be disposed of as an artifact of a grand, failed experiment. Many felt it was a fitting symbol of Doctor Smith's legacy.

Miss Grey had very little hope that they'd find Doctor Smith. She knew he'd been in the south tower, and when the north tower had collapsed, he would have quickly realized he was going to be held responsible for the failure. He'd vacated the building, detonating the explosives surrounding the Omega staff on his way out. His only option after that was to try and disappear, knowing that the US government would never stop looking for him. He could do that on his own, or in conjunction with another country that would have an interest in using him to lead a development team to compete with the US. China, Russia, North Korea, Iran… It was a short list of possibilities.

Based on the animosity between Smith and Xi, she didn't think China would be his first choice. With all the chaos at the World Trade Center, they'd determined that the Chinese team had somehow escaped. The FBI had penned them in the basement of Building 7 and once they had removed the power and made the device inoperable, they had paused to strategize their next move.

However, after the collapse of the twin towers, the order was given to evacuate Building 7, and most of the FBI agents were redeployed to other areas of the campus. The capture of the Chinese became low priority at that point and was not being monitored closely. Essentially, they had been forgotten in the turmoil. It was then that Xi had taken the opportunity to remove the device and exit the building. Where they went was still unknown, although it was presumed they returned to China to avoid capture.

The FBI determined in their after-action review that

Building 7 was destroyed by explosives that Xi had planted to facilitate their exit. When the building collapsed, the US believed the device was buried inside and attempted to recover it before they concluded it wasn't there. There was a lot of blame about how they had let Xi and the Chinese device slip through their fingers, but none of that blame landed on Miss Grey. She had stopped the communication between the Chinese and aliens from occurring, and the rest of the debacle at Building 7 fell on the shoulders of the FBI.

Miss Grey was happy to return to Seattle to close down the temporary office and tie up loose ends with the underground Tacoma facility, TechCom, and at DARPA. The close-knit team members at Tacoma were devastated by the loss of their colleagues in New York but excited to learn that the device had worked as planned. Those remaining at DARPA were reassigned to other projects, and all the data related to Project Poseidon and Project Hermes was secured and sent to another clandestine alphabet agency for review.

The people at TechCom were quickly repairing the exterior of the building after Hoayu's attack. Miss Grey told the local police what little she could, but most of her information was buried in the language of national security. It was blamed on a separate terrorist event under investigation. No comments were made publicly except to assure everyone that all the perpetrators had died due to the heroism of the TechCom security, SPD, and federal authorities working hand in hand.

Maxx, Gabby, Glen, Andres, and Joseph had been given some tickets together behind home plate at the Mariners game with the Anaheim Angels. This was the first game to be played after the tragedy of 9/11, and it was a bittersweet moment for everyone in the crowd. It had personal meaning for many, and for Maxx and Gabby that was especially true. It had been two weeks ago when they had been here with Scott and Glen and had been involved in the intrigue that led up to last week's tragic events.

The Suquamish tribe had given Joseph six tickets as a thank you for the extraordinary work he and Andres had done in helping the tribe recover the Thunderbird device from the shipwreck in Blakely Harbor. They'd been able to recover the device clandestinely and watched as the tribal elders had loaded it securely in the back of Sammy's pickup. He drove off with the device toward the Olympic Mountains. They were curious about where they were taking the device but also confident it would be used wisely.

Maxx signaled to the vendors walking up and down the aisles at the ballgame that they'd take a beer, two dogs, and popcorn. It was a surreal feeling to be doing something so normal and yet knowing that the world had changed so dramatically in the last week. Big things like the increased security, overt patriotism, and the talk of terrorism and war were now part of their lives. The idea of contact with aliens was on no one's mind, as the government had successfully suppressed any idea that didn't fit with the public narrative. It was lost in the sea of information surrounding the tragedy.

When the cold beers were handed out, they took a moment to toast Gabby, who had received a commendation from the Department of Homeland Security on the recommendation of Miss Grey for her work uncovering the Chinese mole and translating the Delta file. None of the details were in the commendation, so it had been given to her in a quiet ceremony at the federal building this morning. Very few people had heard of the DHS until now, so it was easy to keep the small affair discreet.

After toasting Gabby, and during the singing of the national anthem, they had a moment of silence to remember Scott and all that he'd done for them. It was still difficult to believe he was gone.

Later in the first inning, Gabby leaned over and kissed Maxx. "We did it," she said softly as she took his hand in hers.

"I know, right? I'm so proud of us. I think we make a great team."

"I couldn't have done this without you. You always had my back, even when you weren't sure if you could trust me."

"It wasn't you. You always made it easy to trust. It was happening so quickly that it took me a while to sort it out. So what's next for us?"

Gabby laughed and leaned in to kiss him. "Let's enjoy this evening and talk about what's next in the morning."

Maxx nodded, took a sip of his non-alcoholic beer, and kissed her.

Maxx had requested from Miss Grey that his role in the events be minimized. He was embarrassed by the connection to Haoyu through his business. Even though the connection was through Natalie, he didn't want that as part of the official record. Keeping him out of the official narrative also allowed him to avoid the connection to the deaths he'd been responsible for in stopping Haoyu and his allies. It would have been extremely complicated to explain why a civilian was being granted immunity for killing Chinese nationals. It was easier to make Gabby the hero of the story without having to justify Maxx's actions and his role in the ferry incident.

To everyone's surprise, Miss Grey joined them in the third inning. Joseph grinned when Andres asked him if he'd known she was coming, accounting for the empty seat beside him. Clearly there was a spark between Andres and Miss Grey, and Joseph was doing his part to light the ember.

During the seventh-inning stretch, Miss Grey's phone began to vibrate. She'd told the office to contact her only if there was an emergency, having planned to take the night off.

She read the first text and shook her head in disbelief. The first part was exciting and more than a bit shocking. "UPDATED ALPHA AND DELTA FILES RECEIVED. SENT DIRECT TO PRESIDENT. NEED TO BEGIN DECIPHERING ASAP."

In the communication on the morning of 9/11, the aliens had been clear that they wanted to communicate directly with the leader. By sending the information directly to the president, they were apparently leaving no chance for it to be mishandled by an underling this time.

A second text made the hair on her arms stand. "ALSO NEW FILE (LAMDA?) RECEIVED. FILE IS ADDRESSED TO 'MASTERS OF WAR.'"

AFTERWORD

Dear Reader: Listening to music played a significant role in the creation of *Thunderbird Rising*. Below is a list of songs that capture for me the mood of each chapter, either through the music or lyrics. If you'd like additional insight into my imagination as I envisioned the world and characters of Maxx and Gabby, hopefully these songs add an extra dimension to your experience. The complete playlist con be found on Spotify @ **Thunderbird Rising**.

Epigraph:
"All Along the Watchtower" – Bob Dylan
Chapter 1:
"Ruby Tuesday" – The Rolling Stones
Chapter 2:
"Band on the Run" – Paul McCartney and Wings
Chapter 3:
"Spy in the House of Love" – Was (Not Was)
Chapter 4:
"I Gotta Feeling" – Black Eyed Peas
Chapter 5:
"Watching the Sky" – Saxon

Chapter 6:
"Blurred Lines" – Robin Thicke
Chapter 7:
"Where Roads End" – Ramirez
Chapter 8:
"Poems, Prayers and Promises" – John Denver
Chapter 9:
"Come Spy with Me" – Smokey Robinson and the Miracles
Chapter 10:
"Read My Mind" – The Killers
Chapter 11:
"3jane" – EMA
Chapter 12:
"Masters of War" – Bob Dylan
Chapter 13:
"Agent Double O Soul" – Edwin Starr
Chapter 14:
"Underground" – David Bowie
Chapter 15:
"Thunderbird" – Quiet Riot
Chapter 16:
"Deeper Underground" – Jamiroquai
Chapter 17:
"Street Spirit (Fade Out)" – Radiohead
Chapter 18:
"Gimme Shelter" – The Rolling Stones
Chapter 19:
"Smooth Operator" – Sade
Chapter 20:
"I Don't Like Mondays" – The Boomtown Rats
Chapter 21:
"Aqua Boogie" – Parliament
Chapter 22:
"Ghost Riders in the Sky" – Johnny Cash

Chapter 23:
"Trust Nobody" – Hippie Sabotage
Chapter 24:
"I Trust You to Kill Me" – Rocco DeLuca and The Burden
Chapter 25:
"Eve of Destruction" – Barry McGuire
Chapter 26:
"Truth and Honesty" – Aretha Franklin
Chapter 27:
"Mama Said Knock You Out" – LL Cool J;
"You're Going Down" – Sick Puppies
Chapter 28:
"Exit" – U2 "Hands of Love"
Chapter 29:
"Come As You Are" – Nirvana
Chapter 30:
"Blow Me (One Last Kiss)" – Pink

ABOUT THE AUTHOR

John lives in the Seattle area with his wife and the world's sweetest cat: Karmann. Raised in a nomadic military family, he is annoyingly curious, a consumer of whiskey, and a political junkie at heart, but his greatest interests are his family and their collective adventures. And, for the record, he enjoys swimming in the ocean — even if it's with sharks.

Printed in Great Britain
by Amazon

62477634R00208